CARLA NEGGERS

started writing when she climbed a tree with pen and paper in hand at age eleven. Now she is a *New York Times* bestselling author of many novels of romantic suspense and contemporary romance, including *Declan's Cross, Heron's Cove, Saint's Gate, Cider Brook, That Night on Thistle Lane* and *Secrets of the Lost Summer.* An avid traveler, Carla is always plotting her next adventure—whether in life or for one of her novels. She lives with her family on a hilltop in Vermont, near Quechee Gorge, where she is at work on her next novel.

For more information, and to sign up for Carla's newsletter, please visit her at www.carlaneggers.com.

BETH ANDREWS

Romance Writers of America RITA® Award-winning author Beth Andrews writes contemporary romance for the Harlequin Superromance line, checks for her kids' college tuition bills and text messages that somehow end up on her kids' Twitter feeds. She loves coffee, hockey and happy endings. Learn more about Beth and her books by visiting her website, www.bethandrews.net.

New York Times Bestselling Author

CARLA NEGGERS

Trying Patience

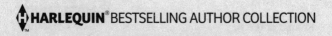

HARLEQUIN BESTSELLING AUTHOR COLLECTION

Recycling programs for this product may not exist in your area.

ISBN-13: 978-0-373-18089-9

TRYING PATIENCE
Copyright © 2014 by Harlequin Books S.A.

The publisher acknowledges the copyright holders of the individual works as follows:

TRYING PATIENCE
Copyright © 1993 by Carla Neggers

A NOT-SO-PERFECT PAST
Copyright © 2009 by Beth Burgoon

Printed in U.S.A.

CONTENTS

Dear Reader,

Thank you for reading *Trying Patience!* I'm thrilled that this funny, sexy story is back in print. If anyone could try a man's patience, it's Patience Madrid. And vice versa: Jake Farr can certainly test a woman's limits. I smile just thinking about this feisty pair. There's no time to waste in the worlds of Jake and Patience.

I love New York City and the beautiful Adirondack Mountains, and I've been to both many times since writing *Trying Patience.* The Northeast, with its diverse geography and endlessly fascinating people and places, continues to be one of my favorite settings. And now Ireland, too! My husband, Joe, and I are frequent travelers to the Emerald Isle. I never know what will spark my imagination, and I've always been a writer who enjoys getting out and about.

Please stop by my website (www.carlaneggers.com) for all my latest news, and to sign up for my newsletter. And drop me a line anytime. I'd love to hear from you!

Happy reading,

Carla Neggers

TRYING PATIENCE
Carla Neggers

CHAPTER ONE

"PATIENCE MADRID, you're becoming a hermit just like Uncle Isaiah."

Taking no offense at Tilly's comment, Patience stretched out on her ratty couch. Contrary to her sister's opinion, she lived comfortably in her two-room log cabin that was situated on a quiet, crystal lake in the southern Adirondack Mountains. Patience pictured her sister on the phone in her elegant condo overlooking Central Park. From her tone, Patience could guess her older sister was already exasperated with her. "The answer is still no."

"Oh, come on, do me a favor. A couple weeks in the city will do you good."

Tilly was nothing if not stubborn. Patience said calmly, "I hate the city."

"You're just saying that to annoy me. You know, Patience, pretty soon you won't know how to talk to anybody but that confounded dog of yours."

"'Confounded'? That must be city talk. Back in the old days, you'd at least have said damned dog."

Tilly sniffed. "That was before Terrence."

Indeed. Scholarships to Smith and Yale and ten years working on Wall Street hadn't changed her sister, but marriage to Terrence Terwilliger and life on Central

Park West certainly had. She even called herself Matilda these days. Said Tilly Terwilliger sounded ridiculous. Patience thought it was impossible to avoid sounding ridiculous with Terwilliger as a last name, but that wasn't her problem: *she* wasn't married to Terrence.

Her sister resumed her argument. "Apollo and Aphrodite are lovely cats."

"I hope they didn't hear you. I've never met a Persian that likes to be called something as ordinary as a cat. Especially your two. Me, I like a good mouser."

Tilly sighed in a ladylike manner. Ladylike sighs were one of the oddities that life among the Terwilligers had taught her. Right now her older sister would be perched on a white chaise longue, dressed delicately in a white satin robe, fingernails and toenails painted. She'd be wearing makeup, expertly applied, and have her hair up, neat and sophisticated. Patience—four inches taller than Tilly, bigger boned, leaner—had on her black trail pants and white fleece pullover she'd worn on her evening trek around the lake with her dog, Jake.

Tilly had said daffodils were blooming in New York City. They weren't blooming in the mountains—the ice was barely melted off the lake.

"You haven't been to New York in ages." The Terwilliger influence hadn't managed to break Tilly's spirit when it came to a fight. "Think of all the fun you could have. I could set up an appointment for you with my hairdresser—"

"For what?"

"For that mop of yours, that's what."

Patience grinned. Matilda Terwilliger was sounding more like the old Tilly Madrid. Even before Terrence, she'd threatened to make an appointment with her hot-shot New York hairdresser to tackle her younger sister's long, wild, frizzy red hair. At two hundred dollars a cut, Patience preferred to stick to trimming her own hair with their late Uncle Isaiah's old barber scissors. Tilly said it looked like it.

"Okay, okay, you win." Tilly sounded frustrated, which she probably was. "Forget I even asked. If you don't want to look after Apollo and Aphrodite for me, I won't make you. I can take a hint."

Patience hadn't been hinting—she'd been out-and-out refusing to cat-sit for her sister.

She sat up, suddenly hearing the wind howling on the lake. It was a familiar sound, sometimes comforting, sometimes downright eerie. Right now it made her feel peculiarly alone. Had her sister's words gotten to her?

"What would I do with Jake?" she asked.

"Jake?"

As if she didn't know. "My dog, Tilly. Can I bring him?"

"No!" Tilly sounded as if she'd nearly choked. "Patience, no, you can't even *think* about bringing that animal to New York. Our neighbors…" She trailed off, leaving Patience to imagine what the neighbors would think. Obviously nothing good. "Jake wouldn't be happy here. He wouldn't fit in."

Patience looked down at Jake. Apparently unaware of his enormous size, he'd squirmed as far as he could under the old-fashioned kitchen woodstove. She didn't know why he didn't burn up. And he looked foolish, which wasn't difficult with his looks. He was a scraggly mutt of no particular charm or beauty. As near as she could figure, he was part black Lab, part German shepherd, with maybe a touch of rottweiler. He'd wandered out to the cabin last spring—a scrawny, parasite-infested, lovable, abandoned puppy. His most endearing trait was a love of canoeing equal to Patience's own. He'd even learned, if the hard way, not to leap out in the middle of the lake. After a few near drownings, he'd managed to cure himself of that particular bit of idiocy. The dog wasn't smart.

"Jake's just an ordinary dog."

"He is *not* an ordinary dog, even by country standards. By city standards—Patience, trust me. It would be a serious mistake to bring him."

"He likes cats."

Tilly was silent. She didn't hiss or curse the way she would have before she'd married Terrence and his Terwilliger trust fund a year ago. She'd even stopped arguing politics. She and Patience and Uncle Isaiah and whatever other Madrids happened to be around used to argue politics all the time, even when they agreed. Now Tilly believed in avoiding subjects likely to cause fights among her guests. What was a party for?

"If I can't bring Jake," Patience went on, a stubborn woman herself, "I can't come."

"Patience…"

There was something in Tilly's voice that hadn't been there before. A tentativeness, even a note of un-Madridlike desperation. Patience got up and walked slowly across Uncle Isaiah's old hand-braided rug to her woodstove, her main source of heat. "Tilly, is something wrong?"

"No, of course not. I mean—" She broke off, uncharacteristically inarticulate. "It's just that I need to get away. I need to relax. And I can't if I'm worried about the cats. You know they hate the kennel."

"What does Terrence say?"

"He says they're my cats," Tilly answered, with a touch of the sharpness that had long been a Madrid trait. It didn't take a great leap of imagination to figure out that Terrence wasn't as fond of Tilly's cats as Tilly herself was.

"Til?"

"Please come."

"Til, are you and Terrence on the outs?"

Not a sound from the New York end of the line.

"He *is* going on this trip with you, isn't he?"

Tilly made a small, pained sound that wasn't like her at all. She was always so confident, so optimistic. "He's going on a trip, but not with me."

Patience kept her initial response—which was unkind, to say the least—to herself. She could read between the lines. Still, she didn't want Tilly to know she'd developed her own suspicions about Terrence Terwilliger III. The man had too much money and had lived in New York too long to be trusted.

"Business?" Patience asked, feigning innocent curiosity.

"He—Terrence needs to get away, too. We agreed to go off alone on—I don't know what you'd call it—a personal retreat, I suppose. I'm going to Arizona, he's going to Florida."

"Ouch."

Patience rummaged in the wood box, not prepared to counsel anyone—even her one and only sister—on matters of the heart. And at Tilly's wedding last year, she'd vowed to mind her own business and stay out of her sister's love life.

"We hope this will be a positive step in our relationship," Tilly said, sounding as if she was quoting her husband, who tended to talk like that. "He would...well, Patience, you know how Terrence feels about your dog."

The first time Terrence Terwilliger III had ventured out to her spot on the mountain lake, Jake had pinned him in his fancy white Jaguar. Jake did look mean and he had a ferocious bark, and although Patience tried to keep him groomed, some things were hopeless. Still, beyond deterrence, he was useless as a guard dog. She'd told Terrence that. "Ter," she'd said, certain she was the only person who'd ever called him that, "Jake wouldn't hurt anything, not even you." He hadn't been reassured. Her brother-in-law, Patience had come to realize, didn't entirely trust her.

"He thinks Jake has fleas," Tilly said.

"I'm insulted."

"And worse."

"I didn't think Terrence was capable of imagining anything worse than fleas."

"He is a bit of a stuffed shirt," Tilly agreed.

"You sure he'll let me tend your precious Persians? How does he know I won't have them stuffed while you two are off on your separate 'retreats'?"

"He knows you're a soft touch for animals. It's men you'd have stuffed."

"Hey, we're discussing your love life, not mine."

"Not that there's a whole lot to discuss," Tilly commented, clearly unable to resist.

Patience wasn't offended. Tilly actually was being kind: there wasn't *anything* to discuss regarding Patience's nonexistent love life, not since she'd broken up eighteen months ago with the geology professor whose idea of a romantic date was collecting rock samples from lake bottoms.

Her tone softened. "You really need to get away, don't you, Til?"

"Yes, and Terrence does, too. We agreed to go off at the same time, to work separately on certain issues in our marriage so that we can better work on them together when we return to New York."

Patience couldn't imagine. During her thirty-two years, she'd had a few of what could be referred to as relationships and she'd always preferred to hash things out up close and personal, right then and there, while she was still piping hot. Which was maybe why her sister had just accused her of being a hermit and there wasn't currently—nor was there likely soon to be—a man of any romantic import in her life.

"So, you'll come?" Tilly asked, not quite pleading. She still had her Madrid pride.

Lifting the grate on her woodstove, Patience shoved a chunk of wood onto the dying fire. She had to be out of her mind. During her last visit to New York, she'd developed a sinus infection from the polluted air. And a cabdriver had screamed at her, when she'd blithely opened her door into oncoming traffic, "Lady, if you want to get yourself killed, not on my meter, okay?" She didn't like New York. She liked her lakeside cabin in the Adirondacks where it was just her and Jake and the occasional stray critter. Give her a lost moose any day over a bunch of dirty pigeons in Central Park. Not to mention the Terrence Terwilligers of the Big Apple.

But she heard herself say, if without enthusiasm, "Yeah, I'll come."

"I'll arrange for a plane ticket—"

"Nope. I'll drive."

Tilly hesitated. "Patience…"

"Don't start on my Jeep next. You want your kitty-cats looked after by family, family is what you get."

LITTLE THINGS had conspired against Jake Putnam Farr, and instead of climbing tall peaks in a warm climate, he found himself standing in an apartment covered with drop cloths and plaster dust. Men in coveralls moved busily around him. Electric tools buzzed and whined. The unfortunate thing was, the chaos was Jake's apartment. He'd occupied the spacious co-op apartment in a corner building on Manhattan's Upper West Side for the past decade, but only recently had he let an architect friend talk him into knocking down a wall or two and generally sprucing the place up. "We'll retain the twenties ambience," Franco had said. He could have said turn-of-the-century flavor and Jake would have believed him for all the attention he paid to such things. In fact, he'd planned to be out of town for the duration of the renovations. But if Jake thought he was in the wrong place at the wrong time, his friend Terrence Terwilliger looked distinctly out of his element amidst the chaos.

"I'm sorry your trip fell through," Terrence said.

"Me, too. March isn't one of New York's finer months."

A carpenter, carrying a sloshing bucket of some sort

of white glop, pushed past Terrence with an irritable grunt. A fat, oozing gob of the stuff just missed splattering onto the knife-creased leg of Terrence's custom-tailored suit. "What're you going to do?" asked Terrence. "Obviously you can't stay here."

Jake shrugged. "I suppose I'll just have to roll out my sleeping bag and camp out on the living room floor—provided there is one. Franco said he'd have made allowances if he'd known I'd be around."

"I'm sure," Terrence said dubiously. He was a man unaccustomed to making do with anything more onerous than a double instead of a king-size bed. At thirty-seven, he was whip-lean, tall, fair, and good-looking in a boyish way—he had dimples women tended to think were adorable. In short, he was the exact opposite of the kind of man people expected would be Jake Putnam Farr's best friend. Jake himself wasn't fair and he wasn't that tall—a couple of inches under six feet—and nobody had ever called him adorable.

"What about Westchester?" Terrence suggested.

Jake's parents resided in Westchester. So did his older brother and sister. He shook his head. "I'd rather hang a hammock from the rafters. I still haven't recovered from Christmas. Mother had an open house and invited every fair-haired damsel within miles. Father grilled me on whether my mountain-climbing was distracting me from business. Lisa introduced me to all her single and divorced friends and kept thrusting babies onto my lap, presumably to show me what I was missing by not being a father. I still haven't managed to get the spit-up stains out of my favorite sweater. And

Jeffrey offered to hunt up debutantes young enough to be my daughter."

Terrence laughed. "Serves you right for remaining one of New York's most eligible bachelors. They just want to see you happy and settled—"

"I *am* happy and settled." A change of subject was in order. "When are you and Matilda leaving on your trip?"

"Tomorrow evening at some ungodly hour. Matilda prefers to travel late in the day. In fact, she suggested that if you want to stay at our place you're perfectly welcome. I think it's a wonderful idea."

"It's nice of you to offer, but if I have to cat-sit—"

"Oh, no. Matilda's arranged for the cats to be boarded in the country while we're out of town."

Terrence said "the" cats rather than "her" cats because of his discreet gentlemanly manner. But Jake knew damned well they were Matilda's cats. He had caught Terrence angrily muttering to himself while he picked their long white hairs off his trousers. Terrence adored his wife, however, and had learned to tolerate her cats. Jake, who preferred his animals wild, couldn't stand them.

"I know you're not terribly fond of cats," Terrence added.

"I hate cats," Jake said.

"They're not so bad once you get used to them."

"Domesticated animals don't appeal to me. I don't even like dogs. The last animal I enjoyed up close was a trout I caught on the Batten Kill. I grilled him over an open fire."

Terrence smiled. "Matilda says you're all bark and

no bite. But if you'd like to stay at our place, you won't have to worry about the cats or animals of any kind. Look, Jake, it's not just the renovations. You're bored. A change of scenery would do you good."

"Bored? Where the hell'd you get that idea?" But Jake already knew. "Matilda."

Terrence neither confirmed nor denied.

"Well, she's wrong. Just because I've advanced my business to the point where my people don't need me breathing down their necks every day, just because I have *time* now to do the things I enjoy—like fly-fishing and mountain-climbing—doesn't mean I'm bored."

"So I've told her."

A carpenter grumpily asked Jake to move aside so he could get by with his stepladder. "I could always pack up and go to a hotel," Jake said, half to himself.

"What for?"

Terrence wasn't one to part with a nickel if he didn't have to. It was a trait that had annoyed every woman in his life until Matilda Madrid, whose attitude toward money was purely pragmatic. And who clearly loved her husband for who he was, not for what she could get out of him.

"To be honest, Jake," Terrence went on, "you'd be doing us a favor if you stayed at our place. We haven't been gone for more than a weekend at a time since we bought it, and we don't have anyone to look after it. I believe our building's quite secure, but I'd rather not find out the hard way. And since Matilda's taken care of the cats, I think you'd enjoy yourself."

The Terwilligers' new apartment on Central Park West, Jake had to admit, was tough to resist. Spacious and beautifully decorated, with incredible views of the park and the city, it also managed to remain very livable. Matilda's doing.

In contrast, Terrence had grown up on a Westchester estate that might have come out of an F. Scott Fitzgerald novel. When he was growing up, kids used to say Buckingham Palace would seem informal to a Terwilliger. In comparison to Terrence's family, Jake's parents were paupers. But Matilda's past remained something of a mystery. Terrence didn't talk much about where he'd found Matilda, nor about her family and the ultraprivate wedding, which, rumor had it, had taken place on a mountain lake up north. Jake had been off scaling peaks in New Zealand at the time. He'd have flown back, but Terrence had urged him not to bother—he and Matilda wanted a quiet wedding. Jake could guess why. He'd heard—not from Terrence—that the Madrid family were an odd bunch. Supposedly there was an uncle who'd been a hermit and a sister who'd once brought home a wounded moose calf—or whatever the devil baby moose were called—with the idea of nursing the creature back to health. Jake took most of the talk with a grain of salt. There was no more normal or sweet a woman than Matilda Madrid Terwilliger.

The carpenter with the bucket of white glop came at them again and rather rudely suggested they remove themselves to the kitchen. Jake was persona non grata in his own apartment.

He relented to his friend's offer.

Terrence beamed, digging out his house keys. "Terrific. I'll inform the doormen. I know you'll have a great time."

Jake accepted the keys, then stopped his friend half-way to the foyer. "You and Matilda have a good trip."

"Thank you. I'm sure we will."

"You'll leave phone numbers?"

"Of course."

"Terrence…everything's okay, isn't it?"

"What?" He seemed surprised by the question. "We're taking our first trip since our honeymoon—what could possibly be wrong?"

Jake had no answer. For a few weeks now, he'd sensed a preoccupation on Matilda's part, a tension that hadn't existed before. It could have been adjusting to life among the Terwilligers. Decorating their new apartment. Giving up her job on Wall Street, which, she insisted, had been totally her idea. Jake didn't know. And he doubted Terrence would tell him. In their long friendship, they'd never intruded in each other's romantic life. If Terrence wanted to talk about any problems he and Matilda were having, he would. But he never had before. One reason could be that Jake Putnam Farr, black sheep of his own family, wasn't the best person to give advice about marriage. Jake considered himself a loner. He did his best work alone. He enjoyed mountain-climbing best when alone. And although he didn't always sleep alone, he had always lived alone. He wasn't about to let the potential troubles of the pretty red-haired wife of his best friend—a woman who liked cats—upset his life. If nothing else, Matilda's troubles were none of his business.

"Enjoy your stay," Terrence said. "I'll send you a postcard from Florida."

"Have fun."

Terrence smiled. "Oh, I will."

"And give Matilda my best."

But Terrence was already out the door.

A few minute later, so was Jake, when a man with a monstrous crowbar asked him if he planned to hang around all day. Central Park West would have to be an improvement, especially if Matilda had shuffled her Persians off to the country. He really didn't care for cats.

PATIENCE ROSE EARLY on the morning she was to leave for New York—a very chilly, but beautifully clear, Saturday. She pulled on jeans, a turtleneck and the Norwegian wool sweater she'd had since college, jumped into a pair of mud boots, called her dog and headed down to the lake. It was a short walk from her cabin. She didn't have anything that resembled a lawn: no Kentucky bluegrass, no trimmed shrubs, no neat perennial borders. What she had were evergreens and oaks and maples and lots of scraggly bushes most people would poison if they found them in their yards. She and her sister had inherited the cabin and thirty-acre parcel from their Uncle Isaiah. He'd used it as a hunting cabin before retiring there for the last years of his life, when he'd become something of a hermit. Patience had cleared out most of the junk he'd left behind, including a stuffed moose head. She wasn't a hunter herself, but hadn't gotten rid of the thing on account of any serious objection to the practice. She'd simply caught herself talking to the damned moose once too often.

Jake walked out with her to the end of the small dock, where the early morning fog still swirled over the quiet lake. There were four other cabins on its shores;

hers was the only one that had been winterized. Town, such as it was, was a relatively easy six-mile drive. Her nearest year-round neighbor was a little more than two miles off. She couldn't even guess how far it was to the nearest mall or department store.

The air smelled of pine and damp earth, and she took in deep lungfuls of it, knowing New York wouldn't be as conducive to deep breathing.

"Well, Jake, what d'you think?" She wondered if talking to a dog was much better than talking to a stuffed moose head. At least Jake was alive. "I'm giving all this up for a couple of weeks in a fancy New York apartment with two fancy New York cats."

Jake rolled onto his back, paws in the air. A friend down in Lake George had agreed to take him in her kennel. Jake had never stayed in a kennel before.

"You'll be a good dog, won't you, Jake?"

He flopped his legs back down onto the dock, coming perilously close to the edge as he rolled onto his side. He wasn't much for water. Those few times he'd leaped from her canoe had been the result of his low IQ, not any desire for a swim. Occasionally Patience could get him in for a morning dip alongside her, but generally he preferred to bark at her from shore.

"You'd hate New York more than a kennel."

But he'd never been to New York. Jake was a sociable dog. What if he liked it? He snapped lazily at something. Knowing Jake, Patience assumed it was just thin air. She'd brushed him for his trip to the kennel. He still looked scraggly and a lot meaner than he was. He just wasn't a neat dog. But, no matter what Terrence

Terwilliger III claimed, he didn't have fleas, and it was no small task keeping a country dog free of parasites.

Terrence and Tilly had left on their separate vacations last night. In a rare concession, her sister had allowed that Apollo and Aphrodite would manage on their own for the night. "But get here as soon as you can tomorrow morning," she'd said in a final, quick call to Patience. "And don't bring that dog of yours!"

Of course, Tilly was at that very moment in Scottsdale, Arizona. She'd never know if Patience had snuck Jake into her apartment.

Jake laid his head on her foot. "If I took you to New York," she said, "you'd behave yourself, wouldn't you?"

He would. She knew he would. How much trouble could a dog like Jake get into?

She rousted him up and headed back to the cabin. To spiff him up for the ride to the city, she tied a red bandanna around his neck. If it lasted until the interstate, she'd be surprised. But he did look a bit less ferocious.

"Come on, Jake."

He followed her outside and off the porch to her old Jeep, hopping automatically into the front seat beside her. The stupid dog did love to ride.

Patience patted him on the head. "You big ugly thing, you. Well, my friend, we're off to the big city."

CHAPTER TWO

SIX HOURS LATER, Patience pulled into Tilly's parking garage amidst the noise, pollution and tall buildings of Manhattan's Upper West Side. The attendant started to make a crack about her Jeep. Then he saw Jake and turned polite. When Patience mentioned the Terwilligers, he straightened up and turned outright gracious. She wasn't sure she liked that. In her worldview, good manners should stem from values and principles, not power and social position. She was about to launch into a discussion of this conviction when the attendant asked her to get out of her Jeep and give him the key. As she did so, Jake leaped out behind her. The attendant backed up a few steps.

"He's harmless," Patience said.

Behind her, a lady jumped back into her Mercedes-Benz. Jake's booming bark echoed in the parking garage. The woman rolled up her window.

New Yorkers, Patience thought as she finished up her business with the nervous attendant, then headed out to the street with Jake loping at her side. He'd never worn a leash, as far as she could recall. Not that he was well-trained—he just didn't need one out by the lake.

"Heel," she said, just in case he would.

Fortunately, New York was a strange enough place,

and Jake did hold a fundamental respect for cars. He stayed at her side. They walked over to Central Park West, as dramatic and busy a street as Patience remembered from her previous brief visits. She loved the American Museum of Natural History at West 79th Street. Tilly's building was within easy walking distance. And Zabar's, a one-of-a-kind deli on Broadway, wasn't that far, either. She and Jake'd manage a couple of weeks in town.

At the entrance to Tilly's building, with its elegant green awning, one of the uniformed doormen opened the door of gleaming glass and polished brass, and didn't object when Jake streaked in ahead of Patience. She'd tied his bandanna back around his neck and he looked quite dapper.

"Heel," she said again, this time to alleviate any fears in people nearby that Jake might not be an obedient New York dog.

"May I help you?" the doorman asked.

"I'm Patience Madrid." At his blank look, she quickly amended, "Matilda Terwilliger's sister."

"Of course. Mrs. Terwilliger left her key for you. Just a moment, please."

He went into a small office adjoining the lobby, which was an impressive place of mirrors, brass, shining wood paneling and porcelain urns of fresh-cut flowers. The Oriental rug would have covered her cabin floor twice. Maybe more. Tilly was a lucky woman, Patience thought; she was living the life she wanted to live. But so was her younger sister. More or less. As much as Patience enjoyed her solitary life in the Adirondacks, she wouldn't have minded having a couple of kids, but that necessitated men and romance, and if there was anything she didn't understand, it was men and romance. Better off just to stick with Jake for company.

She'd almost forgotten him.

"Jake," she called softly.

He was gone. Just like that. There was no sign of him—he hadn't even made a sound. He'd just vanished. Now she'd have to hunt him down and maybe get in trouble with the doormen her first day in town. They'd notify Tilly about her sister's monstrous, undisciplined dog, and Tilly would be furious.

"Jake," Patience said, a little louder.

He didn't come. He never did when she called, unless he really wanted to. She didn't even have a good steak bone on her. It just wasn't the sort of thing one brought to elegant Central Park West.

The doorman handed her an envelope with Tilly's keys inside. "Here you go, Miss Madrid."

She smiled so he wouldn't think anything was up. "Thank you."

Tilly had included a terse note: "Thanks—have a great time in the city! And you damned well better have left that dog home. Til."

Not five minutes in her sister's building and Jake had already gone off solo. This, Patience thought, did not portend well for her stay in the city.

She crumpled up the note, which, at least, had sounded like the Tilly of old.

Behind her, the doorman yelled, "The flowers!"

Whirling around, Patience saw Jake bounding out from under an antique-looking table. The doorman

steadied a teetering urn of flowers before it could top-
ple over. His eyes cut over to Patience.

"Jake's forever squeezing into places where he just
doesn't fit," she explained.

The doorman didn't comment.

Jake trotted up to her. "You old rascal," she said.
Given the mischief he could have created, she was
rather relieved. She reached down to grab his collar, if
only to mollify the still panicky-looking doorman. No
doubt sensing he was about to be marched off like a
recalcitrant toddler, Jake shot past her, slipping on the
Oriental carpet, sliding on the polished floor, hell-bent
for who knew what or where.

"Miss," the doorman said, quiet but firm. "Your
dog."

As if she didn't have eyes. *"Jake!"*

It was a full-blown country yell, but Jake ignored her.

Patience could see Tilly's reputation with the doormen and possibly her entire building in permanent ruin.
"Mrs. Terwilliger, about your sister and her dog..."

Terrence would never understand.

Jake was heading toward the elevator when its brass
doors suddenly opened. Patience hoped this was her
chance. Jake had never seen an elevator before. He'd
be scared and curious. He'd slow down.

She lunged toward him.

Without so much as a split second's hesitation, he
skidded through the parted elevator doors.

"Jake, you rotten *beast!*" Patience yelled, with no
effort to citify her voice.

Then she groaned.

A man—a dark, well-dressed, unamused-looking man—glared out at her from within the elevator.

Completely hyper by now, Jake jumped up on the poor guy and placed two enormous paws on his chest, pressing him against the elevator's far wall, panting into his face. Patience imagined saliva, dog's breath. She had to do something.

But the elevator doors began to close silently, and even as she broke into a run across the carpet, wrinkled and askew from Jake's mad dash across it, she knew she'd never get there in time.

Just before the doors shut with a delicate thud, she saw a thatch of wild dark hair and two wild dark eyes—human eyes, not dog eyes—pinned on her.

"Oh, dear."

Patience watched, impotent, as the floor lights above the elevator flicked on one by one, Jake and his companion ascending to parts unknown of her sister's ritzy building.

The doorman came up behind her. "Miss Madrid—"

She turned, smiling her amiable best, attempting to reassure. "Jake's really very friendly."

The doorman's stern look softened; he seemed almost relieved. "Oh—well, thank heaven you know him."

Patience frowned. Of course she knew him. He was her dog. It wasn't as if she'd tried to deny it. But maybe she *should* disown the incorrigible mutt. Pretend she'd never seen him before. About-face, walk out of the fancy lobby with what shreds of dignity she had intact and never return.

Except then Tilly would come home to a couple of

starved Persians. And Jake? Well, she couldn't leave an entire building of cowardly New Yorkers to her dog.

Squinting up at the floor lights, she saw that the elevator had stopped at the fourteenth floor. That was Tilly's floor. Now it was on its way back down.

What if Jake had panicked and mauled the man?

Nah. It'd never happen. Whatever else Jake was, he wasn't violent. At home he'd lie on the front porch and practically let rabbits and squirrels run over him.

But this was New York....

The elevator came straight down to the lobby. The doors parted, and there was Jake, sitting with his tongue wagging. But for his crooked bandanna, he was the model of an obedient dog.

There was no dark-haired, dark-eyed man.

"What'd you do, Jake," Patience muttered, blocking off any escape and jumping into the elevator with him, "eat the poor guy?"

Not everyone loved dogs. Terrence Terwilliger, for example. Hated dogs. *Really* hated her dog. Tilly used to love dogs, but now she loved cats. Expensive cats.

The doorman peeked uneasily into the elevator. "Where's Jake?"

Assuming she was blocking his view, Patience moved aside as she pressed the button for floor fourteen. "Right here."

The doorman's face went quite pale. Before she could ask him what was wrong, the doors shut and the elevator whisked her and Jake upward.

She collapsed against the elevator wall. "That was a hell of an entrance, Jake," she sighed. At least the worst was over. She'd get Jake safely into Tilly's apartment, buy a leash and avoid every dark-haired, dark-eyed man in the building. In the whole damned city, if she had to.

She'd also probably have to bribe the doormen to keep them quiet about Jake. The last thing she needed— and Tilly, too, she'd guess—was to have him squealing to Terrence and getting him all upset about Tilly's weird family. It might further strain their marriage, and Patience wasn't supposed to aggravate the situation. She wanted to help.

Jake was panting hard.

"I have no sympathy," she told him sternly. "Clearly, Jake, you just can't be trusted."

But he looked at her innocently, and she couldn't help it, she just had to laugh. After that episode, the rest of her visit to New York would be anticlimactic.

Unless she ran into the man from the elevator again. But it was a big building. How likely, really, she thought, was that to happen?

JAKE FARR FIGURED he was lucky to have escaped the elevator with all important body parts intact.

Catching his breath in the Terwilligers' apartment, he then changed into a fresh shirt. The damned dog had soiled his favorite shirt with his muddy paws and spit. If the hairy, slobbering mutt had an owner who could be found, Jake would consider demanding a new shirt. Hell, he'd sue for damages. How much could he get for being trapped in an elevator with an unruly stray? He hadn't actually been *hurt,* but what about mental suffering? It was irresponsible to let such a creature run around loose.

How the hell had the monster gotten past the doormen?

Jake grunted. *In his place, would* you *have tried to stop him?* he asked himself.

Tucking in a fresh, deep blue cotton shirt, he wondered if he should phone downstairs, just in case the doormen didn't know about the slobbering beast running amok in the building. Jake had debated trying to get the dog to follow him into the hall. On their mad ride upward, he'd held steady, managing to creep one hand along the wall of the elevator and press the button to the fourteenth floor. The mutt had collapsed onto Jake's feet. But out in the hall, in safety, Jake had no trouble resisting the temptation to be noble. The dog had shown no sign of wanting to budge, and Jake hadn't been of a mind to insist.

Just as well that Terrence and Matilda were out of town. They'd only left last night and already all hell was breaking loose. Jake could imagine Terrence's reaction to being locked up in an elevator with a salivating dog.

But never mind the damned beast, Jake thought. What about the woman?

He could still see her mass of strawberry hair and hear her yell, *"Jake, you rotten beast!"*

Usually he at least recognized people who held such a low opinion of him. She couldn't have been a recent date. Surely he'd have remembered. The sister or friend of a recent date? But he doubted it. He wasn't known for treating women badly.

There was, however, the ghost of something familiar about her. A client? No way. Though he'd learned to delegate much day-to-day work to his staff, he knew his clients, and none would call him a rotten beast, at least not to his face.

An associate or competitor or employee of a client?

Someone who clearly knew his name and clearly had a bone to pick with him. And knew where to find him, unless that had just been a coincidence.

Now that he'd survived his ordeal with the dog, Jake supposed he should consider himself lucky, given the redhead's low opinion of him. He could have been trapped in an elevator with her instead of the huge mutt.

He sighed. This wasn't a good start to his sojourn on Central Park West.

Deciding just to mention the dog to the doorman on his way out—and perhaps work in an inquiry about the redhead—Jake shooed one of Matilda's cats off the bed. He couldn't tell the damned furballs apart. Finding them prowling about hadn't been a pleasant surprise. So much for Terrence's promise of no cats. Jake had discovered a blithe note from Matilda stuck to the refrigerator with feeding instructions and "THANK YOU" in all caps, implying he'd agreed to do the job of his own free will instead of by default. Terrence had probably told his wife that his old pal Jake was coming and she'd assumed he'd be glad to tend his cats. Terrence, being Terrence, would have neglected to tell her Jake wasn't fond of cats. Especially long-haired white cats. In the bed, no less. But now he was stuck; even he couldn't leave Apollo and Aphrodite to their own devices for a couple of weeks.

And after that wild monster in the elevator, Matilda's mannerly, well-groomed cats looked pretty good. If he could just teach them to keep off his pillow....

As he headed back out into the hall, Jake kept a lookout for the galloping beast presumably still on the loose. He opted for the stairs. Not that he was a coward, but he'd only brought along so many clean shirts. Between cat hairs and dog slobber, he was going through his supply at an alarming rate.

On the stair landing, he heard the elevator slide to a halt down the hall, its doors parting smoothly, quietly.

He heard the distinct sound of dog paws on the hall's polished wood floor.

And a woman humming happily to herself.

If he moved fast, Jake thought, the dog wouldn't find him. He carefully closed the stairwell door behind him; its creak was minimal.

But suppose the mutt had pinned down another hapless victim? Or was about to? Jake hissed in disgust with all animals. Growing up, he'd had only the odd goldfish for a pet, all of whom had come to a bad end.

"Come on, Jake," came a woman's voice. "I haven't got all day. You want to chase strangers, fine. Just don't come whining to me when you're too tired to move. You've had your fun. Now hustle your butt."

This had been one hell of a strange day, and Jake had had enough. He banged open the stairwell door and marched around the corner to the elevator.

The hulking black mutt he'd met earlier loped out to greet him. Jake stood his ground. The dog's boundless energy, however, seemed depleted. He studied Jake a moment, licked his hand, then collapsed on his feet as if the two of them were old friends.

"Jake!"

What the hell was going on? A stray dog stretched

out on his feet, a woman yelling at him. How did she even know he was there?

The annoyed redhead from the lobby came around the corner, hands thrust on her slender hips. She had gorgeous teal blue eyes under a tangle of curls and a tall, fit body. Her boots were caked with dried mud and her clothes reminded him of Paul Bunyan.

"Look, lady," he said, in no mood, "I don't know what your beef is with me—"

"Oh, hello," she said, cutting him off. She fastened her eyes on him and flashed a smile that would have charmed him to no end had she not just told him to hustle his butt and accused him of chasing strangers. Or had she? "You'll have to excuse my dog. He's not used to the city. You're not…um, you weren't by any chance the man in the elevator a few minutes ago?"

Jake smiled, not at all pleasantly.

"Jake really is friendly," she said.

"Jake?"

"My dog."

He stared at the homely beast. Really. He was insulted. "Where'd you get a name like that?"

"I don't know. He just looks like a Jake to me."

She wasn't helping her case any. Jake, however, was noticing she had a very attractive figure beneath her pilled, stretched sweater and near-threadbare jeans. He wished he hadn't noticed. He was certain this woman and her dog had no business in Terrence and Matilda's building on Central Park West. The doorman was probably hunting them down now. No point in his getting involved.

She nudged the beast gently with her muddy boot,

her affection for the dog obvious despite her curmud-geonly way with him.

It was one ugly dog.

"Sorry if he caused you any trouble," she said as if she meant it.

"I survived."

"Do you live on this floor?"

"I'm visiting a friend," he said vaguely.

"I see. Me, too. My name's Patience, by the way," she added, as if she wasn't quite sure whether or not she should introduce herself.

Somehow he had a feeling the woman and the name didn't go together.

Jake pinned his eyes on her. She and her dog had given him a rough time and he wasn't going to let her off scot-free. "Nice to meet you, Patience," he said. "My name's Jake."

Any other self-respecting woman would have been mortified. Would have bit her lip and maybe blushed and at least said she'd had no idea that he and her ugly dog had the same name.

But redheaded Patience threw back her mass of curls and laughed a laugh that left him nearly as breathless as his ride in the elevator with her dog. It was a deli-cious laugh, free and uninhibited, and Jake, caught by surprise, got the hell out of there.

Yet he suspected that this wouldn't be his last en-counter with Miss Patience with the muddy boots and ugly dog.

CHAPTER THREE

PATIENCE SPENT THE REST of the afternoon and early part
of the evening settling into her new, mercifully temporary, quarters. Everything was very fancy. There were
three beautifully decorated bedrooms, each with a private bath. There was a living room twice—maybe three
times—as big as her cabin. It contained a huge television screen, a state-of-the-art—or so she assumed—
sound system and various other electronic gadgets she
made no attempt to identify. The library looked as if
it had been imported from an English country manor.
The kitchen was one heck of a lot more than two people
needed: it had yards and yards of glass-fronted cabinets, granite counters, a restaurant-style stove, three
sinks, two dishwashers and two English porcelain cat
dishes. Jake's pocked and dented aluminum dog dish
looked distinctly out of place next to Apollo and Aphrodite's dining area. The great room had a spectacular
view of Central Park and the New York skyline, a couple of potted trees, original paintings Patience swore
were hung upside down and more places to sit than
she knew people to sit in them. The decor throughout
was remarkably neutral in color, expensive, of the best
quality and very, very tasteful. Things were, she had
to admit, reasonably functional and comfortable. By

comparison, her tube television and Uncle Isaiah's old horsehair mattress looked pretty shabby.

She wondered what had happened to the Tilly Madrid who used to sleep under the Adirondack stars and tell ghost stories around the campfire.

Patience ventured out twice. First, to buy a leash for Jake. A sturdy leash. One that would keep him firmly at her side instead of leaping into elevators with good-looking men who also happened to be named Jake. Had her Jake sensed a human soul mate? Unlikely. The other Jake hadn't looked as if he appreciated dogs. Certainly he hadn't seemed to appreciate the humor in the situation. It wasn't as if her Jake had done any damage— the man had looked impossibly fit and healthy to her, especially for a New Yorker.

The second time she ventured out was to walk Jake about the neighborhood. She discovered people gave them wide berth. She also discovered she felt more damned alone walking the streets of New York, with literally millions of people all around her, than trekking around her isolated lake up in the mountains.

The doorman acted as if nothing had happened that morning.

By nightfall, she was glad to rummage in the Terwilliger library. Not a good potboiler to be found. She settled for a leather-bound, acid-free edition of *The Three Musketeers* and looked around for a spot to curl up and read. Jake, too, was on his feet, pacing, clearly not at home. There wasn't a single ratty afghan or moldy dog bone in the place. Tilly Madrid didn't stand for that sort of thing anymore now that she'd married a Terwilliger. Patience had no intention of suffering a similar fate.

"You wouldn't sacrifice a moldy dog bone for love and romance?" she could hear Tilly arguing.

But moldy dog bones were only a symbol. It was herself Patience wasn't willing to sacrifice.

Was that what Tilly had done? Had she turned into someone else just to please Terrence Terwilliger? Was that why she'd gone to Arizona alone?

You're not responsible for Tilly's happiness, Patience told herself, and, book in hand, headed to the larger of the two guest rooms. She flipped the switch just inside the door. A beautiful porcelain lamp on the Louis Quinze bedside table came on.

And she immediately spotted the wrinkled men's shirt lying on the queen-size bed.

"Oh, Tilly."

She picked the shirt up with one finger and examined it. All cotton, black buttons. Pricey, but of a size and color Terrence would never wear. So were the running shoes poking out from under the bed.

Patience quickly checked the rest of the room.

A leather weekend bag—battered, beaten, ancient, and devoid of the Terwilligers' monogrammed *T*— was jammed into the closet and stuffed with clothes that couldn't possibly belong to her rich, conservative brother-in-law.

"Ah, gee, Tilly, why did you make me have to see this?"

In the adjoining bathroom, a pair of blue gym shorts, a torn white T-shirt and an athletic supporter, not new, dangled from the doorknob.

"I'd take a moldy dog bone over men's exercise clothes any day," Patience muttered.

Especially *used* men's exercise clothes.

A shaving kit was unzipped on the sink. She had a peek. Razor, shaving brush, shaving cup with just a scrap of soap left in it. Toothbrush. No-wax dental floss. Generic mouthwash. After-shave. She uncorked the top and took a sniff: definitely not a Terrence Terwilliger scent. There were other more personal items she chose not to examine more closely.

"Tilly, Tilly."

None of the non-Terrence stuff was well hidden, but maybe that wasn't necessary. Maybe Terrence had already moved out. Maybe Tilly hadn't told her younger sister the truth and her marriage was pretty much over.

Tilly was having an affair.

Patience sank onto the edge of the bed. She warned herself not to jump to conclusions. But if Tilly had gone off the deep end after only a year of marriage and was seeing a man who wore black-buttoned shirts, didn't Patience have an obligation to do something?

Like what? What did *she* know about men?

"Stop!"

Jake fled the room, but Patience was yelling at herself. Tilly was thirty-four years old and had a right to her own life. She could make her own decisions. Her own mistakes. Patience wasn't responsible for her.

Snatching up the offending shirt, she marched over to the closet and stuffed the thing back into the weekender bag.

Would a lover stay in the guest room?

Tilly's would. She was scrupulous that way. Even if she and Terrence were on the outs—even if their marriage was already kaput—Tilly would refuse to entertain a lover in the same room she and her husband had shared.

Suddenly Apollo and Aphrodite appeared on the bed and began pawing the pillows, as cats, fancy Persians or not, would. They did have a peculiar charm. And they were so soft. Not like Jake. Patience could also count on them not to humiliate her the way her damned dog had.

She had to bite her lip to stop herself from laughing just thinking about it, even with the heavier issue weighing on her mind.

A vision of the other Jake—the human one—worked its way to the forefront of her mind, as it had far too often over the course of the day. She didn't want to think about how her Jake seemed to have taken a liking to him—and how she herself kept thinking about him and his dark eyes.

She climbed into bed, determined to enjoy her elegant surroundings and solitude.

But she could see the blue gym shorts hanging on the bathroom doorknob.

Men.

Unable to stand it another second, Patience jumped out of bed, marched into the bathroom, grabbed the toilet brush, and, using the handle, removed the offending articles of clothing from the doorknob. Holding them at arm's length, she deposited them unceremoniously on the closet floor. Then she took a shower, dropping the shampoo bottle on her toe and spilling it. The cap hadn't been screwed on tight. When Tilly got back from Arizona, she told herself, the two of them would go out to dinner and talk. *Really* talk. Not about Patience's love life—or lack thereof—for a change, but about what was going on in Tilly's apparently overactive love life.

How could her sister take up with a man who left the cap loose on the shampoo?

To add to her annoyance, when she climbed out of the shower Patience realized she'd forgotten her nightgown. She'd already turned the heat in the Terwilligers' apartment down to sixty degrees. She hated hot buildings, and there was no point in wasting energy. Why else was flannel invented if not for cool nights? Streaking naked into the guest room, she grabbed a berry-colored T-shirt from the interloper's bag. Definitely not a Terrence Terwilliger color. It wasn't one of her colors, either. It clashed with her hair, but with only two Persian cats and a dog to notice, she put it on and climbed into bed with *The Three Musketeers*.

Jake—all hundred pounds of him—jumped into bed with her and the two cats, who'd already made themselves at home. They didn't seem too sure about her dog, but weren't willing to give up a warm bed.

Ordinarily Patience would have shoved Jake back onto the floor where he belonged, but New York was a strange place for him, and for her, too. She switched on the bedside radio and tried not to feel as if she'd just landed on the moon. Outside, New York was aglow. It wasn't like the Adirondacks at all.

An hour or so later, D'Artagnan was taking France by storm when Jake suddenly leaped off the bed and bounded out of the room. Patience paid no attention. Jake was forever chasing mythical rabbits.

"My God," a man yelled from somewhere in the cavernous apartment, "where did *you* come from?"

Patience bolted upright in bed, her heart racing. She threw down her book. She could hear Jake growling. A burglar? Surely not. Jake would have responded sooner. She'd locked the doors…

But I didn't do the chain lock!

What were doormen for if not to intercept burglars? Maybe it was Tilly's lover.

It was almost midnight. Without making a sound, hoping Jake wouldn't give her away, Patience reached for the bedside phone. She'd call the doorman.

"Nice dog. You remember me, don't you?"

Her hand stopped midair. Remember him?

"Patience?"

"Ah, gee," she muttered, "this can't be."

"Patience, are you in here somewhere? Call off this monster, will you?"

But it was. The man from the elevator. The other Jake. He must be friends with Tilly and Terrence and have his own key. Why the devil hadn't her sister warned her?

She didn't call Jake off right away. This was no time to be jumping to conclusions. He might *not* be a friend of Tilly and Terrence. "What do you want?" she called out.

"What do you mean?" He sounded annoyed. "I want to stay in one piece!"

Obviously he wasn't a dog person. A dog person would have known Jake was harmless. Patience remained wary. "How do I know you're not a criminal?"

Before she could answer, Jake galloped back into the guest room all excited and leaped onto the bed. She thought the slats would give out. He stayed on all fours, breathing in her face. He wasn't one to growl for long. He had no attention span.

The other Jake stood in the doorway. He had his arms crossed over his chest, and his dark eyes focused directly—unswervingly—on Patience.

"You," he said darkly, "must be Matilda's younger sister."

It wasn't easy to be dignified in bed with a dog and two cats and a berry-colored T-shirt that didn't go with her hair, but Patience did her best. She tried not to pay any attention to the way her visitor slouched against the doorjamb, the way his square jaw was set hard as he studied her.

"That's right," she said. She shoved Jake down. "We met earlier today, remember?"

"Oh, I remember." His tone suggested it wasn't anything he was soon likely to forget. "Nobody told me you were coming."

"Should anyone have?"

His dark eyes narrowed even more. He wasn't a happy individual; clearly she and her dog weren't a pleasant surprise. Patience took stock of his blue cotton shirt and canvas pants. *This* was a man who'd hang his exercise clothes on a doorknob.

He said tightly, "I would have thought so."

She tried to be diplomatic. "I don't tell my friends every little thing, either. Now if you don't mind—"

"Obviously, you weren't told anything about me."

She stared, her stomach twisting. "What?"

"If *you* don't mind, I'd like you and those animals out of my bed."

"*Your* bed?" *Oh, Tilly.*

"My bed. The way I see it, first come, first serve. And that's *my* shirt you're wearing. I'd like you out of it, too." He added quickly, not one drop of color coming into his face, "And into something else."

The man was proprietary, to say the least. "What makes you so sure this is your shirt? I know lots of people who have raspberry T-shirts."

His eyes nailed her right to the mattress. "And I'd lay odds with that hair of yours you're not one of them."

"Well, nobody says it's yours—"

"Would you like me to go over there and *prove* it's mine?"

He would do it, too. Patience could see he was at his wits' end, thrown completely off balance by her presence. Not by her necessarily, but by the simple fact of her. As if finding a strange woman in his bed was the last straw.

She, however, wasn't a woman easily intimidated, especially when she had Jake—*her* Jake—licking his chops beside her. He was doing it just because he was tired and thirsty, but that other Jake, not being a dog person, couldn't know that. And he—the four-legged Jake—did look menacing.

Of course, when it came right down to it, so did the human Jake. He wasn't a handsome man. Not ugly by any means. Just no fair-haired Terrence Terwilliger III. He had that square, imposing jaw and those dark, menacing eyes, plus high cheekbones, thick hair, and an athletic build. She tried to picture him in a pin-striped suit and found, oddly, that she could, although it didn't soften him.

She wondered if his temperament and looks were as incongruous as her dog's were.

"And don't think," he said, "that slobbering mutt of yours would stop me."

It was just the sort of know-it-all, authoritative, macho attitude that didn't work with Patience. She stretched out her long legs under the covers and, deliberately and obviously, leaned back against the pillows and yawned. She'd lay odds she and the man in the doorway were the same height. Whoever he was, he wasn't as refined as Tilly's husband, wouldn't limit his library to books by dead authors. He'd have a good international thriller or two on his bookshelves.

Her sister had never fallen for anyone remotely so… Patience couldn't quite put her finger on *what* this Jake character was.

It was almost midnight, and there were animals and a strange woman in what he claimed was his bed. Well, what did he think *she* was feeling? Did he think she enjoyed having a strange man pop in on her and start making demands?

"I've heard all about you," he said ominously. "I'm not backing down."

So her reputation had preceded her. If Tilly had been telling tales, it was no wonder the man hadn't backed off. Tilly liked to paint her younger sister as something of a female Paul Bunyan of the Adirondacks to her New York friends. If Jake believed even half of what Tilly was likely to have told him—and probably not even half was true—he wouldn't worry a whole lot about scaring her half to death, which, Patience suddenly realized, he hadn't.

"Wait in the kitchen," she told him. She wasn't about to let him get away with doing all the ordering. "I'll be out in a minute."

"Make it a fast minute."

A man who liked to have the last word. Patience let him have it. She watched him about-face and head out into the hall. She could have sicced her dog on him, she supposed, but the man was in no mood and her poor mutt had had enough excitement and endured enough insults for one day.

And more to the point, Patience herself wasn't in the mood. Her zest for combat had evaporated.

Tilly's Jake, she thought, was, in addition to everything else, one intensely sexy man. The kind who'd have his way with a wealthy married woman, take her for what he could get and dump her. Tilly just wasn't savvy. She trusted people too easily. If Patience was going to find out what was going on between her sister and this character, *she* had to be savvy.

She also had to be dressed in something besides the man's shirt.

"Oh, Til, what have you gotten yourself into?"

Patience scrambled for her jeans, a sweatshirt and socks. Then she headed to the kitchen with the four-legged Jake at her side, not standing guard, she knew, but just looking for scraps. The other Jake, however, didn't have to know that.

JAKE FOUND A BOTTLE of Saranac beer in the Terwilligers' refrigerator, opened it, took as big a gulp as he could without spilling it all over his face and pulled out a chair at the antique country pine table.

He had never in his life experienced anything like today. Hoodwinked into taking care of Matilda's cats. Trapped in an elevator with a monstrous, ugly, smelly, slobbering hound. Screamed at by a crazy redhead. Only she'd turned out not to be screaming at him, but at her dog, who went by the same name.

Once off Central Park West, he'd had a relatively ordinary Saturday, running errands, checking on his apartment, stopping by his office to do a few things, having dinner and catching a movie with a friend going through a divorce. He'd looked forward to shutting the cats out of his bedroom and having a relaxing hour or two before hitting the sheets.

Now this.

Patience Madrid in his T-shirt and in his bed.

Patience Madrid, a dog and two cats in his bed.

Why the hell hadn't Terrence warned him? It was possible, he supposed, that he and Matilda had gotten their wires crossed and inadvertently neglected to tell Jake he'd have to share their apartment with a nutty redhead and her dog. But why did he feel as if he'd been had?

He drank more of his beer. The redhead with the unruly dog didn't resemble the image he'd had of Matilda Terwilliger's eccentric younger sister. If she did, he might have figured out who she was sooner. But Patience Madrid—Jake didn't think he'd ever heard her name before—was supposed to, well, not have such startlingly teal eyes, such dark lashes, such a mane of untamed strawberry hair. Unlike her older sister, Patience wasn't a delicate woman. Feminine, yes. He'd have had to be blind not to have noticed the soft curves under the T-shirt. But she wasn't fragile. She couldn't be, he supposed, and live the strange life Matilda had described her as leading.

"She's a freelance writer specializing in the environment," he recalled Matilda having told him. "I think she gets along better with animals than she does with people. Sometimes I'm afraid she's going to become a hermit like Uncle Isaiah. Did you know he never ventured further south than the Catskills in his whole life?"

An odd family. From what Jake could gather, Terrence had snapped up the only normal one of the bunch. Uncle Isaiah was dead, but the parents, last Jake had heard, were off on some archaeological dig on the shores of the Black Sea, and there were more uncles, aunts and cousins—none normal.

The dog trotted into the Terwilligers' airy, attractive kitchen, interrupting Jake's thoughts. He refused to let the beast unnerve him. He'd come face to face with a large bear once in the Canadian Rockies and had hardly flinched. Patience Madrid's ratty-looking dog wasn't going to be his undoing. Besides, if the creature hadn't eaten him by now, surely he wouldn't bother in the near future.

"Better watch out," his unexpected roommate said, coming into the kitchen. "Jake likes beer."

"He would," Jake said.

"But he's not particular. I usually keep a six-pack of the cheap stuff around just for him. I guess that's one area where he's different from you."

Jake would suggest there were considerably more areas of difference besides their beer-drinking habits. He had no idea, however, whether or not to believe anything Patience Madrid said. He watched her move to the refrigerator with surprising grace for a woman rumored to chop her own wood and shoot her own game. She got out a beer—for herself or for the dog, Jake wasn't sure. She opened it without struggle and poured a little into a pottery mixing bowl on the floor next to the cats' dishes and a battered aluminum dish filled with dry dog food. Jake thought he remembered Matilda serving pasta in that same bowl—it was made in Portugal, as he recalled—some weeks ago at one of her small dinner parties.

"I didn't bring a water dish," Patience said by way of explanation, then sat across from him at the table and started on the rest of her beer. "I never can drink a whole one."

"So you drink the cheap stuff as well?"

She smiled. Her teeth were white and even and she appeared to have all of them; apparently she believed in modern medicine enough to visit a dentist. Matilda had claimed her sister was an expert in herbal potions. Jake was beginning to suspect she'd exaggerated Patience's lifestyle to spice up dinner-party conversation. Then again, maybe she hadn't.

"I don't have discerning taste buds when it comes to beer," Patience Madrid said.

From what he'd gathered from scraps of conversation with Matilda and Terrence, she didn't have discerning tastes in anything but men. "God forbid you should ever tangle with Matilda's sister," Terrence had said. "Let me tell you, I don't lie awake nights worrying about her living up in the mountains alone. Anyone pestering her—man or beast—is likely to end up hanging on a meat hook in her woodshed."

Apparently her romantic life didn't measure up to bringing home a wounded baby moose or writing articles on the migratory patterns of northeastern songbirds. But she seemed happy enough to Jake. He was something of a loner himself and not inclined to think a person couldn't live a fulfilling life unless married with two-point-three children, or whatever the current average was.

"I'm afraid you have me at something of a disadvantage." Her sudden formality caught him off guard. She looked incredibly *in*formal in her bulky pumpkin sweatshirt and jeans. His T-shirt had been considerably sexier on her. But her teal eyes, he noticed, were soft, curious and—he wasn't a hundred percent sure of this—challenging, even a little unfriendly. What the hell had *he* done? She went on in that same formal tone, "All I know about you is that your name is Jake."

"I see." He was just as glad Matilda hadn't carried north the same sort of stories about him as she'd told about her sister. "I'm Jake Farr, a friend of your sister's."

"Oh, I gathered that much."

Her tone sharpened. Jake finished off the last of his beer, studying her. Definitely a complex woman. There was an air of intelligence and sophistication about her that he just wouldn't have expected from someone who lived the life she lived. "Is something wrong?" he asked.

She bristled. "Mr. Farr, I'll tell you straight out that I don't like to play games."

"Look," he said, attempting to sound reasonable. He pushed back his chair in case she decided to throw something at him, which, given her tone, was entirely possible. "This has been a confusing day for both of us. If you want to spell out just where it is you're coming from, go right ahead. No need for either of us to play games."

Patience sat forward in her chair, but avoided his eyes. "Tilly didn't tell you I was coming?"

Jake tried to hold back a smile. Tilly? He couldn't imagine refined, delicate Matilda Terwilliger answering to a name like Tilly. Of course, he couldn't imagine anyone thinking a hairy mutt like the one who'd lapped up beer and collapsed at his feet looked like a Jake.

He shook his head. "I had no idea."

"She should have told you—or at least told me about you two. Not that I hadn't guessed something was going on."

"I beg your pardon?"

Her cheeks were peachy-red, an accomplishment for a woman who didn't appear to embarrass easily, if at all. "I take it Terrence doesn't know?"

"About me? Of course Terrence knows about me. He and I have been friends since nursery school. He's the one who invited me to stay here while he was away."

"Oh." Patience smiled feebly. "This has been a confusing day."

It wasn't getting any less confusing, either. "Who'd you think I was?"

She waved a hand. "Never mind. Why did Terrence invite you to stay here?"

"My apartment's being renovated and a trip I was supposed to go on fell through." Didn't materialize was more like it, but it was a fine point, too fine a point to try to make at one o'clock in the morning with a giant dog asleep on his feet and a teal-eyed redhead staring him down. "He didn't mention you'd be staying here as well, and I didn't have a chance to see Matilda before they left."

Patience Madrid exhaled, suddenly looking tired. "This is nuts."

"I gather you're supposed to be taking the cats up to the country while Matilda's gone?"

"No, Tilly would never allow her precious kitties to spend ten minutes up north with me. No, she—" But Patience stopped herself midsentence and went tight-lipped on him, apparently unwilling to talk further about her sister. As if Matilda had anything to hide! "The way I see it, all we have here is a failure to communicate. It's no big deal. Doesn't matter what you thought or what I thought. Me and Jake—" this time when she paused she grinned "—have come to the big city to cat-sit. That's all."

"Well," Jake said, rising, "you're welcome to Mr. Apollo and Ms. Aphrodite. I'm not a cat person."

"No kidding." Her tone was richly sarcastic. "What're you going to do?"

He set his empty beer bottle on the counter. Patience, he noticed, hadn't yet finished hers. Maybe she was waiting for him to leave so she could give the rest to the dog. He said, "There's not much I can do tonight. It's late and I'm tired."

She fastened her wide, black-lashed, curiously mesmerizing eyes on him. "I suppose you want your bed back?"

Oh, lady, he thought. Do you know how attractive

you are or do you just not care? "I imagine it's full of dog and cat hair by now."

"Are you allergic or something?"

It amazed him that pet-lovers couldn't fathom how some people might not want to inhale dander and dried saliva and animal hair all night. "You can keep your bed," he said diplomatically. "The other guest room's not made up. I'll just sleep in the den."

She didn't argue with him, and as Jake left the kitchen, wondering why the hell he didn't just cut his losses, go home, uncover his own damned bed and sleep there, he glanced back and saw Patience Madrid pour the rest of her beer in the Terwilligers' handcrafted Portuguese pottery bowl for her ugly dog. Somehow he thought that Terrence didn't have the faintest idea that his sister-in-law had taken up residence in the apartment. So what were Matilda Madrid Terwilliger and her teal-eyed little sister up to?

Jake snuck back into the guest room for his bag and kit, noting with some annoyance that Patience had taken over the bathroom with her glycerin soap, wood-handled toothbrush and non-animal-tested moisturizer. Hadn't the woman seen his stuff and figured there might be another guest staying in her sister's apartment?

He found his sweats in a heap in the closet and gritted his teeth.

And then it hit him.

"She should have told you—or at least told me about you two. Not that I hadn't guessed something was going on."

Good God! The lunatic had thought that he and

Matilda…that he and her sister…that he and Terrence's wife…

He took his things and stomped back to the den, then kicked off his shoes and flopped back on the long leather couch. He and Matilda as…

It was crazy!

And then he began to laugh, hard.

"It's not that damned funny," Patience Madrid yelled from down the hall. "Anybody could've made such a mistake."

Now, how had she known what he was laughing about? Jake sat up straight. "Are you kidding? Terrence and I have been friends for years. I'd never have an affair with his wife."

"How was I supposed to know that? Terrence is such a stuffed shirt and you're…not."

"Couldn't you look at me and know I'm not even remotely your sister's type?"

Patience Madrid didn't answer.

And Jake grinned. This time he really couldn't help himself. He was grinning because, for what was the first and probably the last time, he knew exactly what the crazy, sexy redhead was thinking: he might not be her sister's type, but he sure was *her* type. And that would bother a woman like Patience Madrid a whole lot more than she'd like it to.

As he settled back into the buttery-soft leather cushions, her maddening dog pranced in, collapsing in a heap on the floor just below Jake's nose. He smelled like he'd been chasing New Yorkers all day.

"Go on, you."

The pea-brained beast ignored him.

Jake groaned and rolled onto his back so his nose wouldn't be within smelling range of his unwanted companion.

"Terrence, my friend," he said half-aloud, "do you know what your wife has done to me?"

Or had Terrence been a party to the conspiracy as well? *Was* it a conspiracy? Patience Madrid, her ugly dog Jake, two Persian cats. With friends like the Terwilligers, who the hell needed enemies?

The dog fell asleep first.

Jake had peeled down to his underwear and wrapped himself tightly in a cashmere throw, but he couldn't get warm. It was a damned refrigerator in the apartment. Finally, he checked the thermostat. Sixty degrees! No wonder he was freezing! He knew Terrence was a tightwad, but this was inhuman. He turned the temperature up to sixty-eight and went back to bed, and as he drifted off, he found himself picturing Patience Madrid snuggled under the covers of the bed where he should be sleeping.

It was a disturbing picture, but nothing like a nightmare. He relaxed, his confusion lessening. Perhaps it hadn't been such a rotten, miserable day after all, but only a very interesting one. Then he found himself wondering something that would undoubtedly make his friend Terrence happy since it showed he wasn't bored.

He was wondering, simply, what tomorrow would bring.

CHAPTER FOUR

PATIENCE MADE AN ENORMOUS breakfast of oatmeal pancakes, fresh fruit and coffee. Lots of coffee. She'd had a bad night. The prospect of facing Jake Farr after her erroneous deduction that he and Tilly had something going had kept her tossing and turning. So had her own distrust of her sister. Just because Tilly and Terrence were having marital problems didn't mean she was having an affair! Patience had no idea what had gotten into her. Probably just being in New York.

Jake, the traitor, wandered into the kitchen and dropped onto her feet as she spooned pancakes onto the griddle. He'd never returned to her bedroom, but presumably had spent the night with his human counterpart. She'd only had Tilly's cats for company.

"Yeah," she said, "now that you're hungry you show up."

But she never could hold a grudge and tossed him a pancake. He downed it in a single gulp and stayed close to her in case she had another attack of generosity.

"Is your pal up?" she asked.

She looked at Jake as if he just might answer. It was a bad habit. In her view there was nothing wrong with talking to animals. She didn't want to ignore the dog, risk his getting lonely. Tilly insisted her sister needed human company. "What you need," she'd told Patience at least a thousand times, "is someone who'll talk *back*."

She flipped on the radio to catch the morning news. Who said she didn't have human contact?

In a couple of hours, when Tilly, in Mountain Standard Time, was more likely to be up, she'd receive a call from her younger sister about who else was sharing her Central Park West apartment.

Patience flipped the bubbling pancakes. A good breakfast would help put her in a proper frame of mind.

Jake Farr stumbled into the kitchen and nearly took her breath away with his unbridled masculinity, the intimacy his presence could so easily have implied. He had on jeans with no belt and his blue cotton shirt, unbuttoned, untucked, open at the cuffs, revealing his flat stomach and the dark hairs on his chest.

"Good morning," she said, aware of the catch in her voice. She just wasn't used to having men around at breakfast.

He looked stiff, half-asleep, grumpy. "What the hell time is it?"

Patience glanced at the clock radio. "Seven-thirty."

"It's Sunday morning."

"Yes, it is."

"Don't you sleep late on Sundays?"

"Well, yes. I see you do, too."

"Seven-thirty," he said, "is *not* my idea of late." He squinted at her, his dark eyes obviously not ready to be fully open. "What the hell time do you usually get up?"

She shrugged, refusing to be embarrassed by the routines that had stood her in good stead for thirty-two years. "Five-thirty or sunup, whichever comes first. I get my best writing done in the morning. I woke you up?"

"You woke your dog up, who woke me up by licking my face."

"Licking your face?" She grinned at her dog. "And I thought you were a one-person dog, Jake. You know, he doesn't usually take to strangers."

Clearly not a morning person, Jake Farr grunted, eyeing the coffeepot. Patience told him to help himself, which he did. She wondered if he'd reacted to her as she had to him. Doubtful. She just didn't have the ability to look terrific in a borrowed men's flannel nightshirt—Terrence would probably never forgive her—and wool socks, hair uncombed, face just splashed with cold water. Some women probably could, but not her. She'd pulled her hair back with a rubber band just to keep it off her face while she cooked. Tilly would be horrified. Last Christmas she'd sent Patience a ton of pricey cosmetics, a makeover book and a dozen different kinds of barrettes, ribbons and headbands. Patience had been more amused than insulted. Did Tilly think she didn't know how to dress up? Just because she didn't do it often didn't mean she didn't know how. She wasn't a total hermit. She'd just had a working winter was all.

Nevertheless, she was just as glad she was in no condition to appeal to Jake Farr. That would only complicate matters.

"Would you like some pancakes?" she asked politely.

Standing over her, he studied the griddle dubiously.

"I've got pure maple syrup, too. Made it myself. I stuck a pint in my suitcase when I headed south."

He seemed to be picturing her hauling buckets of

sap, which is exactly what she'd been doing last weekend. She doubted it required a great leap of imagination.

"Sounds good."

Without another word, he set the table, finding his way around the Terwilliger kitchen with little difficulty. He even put out cloth napkins and poured the syrup into a small Bennington pottery pitcher. Patience was impressed.

"No nuts and seeds in the pancakes?" he asked.

"Nope."

They were, in fact, light and sweet, tasting faintly of oatmeal.

After two pancakes, Jake said, "There's no need for me to intrude on your stay in New York. I'll head out this morning and leave you to your dog and your sister's cats."

Patience fought back a totally ridiculous sense of disappointment. What, honestly, had she expected? Or wanted? "Where will you stay?"

"New York has an abundance of hotels."

"You're welcome here, you know." She might as well be polite, since there was obviously no way he'd stay. And wasn't that just as well? He really was a distraction she didn't need right now. "I don't want Terrence accusing me of driving you out. He... Did he not know I'd be here?"

Jake gave her a dry look. "I'd say most certainly not."

"You're sure he'd have told you?"

"If he'd expected us to remain friends, I would hope so."

Patience decided it was just as well she wasn't the touchy type or she might have been insulted. It wasn't as if Jake Farr had found himself camped out with a nest of poisonous snakes. Then again, maybe he'd have preferred snakes to her, her dog and Tilly's cats.

"What about Tilly?" she asked.

"Matilda didn't mention you, either, but I didn't see her before she left." He buttered a third pancake. "I'm assuming this ordeal is simply the result of the right hand not knowing what the left hand's up to."

Ordeal? Patience didn't pursue his assessment of their situation, but in the silence that followed she became aware of Jake Farr's deep brown eyes boring into her. It was decidedly unsettling. Made her wish she'd put a bra on before heading into the kitchen.

She called him on it. "Something on your mind, Mr. Farr?"

He averted his gaze and swallowed another forkful of pancakes. Jake—the dog—moved in closer, looking hopeful.

She'd given up on getting an answer when Jake Farr asked abruptly, "Why did you jump to the conclusion that Matilda and I…that we…"

"Because I'm an idiot," Patience said, not one to air the family laundry in front of strangers.

"You must have been predisposed to think she was—"

Patience jumped up. "I'd forget what I said if I were you. I was flustered and just grasped at straws."

"Well," he said, setting down his fork, "I'm sure Terrence and Matilda are having a wonderful time in Florida."

So Jake Farr didn't know they'd gone on separate vacations. Probably Tilly had confided in Patience just because of her cats, and now she'd blurted out her fears to Terrence's best friend. Or a friend, anyway. How could a "best" friend not know Terrence was having marital troubles?

"I'm sure they are," she said.

Her unexpected roommate sighed and stood up. "I'll do the dishes," he said. "Then I'll be on my way. What are your plans for the day?"

Calling Tilly and doing her best to wring her neck long distance. To him, however, she said, "I don't know. Read the paper and work on an article I brought along. Look, as I said, you don't have to leave. It's not as if there's not enough room for the two of us."

"The five of us," Jake Farr corrected.

Apollo and Aphrodite, Patience had already observed, only entered the kitchen at mealtime. They were pampered and regal—not like real cats at all. They'd probably call 911 if they ever saw a mouse.

"*I* could leave," she offered. "I could bring the cats up north with me. Tilly would never know. Then you could have the place to yourself."

"That would never do."

"I just don't want you to feel as if I've run you out."

Jake Farr looked at her. "Patience, do you want me to stay?"

"Well, if you have no other alternative…"

"Oh, I always have alternatives."

And he smiled a secret, sexy smile that made her wonder just what the man was thinking. Or could he read her thoughts? Did he know that she was reacting to him in a way that could only be explained by the long, cold winter?

He didn't say anything, just rolled up his sleeves and started on the breakfast dishes.

"YOU RAN HIM OFF ALREADY? Honestly, Patience, you're impossible."

Tilly sounded disgusted. Jake Farr had been gone an hour—he'd packed up his shaving kit, sweat clothes, black-buttoned shirt, everything. Patience had been about to put a call through to Arizona when the telephone rang: her sister checking up on her cats.

"I didn't run him off," she said. "He left of his own accord. How come you didn't warn me about him?"

"Because I didn't know he'd be there. It was Terrence's idea—I hadn't told him you'd be cat-sitting."

"Does he know now?"

"Not yet, unless Jake's told him."

"I wouldn't think he'd bother. He seemed to be glad to be out of here."

"What did you do to him?"

"What do you mean, what did I do to him? Tilly, just because my love life isn't the stuff of romance novels doesn't mean I'm a jerk. He thought I stole his bed and—"

"His bed? Patience, what went on there?"

"Don't get any ideas. And if he tells you I stole his shirt, don't believe him. He left with everything he came in with, I assure you."

"I see," Tilly said, clearly not seeing at all.

Patience wished she hadn't even tried to explain. "Jake Farr thinks you and Terrence are in Florida together."

"Terrence doesn't like to discuss his personal problems with anyone, even his best friend." She quickly changed the subject. "How're Apollo and Aphrodite?"

"Just dandy."

"What did you end up doing with Jake?"

"Jake?"

"Your dog, Patience."

"Oh, he—"

But Patience had never been an adept liar, and Tilly was onto her immediately. "You brought him with you, didn't you? Oh, Patience, how could you? No wonder Jake left. Nobody but you can stand that dog."

"He's a great dog."

"Outside, maybe. But not inside. Not in New York, Patience. He didn't— He hasn't done anything, has he?"

Patience had already decided not to tell her sister about Jake's entrance yesterday morning. "On the whole he's been remarkably well behaved."

"That could mean anything. Jake hates dogs—"

"He does not. He's fine with other dogs."

"I don't mean your Jake. Oh, hell." Now she was sounding like the old Tilly. "What a mess."

"It's not a mess. Me and Jake and the cats are all fine. Jake Farr's gone home, or to a hotel, anyway. He's out of here. So you just relax and enjoy your vacation and don't worry about a thing."

"You're sure?"

She sounded almost desperate. Patience's tone softened. "Of course."

"Well, okay."

"Do you have the number where you're staying? I was going to call you earlier, but I realized your cell would be off and I didn't have your number at the hotel. I don't even know the name of your hotel."

"The Hidden Camel Resort in Scottsdale. I'm at the pool, so I don't have the number handy. You can get it from information or I'll give it to you next time I call. Have fun and do *not* give that confounded dog of yours any of our Saranac beer. It's Terrence's favorite."

She and Jake had just split one while she did the *New York Times* crossword puzzle. "Anything else?"

"Enjoy New York."

And for no reason that she could think of, Patience thought of Jake Farr as she hung up the phone. What on earth did he have to do with her enjoying New York? Likely enough, she'd never see the man again.

Which, it had seemed to her, was just fine with him.

She grabbed the new leash. "Come on, Jake. Let's go for a walk."

But he didn't answer back and, much as she liked the hairy mutt, he just didn't have Jake Farr's dark eyes, his square jaw, his muscular thighs.

"Egad," she muttered, "are you sure you're going to be able to stand two weeks of New York if this is what it does to you?"

She snapped the leash onto Jake's collar, and they headed out together.

"JAKE, SOMETHING STRANGE is going on."

It was late Sunday evening and Jake was on the phone in the middle of the unholy mess that had become his apartment. He didn't dare sit anywhere. All day, in fact, he'd felt out of sorts, as if he didn't know where the hell he was welcome, even where he belonged.

"You're not kidding," he told Terrence. "You didn't warn me about Apollo, Aphrodite, Jake and Patience Madrid."

"Jake? Oh, God, she has that damned dog of hers in our apartment! Matilda didn't tell me—" He broke off with a slight growl, regaining his impressive self-control. "I apologize for the confusion. Matilda and I really messed up on this one. Patience came down from the mountains to watch the cats—I didn't realize until we'd already left."

"That's okay. What's done is done. I made good my escape this morning."

And it *had* been an escape, he'd decided. Not the deliberate choice he'd pretended it was. He'd fled from Patience Madrid and her wild red hair, teal eyes and hearty, free laugh. All day he'd been fighting the nagging sense that he'd been a coward. But in what way? It wasn't as if he knew the woman, owed her anything or had done anything to her.

But maybe he'd done something to himself.

"So I gather," Terrence said. "Matilda phoned Patience earlier in the day and, well, to be blunt, she asked me to ask you to look in on her sister while she's in New York. Apparently Patience has been having a tough go of it lately and seems a little depressed. I don't have the specifics, but I gather she's had some trouble with her work and shut herself up in her cabin most of the winter. Matilda hopes she can take advantage of being in the city to relax and see people, have some fun, but so far she shows no indication of wanting to leave the apartment."

Jake contemplated his friend's words, but they just

didn't jive. Something was going on. "Out with it, Terrence. You're leading up to asking a favor, aren't you?"

Terrence sighed in a long-suffering way that Jake imagined was a symptom of living with a Madrid—even one as sweet as Matilda. "Matilda wants you to go back to the apartment. Just be a friend for Patience. I know it's asking a lot, Jake, but I also know staying at your apartment is virtually impossible. Look, there's nothing underhanded here. You've seen Patience. It's not like Matilda would try to fix you two up or anything."

"Then what *is* she trying to do?"

"Help her sister."

"Have *me* help her sister, you mean. Terrence, I don't know the woman, but, if you ask me, there didn't seem a damned thing wrong with Patience Madrid except her choice of names for that ugly dog of hers."

Terrence laughed. "He is homely, isn't he?"

But, in the end, Jake was persuaded. He had no idea why. But he decided he had nothing to lose by offering the woman his company. Besides, Matilda and Terrence had never asked him such a favor before.

"It's important," Terrence stressed.

"What do you think of this Patience character?" Jake asked, trying to shove aside an image of her wide, clear eyes and be more objective.

"I think," his friend said carefully, "that Matilda is probably overreacting, and if I were you I'd watch myself. Patience Madrid is probably the most stubbornly self-sufficient and totally irascible woman I've ever met."

Even with what little he knew about her, Jake was inclined to agree. But he'd have to add curiously beau-

tiful—with her eye-catching curves and mass of red
tangles—something he couldn't have expected Terrence
to notice, married as he was to her older sister.

And, Jake thought, Patience Madrid was a hell of a
lot more interesting than his empty, torn-apart apartment.

"At least she's not boring," Terrence said.

"*That* she's not."

"I owe you, Jake. I wouldn't ask something like this
of you if Matilda didn't seem so desperate. I've never
seen her so worried about her sister."

"But you don't share her concerns?"

"To be honest with you, I don't know. I just think
the whole thing is strange. Patience has always seemed
to me to have life by the tail. You will watch yourself
with her?"

Jake laughed. "It's okay, Terrence. I'm a big boy. I
can handle Patience Madrid."

Terrence Terwilliger made no further comment on
the subject of his sister-in-law, but simply wished him
well—and good luck.

BY EARLY EVENING, Patience was back in Terrence's
nightshirt and had a fire going in the library as she
snuggled under a cashmere throw and pored through
a few more chapters of *The Three Musketeers*. But for
the occasional image of Jake Farr flashing in her mind,
she'd had a good day. She'd gone out to walk Jake and
pick up groceries, but had decided "doing" New York
could wait for another day, if she bothered at all. She
needed time to get over having had and lost her interesting, if hard to figure, roommate.

Then the doorman called up and announced a Mr. Farr was in the lobby and did she want to see him?

"What for?" she asked.

"Just a moment, Miss Madrid, and I'll inquire."

She waited a few moments.

"Mr. Farr, er, wishes to spend the night."

Not one to embarrass easily, Patience nonetheless felt her cheeks heat up. Did Jake think he was funny? Or was he deliberately trying to get to her? *I could send him on his way.* But he was Tilly and Terrence's friend. And she wouldn't mind a chance to prove to her sister that she, Patience, wasn't a total hermit and could stand a roommate for a few days. Even one who hated animals and was as darkly sexy as Jake Farr.

"Send him up," she told the doorman as coolly and smoothly as she could manage.

She decided not to wait for him in the doorway, lest he get the idea she was panting for him or something, but stayed put until he rang the doorbell. With the throw around her shoulders and her four-legged roommates trailing behind her, she walked unhurriedly into the gleaming foyer, undid the series of locks, and, making no self-conscious effort to push the strawberry tangles from her face, let Jake Farr in.

It was like opening the door to the desert wind. The effect of the man hit her full force. He'd exchanged his jeans and cotton shirt for charcoal-gray pants and a black sweater, with a slouchy black leather jacket and scuffed boots. He did not look urbane. He did not look like Terrence Terwilliger III's best friend.

Patience couldn't remember being so affected by a

man. Had to be New York. Too much ozone in the air or something.

She noted the same battered suitcase he'd carried out with him that morning.

"Hi," he said. "I'm back."

No kidding. She managed a smile and hugged the throw around her. She felt like Cinderella before her fairy godmother showed up. Probably should have rubbed ashes on her face before coming to the door. At least her brother-in-law's taste in nightshirts meant heavy flannel. Most of hers were pilled and frayed, but still, at least so far as she was concerned, had plenty of wear.

"Turns out my apartment's unlivable, and there isn't a decent hotel room available in New York. Lots of in-decent ones, but—"

"You don't have to explain," she said, cool, collected, a hell of a lot less naive than Cinderella. "It's not my place to turn you out. I'm Tilly's sister and you're Ter-rence's friend. I guess we both have a right to be here."

Didn't that sound reasonable? So why, she wondered, was her heart skipping along at an alarming rate?

Jake Farr said, "I'll try to find someplace else to stay tomorrow."

"Don't worry about it. Think you can stand Jake?"

Her incorrigible dog had already greeted their visitor in his wholehearted way—by jumping up and placing his paws on Jake's chest. At least he wasn't dirty. Pa-tience had cleaned him up that morning for his sojourn in the big city. Firmly, but reasonably gently, Jake Farr shoved his new friend back down onto all fours and told him to sit. Patience didn't elucidate on the total unlikelihood of Jake's obeying ninety percent of his—or anyone's—commands.

He didn't so much sit as collapse.

"Good dog," Jake Farr said, halfheartedly. He looked at Patience and added without enthusiasm, "I can stand him."

"And Apollo and Aphrodite?"

He nodded curtly, and took his suitcase down to the second guest room, Jake trotting happily behind him. Patience hadn't, of course, made up the bed. And wouldn't. Jake Farr looked perfectly capable of putting sheets on a bed. Before leaving on her private vacation, Tilly had offered to have her housekeeper come by, but Patience had turned her down, preferring to clean up after herself. Also, she'd had her doubts from the start whether she'd be able to leave Jake and hadn't wanted to have any spies reporting back to her sister. Besides, a housekeeper would probably not react well to a four-legged surprise like Jake.

Leaving her roommate to his own devices, she returned to the library with *The Three Musketeers*. Apollo had perched himself on the back of the leather couch. Aphrodite jumped onto Patience's lap and made herself at home. Jake, the traitor, had abandoned her.

It wasn't long—just a few pages of mayhem in seventeenth-century France—before she became aware of a human presence in the library. Looking up from her book, she saw Jake Farr leaning against the doorjamb. Her dog squeezed past him and collapsed on the rug in front of the couch, exhaling as if he'd run around the lake at home instead of just having greeted a guest. One day in New York and already he was getting soft.

New York, however, hadn't seemed to make Jake Farr soft. His sweater loosely outlined the width of his chest and the bulk of his arms.

"Mind tossing another log on the fire?" Patience asked. "I just got comfortable."

"No problem."

"Thanks."

She watched how he moved away from the door—deliberate, with control, even a certain grace. He seemed attuned to his body, aware of himself in an intriguing way that seemed to just skirt arrogance. Patience hoped she'd quickly get used to having him around. She wanted to relax while she was in New York, concentrate on getting some work done, think of how she might help Tilly. Noticing how Jake Farr moved wasn't conducive to anything constructive.

Bending down, he pulled a neat, clean, New York City-type log from the brass wood bin and set it—he didn't toss it as she would have—on the hot coals.

"I chopped that wood myself," she told him. "Had to clean it up before Terrence would let it in his apartment. Brought almost half a cord down in my Jeep. Tilly knows how to chop wood but doesn't do it anymore. What about you?"

He glanced back at her. "I don't have a working fireplace, but I can manage."

"I have a woodstove myself. Better heat distribution."

"So I've heard." Staying close to the fire, he turned back toward her and settled his eyes deliberately on hers. "I was going to offer to take you out to dinner."

"Dinner? It's almost nine o'clock. I ate hours ago.

Made myself an omelet and a salad—there are some eggs in the fridge if you want something to eat. I thought I might make some popcorn in a minute. Don't you New Yorkers get indigestion eating so late?"

"Some of us stay up late, too."

Patience shrugged. She'd already talked too much, chattering on like someone who hadn't seen a human being in months. Well, it had been a few weeks. She'd been finishing up a long, difficult project and hadn't gotten out except for groceries. But yammering on to Jake Farr—well, it was worse than when she'd caught herself talking once too often to Uncle Isaiah's moose head.

"What about a nightcap?" he suggested.

"You mean go out?"

"Sure."

She narrowed her eyes at him, wondering what he was up to. "Why?"

"Because it's a nice evening," he said smoothly, "and I thought you might like to see New York."

"I've seen New York," she said, still suspicious of his motives.

"You come down often? I'm surprised we haven't met—"

"No, I don't come down often, but New York is— well, how often does one have to see it? Big tall buildings are big tall buildings. They're not like trees, you know. Anyway, you shouldn't be surprised we haven't met the few times I have been to the city, because Terrence and I don't exactly get along. I think he'd like to keep me stuffed in a closet when I'm in town."

Jake didn't argue with her nor did he ask her to elaborate. He just looked at her as if he could well understand his friend's attitude.

"Forget the drink," he said, biting back what seemed to her a rather exasperated sigh. "I'll see what I can scrounge up in the kitchen."

Tired as he was, her dog creaked to his feet and followed Jake Farr. Starved for male companionship, Patience decided. Pretty Aphrodite began to purr loudly in her lap, obviously delighted to have Jake—maybe both Jakes—gone.

"I wish I had your sense," Patience muttered.

She was inordinately glad to have Jake Farr back.

She read three pages of *The Three Musketeers* before she realized she hadn't comprehended a single word. She knew why: Jake Farr. He'd shattered her concentration. Annoyed with herself, she flipped back to where she'd started and resumed reading. She couldn't let her imagination get carried away with her.

But she could hear him whistling old rock tunes in the kitchen, and suddenly D'Artagnan and his heroics seemed long ago and very far away.

The two Jakes returned to the library, the two-legged one carrying two beers and a big stainless steel bowl of popcorn. He'd pushed up the sleeves of his black cotton-knit sweater and looked casual, at ease, not as if his heart was thumping madly like hers was. He sat cross-legged on the rug next to the couch and set the bowl on an antique Shaker candlestick table. The dog flopped down beside him.

"I suppose he likes popcorn?" he asked.

"Even more than beer. Is it buttered?"

"Lightly buttered and salted. Otherwise I'd just as soon sit down to a bowl of foam chips. You object?"

"No, I'm on vacation. Besides, I wouldn't want to be an ingrate. Thank you."

"You're welcome." He popped a handful of buttery kernels in his mouth. "What'd you do today?"

"Nothing much."

She reached for a handful of popcorn and noticed he was watching her as if he knew something about her she herself didn't know. That didn't surprise her. She could just imagine what tales Terrence had told him about his sister-in-law. And even Tilly. Being among the Terwilligers and their crowd had given her sister a new twist on the Madrid family. "Patience," she'd said not long ago, "we didn't grow up in a normal family." As if that was news to her. But what was normal? Theirs had been a happy childhood. By Patience's yardstick, that was no mean accomplishment.

"What're you reading?" Jake asked.

She showed him.

"I haven't read that in years."

"Me neither. It hasn't changed though. I never could figure out why it wasn't called *The Four Musketeers*. Porthos, Athos, Aramis and D'Artagnan make four."

"But D'Artagnan was a newcomer."

"True."

Jake tossed a few kernels of popcorn to the other side of the room to lure the dog away from him, but the animal quickly retrieved them and then returned to lay his head on his new friend's lap. It wasn't just the popcorn, Patience knew. Her stupid mutt actually seemed to like Jake Farr, oblivious to the fact that the man clearly wasn't a dog person. Aphrodite blinked up at Patience as if annoyed at these two male interlopers. With a regal yawn, she rose up on all fours, stretched dramatically and jumped off the couch, well clear of the two Jakes. She sauntered off, apparently miffed at having her evening disturbed. Apollo, more of a dope despite his beauty, stayed where he was. Jake didn't comment, but his expression strongly suggested he thought even less of cats—or at least Persian cats— than he did of dogs.

Patience reached for another handful of popcorn. His idea of "lightly" buttered and salted and hers were completely different, but she wasn't about to complain. "Mind if I ask you a question?"

"Not at all."

"Who are you? I know you're Terrence's friend and that your apartment's being redone, but that's about it. If we're going to be roommates, I figure I ought to know a little more about you. I'm not trying to be nosy—"

"That's okay. I'd like to know more about you, too."

Despite how relaxed and casual he looked munching popcorn, Patience observed that his brown eyes were leveled steadily at her, noticing everything. She felt a warm finger of awareness curl up her spine. She resisted it. *Tried* to dismiss it. She was coming off a long winter, and this kind of abrupt, intense physical reaction to virtually the first man she'd seen in months was to be expected. It had nothing, really, to do with Jake Farr himself.

"I own a small consulting business here in New York," he said casually. "JPF Enterprises."

"What's the JPF stand for?"

"Jake Putnam Farr."

As names went, it was almost as elite as Terrence Terwilliger III. "Are you a junior or a third or a fourth or something?"

"No. My parents just liked the name Jake."

"What about Putnam? They didn't just like that, did they?"

He smiled. "My maternal grandmother was a Putnam. How did your parents come up with Matilda and Patience for names?"

"We've never received a straight answer from them on the subject. Mother insists she bought a book of baby names at the grocery checkout and she and Dad each picked a page number and chose the first names they saw. Dad says it was Uncle Isaiah's doing. He was my father's uncle—Tilly's and my great-uncle. According to Dad, he named us after a couple of coonhounds he had. But I don't believe either story."

There she'd gone again, babbling. She could go days without uttering a whole sentence, but not, apparently, around Jake Farr. He didn't seem totally bored, more like bemused. "Your parents and Uncle Isaiah sound... interesting."

She laughed. "Oh, they are. Or were, in Uncle Isaiah's case. He died three years ago. I still miss him." But how had they gotten onto the subject of her and her life when what she wanted to know was about him and his life? "So what do people consult JPF on?"

"Management and leadership problems, mostly in small to medium-sized companies."

"You work long hours?"

"I used to. These days I leave more to my staff. You're a nature writer, aren't you?"

Back to her again. Or was he just being polite? She nodded. "I'm a contributing editor to a natural science magazine of minuscule circulation, and I freelance for a number of other magazines, plus script the occasional documentary, teach the odd community-college journalism course. I've also got a couple of nonfiction books on the environment in the works. I just sold a series for elementary kids on living and working in the woods. It's designed to get them thinking about the natural world around them and also to write about it. I've designed various workbooks to go along with it and—" She caught herself again. "But you're supposed to be telling me about yourself, not listening to me go on."

He shrugged. "There's not much more to tell. I'm thirty-eight, I graduated from New York University, I've never been married, I have an apartment on the Upper West Side and I have parents, a brother, a sister, two nieces and one nephew, all of whom live within an hour's drive of New York."

City birds. Patience grabbed another handful of popcorn, knowing she'd make herself sick if she didn't stop soon.

"You live in the Adirondacks?" he asked.

"Southern Adirondacks, in Uncle Isaiah's old cabin. It's a great place to be a writer."

"Matilda—Tilly—said it was on a lake."

Her mouth full of popcorn, Patience nodded.

"And a ways from the nearest town."

"By Tilly's account, yes. Anything over an hour from the nearest department store she now considers to be in the boonies. But since I hate to shop, that doesn't worry me."

"What do you like to do?"

"Hike, swim, canoe, bird-watch, garden, sew. I've just taken up woodworking. And I read a lot. You?"

"Well, I don't sew," he said, stretching out his long legs, "except for the odd button. And I don't do any woodworking, but the other pastimes you named I do when I've had the chance."

"But what do you do in the city?"

"I enjoy sports, the theater, concerts, and I eat out a lot, like most New Yorkers. Your life seems very solitary."

He seemed more interested in getting her to talk than in talking himself. Behind him, the fire crackled, the glow of its flames seeming to make Jake Farr's eyes darker, mesmerizing. It was quiet in the apartment, almost as quiet as at her mountain cabin. She envisioned him sitting in front of the woodstove in her front room and felt suddenly warm—and a little frightened at her reaction to this man.

She struggled to keep her voice light. "Well, I'm thirty-two and not married. I do have friends and family, but I'm content with my own company. You've been listening to Tilly, haven't you? She thinks I'm another Uncle Isaiah."

"A quasi-hermit, I think is what she said."

"That's because I eat granola and bake my own bread. She should know better. Uncle Isaiah didn't even own a car. Tilly just wants to affirm her own life by comparing mine negatively to hers."

"You two are close?"

"We always have been. We're very direct with each other."

Jake nodded, obviously not surprised. "I can't imagine your being anything but direct. But living alone has to take its toll, especially during a long winter. It must feel good to be in the city."

Diplomatically, Patience withheld comment.

"Look, I don't have a heavy schedule this week. Why don't I show you around?"

"You don't have to—"

"It'd be my pleasure." He gently shoved his canine friend's head off his lap and climbed smoothly to his feet. "Might as well take advantage, Patience. You can sit by a fire reading *The Three Musketeers* in the mountains. And—" he glanced at the sleeping dog "—Jake will get along without you for a few hours."

Patience noticed her throat was dry, her hands clammy. She'd rather have faced a rabid wolf on her doorstep than Jake Putnam Farr offering to show her around town. It wasn't *him* who worried her. It was herself. She needed time to come down off her deadlines and long winter of work before she let a man like this one near her life.

"Thank you for the offer," she said politely, "but, frankly, I don't know what there is to do in the city."

"Then I'll just have to show you the possibilities."

His voice was low and deep, filled with promise and humor, and before she could think of a response, he disappeared down the hall, leaving Patience with a hot finger of awareness trailing slowly, erotically, down her back.

CHAPTER FIVE

As they stood in line at Zabar's, the one-of-a-kind deli on Broadway, it occurred to Jake that Patience Madrid just might be able to beat him in a fistfight.

He grinned at the thought. She looked fit in black pants, a heavy ivory-colored sweater and scarred mud boots with frayed laces. She'd hung a multicolored scarf around her neck, and whenever the wind blew cold off the Hudson River, she'd pull it up around her ears. Even if she did look as if she ought to have an ax strapped to her back, it was a sexy gesture.

"Nice scarf," he commented.

"Thank you." Her teal eyes fastened on him; she had a directness he found captivating. "A friend of mine wove it."

He should have figured.

Whatever else the woman was, she did not seem to him even the slightest bit depressed. They'd spent the entire morning together, so he thought he'd have noticed. She was stubborn and irascible, just as Terrence had promised, but not even remotely what Jake would call depressed. Had Matilda simply been mistaken about her sister? Or was something else going on?

And, more to the point, was it any of Jake's business?

They paid for their cups of fresh-brewed coffee, and

Patience handed Jake his. He noticed her long, slender fingers, the short but manicured nails. There was a small scar below her thumb joint. He couldn't see any noticeable calluses.

"How much further?" she asked when they went back out to the wide, crowded, noisy sidewalk.

"To where?"

She gave him a suspicious look. "To wherever it is we're going."

There was just no use. With anyone else, Jake would have explained—wouldn't have *had* to explain—that they had no destination. They were just walking around the Upper West Side, seeing the sights, getting a feel for the neighborhood. But Patience Madrid wasn't anyone else. If he was uncertain on other points, on that Jake was crystal clear.

His largest point of confusion was why he was so searingly attracted to the woman. God knew it wasn't her boots. And as big and black-lashed and gorgeously teal-blue her eyes were, they weren't the first pair of beautiful eyes he'd seen. The sunlight did have a way of catching the blond highlights in her strawberry hair, and her body, draped in mountain clothes as it was, did have a luscious appeal. But they weren't enough to draw him as inexorably as he was drawn to a woman who didn't like New York, who was argumentative and eccentric, who, for the love of God, dressed like Paul Bunyan.

What was enough, he suspected, was her laugh. It really did have him by the short hairs. Bold and unrestrained, it made him shudder with the pain and mystery of wanting a woman he had no business wanting.

His best friend's sister-in-law. A woman committed to a solitary life in the mountains.

Patience Madrid would be an enormous challenge for any man.

"Well?" she prodded. "We *are* going somewhere, aren't we?"

A goal-oriented woman. Jake had no real agenda. He'd just been showing her around.

"My apartment's just a couple of blocks from here," he said quickly. "I thought you might like to see the renovations."

It was lame, and Patience Madrid seemed to know it. "Sounds fine," she said coolly.

But he saw the spots of color high on her peachy cheeks. It wasn't the cold March wind this time. *So,* he thought, *she's not oblivious to what's going on between us.* Jake took heart, even as he warned himself that if she *was* depressed, he'd better be careful with her emotions. Go easy.

"Let's hope the work crew doesn't kick us out."

She seemed to relax slightly, and Jake wondered if it was because they wouldn't be alone. Yet hadn't they been alone together the last two nights? But that was different. At the Terwilligers', they were on neutral ground. Now they were going to be on his turf.

He turned down West 82nd Street toward the Hudson, then cut up West End Avenue. The wind was brisk and cold, even for unpredictable March. The odd daffodil seemed ready to collapse. Not Patience Madrid, however. They'd been on their feet for two hours, and she seemed as fresh as when they'd started out.

Could she beat him in a fistfight? He grinned thoughtfully.

They came to his corner building, its graceful lines a dead giveaway, his architect had told him, of its twenties construction. Jake had bought his apartment for its airiness, its size and its convenient location. He hadn't even thought about its ambience.

Patience tilted her head back and looked all the way up to the top of the fourteen-story building. "Well," she said, "it's not as ostentatious as Tilly's building."

From her, that was a compliment. Jake led her inside, where he introduced her to the doormen and to a neighbor coming through the lobby with two kids and a dog. Patience got down on one knee and let the cocker spaniel lap her face. She and the kids discussed dog bones and flea remedies. Stephen, the father, eyed Jake. "You didn't find her in New York, did you?"

"Not hardly."

"On one of your mountain-climbing expeditions?"

"She's the sister-in-law of a friend of mine."

Stephen nodded, dubious. "Have fun." He gathered up kids and dog and continued on his way.

"Not bad," Patience said, coming up beside Jake. "It always amazes me that normal people live in New York."

Jake let that one slide. Despite his own misgivings about Matilda and Terrence's assessment of Patience's mental state, he supposed a depressed person might have difficulty seeing the good in anything. He couldn't tell if Patience really believed what she was saying or if she was deliberately trying to goad him. Whatever the case, he'd already decided that however this little adventure ended, the Terwilligers owed him one hell of a huge favor. Cheering up Patience Madrid—particularly when she didn't look in need of it—was no easy task. She seemed to enjoy being curmudgeonly.

They took the elevator up to his apartment. It was still covered in dropcloths, the furniture had been moved around or put in storage and carpenters were everywhere doing their thing. Patience visibly relaxed. She started up conversations with various carpenters, inspected their work, made knowledgable comments. One volunteered to take her on a grand tour. She accepted and Jake tagged along. He listened to her discuss plaster, studs, wiring, the virtues of twenties construction. Was it the scarf, Jake wondered, or the mud boots that made the carpenters take her seriously? Or maybe they were being chivalrous. Humoring her. But when she inquired about kinds of paint and painting procedures, they answered respectfully. It occurred to Jake that no one would humor Patience Madrid.

"It's a great apartment," she told Jake when she'd finished her tour. A carpenter had invited her to have lunch with them, but she'd declined. "You and Terrence have such different tastes. You don't plan to fill up the place with Oriental rugs and priceless urns, do you?"

"They're not my style. Actually, I haven't spent a great deal of time here in the last year."

Her brow furrowed. "Girlfriend?"

"Travels."

"Oh." Was that relief he saw flicker in her eyes? "Well, seeing all these folks working has made me hungry. Is there a decent restaurant around that won't break the bank?"

"One or two," he said, not too sarcastically. "Allow me to treat you."

She didn't even hesitate. "Great. Thanks."

What, he wondered, to make of the woman?

They walked back over to Broadway to a casual, popular restaurant that served great soups and hamburgers, where Patience, in her mud boots, wouldn't be out of place. New York, in fact, was a tough city for anyone to stick out in, even a woodswoman. Jake hoped that by the end of her visit she'd see that. Or at least have had a good time.

Maybe I should just hope we both survive.

She ordered Manhattan clam chowder and a hamburger with nothing on it but raw onions. Jake ordered the chowder and the pasta with calamari.

"You eat squid?" she asked.

"On occasion."

"I'd just as soon sit down to a plate full of rubber bands."

"Are you always so open about your opinions?"

"It's just food," she said, not defensively. "You're welcome to eat whatever you like. It's not like I'm criticizing you or your morals or anything important."

"But you don't acquiesce," he said, "just to avoid conflict."

She frowned. "What do you mean?"

"I mean," he went on carefully, "that some people tend to regard disagreement as a sign of disapproval. They're afraid, for example, that if they say they don't like squid the other person might not like them."

Their cups of steaming chowder arrived, with a brimming bowl of oyster crackers. Patience dumped two large spoonfuls into her soup and added a generous grinding of fresh pepper. She popped a cracker into her mouth and regarded Jake thoughtfully. "I can't imagine why anyone would care if I didn't like squid and he did."

"What about a movie?"

"You mean, if you told me you liked such-and-such a movie and I didn't? Well, I guess I'd say so."

Jake didn't "guess"—he *knew* she'd say so. "And a book?"

"Sure. Why not?"

He tried his chowder. It was very hot, loaded with fresh, not canned, clams. "Okay, what about something more personal—say, if I'd made a special dinner for you and served calamari. Would you tell me you'd just as soon eat rubber bands?"

She shook her head. "That'd be rude."

"Would you eat the calamari?"

"I'd choke a little of it down to be polite."

"Suppose I asked you if you liked calamari?"

"Depends how we got along and whether or not I felt you really wanted to know, really cared what I liked and didn't like. In my case, if I made a friend something for dinner that they hated, I'd hope they'd speak up so I could throw on a hot dog or something. If I cared about them, I'd care what they really thought. But there are times—and I think this is what you're getting at—when the social lie is preferable to the truth."

"But generally you speak your mind," Jake said.

"Generally I do."

His pasta with calamari and her hamburger arrived, and he watched her grind what seemed like two pounds of pepper atop her onions, then add a coating of ketchup. "Well," she challenged, "does this gross you out?"

He smiled. "Not at all."

She smiled back. "Is that the truth or a social lie?"

"It's the truth," he said, and it was.

"I believe in tolerance, you know. I just don't believe it means people always have to agree on everything. We don't. And in my opinion, that's not what tolerance means. You like the city, I like the mountains. That doesn't mean the city's an evil place or the mountains are, well, I don't know what."

"Evil, too?"

She shook her head, but seemed to have difficulty holding back a grin. "Nobody could ever think the mountains were evil."

"You are," he said, "an opinionated woman."

"But tolerant."

"What would you like to do this afternoon?"

She re-covered her hamburger and picked the thing up with both hands. "I don't know. What is there to do? I can always go back to Tilly's and work."

As if there were nothing interesting to do in New York. But she was challenging him, Jake decided, throwing down the proverbial gauntlet, saying to him, "Show me something in this town I actually like."

He *had* promised Terrence. *And this is only our first day together.* Refusing to let her draw him into a heated defense of his city, he suggested they go the Museum of Natural History.

She grinned, surprising him. "Now you're talking."

"I'm determined to find something in this city you

actually like," he said, just to let her know he was onto her.

"I don't know," she said, "the hamburgers are pretty good. 'Course, it's hard to mess up a burger."

"Patience—"

She laughed. "Got you, Mr. Farr. You should have seen Tilly and me in the old days when Uncle Isaiah was alive—he'd disagree with us just to liven up the conversation. How's the calamari?"

"Tasty."

"To each his own."

The air was warmer and the wind had died down when they headed over to West 79th and the Museum of Natural History, Patience commenting on every crocus and daffodil she saw. She was an observant woman, which Jake admired. But would someone suffering from depression be as aware of the world around her? He had his doubts, more and more convinced that Terrence and Matilda had misread Patience.

The planetarium was her idea. It was empty, very dark, hypnotic. Jake could smell the clean scent of Patience's soap and make out the silhouette of her angular face as the stars shone above them. They might have been on an isolated mountaintop. He fought an urge to kiss her. It was there, as unexpected and undeniable and surprising as a shooting star.

He paid no attention whatsoever to the program.

Patience leaned close to him and whispered, "I love the stars."

Her soft voice, the slight pressure of her shoulder against his, the silhouette of her mass of curls—it was more than Jake could handle. He stared at her instead of the stars.

"You should go stargazing in the Adirondacks sometime," she said.

He heard the catch in her voice and knew, in his gut, she was thinking what he was thinking, wanting what he was wanting. She could have turned back around in her seat, but didn't. And neither did he. Raising one hand, he touched his fingertips to her lips. Then, before he could talk himself out of it, followed with his mouth. They might have been alone on an Adirondack mountaintop. Her lips seemed to taste of a cool, clear, nothern lake, tempting and startlingly erotic.

This is madness! How could anything feel so right and yet so wrong? "Patience...." And he made himself pull back, hot and tortured because their kiss had been too brief, too slow, too gentle. He wanted more. He wanted, he thought, everything.

What he needed was a good dip in an Adirondack lake.

When the lights came on, Jake waited for her to say something about what had just happened between them, but Patience was quiet, not looking at him. Thinking? Falling into a state of depression? Jake tensed, waiting, hoping he hadn't been totally stupid.

Then she looked around at him and grinned broadly. "Let's go check out the dinosaur bones."

The woman was definitely hard to figure. If Terrence and Matilda had made a mistake about her, Jake could well understand how.

"Sounds good," he told her, and followed her out of the planetarium in search of tyrannosaurus rex.

ALTHOUGH SHE COULD feel her life—or at least her stay in New York—spinning out of control, Patience found herself rummaging in her sister's massive closet. Tilly owned more clothes than Patience had probably bought in her entire life. Most of them wouldn't fit. Tilly was too short and too skinny. There was a black Lycra dress that would stretch to form to Patience's taller, more athletic figure, but she'd just as soon wear black electrician's tape. And she was restricted in terms of shoes: she'd slipped a pair of black suede flats into her suitcase with her sneakers and boots, just in case. She would not fit into any of Tilly's dozens of pairs of size-six shoes.

Scarves, she thought. Maybe she could dress up her black pants with a nice scarf.

Or just tell Jake Farr she'd rather eat in tonight. On second thought, being alone with him wasn't such a great idea. He'd invited her to dinner. She'd gotten the distinct impression he didn't think she had anything to wear. Of course, she didn't. It wasn't because she didn't own any dresses that would do for a night out in New York City. It was because she hadn't brought any with her. She'd expected to spend her sojourn in the big city holed up in Tilly's apartment with two cats and a dog and her work. She hadn't expected Jake Putnam Farr.

She refused to think about their kiss in the planetarium. Absolutely refused.

Tilly had to have *something* Patience could pass off as her own. Would that be a social lie, she wondered, or a bald-faced lie? Neither, she decided. Just an expedient deception. She didn't like it when people assumed she didn't know how to dress just because she lived up north.

Mercifully, the telephone rang.

"Patience," Tilly said, "I forgot to tell you—I knew you were coming and would be too stubborn to bring anything appropriate to wear, so I bought you an early birthday present. It's in the Bergdorf Goodman's bag in my closet."

Patience carried the cordless phone with her to the closet, where she found the bag. She didn't look inside. "Tilly, I smell a rat."

"What do you mean?"

"To be more precise, I smell a manipulative sister. Did you put Jake Farr up to coming here and showing me around?"

"Jake is Terrence's friend," Tilly said, cool as she always was when guilty. "I hardly know him."

Patience humphed. "I was just hunting for something to wear in your closet because Jake and I are going to dinner, and now you call telling me you bought me clothes. You *are* up to something, Mrs. Terwilliger."

"You have such a suspicious mind. You should write mystery novels. Jake is having his apartment renovated and Terrence let him stay at our place without telling me about it. It's a simple misunderstanding, as I told you. A miscommunication."

"It's just so coincidental, your calling right when I was opening your scarf drawer for something to wear with my pants—"

"It *is* a coincidence, Patience. I was at the pool drinking a margarita when I realized it was getting close to dinnertime in New York and you might have regretted not bringing any decent clothes. So I called."

"I do have decent clothes."

"You know what I mean. Pants and a scarf, Patience? Honestly."

When they'd hung up and Patience dumped out the Bergdorf's bag, she did indeed know what her sister had meant. There was a sleek emerald-green dress, criss-cross suede shoes, a multicolored scarf that picked up the emerald and—Tilly being Tilly—big gold earrings.

Patience dressed, did her face with a mix of her sister's cosmetics and the ones she'd brought and slipped into her shoes. Her hair was pretty much hopeless, but the earrings helped to make her look elegant. She checked her reflection in Tilly's three-sided mirror.

"Hey, not bad," she said aloud.

Jake the dog had wandered into the dressing room and tried to rub against her, but she forbade him. She had no intention of picking dog hair off her dress all through dinner.

The other Jake, the human one, the one who'd upset her equilibrium all day, was waiting for her in the living room, staring out at the New York skyline. It was already seven o'clock. Usually by now she had the dishes done.

Jake turned, and just his eyebrows conveyed that he hadn't expected her to come out dressed the way she was dressed. When he said, "Let's go," she thought his voice sounded huskier than usual. He had on a dark, conservatively cut suit that made him look at once successful, sophisticated and very, very sexy. Was it him? Or had she just been in the woods too long?

They took a taxi to a small, intimate, elegant Italian restaurant on the Upper East Side. The tables were covered with pale yellow cloths and lit with long white candles. The menu was extensive and appetizing. They examined the wine list together and made their choice, Patience noticing the ridiculous markup in price. For dinner, she ordered fresh lemon sole and he picked an eggplant dish. When their bottle of wine came and the waiter filled their glasses, they toasted with a simple "Cheers."

Finally, Patience couldn't stand it any longer. "Jake, what're you up to?"

He uncovered a basket of steaming bread and offered her a piece. When she did not respond, he pulled a piece off the partially cut loaf and spread it with soft butter. "I'm having dinner with an interesting, attractive writer."

It was a smooth answer. "Did Tilly put you up to taking me out?"

"No."

"Well, something's fishy."

Jake looked at her from across the table, the candlelight flickering in his dark eyes. "How so? You came to New York to cat-sit for your sister, only to find her husband had permitted me to stay while my apartment's being renovated. That doesn't strike me as particularly fishy."

"It doesn't?"

He sighed. "I suppose it's a bit coincidental, but—"

"Then taking me around today was your idea?"

"Yes." But before she could decide if she was relieved or not, he added, "And no."

"So you *have* talked to Tilly."

He shook his head. "To Terrence."

Patience almost dropped her wineglass. "*Terrence?* You mean *he* put you up to this?"

"Not exactly. He said you were depressed and—"

"Depressed? Me? I can't believe... I swear that man... Well, I won't say it since he's your friend. But look at me, Jake. Do I look depressed?"

Leaning back in his chair, Jake did look at her for longer than she felt he needed to make his assessment, and more closely than she found comfortable. His expression was impossible to read in the shadows. She hoped her reaction, the heat rushing to her cheeks, was also not apparent.

"No," he said finally, "I wouldn't say you look depressed."

Patience struggled to keep her balance, aware of Jake Farr's eyes still on her. "Where'd he ever get such a loony idea?"

Jake didn't answer.

Putting two and two together, Patience said, "Tilly."

Again Jake diplomatically withheld comment.

"What's gotten into her?" Patience muttered, irritated and embarrassed and just plain surprised. Her sister had plunged right off the deep end without her noticing.

"I have no intention of coming between you and your sister."

"Then don't," she snapped, not angry at him so much as disturbed by this new gulf between her and her sister.

"Patience, I asked you to dinner tonight because I wanted to be with you." His voice was calm, reasonable...and seductive. "I wanted to get to know you bet-

ter. I'd already decided Terrence was mistaken about
your mental state and—"

"My mental state." She nearly choked. "I really don't
appreciate you and my brother-in-law discussing me
behind my back."

Jake didn't retreat. "I don't blame you for being
upset."

"I am not upset," she said testily. Where was her
self-control? "I am *angry,* Jake, and getting angrier by
the second. Don't you get it? Tilly has to know I'm
not depressed. I don't even understand depression. She
just said that because—" She broke off, not wanting
to put her foot in her mouth. In her emotional state,
she knew she'd say something about herself, her sister,
Tilly's marriage. Or she'd say something about how
being around Jake Farr all day—and their kiss—had
catapulted her senses into overdrive. She'd regret it,
whatever she said.

Their dinners arrived, and she smiled at the waiter
and said everything was fine, and so did Jake. Then
the waiter brought freshly grated pepper and Parmesan
cheese, and finally withdrew. Jake refilled their wine-
glasses, looking unperturbed, controlled. Of course, he
wasn't the one having tales told about him.

The fish smelled wonderful. So did Jake's eggplant.

And she was hungry.

"I think I know what's going on," Jake said.

"I thought you might." He was not a stupid man.

Without looking at her, he went on, "Your sister arranged this weekend to get us together."

Bingo.

But Patience didn't say a word. Obviously her sister was trying—consciously or not—to distract herself from her own romantic difficulties. But, as annoyed as she was with Tilly, she refused to confide her sister's most private problems to Terrence's best friend.

"Look," Jake went on, "it's not the first time a friend's done something like this to me, or for me, depending on your point of view."

Patience quickly swallowed some of her wine, wondering if she were just another in a long line of women presented to Jake Farr and rejected by him. The idea didn't sit well with her at all. "If you don't mind," she said coolly, "I need to sort this out in my own mind first. Can we just back-burner this one and enjoy our dinner?"

"That," Jake said, "is a wonderful idea."

And he smiled, a raw, gentle, sensitive, hungry smile that left her ten times as confused as she'd been a moment ago. Should she thank Tilly for putting her and Jake Farr together?

No. Jake had just been decent the past twenty-four hours because he'd thought she was depressed. It was sheer lunacy. The woman he thought he'd been taking around the Upper West Side today—the one he'd seemed attracted to—wasn't her. His actions, his assessment of her, had been colored by having been told she was depressed.

It was just too much. But what was she going to do about it?

Enjoy dinner, she thought. And deal with Tilly Terwilliger the first chance she got.

"YES, I'M SURE I have the name right. The Hidden Camel Resort in Scottsdale, Arizona."

"I'm sorry, ma'am, but there's no listing—"

"There has to be."

"Please check the name and city and try again, ma'am. We'll be glad to assist you."

Patience hung up the phone, frustrated and vaguely worried. Now what? Maybe she just needed to sleep. Look at things fresh in the morning. She'd eaten too much and spent too much time with a certain tall, gorgeous man today. Tomorrow everything would make sense.

Only it wouldn't, and she knew it.

In her stocking feet, she returned to the living room, where her temporary roommate seemed transfixed by the New York skyline. Her breath caught in her throat. He'd taken off his jacket and rolled up the shirtsleeves. The dark hairs of his arms contrasted with the stark white of the expensive fabric. He seemed pensive and as hard to figure as ever. If only Tilly hadn't stuck her big nose into her life…

She might never have gotten around to meeting Jake Farr. And then what? *I wouldn't be feeling so damned out of my element is what.*

"Even my moose head didn't make me this nuts," she muttered.

Jake turned. "I beg your pardon?"

Even as polite as he was, she could hear the huskiness in his voice, the undertone of confusion and irritation. After dinner, they'd taken a taxi back to Central Park West. It must have been a smaller cab than the first one, because Patience didn't remember sitting so close to Jake, feeling his thigh brush up against hers, noticing his hands, his strong chin, the tiny scar at the corner of his right eye. When they arrived at the apartment, she'd fled into her borrowed bedroom to call her sister, hoping whatever had gotten into her in the cab—that shocking, insidious awareness of him—would have gotten out again by the time she had to face him.

It hadn't.

"Nothing," she said. "I can't get hold of Tilly."

"She'll call you back?"

"No, I didn't leave a message."

Technically, she wasn't telling a falsehood; she *hadn't* left a message. But that was only because her rat-fink sister hadn't told her where she was really staying.

"Maybe she and Terrence are still at dinner," Jake suggested. "It's early yet."

Patience didn't disabuse him of his notion that Terrence and Tilly were in Florida together. Until she and Tilly could have a proper heart-to-heart, Patience was unwilling to reveal anything to Terrence's best friend.

Sitting on one of the Terwilligers' elegant couches, Jake asked casually, "Where is the Hidden Flamingo, anyway? I've never heard of it, and I didn't think to ask. I assumed the Orlando area, but—Patience, is something wrong?"

The Hidden Flamingo in Florida.

The Hidden Camel in Arizona.

First, she and Jake Farr had ended up on Central Park West at the same time. Next, Tilly had arranged for Terrence to tell Jake her sister was depressed. But now, the Hidden Flamingo and the Hidden Camel? That was too much for Patience to swallow.

This really was war.

"Patience?"

"I need to think before I tell you more," she said.

She wasn't looking at him, but could feel his eyes boring into her. A curious warmth spread through her. Finally, she gave him a quick glance. Indeed, his eyes were pinned to her. Dark, narrowed, knowing eyes.

"What?" she asked, her tone just this side of demanding.

"I'm just trying to think of a way," he said, "to get you to trust me."

Then he was on his feet, and in two steps was only an inch away. She could smell his cologne and see the stubble of his beard. He studied her face, and she wondered what he could see. Anger? Confusion? Smudged mascara? A woman who desperately wanted to trust him?

He touched the corner of her mouth with his finger briefly, for a fraction of a second. She had no idea why. He didn't explain, she didn't ask. But just that simple breath of a touch ignited the center of her, and she forgot all about her crazy sister's schemes and troubled marriage.

"I trust you," she said, surprised at how certain she sounded. "We've spent the last two nights together, haven't we? I mean, not together-together, which maybe is the whole point...oh, hell, you know what I mean."

"I think I do." His voice was still low, seductive. "But I'm not asking if you trust me to be an ordinary, decent human being and not attack you. I'm asking, do you trust me?"

And his lips touched where his finger had, for half a breath longer.

She knew exactly what he was asking.

But he didn't give her a chance to answer. His mouth

covered hers, pressing his case. He drew her to him, so that she could feel the hardness of him, as his tongue parted her lips. She responded to his urgency, and to her own.

Jake pulled away and asked again in a hoarse voice. "Do you trust me?"

She nodded, unable to speak.

"Good."

Patience found her voice. "Why is it good?"

"Because—" He paused, holding her, but his expression unreadable. "Because I just spent a day with an intriguing woman who's used to making her own decisions and fighting her own battles. Maybe too used to it. I can say that because I'm like that myself, except maybe not so intriguing."

"I don't know about that. I have more questions about you tonight than I did this morning."

"Ditto me about you." He laughed, a rich, deep, free laugh. "Fun, isn't it?"

"I need to think before I tell you more," she said.

"I'm not trying to make you tell me anything you don't want to tell me. I just want you to feel you can trust me. Terrence is a friend, but so is Matilda…Tilly. And I'd like to think you are, too."

Before she could respond, Jake the dog worked his way between them, rubbing hair on her dress and the other Jake's charcoal trousers. He brushed his thigh in disgust.

Patience winced. "I'm sorry—"

He waved off her apology. "I'm flattered he's jealous."

"Actually," she said, "I think he just wants a beer."

Jake laughed. "Then that's two of us."

Feeling strangely unsettled and yet wholly intrigued, Patience watched the two Jakes lope off to the kitchen. When they were out of sight, Apollo and Aphrodite strolled out to greet her, rubbing white hairs against her suede shoes.

Suddenly she knew what she had to do.

Looking out at the New York skyline, the buildings that seemed almost alive with lights against the night sky, she imagined the stars above her cabin, how they'd sparkle on her moonlit lake.

She had to go home. Dog, cats, sister, brother-in-law and attractive New York businessman or not. In the mountains, far away from Jake Putnam Farr, she could think clearly.

On her way to bed, she could hear Jake giving his new canine companion the lowdown on a long list of domestic and imported beers, and she smiled, genuinely liking the man.

Which was as good a reason as any, in her view, to get the hell out of New York.

CHAPTER SIX

JAKE HEARD PATIENCE fumbling around the apartment, collecting cats and dog, throwing her things together, preparing to make her exit. Folding his hands under his neck, he settled back against the multitude of pillows on the big bed. He debated going out and saying goodbye. But it was six o'clock in the morning and she was deliberately trying to sneak out before he got up.

He'd let her.

There was no good reason for her to be leaving. So what if Matilda had engineered their week together? He'd been the victim of far worse would-be matchmakers. And it wasn't as if he and Patience Madrid hadn't been getting along. They had.

Which no doubt was the real reason for this mad exit. He'd touched a raw nerve and now she was making good her escape.

Or was he being arrogant?

Her departure could also have damned little to do with him. He recalled her reaction to his question about the Hidden Flamingo. Terrence hadn't left a number as he'd promised, otherwise Jake would have called him and demanded to know what in blazes was going on. But why had Patience looked so shocked and suspicious when he'd mentioned where her sister and brother-in-law were staying?

"I need to think before I tell you more."

Well, apparently she'd done her thinking and had decided *not* to tell him more.

"Jake," she called in a loud whisper. He knew she didn't mean him. "Jake, no, you can't go in there. Now come on."

He could hear the dog sniffing at his bedroom door. He'd miss the ugly hound.

But they'd see each other again soon. Jake was confident of that. He and Patience Madrid had unfinished business, whether she'd admit it or not.

When he was sure she was gone, he rolled out of bed and wandered into the kitchen, where he wasn't surprised to find a curt note from his ex-roommate.

Dear Jake,
I decided to return home—I've taken the cats with me, so you needn't worry about them. I'll let Tilly know. Help yourself to the groceries I left.
    And thanks for showing me around NYC. It was more fun than I'd expected.
Patience

It wasn't the sort of note worth keeping for posterity. He crumpled it up and tossed it in the trash can, only to notice a small heap of crumpled-up notes. He scooped them out and dumped them on the table, then smoothed them one by one. Each was an aborted attempt at a note to him. There were seven tries in all.

"Dear Jake, Sorry I didn't say goodbye, but I didn't want to wake you."

"Dear Jake, It's been fun, but"

"Dear Jake, I'm sure I must seem a coward to you sneaking off at the crack of dawn, but I wanted to beat rush hour and"

"Jake, Apollo, Aphrodite and I have gone to the mountains. See you. P.M."

"Jake:"

"Jake: Decided to head home, but not on account of you or anything we"

"Dear Jake, I had a great time with you in New York, but decided to head home. Took the animals with me. Enjoy your stay on Central Park West. I'll be in touch. No, I won't."

So. She'd struggled to find the right words for her goodbye note. He was amused. Flattered. *Challenged.*

Where in the Adirondacks did Terrence say his unusual sister-in-law lived?

He found a map of New York on his phone, and, over a pot of coffee, scoured the northeast corner of the state for a town, village, mountaintop, route number or lake that sounded familiar.

Patience Madrid hadn't heard the last of him.

SIX HOURS AFTER she'd arrived back at her lakeside cabin, Patience had been for a walk around the lake with Jake, filled her wood box, lit the stove, made a pot of chili and given up on keeping her visitors from New York fluffy and white. They'd appropriated Jake's spot under the woodstove. He hadn't minded at first; three nights in the big city had given him a taste for human beds.

But after Patience kicked him off her bed the third time and threatened to throw him outside for the balance of Apollo and Aphrodite's visit, he decided he wanted back his spot under the stove. The cats, however, wouldn't budge. It didn't seem to occur to any of the three animals that Jake was big enough to insist.

Leaving well enough alone, Patience curled up on her sofa with a notepad for a brainstorming session. Nothing like work to ease one's mind.

She wondered what Jake Farr had done when he'd found her note. For a while she'd entertained the fantasy—a word she never thought she'd associate with her feet-flat-on-the-floor self—that he'd immediately set out for the Adirondacks. But he'd have been here by now. Unless he'd gotten lost....

"Nope," she said aloud, "he's not the type to get lost."

So what had he done?

Tossed out her note, eaten breakfast and gotten on with his life.

She sighed, and then the telephone rang.

Tilly was in a rage. "Patience, I don't believe you. You have Apollo and Aphrodite in the *mountains!*"

It wasn't a question. Obviously Tilly already knew the answer. It was more an expression of outrage and incredulity. Nevertheless, Patience reined in her own annoyance and said, "Sure. They're having a ball."

"Doing what?"

Patience didn't appreciate the unrepentant note of suspicion in her sister's voice. "Enjoying life in the beautiful Adirondacks."

"You haven't let them outside, have you?"

"No, of course not." She'd tried; they wouldn't go.

Nothing irritated her more than house cats. "Tilly, quit worrying. You know I'd never let anything happen to them."

"They're not country cats."

This was not news to Patience.

Tilly groaned. "I wish you'd told me you were taking them up to the cabin with you."

"I would have," Patience said coolly, "but I didn't have your number."

"Yes, I know."

Again, not even a hint of guilt. "How did you know I was here?"

"How do you think? Jake Farr told me when I tried to reach you a little while ago."

Patience licked her lips. She didn't want to give away her confused feelings toward her brother-in-law's best friend. Coming home hadn't put him out of her mind, as she'd hoped. "Then he's staying on at your apartment?"

"For now." Tilly paused, then cleared her throat. "How much does he know?"

"Nothing."

"How'd you find me out?"

"The Hidden Camel and the Hidden Flamingo, Til? Come on, you could have done better."

"So I'm not a writer like you."

"I deal in nonfiction, Tilly. Facts, not make-believe, not *lies*. The hurting marriage, the separate vacations— all a ruse to get me and Jake Farr together?"

There was a silence on the other end—wherever it was—of the phone.

Then Tilly said softly, "Not entirely."

Patience felt a knife-stab of guilt. "You want to tell me what really is going on?"

"I can't."

"Can't or won't?"

"A little of both. I don't mean to be closemouthed, Patience, but I'm in an awkward position. I'll tell you everything when I get back. I promise."

"What about Terrence?"

"He's still my husband," Tilly said vaguely and, Patience thought, a little desperately.

"I'll tend Apollo and Aphrodite," Patience said. "Don't worry about them, okay?"

"What about Jake?"

"Well, if the cats give him his place back under the stove I think they'll get along well."

Tilly gave a small hiss of pure, sisterly irritation. "I didn't mean your confounded dog, Patience. I meant Jake Farr."

"Oh."

"When I spoke with him, he sounded, I don't know, not annoyed with you, really. Just determined."

"Determined to do what?"

"I couldn't say."

Apollo slithered out from under the woodstove, stretched and hopped onto Patience's lap. He was covered with soot, sawdust and wood chips. Nothing like a white cat to point out one's housekeeping deficiencies.

"Well," Patience said, "it doesn't matter. He's in New York and I'm up here at the lake. By the way, was my being depressed your idea or Terrence's?"

"Your being what?"

"Depressed, Tilly. Don't act as if you don't know.

Terrence told his pal Jake that his weird sister-in-law was depressed and could he please show her around New York."

"Are you serious? Patience, you've never been depressed in your life. It's just not your style."

"I know that," she snapped, really confused now.

Tilly sighed. "No, telling Jake you were depressed was not my idea."

"Look, you and Terrence just get your act together where I'm concerned, okay? I don't need you messing around in my life."

"I understand. Really I do. But…you can't blame Terrence for thinking—if it is what he thought—that Jake was your type, can you?"

"How can a New York businessman be my type?"

"It's not as if he's an ordinary New York businessman. Good Lord, Patience, Jake Farr's climbed more mountains than you have!"

And on that note Tilly said goodbye and hung up without mentioning where she was staying or what, exactly, she and Terrence were up to. Patience resisted the urge to throw her phone across the room.

Why did she feel as if the heavy hand of fate had given her life a good swat?

She patted Apollo, and he immediately began to purr. Jake had wormed his way underneath the stove, and Aphrodite, as filthy as her fellow Persian, had curled up on his stomach.

"Good Lord, Patience, Jake Farr's climbed more mountains than you have!"

"Well," she said aloud, "I've never claimed to be a terrific judge of people."

Male people in particular.

Had she misjudged Jake Putnam Farr?

No, she thought. She hadn't misjudged him. She hadn't judged him at all. She'd fled New York before she'd given herself that chance.

"So, what next?"

A good night's sleep. Cabin-scrubbing in the morning. Then baths for the cats and maybe Jake as well.

There was nothing like physical labor and fresh mountain air to stimulate the brain. By tomorrow afteroon, she'd have a plan of action to figure out what to do about her sister, her brother-in-law and the mountain-climbing New York businessman.

Jake Farr wasn't the only one who knew how to be determined.

IT WAS DARKER than the pits of hell at midnight in the Adirondack Mountains.

Jake crept along the narrow dirt road in his Acura, grateful he didn't go for low-slung sports cars. As it was, he'd gone into a few potholes he'd thought he'd never come out of again. Matilda had warned him.

"It's a rough road," she'd said. "Patience loses her muffler every spring."

He'd thought Tilly had been exaggerating.

He hoped to hell he had the right dirt road.

"It winds around through the woods for a mile or so before you come to the lake, which kind of sneaks up on you."

Seeing how the Adirondack State Park was six million acres' worth of forest, Jake had had no trouble finding a dirt road through the woods. And there were thousands of lakes. Chances were this dirt road, even if the wrong one, would land him on the shores of a lake.

A furry creature scurried in front of his car. Jake could see bright eyes reflected in his headlights and a black silhouette that was too big for a raccoon and too small for a bear. It disappeared into the woods, and he didn't contemplate what species it might be. He checked his gas tank. Half-full. He hadn't thought to pack any camping gear in the trunk. What if he didn't come upon the Madrid cabin soon? What if he had to spend the night out in the wilderness? He'd survive, of course. He knew his way around the woods. But he doubted he'd be in any temper to deal with Miss Patience Madrid in the morning.

"Trust me," her sister had said, "she lives *way* out in the woods."

He hadn't seen any evidence of human habitation since the exit off the interstate, over forty minutes ago.

What had he gotten himself into this time?

"I wouldn't ask this of you, Jake, but I'm really worried about my sister."

Yes, yes. And what a good soul he was to drag himself off to the wilderness to find her. He'd had tickets to the Rangers game that evening. Behind the penalty box.

Why didn't the Patience Madrid he'd kissed and the Patience Madrid her sister described not jive? Those two Patiences were why he'd headed north. He had to reconcile them. He had to know who he'd kissed last night, who he'd dreamed about, who he couldn't get out of his mind. He had to find out who Terrence's strawberry-haired sister-in-law was and whether or not he should leave her in the woods with her animals.

"Holy—"

He crashed on his brakes and came to a screeching halt inches, it seemed, from a glass-still lake. His heart pounding, he sat with his foot hard on the brake and stared across the quiet waters that reflected the star-dotted night sky. He loosened his grip on the steering wheel. Swallowed. Breathed again.

He was here, in Madrid country. And it was as startlingly beautiful, as eerily seductive as he ever could have imagined. If he were going to be a hermit, he should be so lucky to pick a spot as breathtaking as this one.

"Make a ninety-degree turn to the right," Tilly Terwilliger had directed. "Follow the road all the way around to the other side of the lake. You'll go past a couple of summer cabins. Patience's will be the last one you come to—she has the whole north side of the lake to herself. If it's cold, it'll probably have smoke coming out of the chimney."

Following her sister's instructions, Jake backed up and made the turn. If possible, the road narrowed even more. There were ruts, rocks, holes, the odd branch, more scurrying creatures. A lovely cabin with a huge deck on his left. A steep incline, then another cabin. Both were deserted for the winter. The road veered off into the woods again, away from the lake, and after another half mile there was another cabin, this one older, less attractive. He bounced through three holes in quick succession. He thought his muffler was gone for sure, but it held fast.

What did Patience do when she ran out of milk?

How had he let Tilly talk him into this escapade?

She didn't. You'd already decided to go. She just gave you an excuse.

"Madness," he said, negotiating a steep downhill turn.

Once more, through the dark silhouettes of the tall evergreens, he could see the starlit mirror of the lake. He had to be getting close.

Then an old log cabin came into view, nestled into the woods not far from shore. A dim light burned somewhere inside. And smoke was, indeed, curling from the stone chimney. Jake turned into the narrow driveway and parked, debating for a few seconds before turning off his engine whether or not to head back to New York. Patience had sneaked out on him that morning. Maybe it had been a difficult decision, but she'd made it, stuck to it. What right did he have barging in on her? Hadn't she denied being even remotely depressed?

"Of course she denied it!" Tilly had groaned. "Patience would never admit a weakness."

So, Jake thought, he'd made *his* difficult decision. And now he had to stick to it.

He shut off his car engine and climbed out, the crisp, cold Adirondack air instantly reinvigorating him. He grabbed his knapsack from the back seat, slung it over one shoulder and started along a flagstone path to the front of the cabin. He moved with care. If Jake were an outdoor dog, he might not recognize him right away and attack. Or there could be other nocturnal creatures lurking about.

In any case, he was definitely in Madrid country and prepared for anything.

He felt only slightly guilty about showing up on Patience's doorstep in the middle of the night. After all, within the past few days he'd been accosted by her dog in an elevator and had his bed confiscated by her and her creatures.

He climbed up onto the porch and knocked on her solid, rough-wood door. "Patience?"

"It's a good thing," her voice said behind him, "that I look before I shoot."

He turned slowly, carefully, and sure enough, there she stood behind him in a red union suit, her hair sticking out everywhere, pointing a shotgun at him.

"Your teeth are chattering," he said.

She lowered her gun. "Wouldn't affect my aim."

"Hello, Patience."

"Hello, Jake."

"Mind if I come in?"

She didn't answer right away. "Door's open. Don't let the cats out."

He went inside, and she followed, shutting the door hard behind her. She leaned her shotgun up against the wall. It looked maybe eighty years old.

"Is it loaded?" he asked.

"Nope. If you'd been a stranger up to no good I'd have just whacked you over the head. I don't need ammunition to do that. I heard you coming about fifteen minutes ago and snuck outside, just in case."

The contradictions Jake had come to expect from Patience Madrid were in evidence. The chattering teeth coupled with the tough talk. The long, slender fingers and feminine curves under the well-worn, purely functional union suit. The wild hair framing the clear, peachy skin and wide, sensitive eyes. She seemed absolutely, incontrovertibly confident, and, at the same time, curiously, agonizingly vulnerable.

Jake had never met a woman he wanted to know more.

She flipped on a copper lamp above a small, round oak table in what passed for a dining area. As far as he could tell, her cabin consisted of two cozy, charming rooms. The kitchen, dining and living areas formed an L. The furnishings were a mix of flea market and hand-crafted pieces. Tilly's two cats and Patience's dog were asleep together under the woodstove. How they all fit Jake couldn't have said. He duly noted the state-of-the-art computer and printer on the far wall, under a portrait of an old man with a white bushy beard standing next to a dog or a bear, Jake couldn't tell which. The infamous Uncle Isaiah, he presumed.

Through an open doorway, he caught a peek of an unmade bed.

"Sorry I woke you," he said.

"I wasn't asleep. Mind telling me what you're doing here?"

In the dim light, he could see the clear teal of her eyes, the stubborn set of her jaw. Patience Madrid didn't trust him. She wasn't afraid of him—she just didn't trust him.

"I spoke to your sister. She's worried about you."

"Horsefeathers."

"It's true. She asked me to check on you."

Patience sighed. "Because I'm depressed?"

"On the verge of becoming a misanthropic hermit. She wouldn't call it depression."

Grumbling, Patience pulled a pitted kettle off the

woodstove and, with her free hand, grabbed two mugs from an open shelf. "Tea?" she asked.

"I'd love some."

He almost changed his mind when she dumped a tablespoon of what looked like bird food in each of the mugs. She added water, banged the kettle back down on the stove and threw on another log. Definitely a woman who could fend for herself.

She set the two mugs on the table, next to a stack of newspapers and magazines. Jake pulled out a chair, but didn't sit down right away. Most of whatever Patience had dumped in his cup had settled to the bottom, but a few odd pods and leaves were floating on the surface.

"It's a soothing mixture of herbs," she said. "I forget what all kinds."

"Don't you have a strainer?"

"Somewhere."

But she sat down and sipped at her brew, and Jake decided he'd best make do.

The stuff was dreadful.

"I've been working hard," Patience said, "and I haven't been out much this winter. But I'm not depressed and I'm not a 'misanthropic hermit.' Can't you see what Tilly's doing?"

Truthfully, he couldn't. He'd given up on trying to figure out the Madrid sisters at all. In fact, as certain as he was driving up from New York that he was doing the right thing, now he couldn't imagine how he'd swallowed Matilda Madrid Terwilliger's line. Her sister seemed fine.

"What do *you* think she's doing?" he asked, keeping his calm.

"Trying to keep us together. Physically together. I mean…" She blushed, which, Jake would guess, was an unusual experience for her. "She's matchmaking."

"I see."

"I told you that before."

"Yes, but she insists she can't imagine any two people more unsuited for each other than the two of us, that she's not matchmaking but trying to keep you from becoming another Uncle Isaiah."

Patience looked at him. "Oh."

"I'm at a loss as to whom to believe."

"Well, it's not as if *I* think we're suited for each other.…"

He smiled. It clearly had crossed her mind.

Her spine ramrod-straight, she rose, mug in hand. "I'm going to bed. You're welcome to spend the night—the couch is reasonably comfortable. If you need another blanket, give a yell. We'll figure out this mess in the morning."

She crammed another log onto the fire, then headed off to bed, firmly closing the door behind her.

Alone in the L-shaped room, Jake could hear animals breathing, the fire crackling. How the hell had he ended up here? He poured his "tea" down the drain. Through the window above the sink he could see the shadows of the tall evergreens around the cabin, the seemingly endless night. Not even in the distance could he hear the scream of a police or ambulance siren, the honking of taxi horns.

The couch *was* only reasonably comfortable.

He kicked off his shoes but left on his jeans lest God-knew-what disturbed him in the night, then pulled the thick, soft, worn afghan up over him.

Jake the dog crept out from under the woodstove and licked his face, flopping down alongside the couch. He smelled of pine and long-dead leaves. Apollo and Aphrodite, no longer snow-white, peered suspiciously at the two Jakes from under the stove.

All in all, Jake had to admit Patience Madrid didn't have a bad life in the mountains. But what did she do when she tired of four-legged company?

CHAPTER SEVEN

PATIENCE WOKE at six o'clock, glad she was in her own bed in her own house. There was no danger, however, of her barging in on Jake Farr in the next room. She had not forgotten he was there.

"Not bloody likely I would," she muttered, throwing back the covers.

She got dressed and crept across her small bedroom. After sharing the Terwilligers' apartment with Mr. New York, she was well aware he didn't keep the same hours she did. She cracked the bedroom door and peered into the front room. All seemed quiet and peaceful. She had no idea how late Jake would sleep. He'd seemed pretty tired last night and wasn't conditioned to early rising the way she was. She'd *tried* to sleep late.

Opening the door a bit wider, she looked left to where the couch was pushed up against the wall. She didn't know how long she could stand being confined to her room. She had things to do.

Jake looked twisted and uncomfortable, one black-stockinged foot poking out from the end of her afghan, his arms at odd angles. His eyes were closed. Patience noticed the dark shadow of beard on his square, upper-class jaw.

How did Jake Putnam Farr end up asleep on her couch?

"Better than asleep in your bed," she grumbled well under her breath. "Or worse."

He stirred.

"I'm awake," he said, not sounding pleased.

"Awake-awake or getting there?"

"Neither." He still hadn't opened his eyes. "I can't say I've been asleep."

"Rough night?"

"Your dog wanted to go out sometime around five o'clock."

"He's a little off his schedule because of New York. Usually he waits until five-thirty or even six."

"How charming."

"Did you let him out?"

His eyes opened. "I walked him."

She laughed. She couldn't help it.

Jake Farr glared at her. "What the hell's so funny?"

"Well…" She tried to control herself. "You don't walk dogs up here. You just open the door and let them go do their thing. You walk dogs in New York."

She went over to the stove, noticing her Jake squished up under it, looking very pleased with himself. Obviously he enjoyed putting one over on a rich New Yorker. Patience tried not to share too much in his amusement; Jake Farr *was* her guest. She noticed it was foggy out. Ahh, March.

Heat—plenty of it—radiated from the stove. Or was it having Jake Farr's eyes on her? She'd put on heavy dark leggings and a long roll-top yellow sweater, a concession to her intensely male guest. Or her reaction to him.

"I kept the fire going," he said.

"Thank you."

"You're welcome, but it was just self-preservation."

He'd sat up, thrown off the afghan. He looked rumpled and about as egregiously sexy as any man had a right to look. He ran one hand through his hair, a gesture Patience found irresistibly masculine. Her physical response to him, from the tingling in her lips right down to her toenails, was way out of bounds. She had to regain some control before she did something she regretted. She knew she could count on her good sense to stop her. But it was that feeling that she'd *like* to do something she'd regret that ate at her.

That and Jake Farr's overwhelming physical presence.

"I'm surprised I didn't hear you," she said. "I must have slept more soundly than I thought."

Soundly, but not easily. She'd had full-color dreams of her and Jake Farr. She refused to analyze them, at least not while he was camped out on her couch. Right now, Jake was too real—too much of a threat to her stability—for her to examine her subconscious thoughts about him.

"Something hot to drink?" she asked.

"Such as?"

He sounded suspicious. Obviously he hadn't liked her tea last night. "Coffee."

She ground some mocha java beans, got out an unbleached filter, dumped in the coffee and poured on boiling water. She flipped on the public radio station broadcast out of Albany and listened to "Morning Edition." Jake emerged from under the stove and she let him out. Then the cats deigned to show their presence, rubbing up against her legs and purring until she finally fed them. No fancy cat dishes in her house. They got a couple of tin plates Uncle Isaiah had left behind.

While she rinsed out the can of cat food for recycling, she sensed Jake's presence behind her. She said idly, "Apollo and Aphrodite are beginning to look like real cats, don't you think?"

"You'll bathe them before you return them to your sister?"

"I suppose I'll have to."

The coffee made, Patience poured two mugs and sliced a couple of bagels she'd brought with her from New York. She placed them in the woodstove oven to heat up, then banged the door shut with her foot. She didn't have any cream cheese, so she put out butter and natural peanut butter. To make room for her company, she piled up her newspapers and magazines and shoved them to one side.

"What did you think you'd accomplish by coming here?" she asked, trying to sound casual, as if she didn't much care.

Jake shrugged. She thought she detected the same level of forced casualness in him. "I don't know."

"Tilly had you worried?"

"Not really. She's the one who was worried. Even if she was exaggerating—"

"She was *lying,* Jake."

He sat down at the table and sipped his coffee before answering. "I couldn't take that chance."

"Why not? It's not as if you owe me anything. We only just met."

"True, but Terrence and your sister are my friends. I felt I owed them at least the effort of looking in on you and reassuring them you were fine."

Patience didn't know whether or not to be insulted, or even just slightly miffed. Did she want Jake Farr to tell her he'd headed north because he wanted to see her again?

She leaped up suddenly and snatched the bagels out of the oven. She'd almost let them burn.

"They're a little crisp," she said, "but they'll do."

Jake was smiling. "You seem at home here."

"I *am* at home here."

"But you seemed just as at home on Central Park West. Cooking on a woodstove or a restaurant-style stove doesn't seem to make much difference to you."

She pointed her knife at her small kitchen area. "I have a regular stove here, too."

It wasn't, however, anything like the Terwilligers' expensive, state-of-the-art stove.

"You don't need to be defensive."

"I'm not."

"I'm merely suggesting that you have the ability to adapt, to make the best of any given situation, that your surroundings—material things—aren't all that important to you."

She laughed. "Good thing, huh?"

"Yes," he said, taking in her modest accommodations, "one could say that."

"What about you?"

"Given a choice between an expensive apartment

and a great view, I'll take the view. But it depends on the circumstances."

"Tilly says you like to climb mountains." Of course, Tilly had also adamantly denied having told Jake Farr her sister was depressed.

"It's a hobby of mine, yes."

"What kind of mountains?"

"Virtually any kind. I've done all the peaks in the Adirondacks. In fact, I was supposed to have gone climbing in New Zealand during the renovations on my apartment, but that trip fell through, which is how I ended up at your sister's."

Mountain-climbing in New Zealand. The man did defy expectations. Patience wished she'd spent more time grilling Tilly on Jake Farr's background.

After breakfast, he insisted on cleaning up, and she was happy to let him at her kitchen. Grabbing a jacket, she headed outside. She needed a dose of fresh, cold mountain air to regain her equilibrium.

She'd enjoyed having Jake Farr across her breakfast table. She'd thought too much about rubbing the back of her hand across his stubble of beard. Thought too much about where he might sleep tonight, if he stayed.

What had happened to her peaceful, orderly, productive life?

She headed down to the lake and walked out to the end of the dock, the four-legged Jake at her heels. Morning fog swirled over the water. The air was downright springlike. She inhaled deep lungfuls of it, glad to be home, away from New York and—

"And its excitement," she finished aloud, forcing herself to be honest.

New York City was an energetic place. She remembered the glittering skyline outside Tilly's apartment, the rush she'd felt when she'd seen Jake's renovations, the elegant dinner they'd had together and how sophisticated she'd felt. Contrary to popular belief, she did enjoy dressing up and going out once in a while. Putting on evening clothes, makeup, panty hose, heels. So she'd been holed up all winter working. Did that mean she was a hermit? It wasn't as if she holed up *every* winter.

Or was it Jake Putnam Farr who had made her see New York in a different light? The man had worked his way under her skin and was hell-bent, it seemed, for her soul. And she didn't know why. *Why* was she so attracted to him?

And was he attracted to her? Or was she just a curiosity to him? A woman who could get along on her own in the mountains. Who knew how to chop wood, build a fire and shoot a gun.

Her mutt had dragged a wet, muddy stick down to the dock. She got it away from him and flung it into the lake. "Fetch, Jake," she urged. "Come on, fetch."

He didn't move.

"You slug, Jake."

"I'm assuming you're speaking to your dog," Jake Farr said, joining her on the dock. "But if you ask me, I wouldn't jump in that cold water to go after a stupid stick, either."

Again Patience felt a surge of warmth at seeing him. It was getting worse, not better, each time he came close to her. And he was close. If she tried to put a few more inches between them she'd land up in the icy lake herself.

"Swimming's good exercise," she said.

"No doubt. When do you take your first dip?"

"Memorial Day, just to say I've done it. I last about ten seconds. I'm not into frostbite swimming."

"When does the water get warm?"

"It doesn't. It gets comfortable, though, around mid-July."

He nodded, acknowledging her words. He seemed content as he looked out across the quiet lake. "Do you go canoeing?"

"Every chance I get. Jake and I go together."

His smile settled on her. "Sounds fun. Think it'll be warm enough to get out on the water today?"

Before she could think—before she could come to her senses—she nodded and said sure. In another minute, she and Jake Farr were heading up to her shed to get out her canoe and paddles and make sure they were lakeworthy.

If she'd been aware of him in her cabin, out on the dock, what would happen when she got into a canoe with him? Then for sure she'd have no place to run. She'd just have to sit there and paddle along and...

"Can you steer a canoe?" she asked.

"Uh-huh."

Good, she thought. At least then she'd have her back to him.

IT WAS A MISTAKE.

Jake steered fine. It wasn't that. And she didn't have to worry about being distracted by having to look at his strong back and dark hair. No, not at all. Instead she was distracted with imagining what *he* was thinking in the stern of the canoe looking at *her*.

In the middle of the quiet, still lake, with a clear, sunny sky overhead and the mountains all around them, she could feel Jake Farr's eyes on her. It was all she could do not to swing around suddenly and catch him at it. But she didn't want to capsize the canoe.

Jake was on the end of the dock, barking at them. His human counterpart had refused to take him along on his first outing on the unfamiliar lake. Patience had concurred. Her dog had not, however, and made his displeasure known.

"Does anyone in the Madrid household suffer in silence?" Jake asked.

"People say you always know where you stand with a Madrid."

"I can see why."

Her voice was a little hoarse and that tingling of pure sexual awareness was back, throwing off her paddling rhythm. She wondered if she was just imagining things. Maybe Jake Farr wasn't looking at her in that way at all. Maybe all she was to him was Terrence Terwilliger's nutty sister-in-law.

Then again, maybe not.

She wondered how long he planned to stick around. And what she'd do with herself when he was gone.

The wind picked up, rocking the canoe and penetrating Patience's sweater. She'd skipped her Windbreaker. For March it was a warm wind—which meant it didn't freeze her skin on contact—and she didn't mind it. Also, given the male presence behind her, she welcomed the cool air on her overheated body. Between the exercise of paddling the canoe and the effort to control her vigorous imagination, she was close to melting.

"Shall we head closer to shore?" Jake suggested.

"Sounds good."

With strong, rhythmic strokes, he steered the canoe across the lake. Patience hardly had to paddle at all. It was a nice change from her outings with her lazy dog, who continuously had to be reminded to keep still and not jump out. She pointed out the other cabins on the lake.

"Yes," Jake said dryly, "I saw them last night."

"Oh, that's right. Tilly sent you the long way round, you know."

"What do you mean?"

"It's easier to go up one more exit on the interstate—it's not so remote—and to take the second left off the main road instead of the first. You'd have come to my cabin from the north—it's only about a half mile. Tilly obviously wanted you to think I lived further out in the sticks than I really do."

"Why?"

"How do I know?"

She was more frustrated with her sister than irritated. What was she supposed to do about Tilly? Wait until she returned to New York and wring her neck? Worry?

"You're worried about your sister, aren't you?" Jake asked.

Patience sighed. "I don't know. She's so wrong about me that maybe I'm wrong about her, too. But no matter what, she's acting weird. I…" She clammed up. She'd almost confided in Jake her sister's comments about her marriage. Feeling his eyes boring through her layers of clothes didn't mean she should forget family loyalty. "I don't know what to do, frankly."

"Let's head back to the cabin," Jake said in a quiet, undemanding way. "We can talk there."

She shuddered with a sudden, strange and wholly inappropriate sense of loneliness and longing. To have someone to talk to. To share her troubles and concerns with. To laugh with. Six months ago, she'd have snorted at such sentimentality. She'd relished her winter alone in the cabin with her computer and her work. She had friends. Her parents. Tilly. The Madrid cousins. It wasn't as if she didn't have anyone.

But she didn't have a man in her life.

And men were different.

Paddling slowly, they stayed close to shore. Patience could see the signs of spring in the melted snow, the green shoots poking up out of the mud and dead, wet leaves, the tight red buds on the trees. Before too long the weekend and summer people would be making their way north, telling themselves that someday they would live in the Adirondacks year-round when really they wouldn't. It was just as well. The land was fragile. Patience sometimes thought of herself as an intruder in a wilderness so many, including herself, worked to preserve. She tried never to indulge in the arrogance that she wasn't a part of the problem. But how could she stand to give up this life and live in the city year-round?

In an apartment like Jake Farr's...*with* Jake Farr...

She dropped her paddle in the lake, swearing under her breath.

Jake scooped it up as it floated by his end of the canoe and handed it to her. She had to twist around to take it from him, and nearly dropped it all over again. Never had she met a man who was even more drop-dead sexy in real life than in her imagination. Seeing him was far more unsettling than simply thinking about him.

His expression was something between knowing and amused. "Distracted?"

She smiled feebly. "It's been one of those days."

And it wasn't even noon, she thought. Her hands were shaking. In the bright sunlight, his eyes seemed even darker, and she noticed the muscles in his arms and shoulders, the flatness of his abdomen, the close fit of his jeans on his thighs. He didn't look at all like what she thought a New York businessman ought to look like.

Facing front, she paddled furiously, but her rhythm was off and she wished she'd steered after all. Finally Jake quietly suggested she just let him get them ashore. Annoyed with herself, she set her dripping paddle in the canoe and placed her hands on her lap. She was unaccustomed to letting anyone have so much control over her, even if it was just a few yards to the dock.

The hound was barking up a storm.

"Oh, you're just jealous," she called to him.

Jake steered the canoe parallel to the dock, holding on to the post. "Why don't you get out here and I'll pull up on shore?"

She said sure. She'd had about enough of canoeing with Jake Farr, anyway. It wasn't him. He wasn't doing anything except being himself. It was her. Her reaction to him. Her disturbing questions about her own life, her own choices. Whether he'd meant to or not, the man had thrown a big fat monkey wrench into her world.

Of course, it wasn't *his* intentions that had landed

them on Central Park West and now in the Adirondacks together. It was Tilly's. *She'd* thrown a monkey wrench into her sister's world.

Patience needed a warm fire, hot tea and a cold shower.

And her cabin to herself.

Grabbing hold of the post, she hoisted herself up onto the dock. Her feet were still in the canoe when her idiotic dog pushed past her, throwing her off balance. Then he jumped over her, and she realized he was heading for the canoe.

"Jake," Patience yelled, "you idiot!"

Naturally Jake Farr thought she was talking to him. "What?" he asked, confused, until his canine friend leaped into—or partly into—the canoe. "Good God, you won't fit, you nut."

But it was too late.

The canoe tipped. First the dog went. Then Jake Farr yelled something very pointed and non-urbane as he went head-over-heels into the water. Patience, half horrified, half hysterical with laughter, was left hanging on to the dock. Her feet splashed into the water up to her knees, but damned if she'd let go and submerge herself in the icy lake. The dog immediately beelined for shore, looking confused and a little insulted. He wouldn't have any idea that he'd caused his own dunking.

She'd lost Jake Farr.

Then there was a splash behind her, and a colorful description of just what body parts were about to freeze and fall off into "this godforsaken lake."

Patience tried not to laugh. She didn't try too hard because she was more concerned with keeping her own precious body parts out of the frigid water. But she did try. Hooking one leg up onto the dock, she glanced back, just in time to see Jake Farr tearing for shore in the thigh-deep water. He was drenched head to toe and cursing soundly. The other Jake was barking furiously at him. When Jake got to shore, the dog decided to shake off, soaking him further. Jake threatened to cook him over a spit for dinner.

It was more than Patience could stand. She positively howled with laughter at the sight of Jake Putnam Farr of New York City soaked to the bone, having it out with a waterlogged dog. She would have doubled over if she hadn't been trying to keep herself from getting just as wet.

The two Jakes heard her laughing. The human one was clearly not amused.

"That's it," he said, and bounded toward her.

Patience struggled to get herself up onto the dock, but she was weak with laughter, barely able to hold on, and now she had the added pressure of Jake Farr coming after her.

He planted his squishy sneakers right at the post to which she was so desperately clinging and squatted down on one knee. He was breathing hard and there were droplets of water clinging to his face. If possible, he was even sexier dripping Adirondack lake water. Breathtaking, really.

"Having a little trouble?" His tone was downright menacing.

"I'd rather not get any wetter than I already am...."

"Oh, I'm sure."

He made no move to help her.

She noticed his dark, wet hair and the way his shirt clung to his chest and arms. "If you'd move," she said, "I could give a good heave and get out of this position."

"Is that right?"

"Jake, it wasn't my fault—"

"You laughed," he pointed out.

"It was *funny*."

"Do you know how cold that water is?"

"Yes. My left foot is still in it."

"But not your whole body."

She was doomed. The man was definitely an eye-for-an-eye type. She ought to just give up and drop in the water, get it over with. But she wasn't the type to surrender without a fight.

"I'm innocent," she said.

He grunted in disbelief. "Sweetheart," he said in a low, seductive voice that further loosened her grip, "you're a lot of things, but innocent isn't one of them."

Then he grabbed her arm, held her suspended, neither pulling her up onto the dock nor pushing her all the way into the lake.

"Debating whether to toss me in headfirst or feetfirst?"

"Neither."

He took her other arm and hoisted her up as if she was no heavier than a sack of onions and held her close against his cold, wet chest.

"I was just debating," he said, "whether we should warm up by the fire."

"Or?"

He gave her a slow, piratical smile. "Or not."

CHAPTER EIGHT

IF IT HAD BEEN any warmer out, Patience was convinced they'd have made love right out there on the dock. As it was, Jake had no choice but to release her, and she dashed up to the cabin ahead of him, half-frozen by the time she got there. She consoled herself that Jake Farr was even colder than she was. She quickly shoved two logs on the fire and peeled off her icy socks, hanging them on a pot-warmer above the woodstove. A sense of responsibility—that, at the moment, had nothing to do with affection—compelled her to towel off her dog, who dove under the stove at first opportunity. Apollo and Aphrodite had already vacated the front room for her bedroom and were probably happy to have avoided the commotion.

Jake Farr could have passed for a big, cold, wet dog himself with all his growling.

"Better get those wet things off," Patience told him unnecessarily. "Wouldn't want you to get hypothermia."

He glared at her, tearing off his layers of upscale mountain clothes. Patience tried not to stare. It was difficult. He had truly impressive shoulders and his abdomen was flat and obviously hard.

He threw down his heavy, soaked sweater and unfastened the top button of his pants.

Patience turned away abruptly. She wasn't used to having a half-frozen man undressing in her cabin.

Jake laughed. His laugh was soft, amused, sexy. An invitation.

"I can go into the bathroom," he said.

"It's colder in there. I—I'll duck into my bedroom and get some dry clothes on myself."

He watched her a moment. "Suit yourself."

As she walked past him, she noticed the purple tint to his lips. "You'd better get some warm liquids in you, too."

"You know the best cure for hypothermia, don't you?"

She did, but chose not to say so.

"Another person's warm body," he answered for her.

"Well, I'm not that warm myself."

That laugh again. A touch of incredulity had crept in. "Oh, I don't know about that."

She dashed into her bedroom and shut her door quickly and firmly behind her. She *was* warm, all right. Burning up. Never mind that her feet ached as they began to thaw. The rest of her—the crucial parts—might just have come out of the woodstove they were so hot.

"Tilly," she breathed, "what have you done to me?"

Her life had been so ordered. So sensible. A little eccentric by other people's accounts, perhaps, but she'd been free. No more. Jake Farr had turned her peaceful existence on its head and given it a ferocious shake.

It wasn't his fault. He hadn't meant to do anything of the sort. He was Tilly's victim, as well. Probably out in the front room cursing his fate. Wondering how the hell he'd ended up flipped out of a canoe by a dog into a cold Adirondack lake. Thinking he couldn't get back to New York fast enough.

Then again, who knew what a good head-to-toe dunking in forty-degree water did to a man?

You know the best cure for hypothermia, don't you?

Probably didn't matter who she was. Not right now when he was cold and she was the only woman around. Maybe she wasn't being fair to him, but since when were sex and romance and hormones fair? Because it wasn't just his obvious, if dubious, attraction to her that was troubling her. It was her attraction to him. It went beyond dreams and fantasies. It had begun to involve not who she thought Jake Farr could be, but who he was.

With a groan of pure frustration—physical *and* mental—she changed her clothes top to bottom, putting on her oldest, baggiest jeans, a cheap sweatshirt and Uncle Isaiah's ancient red chamois shirt. She braided her hair. Any number of curly strands wouldn't stay in the braid, but she ignored them, letting them poke out and fall where they would. If nothing else, she'd obliterate any lingering image Jake Farr had of her at dinner in New York—elegant, feminine, sophisticated. She peeked in the mirror. This was who she was—sloppy, casual, down-to-earth.

"Are you dressed?" she called out to the front room.

"More or less. You can come out now."

What did "more or less" mean? Feeling more nervous than the time she'd had to roust a potentially rabid fox off her porch, Patience ventured into the front room. Her knees were weak, and not from her morning adventures. She balled her hands up inside Uncle Isaiah's soft, tattered sleeves, which were several inches too long even for her. The heat from the stove immediately warmed her body.

And so did the sight of Jake Farr.

He'd pulled a chair from the table up close to the fire and sat with his legs stretched out. His bare feet were tucked up under her dog, who'd collapsed in total exhaustion from his role in their ordeal. He had on a black chamois shirt which he'd left unbuttoned, nothing but dark chest hairs and taut abdomen underneath. He'd put on black sweatpants. She had a sudden impulse to run her hand over his thigh to feel the juxtaposition of the soft, fleecy fabric over his hard muscles.

"I had visions of a mountain run," he told her, explaining his sweatpants.

"I'm sorry things aren't working out the way you'd planned."

"I don't know if I had any plans. Hopes, perhaps. Expectations, dreads. But not plans. Your sister had me thinking I might have to cart you off to the loony bin." He studied her a moment. "You okay?"

She nodded, feigning—probably badly—calm. "Fine."

Before she could see in his eyes whether or not he knew she was lying, she walked around his chair and checked the fire in the woodstove. It was cooking right along, but she added another log, anyway, just to have something to do. Her only hope was to keep busy.

"Still cold?" he asked from behind her.

"A little."

"Sit by the fire, then. There's room."

She looked around at him. "No, there isn't. But it's okay."

"Sure there is," he said in a low, husky voice.

Without another word, he swung one arm around her waist and pulled her down onto his lap. She'd never sat on a man's lap before. Never. It wasn't something she did—hadn't done even in her youth. She landed awkwardly, her heart thudding, and automatically balanced herself by placing a hand on his chest. Another mistake. Despite his unexpected dip in the lake, his skin was warm to the touch, and the muscles were as solid as she'd imagined.

"You, um, seem to have warmed up."

"My feet are still ice blocks, but they'll recover."

She sat rock-still. "I'm not a small woman—you must be uncomfortable."

There came that spine-melting laugh again. "You could call it that."

She blushed. She who had grown up among the free-wheeling, freethinking, free-speaking Madrids. She who had been on her own for more than a decade and had grown up around animals and men and knew what was what. She was not what anyone would call an ignorant innocent. She wasn't unworldly.

But she wasn't stupid, either.

She knew she was blushing not because of what Jake had said but because she'd thought it even before he'd said it. She'd noticed what the rugby-weight fabric of his sweatpants did nothing to hide. He was aroused.

"You're not an easy woman to figure out, Patience Madrid," he said quietly.

"I'm just…" She paused and licked her lips, aware that he was watching her. "I'm just trying to be myself."

"I know." He shifted so that she was thrown up closer to his chest; his arms were wrapped around her waist. She felt warm, feminine even, in Uncle Isaiah's old shirt. "That's what's so intriguing."

They were eye to eye, the man from New York and the woman from the mountains, and all Patience could think was how much she wanted to kiss him, wanted him to kiss her. She could almost feel it happening. She could taste the moistness of his mouth. Feel his warm tongue circling and melding with hers.

"Jake…"

And then it was happening. She couldn't have said who made the first move, didn't care, only closed her eyes and allowed herself to be enveloped by the sensation of the kiss.

His hand curved around her bottom, and the intimacy of his touch electrified her. She relaxed against him, her breasts crushed against his chest, as their kiss became more deep, more abandoned. Its effects spread throughout her whole body. She could feel its effect on him pressing against her thigh.

"Jake…I didn't mean for this to happen."

His eyes were so dark, liquid with wanting. "Do you want it to?"

She didn't hesitate. "Yes." He lifted her easily— she might have been an armload of wood—and she laughed. "Does passion give you superhuman strength, Mr. Farr?"

He smiled. "You're fit, Miss Madrid, but you're not even close to being heavy." He drew her up higher in his arms, tight against his chest, so that she could feel his heart beating along with her own. For a second she didn't know where his began and hers ended. "I could carry you all day."

She wasn't sure if it was bravado, kindness or the truth. "Pray you never have to."

Bursting into her bedroom, he carried her to the bed. She still used Uncle Isaiah's old horsehair mattress and cast-iron frame, but she'd added her own touches to her bedroom—a slate-blue handwoven spread, appliquéd pillows, pottery lamps, antique cross-stitched samplers, a collection of scented candles in a wide variety of holders. It was an eclectic room, feminine and cheerful, and she saw Jake looking around in obvious surprise.

"What did you expect?" she asked, amused. "Gun racks and trophies?"

"I had heard stories."

"There's a lot of Uncle Isaiah here still, but a lot of me, too. Things don't have to stay the same. I can accommodate change."

Could you accommodate Jake Farr? Add him to Uncle Isaiah's old cabin?

But she only formed the question, didn't bother with an answer, as Jake laid her on the bed and settled alongside her, their two shapes oddly, perfectly suited. He lifted her arm and started to roll up the frayed, dangling sleeve, then broke off. "Let's just get rid of this thing altogether."

"I know it's not very sexy—"

"On the contrary," he murmured, sliding the old shirt off her shoulders. "It invites one to speculate on the possibilities."

She wasn't entirely sure what he meant, but his voice, his touch, his eyes all combined to make her feel sensual and wanted, connected to him in a way that made her ache with a wild mix of emotions she couldn't pin down or separate. But she didn't care.

"Actually," he went on, "it's your socks. There's something curiously erotic about a woman in her stocking feet."

She smiled. "You're an unusual man, Jake Farr."

"I accept that as a compliment."

But she could see he was distracted, not really paying attention to what he was saying. He dropped Uncle Isaiah's shirt off her side of the bed onto the floor, which entailed rolling half on top of her. He was reasonably warm all over, except for his feet, which might have just come from the icebox. She rubbed her woolen socks over them.

She said, "If you're cold—"

"Getting warmer every second."

Jake held her closely against him. His breath tickled her face and the weight of his broad chest pressed against her breasts. Their hips were locked. He'd hooked one leg over hers, and they were united almost as if they were one body. With his finger, he brushed stray hairs from her forehead, but they flopped back, and he moved on, slowly tracing a path down her hairline to her ear, then across her jaw to her mouth. He outlined her lips. She kissed the tip of his finger and smiled.

"Oh, Patience," he whispered, lowering his mouth to hers.

It was a slow, romantic, generous kiss, giving more than taking, asking more than demanding. Patience drank in its every nuance, trying to discover the man lying next to her through his kiss. He tightened his arms around her, drew her solidly against him. Her shirt had come untucked. He slid his fingers underneath it. She shivered.

"Are my hands cold?" he asked.

"Not cold—just a bit cool. But that's not why I shivered."

He smiled. "I didn't think so."

"Sure of yourself, aren't you?"

Her tone was teasing, but his expression turned serious and he shook his head, gently rubbing his thumbs along her sides. "No, not at all. I'm just sure that this is what I want—that I've been waiting a long, long time for you to come into my life." His eyes seemed to darken as he shifted next to her. She had to roll onto her back to maintain the close view she wanted of him, of his square jaw and strong shoulders. "And when you respond to me...when I feel your need..." He shrugged. "It gives me hope."

Her throat was dry, constricted, but she couldn't figure out why, and when she spoke, her words came out in an unexpected hoarse whisper. "Hope for what?"

"For us."

And his mouth descended to hers once more, as his palms slid up her stomach to her breasts, lifting her shirt. His fingers skimmed her lacy bra. She sensed his surprise. Pulling his mouth from hers, he glanced down. Her bra had a fairly racy cut and was the color of pumpkins.

"I don't think anyone makes woodswoman bras," she said.

"What other surprises do you have in store?"

Matching bikini underpants, something he could discover in due time. "Oh," she said evasively, "you never know."

He'd started to unclasp her bra when their four-legged friend wandered into the bedroom and barked, obviously not sure what was going on. Patience tried to get rid of him. But Jake was a stubborn beast, and New York had spoiled him if not, as she feared, completely ruined him. He leaped onto the bed. He was still damp from his dip in the lake and smelled like wet mittens.

Patience jerked up straight. "*No!* Jake—Jake, off the bed. Now. You know it can't take this much weight."

He stood up on all fours and panted in their faces.

"Good Lord," Jake Farr said, and rolled sideways off the bed.

"Off, you mutt!"

She gave him a good shove, and finally he got the hint and, with a dangerous creaking of slats, bounded onto the floor. Patience groaned and fell back onto her pillows. Now she also smelled like wet wool.

Jake—the one she *wanted* on her bed—reached down and tugged her shirt back over her pumpkin bra. "Your dog has a point."

"What? What kind of point? The stupid mutt has no sense of timing—"

"Not intentionally, no." Jake straightened, his eyes not on her now, but focused on the hemlock outside her window. Without looking at her, he said, "The point is, we haven't talked."

"Talked," she repeated.

He nodded.

And, with a long sigh of exasperation, she agreed.

"I'll put the kettle on for tea," he said, and withdrew from her bedroom.

Patience glared at her dog. Unrepentant—indeed, probably unaware he'd done a thing wrong all day— he followed his new friend out to the front room. She heard the clattering of the woodstove, the running of water. Humming. Well, she wondered, when Jake Farr said they needed to talk, did he mean he, she or they should do the talking?

And was he being noble or had her dog's intrusion catapulted him back to his senses, reminding him that he was on a horsehair mattress in the middle of the woods with the younger sister of his best friend's wife?

"Well," she muttered, "everyone says if it's one thing you've got it's guts. So go find out."

After all, she'd never been one to shy from reality.

But she'd never had such a pleasant, tempting fantasy as making love with Jake Putnam Farr. It wouldn't be an easy one to surrender to reality.

"I'M WORRIED ABOUT TILLY," Patience said.

Jake studied her from across the table. He'd made English breakfast tea. For lunch, he'd grilled a couple of cheese sandwiches on the wood stove and opened a can of pineapple. "Why?" he asked.

"She hasn't been herself."

"That's what she says about you."

Patience waved a hand. "Yeah, but she's wrong about me. Saying I'm depressed—well, if it wasn't some hare-brained scheme to get us together—"

"Considering what we were just about to do," Jake

interrupted quietly, "I'm not sure 'harebrained' is the word I'd choose."

"Harebrained in the sense it was too obvious, too unlikely to work. Not that it didn't work..." She groaned. "Oh, never mind. The point is, I'm *not* depressed. I think Tilly's projecting her own depression onto me. You know, misery loves company."

Jake bit into the second half of his sandwich, which oozed melted cheese. He seemed content with their simple lunch. He said, "I don't see Matilda as being depressed."

"Troubled, then."

He said nothing.

Patience sighed, wishing she hadn't started on this subject. Divulging family problems just wasn't the Madrid style. But Jake had begun to feel like family....

"I think she and Terrence are having marital problems."

"What makes you think that?"

"Tilly said so."

"I see."

Patience used her fork to lift a slice of pineapple out of the can and set it on the edge of her plate. Inelegant, but functional. "She told me they were going on separate vacations to work on certain issues in their marriage—she to Arizona, Terrence to Florida. But now I know there's more to it than she's telling me." Patience went on to explain the lie about the Hidden Camel and Hidden Flamingo resorts.

"Why do you think she made them up?" he asked.

"She wouldn't level with me when we talked. I think it's just a symptom of her confused state of mind, her lack of trust. I don't know. If I knew, maybe I wouldn't be so worried." She exhaled, suddenly no longer hungry. "But I don't know."

"So you are worried."

"I can't help it."

"You and your sister are close?"

She nodded. "Always have been."

"That's nice. My brother and sister and I…well, we have our moments. But since I'm not married and producing children, don't live in the suburbs, don't work nine to five—we don't have as much in common as we once did. Sometimes it gets in the way of our relationship. Sometimes it enhances our relationship. It just depends."

Patience narrowed her eyes at him, thinking. "Are you suggesting that because my life and Tilly's are so different we're no longer communicating? That we have nothing in common?"

"I'm saying," he paused, pushing back his chair, "that you and your sister maybe don't have as much in common as you once did. Your lives are different. That could skew the way you see each other."

"It could."

"You sound dubious."

"That's because I *am* dubious. Jake, you have to understand the Madrid family. We never were like other people. We had Uncle Isaiah, the hermit, and eccentric archaeologist parents who really weren't like other parents at all. I mean, we never went to amusement parks. We went on treks in the woods to hunt for arrowheads. We didn't even have a television set—I still don't. I could always count on Tilly to understand me, and she could count on me to understand her. We weren't like normal suburban families."

"Just what *is* a normal suburban family? I'm not sure there is such a thing. All families are by definition unique in some way." He grabbed the pineapple can and lifted out a couple slices. "But I'm not denying the uniqueness or the peculiarities of your upbringing. I'm just suggesting that perhaps you and your sister's lives have taken such different paths that you can't count on each other always to understand. Maybe this time you don't. And she doesn't."

Patience was still reluctant to see his point, despite the voice inside her that said it was a valid one. "What's there not to understand? I'm not depressed. She said so herself. And she's the one who told me her marriage was on the outs."

"Her words?"

"Well, she doesn't say things like 'on the outs' anymore. I don't remember her exact words."

"Isn't it a possibility," he said carefully, "that you and your sister are both jumping to erroneous conclusions about each other?"

"*I* didn't lie about where I was staying."

He sighed. "That is a bit odd, I agree, but perhaps there's an innocent explanation."

"Such as?"

He thought a moment, then shook his head. "Can't think of one."

"I wish I knew where they really were staying, together *or* separately. I don't think I can stand another week of not knowing. Next she'll call you and tell you I—who knows what? Depressed is bad enough."

"That you've taken up wearing sexy pumpkin underclothes?"

"Jake Farr, if you tell her that—"

He laughed. "It's our secret, I promise."

Their secret. It sounded delicious. And scary.

But Jake had grown thoughtful again. "I don't know if I should suggest this…"

At his hesitation, Patience, her curiosity piqued, prodded him. "Suggest what?"

He looked at her. "There's a chance I can find out where they're staying."

"How?"

"Terrence and I use the same travel agent who's a mutual friend. It's not a guarantee, but I could ask."

"Could," Patience observed, "but does that mean you will?"

"If we *are* the victims of an elaborate scheme by either Terrence or Matilda, I think we owe it to ourselves to find out sooner rather than later, don't you?"

"What do you mean?"

"I mean," he said, leaning over the table, his dark eyes commanding her undivided attention, "that your concern for your sister and her role in our coming together is a distraction. For both of us. I want to get to the bottom of it before—" He shook his head, not finishing. "Let's just leave it at that."

It wasn't easy, but she did. She thought of how close they'd come to making love on her horsehair mattress in the next room. Of how close—how damned close—she was to falling in love with this man. Where would they be in another week when Tilly came home?

"This travel agent's in New York?"

"Yes."

"Can you call?"

He shook his head, rising. "I think this is something I should handle face to face. If I get moving, I can reach her before she leaves the office."

Patience couldn't understand her sudden disappointment—she felt devastated that he was leaving. Her cabin was her home. Her space. And she wanted him in it.

It just didn't make sense.

"You'll call me when you get an answer?"

"Call you?" He frowned at her. "I was assuming you and your entourage would be coming with me. We can take your car since I assume it's set up for animals."

From his enthusiasm, Patience guessed he hadn't really noticed her Jeep in the driveway. She'd noticed his Acura. Her dog would have loved to ride in the passenger seat. But she supposed that with a little imagination she and the two Jakes and the two cats could all fit in her Jeep, although it would be a struggle. Regardless of how they traveled, she couldn't believe how excited she was at the prospect of heading back to the Big Apple.

She tossed her sandwich crust under the stove for Jake. "Did you hear that, you hairy beast? It's off to the big city again."

"Yes," Jake Farr said, "and let's not forget a leash, shall we?"

CHAPTER NINE

THERE WERE THINGS in his life Jake Farr wished he could go back and undo. The time in college he'd gone to a football game instead of studying for his economics exam. The relationship he'd maintained for far too long in his early twenties with a woman who hated mountain-climbing, hated Wall Street, and really, she finally admitted, hated him. The ten thousand dollars he'd thrown down the tubes on a friend's nutso idea for a doomed company. Stupid bets on hockey games. Bad decisions.

They paled in comparison to having told Patience Madrid they could all go to New York in her Jeep. Definitely something he'd undo if he had the chance.

He should have inspected her Jeep before making such a daring suggestion. He should have asked to sample her driving style. Taken a cruise around the lake with her at the wheel. Experienced how a mountain woman drove before ending up on the interstate with her.

He should have considered her hairy, muddy dog and her temporary custody of her sister's two New York cats. Asked himself where he thought the animals were supposed to sit.

Where the hell had his head been?

He knew. His head—his entire body—was still feeling the effects of having come so close to making love to this wild, teal-eyed redhead.

It wasn't that she was a bad driver. She stayed between the lines on the interstate and only exceeded the speed limit when she passed, if simply because her rusting hulk of a Jeep couldn't be trusted to maintain a high rate of speed. But she didn't sit still behind the wheel. At unpredictable moments she'd pluck a cat off her lap or reach back and scrounge around for a dropped dog bone or stick an arm in front of Jake for a tattered map in the overflowing glove compartment. It was nerve-racking.

"If you'll just tell me," he would say, "I can do things for you."

"Oh. Right. I'm not used to having a passenger."

Patience Madrid, he decided, was used to doing everything on her own. He wondered if she could change, if she *wanted* to change. Not give up her independence, but merely share it with another person. Him, for instance.

He shifted uncomfortably at the thought. Maybe he was allergic to cats and his mind wasn't working properly. Aphrodite was curled up on his lap, purring. Apollo had perched himself on the headrest of his seat; a sudden braking and Jake would have the beast clinging—claws out, no doubt—to the back of his neck. Jake the dog had the backseat to himself. Even so, he would give his human counterpart sullen, jealous looks for confiscating the passenger seat.

Never was Jake so delighted to see the New York skyline.

Patience's Jeep being what it was, he felt every pothole, every bump, grate, crack in the road. And in New York there were many. He didn't care. He was home. She stopped in front of the Terwilligers' building on Central Park West, and Jake offered to park her Jeep while she tended her animals.

"Hope it goes better than last time," she said, grinning.

He remembered—he would never forget—Saturday morning, the elevator doors parting, and the big, hairy, ugly, slobbering dog leaping inside with him. He'd thought he was a dead man. And he'd seen Patience Madrid for the first time as he was pinned to the elevator wall. Had it been fate?

More likely, the hand of Matilda Terwilliger.

Cats, dog and redhead disembarked from the Jeep. Jake thought he saw the doorman blanch.

Parking the Jeep was an adventure. It handled better than he expected, but for the first time in all his years in New York, pedestrians actually got out of the way when they saw him coming. The skinny parking attendant recognized the all-too-memorable vehicle. "What happened to the lady and the dog?"

Jake battled an inclination to disavow any knowledge of Patience Madrid and her dog. But he said, "They're back at her sister's apartment."

"So she really is Mrs. Terwilliger's sister?"

"She is."

The attendant shook his head, the New Yorker who'd now seen everything. "Well, I guess you never know."

"I guess you don't."

At the Terwilligers' building, one of the doormen asked him how long he and Miss Madrid would be staying. Jake noticed white cat hair on the man's uniform and assumed Patience's entrance had not been uneventful. "Her dog…" the doorman said, but shook his head, not going on.

Jake found Patience in the cavernous master bathroom attempting to bathe Apollo and Aphrodite. Two monogrammed pure white Egyptian cotton towels, undoubtedly never intended for cat use, were set out on the counter.

"You made it up here all right?" he asked.

"Oh, sure. Aphrodite tried to claw my ear off and Jake got loose, but the doorman grabbed him and offered to take Aphrodite for me. Nice, huh?"

Jake doubted the doorman had tried to be nice. More likely he'd tried to avoid having the entire lobby destroyed by the three animals.

"Now, Apollo," Patience said, plopping an unhappy cat onto one of the towels, which she proceeded to unfold around him. "You'll live. That wasn't even a real bath."

From the look of him, Apollo didn't agree. He quickly made his escape past Jake. Before Aphrodite could follow him through the door, Patience snatched her up, plopped her in the tub and unceremoniously removed any traces of her Adirondack sojourn from her beautiful fur.

It occurred to Jake he could stand there and watch Patience Madrid the rest of the day. But he said, "I'm off to see what I can find out about Terrence and your sister's whereabouts. You'll be okay here?"

Aphrodite twisted free and raced out of the bathroom, dripping suds and water. Patience laughed, though Jake could see scratches on her forearms. "If I don't have a rebellion on my hands. See you soon?"

He sensed an awkwardness, a reserve, she hadn't exhibited on her turf up north or even sitting so close to him on the trip south. Perhaps it was just being alone with him in the huge bathroom, a tub plenty big enough for two right behind her. His mouth went dry as he considered the possibilities.

"I'll be back ASAP," he said and dashed out of the bathroom before he could stop himself from exploring those possibilities.

First things first, he told himself. If he was ever to have Patience's full attention, he first had to track down her sister and brother-in-law. After that...

Well, who knew?

One thing was certain: his apartment renovations would include a tub just as big as the one on Central Park West.

"You're sure?" Jake asked his friend an hour later.

Emmie Dalton sighed, exercising more patience with him than he probably deserved, considering what he'd just talked her into doing. "Of course I'm sure. I made the reservations myself. Just how sick is Matilda's sister?"

Jake bit his lower lip. He'd hated lying. "Emmie—"

She narrowed her eyes at him. She was slim and petite, with neat black hair and a deceptively cute smile. Her black designer suit gave a more accurate impression of the imposing, successful and smart woman that she was. She'd become a top Madison Avenue travel agent through her own guts and hard work. Jake had been friends with her for years.

She sighed, watching him with knowing eyes. "Jake Putnam, you lied to me."

He nodded.

"Rat."

"I'm sorry."

"Did you have a good reason?"

"I think so."

"The Terwilligers are good clients. *And* they're friends." She leaned back in her ergonomically correct chair, rattling a cheap ballpoint between two fingers. "If I didn't rat them out over sickness and death, it'd better be over love and romance. I like a happy ending."

He cleared his throat. "I'll explain when this thing's resolved."

She wasn't going to let him off that easily. "Does this 'thing' involve the sister?"

Jake pretended not to hear her. "Thanks, Emmie." He was on his feet. "I promise I'll keep your name out of it."

"She's always sounded like your type to me. Mountain woman—skins animals herself, from what I hear."

The Patience Madrid myth. Jake had seen no evidence of hunting or trapping in her cabin. He'd even checked her freezer—what meat was there had come from the grocery store.

"I'll talk to you soon," he said.

"Jake Farr, are you in love?"

She was grinning. His own friends wouldn't sympathize with his dilemma. They'd be amused, entertained because he'd fallen head over heels for—

Just who the devil *was* Patience Madrid?

"Well," Emmie said, "if you ask me, it's about time."

Since she'd just done him a remarkable favor, Jake didn't point out that he hadn't asked.

She continued. "You end up on New York's list of most eligible bachelors one more time and we women are going to start a hall of fame for all you incorrigible bastards who're determined to remain unattached. Disqualify you from getting on the list. 'Eligible' implies a certain willingness to engage in a long-term relationship."

This from a woman who regularly stated her own determination to avoid marriage. "Look who's talking…"

"Don't start on my love life when I'm lecturing you on yours. Besides, I've got real work to do around here." She reached for her telephone and waved a hand at him in dismissal. "Go."

Jake went, glad for his friends in New York, his life here. Could he give them all up for an isolated mountain cabin?

On his way back to Central Park West, he stopped in at his office. All was well there. Naturally. He returned a few calls and headed back to the apartment.

Patience was in the kitchen, unloading a monstrous bag from Zabar's that included, she informed him, a sample of ten different dishes she couldn't resist and six kinds of dessert.

"Any luck?" she asked.

"If you mean did I find out where they're staying, yes, I did."

"And?"

Taking her by the wrist, he led her into the living

room with its magnificent view of Central Park. He pointed south. "There."

"What do mean? Florida, the moon, where?"

"The Plaza."

"What plaza?"

"The Plaza Hotel, Patience."

"You mean the *New York* Plaza?"

He nodded. He could tell she was shocked. He had been, too. And angry. Instantly angry. Patience Madrid wasn't one to ponder how she felt. Jake himself was still deciding whether or not he wanted to strangle the Terwilligers or fall down laughing.

Or whether he should worry. This kind of subterfuge wasn't like Terrence. *Was* his marriage on the rocks?

"We should discuss this," he said.

She shot him a look, in no mood to discuss anything. "What's there to discuss? My sister lied to me. She's made me the victim of some elaborate scam. She— she's acting weird."

But, Jake noticed, Patience didn't seem particularly surprised that her sister had never left New York, nor particularly insulted, and not the least bit hurt. She was just angry. Jake couldn't tell how angry. He judiciously kept silent, following her as she stamped into the guest room she'd appropriated from him.

"What're you doing?" he asked.

"Packing."

"Patience…" He sighed, watching her stuff things back into a large canvas tote bag. "Look, you don't have to leave. Let's have dinner and talk this over. It's a long drive back to the mountains."

She angled her hot teal eyes at him. "Who said I was heading home? *That* would be surrendering."

Pulling her bag off the bed, she carried it past him, out into the hall, where she dropped it on the polished wood floor and shoved it against the wall. She was breathing hard. Her cheeks were peachy red. "Then where are you going?" Jake asked calmly.

Her eyes met his. They were glittering, fiery. She caught her breath and seemed to relax, if only a little. And instead of out-and-out anger in her expression, he saw her zest for adventure, her determination, the years of affection and trust between two sisters that virtually nothing would shatter.

But she smiled, a small, self-deprecating smile. "I'm going to check into the Plaza Hotel."

He'd been afraid of something like that. "Patience—"

But he stopped himself. He remembered something Terrence had said not long after he and Matilda had married. *"There's one thing I've learned, Jake—it's never to come between my wife and her sister. There's a bond between them that you rarely get to see between two people. They're different as night and day, but I've never seen two sisters more devoted to each other, who know each other better. It's really something."*

Indeed it was.

"If my sister's in trouble," Patience said, "I need to know."

"What if she's not?"

Her jaw tightened. "Then I need to know that, too."

"For what purpose?"

She headed back toward the kitchen. Without turning, she said, "So I can figure out whether her death ought to be slow or quick!"

Bravado, Jake decided. "I think you're like your dog," he called to her. "All bark and no bite."

Dead silence. Not even a peep from the kitchen.

A woman to be reckoned with, Patience Madrid. Whistling to show just how unconcerned he was at the host of possible reactions she might have at his comment, he sauntered down the hall.

Diving headfirst from the kitchen doorway, she blindsided him with a massive tackle, pushing him against the wall. She was strong. And fit. Willing to take risks. And she had the element of surprise in her favor. But in her actions Jake clearly saw a woman who still thought of him as Terrence Terwilliger's best friend, a New Yorker, which, in her estimation, wasn't up to a good fight with a woman who knew how to fell trees and build fires.

"All right, Jake Farr, I'll show you bark and bite."

But she'd underestimated him. Jake knew it.

"Mmm," he said, "I wish you would."

She glanced up at him, and in her eyes he saw that she knew she'd made a mistake.

"Don't you dare," she said.

He laughed. "Too late."

With more ease than doubtlessly she'd have liked, he caught her around the torso in an old wrestler's hold, about-faced her and propelled her across the hall, where he pinned her up against the opposite wall. It took some effort, but he'd thought before he'd acted. He'd known he'd succeed.

"I should have kicked you when I had the chance,"

Patience told him matter-of-factly. "Never let up on an opponent, right?"

"Right," he said. "You should never have pegged me for a weakling."

"Now, Jake, I never—*No! Don't you dare! No tickling!*"

But her sweater had gotten scrunched up under her breasts, exposing a tempting expanse of bare midriff, and how could he have resisted? She was laughing, pummeling him with her elbows, until finally, with a massive burst of energy and willpower, she spun around against his chest and had at him, seeming instinctively to know all his ticklish spots. They fell to the floor together, legs intertwined, neither willing to give up.

He could have made love to her then and there.

But he didn't. It wasn't willpower or nobility or common sense or even hunger.

It was, he thought, because he cared so damned much about her. She had to put her mind at ease about her sister. Then...

Distracted, he'd let her manage to flip him over on his back and climb onto his stomach, straddling him. Her hair had come out of its pins and braid, thick, curly strands of it dangling in her face. She was panting for air. From his vantage point on the floor, he could see her breasts heaving with each gulp of air.

First, her sister.

Then there'd be no stopping him.

PATIENCE LEFT shortly after dinner, looking urban and perfectly capable of getting along on her own in the big city. Jake walked with her out to her cab. He'd offered to carry her bag, but she'd declined. He wondered how many Plaza guests arrived with such unprepossessing luggage.

He noticed the monogram for the first time. "MMT?"

"Matilda Madrid Terwilliger." Patience grinned around at him and she pulled open the cab door. "Her mother-in-law and sister-in-law both gave her monogrammed canvas bags. Do you believe it?"

Knowing the Terwilligers as he did, Jake believed it.

"'Course," Patience said, "Tilly just uses hers for the beach and picnics. I use mine for whatever."

Apparently a night at one of New York City's priciest hotels constituted "whatever."

Which reminded him. "You had no trouble getting a reservation?"

"Huh?"

"A reservation, Patience."

"Hell, it's a big hotel, there won't be a problem."

He sighed.

Shoving her tote bag onto the cab seat, she turned to him and frowned. "Jake Farr, I'm not some kind of a rube. I know the Plaza's not your average roadside motel. I didn't call ahead for a reservation because…" Her frown intensified to a glare. "Because I was *distracted,* okay? But don't you worry, I'll manage just fine."

Since there was no delicate way to ask his next question, he didn't bother trying to be discreet. "You're all right for money?"

"I should be. I brought a ton of cash."

He didn't say a word, just imagined her whisking out a pile of crumpled bills and plopping her mono-

grammed canvas tote bag on the reservation desk at
the Plaza Hotel. At least she'd decided to leave her dog
with him. But her chances were still less than even that
she'd land a room, even if there was one available. He
wondered what she meant by "a ton of cash," but didn't
ask. As she'd said, she wasn't a rube. She was a talented,
intelligent writer specializing in environmental topics.
She'd just penned her first book. She knew how to book
a room in a hotel.

But she was worried about her sister, confused by
her feelings for him, and this was New York. It wasn't
like other places.

She climbed into the cab, and Jake shut the door
behind her, wishing her well. She grinned and waved.

An intrepid woman.

He went back up to the Terwilligers' apartment and,
kicking all animals out of the den and shutting himself
in, called Emmie Dalton at home.

"I need a big favor," he told her.

"Two in one day? Gosh, the gossip columnists get
hold of this—"

"Emmie, please, this is painful enough as it is."

"Ah, male pride. Well, my friend, don't you worry,
one of these days you will, I assure you, be called upon
to return these favors. What can I do for you?"

"A room at the Plaza."

"For when?"

"Now. Tonight."

"Well, hell, Jake, you don't ask for much. While I'm
at it, you want a five-room suite, champagne, choco-
lates, a masseuse?"

"Just a room, Emmie," he said patiently. "Can you do it?"

"Of course I can do it," she hissed, insulted. "But you owe me, Jake Putnam Farr."

"I'll remember."

"Damned right you'll remember."

He gave her the details she needed and five minutes later she rang him back. "Done," she said, and hung up.

Mission accomplished, Jake resisted the temptation to build a fire, find a good book and spend the rest of the evening alone in the den. Instead he returned to the outer rooms and dutifully took Patience Madrid's ugly dog for a walk. He was definitely not a New York dog. No one stopped to pet him, no one called him a handsome beast. Mostly people gave them wide berth, if only because Jake looked as if he'd break free of his leash at any moment and turn the city upside down. He wasn't used to the pace of the city, the rules, the tricks of getting along and enjoying life there. Like his mistress, he was used to the freedom of the mountains.

After ten blocks, Jake suspected his canine counterpart would never really feel at home in the city. He'd never belong.

He patted the tired old dog on the head. "What about Patience huh, boy? Think she could ever feel at home here?"

But the dog had no answers, and neither did Jake. So finally, at a slow pace, they headed back to Central Park West.

"YES, MISS MADRID," the formal man behind the Plaza reception desk said, "I have your reservation right here."

"But I don't have a reservation."

He smiled and leaned over, saying in a quiet, conspiratorial voice, "Emmie Dalton said you might be surprised. I spoke to her myself a few minutes ago. She's taken care of everything."

Patience's bag bounced against her knee. "Everything?"

"Your entire tab is taken care of, including any room service you might wish to order."

Who the hell was Emmie Dalton?

Patience looked around the elegant lobby, remembering the time she and Tilly had come to New York in high school to see the Christmas tree at Rockefeller Center and had ducked into the Plaza, just to see what it was like. As far as she could see, it hadn't changed much.

"Might I ask," she said to the man behind the counter, "how much a room in this place costs?"

He told her how much her room would have cost her. *Was* costing someone else. Patience had a damned good idea who that someone was.

She managed not to choke. She had just enough cash to cover the tab, but she would have had to break out the plastic to eat. Her New Year's resolution had been to send her credit cards back to their appropriate banks in small pieces.

Pride had never gotten in the way of a Madrid and a free meal, never mind a free night in Manhattan. They were a practical lot. They also never judged their self-worth or anyone else's by the size of their bank accounts.

She got her room assignment and key and thanked the man who'd introduced himself as Frank.

Patience carried her own bag up to her room.

It had no view and she'd hate to figure out what it was costing Jake Putnam Farr per square foot. But it was the Plaza, elegant, unique, hard not to appreciate.

She called her sister's apartment. Jake answered on the fourth ring; she hadn't realized that she'd counted. "What if I told you I don't accept charity?"

"I'd say fine, you're on your own."

"You wouldn't argue with me?"

"No."

"You wouldn't make me feel like I couldn't get along without you?"

"Well, I'd like to think you can't," he said, his voice low, deliberately sexy, "but not because of money."

She refused to let him think he'd gotten to her, although he had. "You're worth a lot?"

"I'm used to paying New York prices."

She wasn't. In fact, she hated to part with a nickel. Frugality was a way of life for her, a choice more than a necessity, although she suspected environmental writing didn't pay as well as management consulting or whatever it was Jake Farr did for a living. Not much, so far as she could see. And it wasn't just New York prices he was used to. It was his New York lifestyle.

"Who's Emmie Dalton?" she asked.

"The travel agent friend who told me where your sister and Terrence are staying."

"Oh. Think she can find out what room they're in? I don't think hotel security would take to my peeking in keyholes. Hate to have Tilly need to haul me out of jail."

"I can ask, but I've called in all my chips with her—"

"Then it's okay. I wouldn't want to put you on the spot. I'll figure out something."

He grumbled something she couldn't make out.

"You okay?" she asked.

"Yes. It's this dog of yours. He insists on climbing in bed with me."

"You're in bed?"

"With a book, yes. But *The Three Musketeers* is no match for what I had in mind before you decided to spend the night at the Plaza."

She felt a rush of heat in a few strategic places, reminding her of how easily she reacted physically to Jake Putnam Farr. It had nothing to do with common sense. It wasn't even anything she could control. She could control what she *did* about it—getting into bed with him, for instance—but not its existence. It was so damned complicated, and yet, in its essence, so very simple. She wanted to make love to him. Wanted him to make love to her.

"Patience, are you there?"

She cleared her throat. "Mmm, yes."

"Sleep well," he murmured.

Now that, she thought as she hung up, would be a trick.

CHAPTER TEN

"I'M SORRY," the woman at the front desk said, "we have no one at all registered under the name Terwilliger."

Hunching her shoulder to hold the phone, Patience tucked her feet under the covers of her Plaza Hotel bed. So far, she'd drawn a blank with Terrence and Matilda Terwilliger or any combination of names ending with Terwilliger.

"What about Madrid?" she asked.

"First name?"

She leaned forward anxiously. "Matilda or Tilly."

"I'm sorry, no."

Damn! "Patience. You do—"

"Yes, ma'am, I am trying to be patient."

"No, no, I'm not criticizing you. I'm just making sure you do have a Patience Madrid registered."

A short pause. "Let me see…yes. I do have a Patience Madrid registered. I had no idea…it's an unusual name."

"I'll agree with you there since I've put up with it for thirty-two years. Look—" But she hesitated. There'd been something about the woman's tone. Patience took the receiver in one hand and pulled the blankets up over her knees. She'd ordered a bottle of very expensive champagne—Jake Farr would learn not to be so generous. Not one to waste anything, she'd already drunk two glasses herself. But she was feeling sleepy now. Possibly she'd just imagined hearing something in the woman's tone.

Then it hit her—why had she needed a *first* name?

Because there was more than one Madrid registered.

If not Tilly, who?

"Is there a Sarah or Jebediah Madrid registered?"

"I'm sorry, no."

Those were the names of her parents. Patience considered. "Isaiah Madrid?"

The woman on the other end was silent. "Miss Madrid, I'm not sure I should reveal—"

"So good ol' Uncle Isaiah *is* here! Terrific." She had to think fast. "Can you connect me to his room? Gosh, it's been years. We're having a family reunion here in New York, you know, and I just wasn't sure who all was coming and staying at the Plaza. Well, it's been confusing, but you can understand."

"Yes," she said dubiously, "I suppose I can. I'll put you through."

Isaiah Madrid.

When she got hold of her sister...

But after two rings, she hung up.

This was too easy. Not on her. On *them.*

Her hands were shaking. The Hidden Camel, the Hidden Flamingo, depression, Jake Putnam Farr. Her sister and brother-in-law had put her through a lot. They'd taken advantage of her. Made assumptions about her and the life she'd led.

They'd put her in one hell of a spot. She wanted revenge.

She called the Terwilligers' apartment on the west

side of the park. The phone rang and rang and rang, but there was no answer. She hung up, wondering if she'd dialed the right number. She'd never thought to ask for Jake's cell phone number. She was feeling the effects of the champagne. Her eyelids heavy, she tried once more.

Still no answer.

Were the two Jakes out for an evening walk? Had Jake Farr decided he'd had a big enough dose of the Madrid family and retreated to his own apartment? Just abandoned dog and cats and headed home?

She wouldn't blame him.

Restless and a little dopey, Patience jumped out of bed and marched into the bathroom. Turning on the water good and hot, she filled the tub. The hell with "Mr. and Mrs. Isaiah Madrid." The hell with Jake Putnam Farr. How often did she get to spend a night in a fancy hotel on someone's else's tab? She didn't have a bathtub in the mountains. She added some bath oil she'd scrounged from room service. Lord only knew how much it'd cost Jake. Served him right, too, although she didn't know why she was mad at *him*.

She'd soak, think, get a good night's sleep, and in the morning she'd deal with her sister, her brother-in-law and maybe even Jake Farr.

Before she climbed into the tub, she tried him one more time.

Zip.

What if he'd been manipulated by Tilly again? What if she'd called him with another wild tale about her lunatic sister and he'd swallowed every word?

"You're getting paranoid," she said aloud.

And why not? Wasn't she seven floors up in one

of New York City's ritziest hotels hunting for her sister who was registered under their dead uncle's name?

She poured herself another glass of champagne, shut the bathroom door, locked it and climbed into the tub, easing herself into the steaming, fragrant water. She sipped from the glass.

"Just think," she said aloud. "I could be home cutting snarls out of Jake's fur."

Life in New York among the Farrs and Terwilligers could be confusing, she thought, leaning back, but it did have its moments.

TERRENCE TERWILLIGER III climbed into the cab Jake had taken from Central Park West and was now parked in front of the Plaza. The dog was flopped between them. Dressed in an elegant evening suit, Terrence eyed the hound with distaste. "Good dog," he said dubiously.

"Patience says you don't like him."

"How astute of her."

"I didn't want to leave him alone too long in the apartment with your cats."

"Matilda's cats," Terrence corrected dryly, his tolerance on a low ebb. "How the devil did we get mixed up with the Madrid family?"

"Fate, I think."

"Maybe someone put a curse on us back in nursery school."

"Were they born then?"

"Doesn't matter. Had to have been a witch that thought them up."

Jake smiled. In spite of Terrence's dark words, the man was plainly and hopelessly in love with his wife.

Jake had just witnessed them walking hand in hand into the Plaza Hotel like a couple of dewy-eyed kids. It was obvious their marriage was *not* in trouble. If Jake could be sure of anything about the past few days, he could be certain of that.

"I thought for a minute you hadn't seen me," Jake said.

"Recognized the dog."

It wasn't a point of pride for Terrence. He did not like his sister-in-law's dog and seemed not at all pleased to have spotted him outside the Plaza Hotel. Patience Madrid was obviously a lot more than Terrence Terwilliger was used to dealing with. As for her dog, the cab driver had agreed to let him come along on the grounds a window was kept open. It had been a chilly ride. Naturally the homely beast had enjoyed every minute of it, keeping his head poked out the entire way.

"I put Matilda on the elevator and told her I thought I'd seen a business associate and wanted to say hello," Terrence said, unusually formal. "I don't normally lie, but this time…" He exhaled, loosening his tie. "Jake, what the hell's going on?"

The question of the hour. "I was hoping you'd tell me."

Terrence shook his head. "All I know is Matilda made plans for us to go to Florida and we ended up staying in New York. She said it was a surprise. Then she had me call you about her sister." He squinted at Jake. "*Is* she depressed?"

"No."

"I didn't think so. Depression…well, it's just not a state of mind I associate with Patience. She has her ups and downs like anyone else—she just handles them differently."

"What about recently?"

"I haven't seen her in ages. I know she's had a hard winter, workwise. Several deadlines in a row, that sort of thing, but it was my understanding that she was thriving up north in that cabin of hers...until Matilda told me otherwise."

"Terrence," Jake said carefully, "has it occurred to you that you and I might be the victims of your wife's little scheme to get your sister-in-law and me together?"

"What do you mean?"

Although Jake thought his friend already knew, he said, "Matilda's been playing matchmaker."

Terrence winced. "But isn't this awfully elaborate? Telling me we were going to Florida, then having us stay here in New York, calling you about Patience being depressed.... Really, it's a bit much."

"You haven't heard the half of it. Tilly—Matilda also led Patience to believe your marriage was on the rocks."

At that, Terrence laughed, incredulous.

"That's how she got her to come to New York and take care of the cats in the first place," Jake went on. "And as for the Florida ruse, she must have known Patience would come after her once she figured out what was going on." He paused. "And she was right."

Terrence paled, his worst suspicions confirmed. "You mean Patience is *here?*"

"Here and loaded for bear, Terrence."

"But this is all so...so ridiculous. For heaven's sake, Jake, you were supposed to be out of town this week.

Who could have predicted your mountain-climbing trip would fall through? It was a coincidence."

Jake looked at his longtime friend. "Was it?"

The dog shifted between them as Terrence thought for a moment. Then he said, ominously, "Emmie Dalton."

"Bingo."

Taking a few minutes to digest the likelihood that he'd been had by the woman in his life, Terrence finally turned back to his friend. "What now?"

"I haven't the faintest idea."

Terrence patted his sister-in-law's dog. "Those Madrid sisters are quite a pair."

"I agree," Jake said. "But in this case I'd say Patience is Matilda's unwitting victim."

"Perhaps, but she was due."

"What do you mean?"

"I've never told you how Matilda and I met, have I?" But before Jake could answer, Terrence leaned over the front seat and spoke to the cabbie. "Drive—my friend and I need to talk. Take us down Fifth Avenue to the Metropolitan Museum of Art and back, will you?"

"Just keep the window open."

As the cab pulled away from the curb, the dog lunged onto Terrence's lap and stuck his hairy head out the window, his ears pinned back in the wind, dog slobber flying. Terrence gave the beast room.

"You'd think Patience could have come up with a different name," he said. "But she knew what she was doing."

Jake stiffened. "What do you mean?"

Terrence rubbed his jaw, clearly ill at ease. "That's

another story you don't know about—and I'm not sure if I should tell you. If you tell Matilda…"

"I won't."

Jake understood his friend's strong penchant for privacy. It had led some—including, apparently, his own sister-in-law—to think he was something of a stuffed shirt.

Terrence reluctantly began to talk.

HER SKIN HAD BEGUN to shrivel and wrinkle, and Patience knew if she didn't haul herself out of the tub soon she'd fall asleep and drown. She'd finished her third glass of champagne.

Yawning, she decided her revenge plot could wait until morning. She needed sleep.

But as she flicked the drain open with her toe, she heard a commotion in her room and shot up straight, instantly alert.

Nothing. Just silence.

Had she imagined an intrusion? No one could have gotten into her room. She'd latched the chain lock.

Hadn't she?

"I can't remember," she whispered, feeling a stab of panic.

Without a sound—unless the whole damned building could hear her heart pounding—she carefully climbed out of the tub. She'd left her clothes in the outer room. Why be modest when she was supposed to be alone? Without bothering to dry off, she wrapped up in the terrycloth robe the hotel provided.

Still nothing from the outer room.

Was she getting paranoid?

She pressed her ear to the bathroom door, held her breath and listened.

There was a distinctly male grunt. And panting. She was sure of it. It sounded canine to her, but how would a dog get into the Plaza Hotel?

Then, *"Dom Pérignon!"*

It was an angry bellow from a man who perhaps wasn't as accustomed to high New York living as she liked to believe.

"Jake? Jake Farr, is that you?"

Jake the dog barked.

"Quiet," the other Jake said, "before you get us all tossed."

She could hear footsteps.

Then, close to the bathroom door, Jake Farr said seductively, "Hello, Patience. I see you've been having quite an evening for yourself. Why didn't you order caviar to go with your champagne?"

"Wish I'd thought of it." Her heart was pounding even faster than when she'd thought he was a mere burglar. And the rush in her head was not the alcohol. "What're you doing here?"

"I had nightmares someone was spending all my money."

She grinned. "Thought you were used to New York prices."

"Dom Pérignon is expensive wherever you go. You could've exercised some restraint, you know."

"I did."

"How?"

She pulled open the door. "I could have ordered *two* bottles of champagne."

Jake was standing on the threshold, barring the door with his solid, masculine body, devastingly handsome in jeans and a deep burgundy shirt. Deeply aware of her own near-nakedness, Patience noticed his dark, probing eyes. He inhaled.

"Evening," she said and hiccuped.

He slowly let out his breath. "Good thing you didn't order that second bottle."

"Guess you shouldn't have bragged about the size of your bank account—"

"I didn't."

She shrugged. "It was implied bragging."

"There's no such thing. You should be grateful, you know. I know you'd never admit it, but you'd never have gotten a room without my help. Emmie had to pull strings."

"Listen here, Jake Putnam Farr, nothing—not the price or availability of a room at the Plaza Hotel—*nothing* would keep me from tracking down my sister once I'd put my mind to it."

Jake's eyes didn't quaver. "No doubt."

She thrust her hands onto her hips. "Are you patronizing me?"

"Wouldn't dream of it."

His voice was mild and, as far as she could tell, perfectly sincere. But, as he stood with his gaze upon her, she had the distinct impression that he wasn't really paying attention to their conversation. Suddenly self-conscious, Patience felt water dripping from her hair, down her neck and between her breasts. She felt the moistness between her legs. She felt dizzy.

"I need to get a towel…"

His gaze lingered where the droplets of water gleamed at her cleavage.

Intensely aware of her every move, she grabbed a folded towel, patted dry her face and toweled her hair. Jake didn't move from the doorway. He wasn't menacing or leering or anything like that. He was just *there*. And that, for Patience, was enough.

"How'd you get Jake in?" she asked to break the silence.

"I bribed a bellhop—cost me a pair of hockey tickets." The dog chose that moment to squeeze into the bathroom and drink from the toilet. "I had considered leaving him at your sister's for the night."

Patience swung around. "For the *night?* Jake—"

"It was lonely in that big apartment with just me and Jake and the cats."

He didn't sound lonely. He sounded like he was making a lame excuse. His grin said he wasn't trying too hard. Patience hung up the towel and followed her dog out of the bathroom. The air in the outer room felt cool on her overheated skin and helped to clear her fuzzy head.

"Besides," Jake said, "I didn't know how you'd take to being without your dog for a whole night in the big city."

She turned to look at him. "Jake Farr, are you serious?"

He laughed. "No."

"Then why are you here?"

His grin fading, he moved toward her. "Why do you think?"

"To be honest, I don't know—"

"Don't you?"

He was close enough now that she could see the fine lines at the corners of his eyes and the few gray strands in his dark hair. He was close enough that she could smell the heady cologne she'd found in his shaving kit when she'd thought he and Tilly....

It seemed so silly now, what she'd thought. Tilly would never have an affair. If she and Terrence were having problems, Tilly would confront Terrence about them. She was like Patience in that one way—not afraid of confrontation.

No, confrontation is easy compared to this. Compared to telling a man that you think you're falling for him...that you're afraid you already have.

She exhaled, trying to smile. "I know it's been a strange week—"

"Patience." He moved even closer, placing his palms gently on her shoulders. "Patience, if you want me to leave, I'll leave."

"No, it's not that. There're two beds—"

"Patience," he said.

"Did you come here just because...just to..."

He sighed. "Let's say you are definitely on my mind."

"But?"

"They're on the tenth floor. I've got the room number written down here somewhere."

She grinned. "You're kidding! Emmie Dalton again? You'll have to thank her for me. And thank *you*, Jake. I know you must think this is weird, but Tilly and I— well, I just have to put my mind at ease that she's not crazy."

"I understand," he said.

But there was something about his expression. If the champagne hadn't dulled her wits, she might have been able to discern what it was. "Jake, are you all right? Is there something else you need to tell me?"

"No."

"Look, I know Tilly and I must seem as different as night and day. Most people probably do think our lives have drifted apart, that we don't have as much in common as we once did. But that's not what's going on here. It's something else. Tilly and I are sisters, Jake. We'll always be sisters. If I'm worried it's because I have cause to be worried."

"I'm beginning to see," he said carefully, "that you and your sister have a hell of a lot more in common than I'd ever have believed."

"Because of whatever scam she's got going on me? The Hidden Flamingo, the Hidden Camel. And now the Plaza Hotel…" Patience laughed languidly. "What do you suppose she could be up to?"

"Whatever it is, it can wait until morning. Fiery though your soul may yet be, Miss Madrid, you look about done in. It's been a long day."

"It really has."

And when they turned around, Jake—the big black, hairy one—had made himself at home in the middle of the second bed. Patience had taken the one near the window.

"You scroungy dog," Jake said. "Off the bed."

Jake didn't budge.

"He probably blames you for getting him dunked," Patience said.

"Me? It wasn't my fault. The stupid mutt… Come on, off the bed."

Jake yawned and stretched out his long, bony legs.

"You've spoiled him," Patience said. "You should never have fed him from the table. Now he won't do anything you say."

"Then *you* get him off my bed."

"What makes you think that one's your bed?"

"Because you've already camped out in the other one."

"But I thought you came here for—"

He looked at her, and his eyes, usually so dark and impenetrable, were shining, tender, an open door to his soul. "I came here for what you want, for what you're ready for," he said softly. "Nothing more."

"That's it?" she asked. Her voice, too, was soft, and she wondered if her eyes were as affectionate and trusting. She wanted this man to know her. To like her for who she really was.

"And just to be with you," he said simply. "We're allies, soul mates in this little venture." His eyes narrowed a little, betraying just that hint of suspicion she'd detected earlier. But suspicion of what? "You *have* told me everything, haven't you?"

"About Tilly and Terrence? Yes—yes, I have."

He smiled, but the hint of suspicion was still there.

"Jake, is something on your mind?"

"Oh, yes." And the suspicion vanished, so quickly Patience wasn't sure she hadn't just imagined it. It was replaced by a devilish grin and a low laugh, as he scooped her against him with one arm. "There's definitely something on my mind."

She pretended not to understand. "What? You know you can tell me anything."

He lowered his mouth close to hers, so that their breath mingled.

"What do you want to hear?" he asked.

"Whatever you want to say."

"I want to say…" he paused, licking his lower lip, his tongue almost touching her mouth "…I want to make love to you, Patience Madrid."

For a moment, she was lost for words. Then she murmured, "I thought that's what you might say."

He didn't back down. "It's the truth."

She nodded, slipping her hands around his waist, locking her fingers at the small of his back. Their bodies fit together so well. They might have been made for each other, except Patience didn't think like that. Love was too special for her to believe she and Jake didn't have anything to do with where they were, how they were feeling, at this moment. It was too easy to say it was destiny. It made what she was feeling right now—a mixture of passion and a desire to love and be loved—seem trivial, outside her control. As if what she and Jake did, who they were, didn't matter.

But all that *did* matter. Love wasn't just about bells and whistles going off that first moment two people destined for each other met. The only bells and whistles likely to have gone off when Patience saw Jake Farr being thrown back against the elevator by her big dog were alarms and sirens.

Was she in love with him?

"Jake's had a rough day," she whispered, and they both knew she meant her dog. "Let's let him have the other bed. If he wrecks the bedspread, I'll reimburse the Plaza myself."

"Are you sure?"

"Oh, yes. How expensive can a bedspread be?"

He tightened his grip on her. "Not about the damned dog, Patience. About *us*."

She smiled. "I know what you meant. I was just…" She stopped, realizing this wasn't the time for teasing. "Yes—yes, Jake, I'm sure." Her hands drifted up his back, and she pressed herself against him, the robe falling open. "Thank you for asking."

It was the last thing she said before his mouth captured hers.

Her robe dropped to the floor.

She could feel that his breath had stopped. She drew herself against him, until his hands drifted down her spine and caught the curve of her hips. She gave a small gasp.

He smiled against her mouth. "I'd given up on finding someone like you."

"I'm not sure I ever dared hope I'd find you."

His eyes sparkled, his hands smoothing lower, down her bottom, to the tops of her thighs. "I thought you weren't afraid of anything."

Slowly, erotically, one hand slipped between his body and hers, between her legs.

Now her breath stopped.

"Everybody's afraid of something," she whispered.

Her thighs parted and his fingers touched her hot, moist center.

His mouth found hers again, and she responded immediately, eagerly, her tongue matching the erotic, primitive rhythm of his. He kissed her chin, her throat, igniting her. He bent his head and his tongue flicked against one hardened nipple, then the other, then back again, until she moaned, aroused and excited. Between her legs, his fingers moved deeper, until she moved against them, responding.

She could hear his sharp, tortured intake of breath.

Then he pulled away and began tearing off clothes. His shirt, his pants, his underclothes. He moved fast, unselfconsciously, unblushingly. Patience watched. He caught her and grinned. In a moment, he was naked. Magnificently naked. Solid, sleek, muscled.

They fell together on the big hotel bed, kissing each other, exploring, exulting in the passion they shared, until finally she was on top of him and he was lifting her, and she knew it was time. Every fiber of her body and being wanted him.

"Patience," he breathed, "oh, Patience."

She murmured his name and felt him come into her. She heard his soft, welcoming groan as he wrapped his arms around her and she drew him deeper into her.

She couldn't speak, couldn't make a sound.

Then the control disappeared. Where there had been a quiet, romantic fire now there was a conflagration, hot flames erupting all around them. Patience thought she would explode.

Together, they rolled over, until she was on her back, knowing only that she wanted more, all of him. He thrust hard and fast, and she realized her fingers were dug into the hard muscles of his thighs. She wanted more heat. More fire. More explosions.

And when the final one came, it rocked her to her very soul.

There had never been anyone remotely like Jake Putnam Farr in her life. He was the spark that set her ablaze. Together they were unstoppable, a flame that no one—nothing—could extinguish.

Or so it was in the darkness of the New York night, when Jake was with her. Right now the mountains, where she'd always felt she belonged, were far away. Come morning, she just didn't know where she'd feel she belonged. Anywhere so long as it was with Jake Farr? But that was too easy, and life, she knew, just wasn't that easy.

He held her, kissed her gently. "Good night, Patience Madrid. Sleep well."

Laying her head against his shoulder, she knew she'd be lucky to sleep at all.

A LONG TIME LATER, she became aware that he, too, was still awake. She raised herself up and looked down at him, his long, lean figure outlined in the darkness. She touched the long, jagged scar above his right knee. "I noticed this earlier," she said, half smiling, "but didn't think it exactly the right time to comment."

He trailed one finger down her left thigh, where she had a scar. "Same here."

"One little mistake with a chain saw. You?"

"Mountain-climbing in the Alps. Were you alone?"

"Yes."

"You're lucky you didn't bleed to death."

"Uncle Isaiah was still alive then. He was off fishing or something. He hauled me off to the hospital when he got back, lecturing me the whole way on what I'd done wrong. It's not a mistake I'll ever make again."

"One would hope."

"How'd you manage in the mountains?"

"I had a friend with me."

"Terrence?"

"Yes. He hadn't met your sister yet. He patched me up and went for help."

"You're good friends, aren't you?"

There was no hesitation. "Yes."

She smiled and kissed his scar.

When she finished, he kissed hers, and it was a long time again before, at last, they slept.

CHAPTER ELEVEN

PATIENCE WAS UP EARLY. She showered, got dressed, kicked her dog off the extra bed and ordered room service before Jake even stirred. "Sleeping past sunup's abnormal," Uncle Isaiah used to say. For a long time Patience had believed him. Now she believed in tolerance.

But it *was* getting late. Almost eight o'clock. She hoped a newspaper would come with her breakfast. Usually by now she knew what was going on in the world.

She considered putting Jake up to licking his new friend's face, but decided that was mean. After last night, the man needed his sleep. So did Patience. Habit and a guilty conscience had gotten her up earlier than her body had wanted.

She had a fair idea that Jake Farr had figured out she hadn't quite told him everything about Tilly's little matchmaking scheme. Like that Patience might know her sister's motive for doing it.

There was a quiet knock at the door. Expecting room service, Patience opened it up. She was shocked to see her sister standing on the threshold in a designer pantsuit.

"Tilly, how in the world did you know I was here?" she blurted out.

She brushed off her younger sister's question. "That's the least of your worries right now. Patience, you're not going to believe—"

Patience quickly shushed her. "No, Til, *you're* not going to believe." Looking behind her, she saw that Jake Farr was still sound asleep. She scooted out the door. "I've got company."

"Who?"

"Don't be an idiot, Tilly."

"You mean *Jake?*"

"Both Jakes."

"Oh, my…" Tilly shook her head, looking a bit pale. "If I get out of this alive, I'm going to pretend I've never heard of either of you."

"A little late for that, don't you think?"

"You weren't supposed to fall for the guy!"

Patience frowned, unwilling to discuss her love life, even with her sister, in the seventh floor hall of the Plaza Hotel.

Tilly sighed. She was an attractive woman, shorter and more fine-boned than Patience, less prone these days to wielding an ax. Her hair was a more demure shade of red, and her two-hundred-dollar cuts had it nicely tamed. Her nails were painted a pretty coral, and Patience knew for a fact she didn't have any chainsaw scars on her. But she was Uncle Isaiah's niece, Sarah and Jebediah Madrid's older daughter. She was not all Terwilliger.

"Terrence is onto me," she announced.

"So I guess this means that he wasn't in on your little scheme. It must have been a surprise when he thought he was going to Florida and ended up around the corner from where he lives in the Big Apple."

"I wouldn't be sarcastic if I were you. Did your buddy in there tell you he saw Terrence last night?"

Patience felt her own face lose its color.

"There," Tilly said, not particularly enjoying her small victory. "See? We should have listened to Uncle Isaiah and never gotten ourselves mixed up with New York men."

"Meeting Jake wasn't my idea."

Tilly's eyes—as teal as her younger sister's—flashed. "Don't tell me you didn't know I'd have my revenge one of these days, Patience Madrid. *You* started this."

She bit her lip, knowing she had.

"I saw Jake Farr and your damned dog in a cab outside the Plaza last night. Terrence brushed me off. He thought I didn't know what was going on, but he's the worst liar. I looked out the window and saw him getting into the cab. He and Farr must have had a good long talk. They…" She shrugged. "Well, they obviously will look upon themselves as victims in this whole thing."

"They would," Patience said.

"We have to do something."

"Like what?"

Obviously Tilly didn't have the faintest idea.

"How'd you find me?" Patience asked.

"Emmie Dalton. I called the rat fink after I saw Terrence and Jake together. She confessed everything and said we all owed her for putting her on the spot the way we did. I guess she has a point." She chewed her lower lip. "Well, what're we going to do?"

"We're Madrids, Til. What do we always do in a crisis?"

She looked at her sister. Then the panic faded, and she smiled. "Wing it."

JAKE AWOKE to the delivery of the most enormous breakfast he'd ever seen. There were also two messages for him. The first was in the form of a scrap of a note in Patience's distinctive scrawl: "I'm walking Jake. Enjoy your breakfast. Hope you're hungry." He had to call downstairs for the second message.

"There's a note here from Mr. Terwilliger," the woman at the front desk said.

"Can you read it to me?"

"Certainly. 'Jake: I'll be getting Matilda out of the picture today as planned. Is Paris far enough?'"

Jake laughed. "Thanks."

He turned to the breakfast tray. Patience Madrid was not shy about her appetite. She'd ordered eggs, yogurt, a basket of muffins and sweet rolls, fresh fruit, a pot of coffee and—a bottle of champagne. Not, he noted, Dom Pérignon. Still, he could have eaten for a week on what that one breakfast cost.

He poured himself a cup of coffee and contemplated the fate of the Madrid sisters.

Ahh, sweet revenge.

Patience returned a few minutes later, red-faced and out of breath, her dog panting beside her. "We've been asked to leave."

"Got caught, did you?"

"I guess I don't have your gift for having my way in the big city." She pushed back her wild hair. She'd dressed in jeans and her Norwegian wool sweater. At least she'd left her dead uncle's shirt up in the woods. "I've got fifteen minutes to pack up me and my dog and hit the road. How's breakfast?"

"There's enough here to feed half the hotel."

"One would hope—it cost a fortune."

Jake judiciously withheld comment. He swallowed a bite of blueberry muffin as he stood at the window. Patience whirled around their room, throwing her things together and grumbling at Jake—they'd really have to come up with another name for that beast—for being so obtuse as to try to make friends with a woman wearing *that* many diamonds. Jake didn't ask how many. She'd gone into her salt-of-the-earth mode and only would fuss at him for having money, which he did and wasn't about to pretend he didn't.

Carefully, he watched the street below. Then suddenly there they were. He stiffened with the incipient thrill of victory.

"Patience," he said, "come here a minute. I think I see your sister."

"What? Are you serious?"

She raced to the window and peered down, frowning when she spotted Terrence and Matilda Terwilliger climbing into a cab. Jake noted that Terrence took his time, making sure anyone watching from up above would get a good look at his wife.

"Where do you suppose they're going?" Jake asked mildly.

"Could be just out shopping."

But a bellhop came out and put the Terwilligers' luggage into the trunk of the cab.

"They're leaving!"

She started for the door, but Jake grabbed her by the elbow, stopping her in her conspiratorial tracks. "You'll never make it in time."

"But I promised—I told Tilly I wouldn't abandon her to Terrence and…"

Jake was enjoying himself. Oh, but he did like knowing what was going on. "You told Tilly, did you? What and when exactly did you tell her?"

Patience bit her lip. He could see she knew she'd blown it.

"Patience?"

Her beautiful teal eyes fastened on him. He refused to be swayed into feeling any pity. The Madrid sisters had this coming. If anyone should be pitied, Jake thought, it was Terrence and himself.

Of course, after last night…

"How much do you know?" she asked.

"Everything."

Freeing her arm, she walked over to the breakfast tray and poured herself a cup of coffee and popped a chunk of fresh pineapple into her mouth. He admired her calm. The woman did have a certain way of handling the unexpected.

"Where's Terrence taking my sister?"

"Paris."

She nodded. "I'd have thought a desert island."

"I'm sure it's something he considered, but since he's going with her, he didn't want to have to suffer."

"Is he mad at her?"

"Let's just say he's been waiting for the other shoe to drop for more than a year."

He thought he saw Patience's calm falter. Apparently when he'd said "everything" she didn't expect he meant *everything.* But he did.

She cleared her throat. "Um—I guess I don't know what to say."

Jake wondered if that was a first. "It didn't occur to you that Tilly was getting her revenge?"

"Not soon enough. I figured since she and Terrence ended up getting married that she'd let bygones be bygones and wouldn't come after me." She ate a couple of grapes. "And I guess when she indicated she and Terrence were having marital problems I blamed myself, so my guard went down. I fell for her scheme hook, line and sinker."

So had Jake. Only he had been at a great disadvantage. He hadn't known—as everyone else involved had—the true circumstances of how Terrence Terwilliger and Matilda Madrid had met.

"You picked Terrence's name out of the *Wall Street Journal?*"

Patience nodded. If she had any regrets, Jake couldn't see a sign of them in her matter-of-fact expression. It was as if she set people up every day. "It was in an announcement of promotions at his firm. I mean, Terrence Terwilliger III? How could I resist?"

Jake chose not to answer. Of course she hadn't resisted. She'd made up some fake stationery on her expensive computer in the mountains and dashed off a letter, ostensibly from Terrence, to her sister threatening to sue her on some specious grounds. One thing had led to another.

"I thought 'Tilly Terwilliger' sounded so ridiculous

that one or the other of them would catch on before anything happened."

"Like their getting married."

"Precisely."

"So when Tilly implied she and Terrence were having problems, you were quick to blame yourself for ever having 'introduced' them."

Sinking onto the edge of the bed, she exhaled. "They're so different. Of course, Tilly—she's no dummy, you know—she counted on guilt to keep me from getting suspicious."

"It worked," Jake pointed out, walking over and sitting down beside her. Life with the Madrid sisters, Terrence had said, was never dull. Jake thought he knew what he meant.

"Terrence vowed he'd never tell a soul."

"He finally had to—we *are* friends, you know."

"Are you mad?"

"At your sister? No. She owed me, too, you know. I played a practical joke on her last Christmas and she promised revenge. I never thought she'd throw me to her little sister." He grinned. "But I think I handled it."

He thought he saw Patience shiver. "What now?" she said.

"Well, Terrence has seen to it your sister's out of the way." Jake leaned over for the coffeepot and poured himself another cup. "You and your hairy mutt have been thrown out of the Plaza Hotel. We've got two neglected cats back on Central Park West."

"So it's back to normal."

"No, I wouldn't say that. I don't think we'll ever go back to where we were before my elevator hit the lobby on Saturday morning. We'll have to fashion a new normal for ourselves."

"Jake—"

"It's just us now, Patience. You and me and your critters. The question is, what're *you* going to do?"

WHAT PATIENCE DID was fall in love with Jake Putnam Farr.

Terrence kept Tilly out of New York for three more weeks. Patience received postcards from Paris, then Rome, then Vienna, Copenhagen, Amsterdam. They all begged Patience to be patient and tend her cats. They all sounded like Terrence's idea of revenge suited Tilly fine.

Patience took care of Apollo and Aphrodite. They even became friends of sorts. Aphrodite developed a taste for beer. Apollo learned to fetch, which was more than Jake had ever done. All the animals learned to stay out of the bedroom when Jake Farr was in it. Not Patience, however. She was in Jake Farr's bedroom every night. It wasn't really *his,* she'd point out, nor hers, nor theirs.

They did not, it became painfully obvious, have a place of their own.

She resumed working. So, to her mild surprise, did he. Evenings they went to dinner or cooked together. They saw shows and hockey games and movies and walked through Central Park hand in hand. They had long talks about politics and the economy and philosophy and romance and the environment. They argued. They made love. Patience was convinced she would never get enough of him. Every time they were together seemed more remarkable—more transforming—than the last. There was always more to discover, always more to give.

And then it was time for Patience to head back to the mountains. Just like that. Terrence and Tilly were coming home.

And so it was on the first day of April that Patience woke up all alone on Uncle Isaiah's old horsehair mattress. She built a fire to take the chill out of the air. Then let Jake out. Got into her exercise clothes and went for a fast, hard walk around the lake, trying to get back into the spirit of her isolated existence.

"I can't come," Jake had told her.

He'd been honest, at least. He had an important business meeting in the city. He had to meet with his architect. His architect for *his* apartment. Just as it was *her* log cabin.

Did whatever they had together necessitate separate lives?

Did he need to keep his apartment, she her cabin?

She walked faster, harder, her lungs burning, the mud squishing under her sneakers. Four days she'd been back. There'd been an enraged phone call from Tilly about Aphrodite's sudden interest in beer, but nothing from Jake. Nor had Patience called him. Perhaps they needed to know what it was they had apart in order to better understand what it was they had together.

Then again, Jake Farr was independent, a man accustomed to keeping his own company, having his own space. Patience understood. They weren't, she thought, as different as her sister had thought when she'd set them up.

At the end of her walk, she did a few stretches out on the dock and threw rocks in the water, smiling at the memory of Jake Farr going head over heels into the frigid lake.

In the distance, she could hear the engine of an approaching vehicle. Her heart pounded. It was still too early for tourists. Jake?

She raced up to her cabin, only to see a delivery truck backing into her driveway. She ran up to him. "I'm sorry, but you must have the wrong house—"

"You're Patience Madrid, aren't you?"

The burly man looked confident that she was, and she nodded as he climbed out of the truck. "What do you have?" she asked.

But he was working, obviously not one for chitchat, and opened the back of the truck and slid out a new mattress and box spring.

"I didn't order a mattress!"

"It's paid for," the man said. "Where do you want me to put it?"

Clearly he was going to leave her with his cargo whether she wanted it or not. She pointed to the porch. With remarkably little effort, he hauled the mattress and then the box spring out of the truck, up the steps and leaned them against the porch rail. They were at least queen-size.

She signed on the line the man indicated, and he departed.

She scratched Jake's head. "Well, what're we going to do with a new bed?"

"I hope by *we,*" Jake Farr said behind her, "you mean you and me, not you and him."

Startled, she swung around, and Jake walked down from the driveway. With the loud truck, she hadn't heard his car. The sunlight seemed to dance on his dark hair, in his dark eyes. It was a bright, warm day, and he'd just worn a pullover and jeans. She felt a rush of emotion. Tears sprang to her eyes. That had never happened to her. She was Patience Madrid. The mountain woman. The hard case who could damned well take care of herself. But she also knew now that she didn't have to prove that to anyone—herself and Jake Farr included.

"Jake…"

"Do you mean me or that scroungy hound?"

"You. I'm training him to go by a different name."

His eyes narrowed suspiciously. "What?"

"Zeke. It sounds enough like Jake that he's not that confused."

"You don't happen to know a Zeke, do you?"

She shook her head.

He moved closer. "You named that damned dog after me, didn't you?"

"I didn't know you—"

"You might as well fess up." He stood toe-to-toe with her now; they were only inches apart. "You found out Terrence's best friend was named Jake, and when this skinny, ugly hound wandered into your cabin, you couldn't resist. You named him Jake just to irritate your brother-in-law."

"Did he tell you that?"

"Nope."

"Tilly?"

"No, I figured it out all by myself. Terrence warned

me this kind of thinking is a direct result of life with a Madrid."

"Well..."

He slipped his arms around her waist. "I'm right."

He was right. And he *knew* he was right. So Patience saw no need to tell him.

"If you don't fess up," he said in a low, menacing whisper into her ear, "I am going to toss your pretty behind into the lake."

"Now listen here, Jake Farr, just who do you think you are, extracting confessions from me? I can be stubborn, you know—"

"Oh, I know."

And he picked her up off her feet.

"Don't you dare!"

"Confess."

"You can't ask a person to incriminate herself."

He took a few steps toward the lake.

"Jake, I mean it. If you throw me into that water, you'll regret it. I promise you'll regret it—"

Clearly the man wasn't listening. He hoisted her up onto his shoulder like an old rug and hauled her out to the end of the dock.

"Did you or did you not name that dog after me?"

"I'd never even met you."

He sighed. "How cold do you think that water is?"

"Freezing."

"Good."

"Okay, okay," she yelled. "It's true. I named Jake after you. I made...certain assumptions about your character."

He didn't say a word. Nor did he lower her back down to the dock.

Then her dog had to join them. He was muddy and slobbery from their trek around the lake and looked even hairier and uglier than usual.

The two Jakes stared at each other. The four-legged one flopped down and started scratching and licking himself. It was a sight.

Patience knew she was doomed. With a low growl, Jake Farr pitched her feetfirst into the lake.

Which was a mistake. Headfirst and she wouldn't have made a quick recovery—the shock of hitting the water would have been too much. But feetfirst she could handle. She hit bottom and popped up like a missile out of a submarine and got him by the leg, knocking him off balance and right into the water with her.

He landed with a yell and a huge splash.

Before he came up for air, she scrambled for shore and beelined for the front porch.

If the damned mattress and box spring hadn't been in the way, she'd have made it. As it was, Jake caught up with her.

"I'm soaked head to toe," she said. "There's nothing you can do to me now."

"Want to make a bet?"

His eyes now blazed with the desire for something other than vengeance, and his grip on her waist softened. Wet and shivering, she smiled and pressed a wet finger to his mouth. "I don't think I'll take that bet."

"Oh, Patience," he breathed.

"I know. Four days—it seems like forever."

"The mattress…" He pushed back his dripping hair.

"If you object, I'll send it back. I remember when you said you'd made Uncle Isaiah's place your own by adding a few personal touches. As far as I'm concerned, everything can stay the same—except for that damned horsehair mattress. There, my love, I draw the line."

"Jake—"

He shook his head, not letting her interrupt. "And we have an appointment in New York next week with an interior decorator. I figure neither of us is good at that sort of thing, but I'd like to make my apartment *our* apartment. I want you to add your touches there, too. But if you don't want to live in New York at all, even part-time, it's okay. We'll work something out." He smiled. "I'm talking fast because if I don't I'll freeze to death and then none of this will matter. Patience, I love you. I want to be a part of your life. I want you to be a part of my life. Damn it, if I have to thank your sister for putting us together I will—"

"Jake—oh, Jake." She smiled, feeling warm all of a sudden. "I...I don't know what to say."

"Say you love me."

She laughed. "I love you."

"For all time?"

"And beyond."

"Good." He scooped her up. "Then shall we find out what it's like to warm up on a horsehair mattress?"

WEEKS LATER, on a warm afternoon in early June, Jake met Terrence for lunch. They both looked very Wall Street. Dressed in pinstripes, carrying expensive leather briefcases.

Terrence surreptitiously withdrew a flaming orange card from his suitcoat pocket. "Did you get one of these?"

Jake nodded, and withdrew his. He figured Patience had done them up on her computer. She had one in the mountains, one in New York.

"What the hell is it?" Terrence asked.

"It's an invitation to the Madrid family reunion in September."

Terrence shook his head, adamant. "No, please don't say that."

"Then what do you think it is?"

"Do you know how many Madrids there are? Scores, Jake. All of them with names like Patience and Matilda and Jebediah and Isaiah. They're all smart and stubborn and weird. No, this isn't any ordinary family reunion." Terrence's face darkened. "This, my friend, is our wives' revenge."

"You mean they arranged it just to torture us?"

"Oh, yes."

Jake threw back his head and laughed, because he knew Terrence was right. The Madrid sisters always had the last word, and they never gave up.

But, in Terrence Terwilliger III and Jake Putnam Farr, they'd more than met their match.

"Any question of just calling it even?"

"Nope," Jake said, setting down his briefcase. "Not a one."

The two men rolled up their sleeves, and with conversations on the stock market and deficits and bond ratings going on around them, they plotted their next move.

"Think we'll be doing this when we're eighty?" Terrence asked.

Jake had to smile, just thinking of it.

* * * * *

Dear Reader,

I am thrilled Harlequin chose to include *A Not-So-Perfect Past* as the bonus book for this Bestselling Author Collection release! As a reader and fan of Carla Neggers' wonderful, heartwarming stories, I'm honored to be released along with *Trying Patience*. As an author, I'm beyond excited to share *A Not-So-Perfect Past* with you.

When I originally wrote this story, I had three teenagers underfoot, spent most of my free time watching those teens play various sports and had just taught my son how to drive. I was at the very beginning of my career and there were many things I still had to learn, but the one thing I knew for sure was that I wanted to write for a living. More than that, I wanted to tell stories about people overcoming challenges, facing disappointment head-on and learning from their mistakes. Stories where the characters grew and changed to become their best selves. Stories that celebrated the importance of friends and family.

Stories of redemption, self-acceptance and, best of all, love.

Yes, many things have changed in my life since then. Two of those three teenagers are now on their own, I have more time for my own interests and pursuits and I no longer slam on an invisible brake while one of my children is driving.

But some things are still the same. I'm still writing. And I still believe there's nothing better than a happy ending and nothing stronger than the power of love.

I hope you'll look for the next book in my In Shady Grove series for Harlequin Superromance out this December.

Please visit my website, www.bethandrews.net, or drop me a line at beth@bethandrews.net. I'd love to hear from you.

Happy reading!

Beth

A NOT-SO-PERFECT PAST
Beth Andrews

For Andy.

CHAPTER ONE

Aw, HELL. NOT "Jingle Bells."

Dillon Ward grit his teeth as he entered the brightly lit bakery. Red and green decorations and twinkling colored lights took up every inch of the large room. The effect was cheerful, bright and filled with so much Christmas spirit, it hurt his head.

He stomped his boots harder than necessary and brushed snow off his jacket. Luckily, the smells of yeasty bread and sweet pastries and chocolate helped ease the shock of the faux Christmas wonderland.

He scanned the room as he crossed to the front counter. Only two of the dozen or so small tables had customers, but Dillon figured that had more to do with it being twenty minutes before closing time on a Sunday afternoon, and less to do with the snow falling steadily outside.

It'd take more than an early December storm to keep the citizens of Serenity Springs, New York, from their donuts.

An elderly lady turned from the counter, her step faltering when she noticed him. She clutched her white bakery bag to her chest, lowered her head and scurried out.

Dillon took off his knit cap and pushed a gloved

hand through his hair. Even though he'd lived here for almost two years, people were still wary of him. Still looked at him with the mix of curiosity, fear and revulsion usually reserved for circus acts.

Or killers.

He took off his gloves, stuffing them in his pocket. "This month's rent," he said, holding an envelope out to Nina Carlson.

From behind her cash register, the curvy blonde looked past him to the large picture window. "You didn't have to shovel the walk."

He shrugged. "It needed it."

Because she hadn't reached over for the rent check, and because he was tired of holding it out, he set it on the top of the pastry-display case and slid it toward her.

"Well, I appreciate it." She cleared her throat. "Why don't I get you some lunch? As a thank-you?"

Usually his cupcake of a landlord could barely meet his eyes, let alone stammer out a few words to him. Now she wanted to give him lunch? "Why don't I just take ten dollars off next month's rent? And we'll call it even."

Staring at the counter, she picked up the check. "Actually, I was hoping to talk to you…"

"About?"

She blinked several times. "Just a few things. About the apartment."

"If you're raising the rent—"

"I'm not. It's more complicated than that. If you can't stick around until closing, I could come up to the apartment when I'm done working."

To his place? Alone? Wouldn't that go over well with

Serenity Springs' moral majority? Sweet single mother Nina Carlson going to the lion's den.

Or in this case, the ex-convict's lair.

He doubted she even had the courage to climb the stairs.

Whatever she wanted to talk to him about must be important. And as always, his curiosity got the better of him. Never a good thing.

"I'll wait," he said, noting the relief on her face.

Dillon picked a table by the far window on the opposite side of the room from the middle-aged couple finishing their coffee. He sat with the window to his right, allowing him a clear view of the entrance, the kitchen and out onto the street.

Prison had taught him to protect his back.

A few minutes later, the kitchen door swung open and Nina came out, a coffeepot in one hand, a tray of food in the other.

She set the tray in front of him. "I'm finishing up with your sister in the kitchen—she's tasting wedding cake samples—and I thought I'd bring you something to eat while you wait."

He slouched in his seat and hoped Kelsey stayed in the kitchen. At least until he was gone.

Nina leaned over and poured a cup of coffee he hadn't asked for and didn't particularly want, and he caught a tantalizing glimpse of cleavage. He frowned. He'd bet his brand-new nail gun she'd run screaming from the room if she knew where his thoughts went at the sight.

"It's today's lunch special," she continued, placing a shallow bowl and a large plate on the table. "Tomato parmesan soup, a ham and provolone Panini on my honey wheat bread and a raspberry bear claw."

She tucked the tray under her arm and watched him expectantly. He almost refused the food, but his stomach chose that moment to remind him the only thing he'd eaten all day were two slices of cold, leftover pizza.

His resolve was nothing up against hunger. Or a pretty blonde.

Especially this woman, with her big gray eyes. She was wearing a pair of faded jeans that accentuated her generous curves and a bright pink, V-neck top that clung to her breasts like frosting on a cake. Knowing he was beat, he picked up his spoon, sampled the steaming soup and grunted in appreciation. She smiled, producing a small dimple in her left cheek. Her loose braid swung in time with her hips as she walked away.

He'd gotten the better part of this deal. Great food and a full stomach while all she'd gotten was a cleared sidewalk. He glanced out the window. A sidewalk that would be covered again within the hour.

Halfway through his sandwich, the nape of his neck prickled, telling him he was being watched. He slowly shifted his gaze to the left and stared into a pair of guileless blue eyes.

Emma Martin, with her soft halo of blond hair, grinned up at him. "Hi, Uncle Dillon," she said around a mouthful of chocolate chip cookie. "What're you doing here?"

He scowled at her. Not that it would deter Emma any. She was high-strung, affectionate and could talk you into a coma.

She also scared the hell out of him.

"I'm not your uncle," he pointed out gruffly.

"You will be," she said, "once Kelsey marries my daddy and becomes my mom."

The kid was a little young to be getting so technical about things, wasn't she?

"Where's your dad?" he asked, surprised to find the room empty except for him and Emma.

"Working." She wiped her hands on her legs leaving a trail of cookie crumbs across the light blue pants. Before he knew what she was doing, she nudged her way under his elbow and climbed onto his lap. "Me and Kelsey are picking out wedding cakes."

Dillon shifted his leg but she didn't budge. Over Emma's head he saw his sister's bright red hair through the small window into the kitchen. He opened his mouth but the mini-queen of gab kept right on talking.

"Kelsey said they couldn't have a Princess Barbie cake for the wedding but that I could get one for my very own when they got back from their honin' moon."

He glared at the top of Kelsey's head. Felt a trickle of sweat form between his shoulder blades. *Come on.* He didn't doubt Kelsey knew he was staring at her.

"I want to go on the honin' moon, too, but Daddy says I have to stay at Grandma Helen's, even though I promised to be real good and not bother them when they lock the bedroom door so they can make my baby brother."

His mouth dropped open. "What?" he croaked.

"I asked Daddy if they could make me a baby brother on their honin' moon," she told him patiently. "Daddy laughed and said it would take lots and lots of practice to make me a brother."

"I don't need to know any more," he said with a quick shake of his head.

"Kelsey just sort of made this weird sound, like she was choking." Emma widened her eyes and made gagging sounds. "Like she'd just tasted something really yucky like olives, but then Daddy whispered a secret to her and they kissed, so I guess she was okay."

Dillon sat frozen for a moment, wondering what the kid might tell him next. Abruptly he jumped to his feet, tucked Emma under his arm like a very large, very talkative football and stalked toward the kitchen.

"ARE YOU SURE she's okay out there?" Nina asked as she boxed up cake samples for Kelsey Reagan. Nina wished she could see how Dillon was handling his alone time with Emma but she didn't have a clear view of his table, only the front door.

"Emma's fine," the redhead assured her. "Besides, Dillon has to get used to having his new niece around."

Nina placed a square of German chocolate cake with coconut/pecan frosting into the box. "It's just that your brother doesn't seem like the type to be…comfortable around children."

Actually, the coolly enigmatic Dillon Ward didn't seem as if he'd be comfortable around anyone. From what she could tell, he seemed more likely to make people uncomfortable. And enjoy doing it.

Kelsey leaned back against the counter and waved Nina's concern away, the stunning diamond on her left hand catching the light. "Dillon's got tons of experience with little girls. He raised me, remember?"

Nina tucked in the flaps of the bakery box and taped it shut.

She didn't know all that much about her tenant—the tenant she'd acquired with her purchase of Sweet Suggestions six months ago from her grandparents when they'd retired and moved south. She knew Dillon lived alone. Paid his rent on time. Took care of any problems in the apartment. And except for the time he spent with Allie Martin, a local bar owner, he kept to himself.

Oh, yeah. She also knew Dillon had served prison time for killing his stepfather.

A fact which Nina became aware of before most people in town—including her family and ex-husband—when Police Chief Jack Martin informed Nina and her grandparents of Dillon's past shortly after he moved in above the bakery. Her grandparents opted to let him rent from them anyway.

After all, her devoutly Christian grandparents had told her, to forgive is divine.

A sentiment that sounded good but was hard to pull off.

But, despite Nina's misgivings, Dillon hadn't caused any problems and had never been anything other than polite to her or her grandparents.

The kitchen door swung open and Dillon—a giggling Emma in tow—headed straight for his sister. "This yours?"

Kelsey tilted her head. "Hmm…might be. What are you willing to give me to take her off your hands?"

Nina couldn't believe Kelsey was teasing Dillon. He was so…hard. His work boots added two inches to his already impressive height, and the sleeves of his dark green chambray shirt were rolled up to his elbows revealing muscular forearms. His brown eyes, as usual, were guarded. And watchful. His mouth set.

She wondered if he even knew how to smile.

Of course Kelsey—with her confidence and bad-girl attitude—didn't seem the least bit fazed. Her multiple ear piercings and short, spiky hair proclaimed her a rebel. Really, she was everything Nina "the good girl" wasn't. And had long ago given up ever becoming.

Dillon attempted to set Emma down, but she giggled even louder and lifted her feet to keep them from touching the floor. "If you don't want her," he said, "maybe I'll just take her out back. Toss her in the Dumpster."

Kelsey shrugged and studied her cuticles. "Seems like a waste of a perfectly good kid, but if that's what you want to do…"

Nina started to laugh, but Dillon shot her a look so she cleared her throat and struggled to keep a straight face.

After another long, intense look at his sister, Dillon turned on his heel and crossed the kitchen, Emma shrieking in delight. He stopped at the back door without opening it—thank God. Not that she believed he'd toss Emma out into a snowbank or anything, but it was brutally cold out and Emma didn't even have her coat on.

Emma didn't waste the opportunity, squirming around and climbing up Dillon's back where she clung to him like a monkey. *Uh-oh.* This was getting out of hand. *Why wasn't Kelsey stepping in?*

"Kelsey," he said, a threat and—if Nina wasn't mistaken—panic clear in his low voice.

Which she didn't understand. If someone had messed with her ex-husband, Trey, this way, he would've lost his patience—and his temper.

"You know," Kelsey said, tapping a finger to her chin, "my wedding's in less than two weeks and I don't recall receiving your RSVP. You are coming, aren't you?"

While Nina couldn't understand how Kelsey stood her ground, she did admire the other woman for it.

"The kid," he muttered. Nina noticed he had one arm bent at an awkward angle behind him so Emma wouldn't fall.

"Yeah, Emma's a great kid." Kelsey clapped her hands. "Oh, I know. Emma, how would you like to hang out with Uncle Dillon for a while? We're not quite done here, are we, Nina?"

Brother and sister both stared at her. She was trapped, solidly stuck to the spot by Kelsey's shrewd green eyes and Dillon's hooded, flat gaze.

She hated being put in the middle almost as much as she hated confrontations. Whichever side she took would probably be the wrong side. Besides, she'd end up disappointing someone.

"Uh…no? I mean…we still have a few things to go over."

Kelsey's face lit up. "See? Much to do. Many, many cakes to sample and decisions to make. It could take as long as a few hours—"

"Okay," he said. "I'll be there."

But Kelsey didn't budge. Just raised an eyebrow. "Promise?"

Dillon pressed his lips together. "Promise."

Kelsey grinned and motioned for him to turn around. When he did, she pulled Emma off his back.

"It worked, Kelsey," Emma said wiggling with excitement in Kelsey's arms.

"It sure did. You were great." She hugged Emma and set her down.

Nina's jaw dropped. They'd set Dillon up. Not only that, but they'd just admitted it. In front of him. Her stomach cramped as she waited for the explosion of temper. When a man had been so neatly played, so easily boxed into a corner, he was going to lash out.

Except nothing happened. Dillon didn't curse or threaten or call his sister names. Didn't pick up the nearest object and throw it at the wall. He just shook his head in disgust.

He must not be as angry as she thought. Or else he had a better hold on his control than she'd realized. Which was good, seeing as how he probably wasn't going to be too happy with her once she told him her news.

Kelsey stuffed Emma into her coat, tugged a hat over the little girl's head and grabbed the box of cake samples for Jack. "The wedding's at two," she told Dillon. "Reception's at the ski resort."

"I got an invitation."

She winked at him. "So you did. See you there. Thanks for these," she said to Nina. "I'll let you know in the morning which one we choose."

Hand in hand, she and Emma walked out the back door. It took a full minute, staring at the closed door, for Nina to realize she was alone.

With Dillon Ward.

She had to talk to him about her decision regarding the apartment. But for the love of all that was sweet and holy, she just wasn't certain she could deal with his potentially violent reaction to what she had to say. No matter how surprisingly calm he'd been so far.

As usual, his expression gave none of his thoughts away. She licked her lips, and didn't miss the way his gaze dropped to her mouth. The way his jaw tightened.

Her heart fluttered and she placed her hand on her chest. She hoped she wasn't having a heart attack or something. Wouldn't that be perfectly embarrassing? She could see the headlines of the *Serenity Springs Gazette* now: Local Business Owner Scared of Her Own Shadow. Has Heart Attack Because She Was Alone With A Sexy Man. Complete story on page 12.

"Aren't you mad?" she asked, her curiosity getting the best of her.

"About what?"

She picked up a dish towel and carefully folded it. "Kelsey," she said, unable to look at him. "The way she tricked you into going to her wedding."

"She's sneaky. You have to watch out for her."

Nina raised her head but she couldn't tell if he was joking or not. "Uh, well, it's not like you have to go…"

The look in his eyes seared her. "I promised."

"I know, but she did trick you—"

"I don't make promises I don't intend to keep."

She swallowed but her throat remained dry. The way he said it made her believe him.

Someone like Dillon Ward couldn't be trusted. She knew that. And if she didn't, her family warning her—

repeatedly—how dangerous and unpredictable he was should be enough to convince her.

Except, every once and a while, she had her doubts. But then she'd remember how Trey always said her naivety would be her downfall.

Dillon stepped toward her and she couldn't stop herself from backing up. He motioned to the towel twisted tightly in her hands. "That do something to you?"

Warmth climbed up her neck into her cheeks. She tossed the towel on the counter. "No. It's just been a long day."

He nodded as if that explanation was good enough reason for her to be acting like a complete moron. But at least he wasn't looking at her like most people did—with pity.

"I'm sure you're in a hurry to close up and get home, then," he said.

"Not particularly. I mean, I can't go home. Trey, my ex, is dropping our kids—"

"Still, I'm sure you have things to do. I know I do," he said pointedly. "So why don't you tell me what it is you wanted to tell me and I'll get out of your way."

"I'm sorry. I didn't mean to keep you from anything. I just wanted…that is…things have changed. In regards to your apartment. Since buying the bakery, I've had some time to think about what's best for my business and with costs rising the way they are—"

"So you do want to raise the rent."

"No, that's not it. It's not just about the money. Not really. I mean, it's partly the money, but more than that, what I need—"

"Would you just spit it out?" he snapped.

"I need you to move out."

DILLON SHOOK HIS HEAD. "What?"

She stepped back, her eyes darting around the empty room. He shoved his hands into his front pockets to keep from fisting them. Yeah, he towered over her and he'd just snapped at her, but he was really getting tired of everyone in town treating him like the spawn of Satan.

"I need you to move out," she squeaked, "by the end of the month."

"Let me get this straight." For some reason, he simply could not wrap his mind around the fact that this pretty little piece of fluff was giving him the boot. "You're evicting me?"

She swallowed and nodded. "It's just that if I want to increase my business—which I do—I have to think about expansion."

"You're going to expand the bakery into my apartment?"

She blushed deeper and dropped her gaze and just like that, he knew whatever she was about to tell him was a pile of crap.

Figures. You couldn't even trust someone as sweet as a cupcake to tell you the truth.

"I want to convert the apartment into a tearoom. A place I can rent out for parties or book clubs—"

"Serenity Springs has a book club?"

She frowned. "Local clubs could have meetings up there or I could serve special lunches and have tea tastings. It'll be nice…"

Sure. For her. And everyone else in town who wanted

him gone since the *Serenity Springs Gazette* ran that article about his five years in a maximum security prison.

But for him? Not so freaking nice.

"My lease says you have to give me thirty days and written notice."

Nina rubbed her thumb across the base of her left ring finger. "I'm giving you thirty days. And this—" she reached into her back pocket and pulled out a folded-up envelope "—is the notice."

He took the envelope from her. Noticed the unsteadiness of her hand. Great. He'd obviously scared her. He wanted to tell her to develop a backbone so the world didn't eat her alive. But then he supposed he should stop scowling at her and giving her a hard time. Try to put her at ease, like a nice guy would.

Then again, he'd stopped being a nice guy a long time ago.

He ripped open the envelope and quickly skimmed the paper while his mind turned with questions. If she was kicking him out because of his past, did he have legal recourse? Could he prove it? And the big question: where could he go?

He doubted anyone else would rent to him. After the police had suspected him of killing a woman a few months ago and that damn article ran in the paper, he'd lost two jobs he'd hoped would pull him through the winter. Despite being cleared of any wrongdoing.

He scratched his cheek. Wait a minute. What was he getting angry about? He'd be done at The Summit, a local bar he was renovating, any day now. He could blow this town. Truth be told, he should've been done two weeks ago but Allie Martin, the bar owner, kept giving him small jobs to do. More than likely because she knew he didn't have any other work.

Not that he liked charity, but he did like working for Allie. It was hard not to. She was smart, funny and gorgeous. Almost too bad they were better suited as friends than lovers.

And he hadn't had any real friends since before he'd been sent away. He didn't want to do anything to ruin his friendship with Allie.

He wasn't really surprised Nina was kicking him out. Ever since she'd bought the bakery from her grandparents, he'd known this day was coming. He supposed after having it *not* come for so many months, he'd grown complacent. Too comfortable. Too secure.

No, this wasn't something to get angry about or fight over. This was an opportunity. Or fate's way of telling him to get his ass in gear and get out of Serenity Springs.

He placed the eviction notice in the envelope and tucked it in his back pocket. "I'll be out after Kelsey's wedding," he promised before pushing open the kitchen door.

"You don't have to move out so soon," Nina said, following him into the dining room. "You can stay the full thirty—"

"No need." He grabbed his coat off the back of the chair and put it on. "Besides, I'm sure you want to get started on that tearoom as soon as possible."

"Of course I do," she said unconvincingly. "It's just I don't want to rush you. It might be difficult to find another place in two weeks—"

"Don't worry about it." He pulled his hat on. "I'm not going to."

He reached for the door when it swung open. Nina's kids, Hayley and Marcus, came barreling inside. The little girl spotted Dillon immediately and skidded to a stop. Unfortunately, Marcus kept going, plowing into his sister and knocking her down.

Sitting on the floor, Hayley's lower lip quivered and her eyes welled with tears, but she didn't make a sound.

"Honey, are you okay?" Nina asked, bending to pick up her daughter. Dillon couldn't help but notice her shapely backside.

"Everything all right in here, Nina?"

Trey Carlson, Nina's pretty-boy ex-husband, stood in the open doorway. And from the expression on the guy's face, he'd noticed Dillon checking out his ex-wife.

Great.

Before Nina could answer, Dillon zipped up his coat and said, "If that's all you wanted, I'm heading out."

"Oh. Yes, that's all." She looked like she wanted to say something else but didn't. Her daughter had her face buried in Nina's neck. Her son had taken off his hat and his pale blond hair stuck up all around his head. The boy's eyes were huge in his round face as he sidled next to his mother and put his arm around her leg.

"Thanks for lunch." A stupid thing to say considering she'd only fed him so he'd stick around long enough to be evicted.

At the door, Carlson blocked his way. Perfect. Just what he needed. A pissing contest with the town's self-important, arrogant psychologist.

Dillon didn't move. And he sure wasn't going to say

"excuse me" or anything civil to this guy. Carlson had made his displeasure about Dillon living above the bakery known to anyone and everyone who would listen. He'd even written an article for the *Gazette* about the psychology of a killer.

It hadn't taken much to deduce which particular killer he was referring to.

After a long, silent stare-down, Carlson stepped aside.

Dillon smirked. Yeah. That's what he thought. All flash. No substance.

He lowered his head against the driving snow and walked around the building to the entrance to his apartment.

He couldn't wait to get as far from Serenity Springs as possible.

CHAPTER TWO

THE MUSIC SWITCHED to Bing Crosby crooning "White Christmas." The sentimentality of it would've fit Nina's current circumstances perfectly—snow was falling, Christmas was approaching and she was with her kids. Except she was also with Trey. The man she once thought she'd be spending the rest of her life with. The man she had once been afraid she'd never escape.

Trey took his time closing the door and brushing the snow off his shoulders. Closing in on forty, he could pass for ten years younger. Nina wondered if his patients knew their psychologist was afraid of growing older—or at least, looking older—so much that he had his tawny hair professionally highlighted once a month.

Or that he went to a salon two towns away to keep them from finding out.

But not even a bit of gray or the few lines bracketing Trey's blue eyes could detract from his movie-star looks with his conservative haircut, perfect tan, suede jacket and dark designer jeans. And he still had the sense of privilege and entitlement he'd had when they'd first met ten years ago.

At nineteen she'd been way too young. Too young, naive and, if she was honest with herself, stupid to ever get involved with Serenity Springs' supposed golden boy.

Live and learn.

"Nina, put her down," Trey said in what she thought of as his professional voice—soft and carefully modulated. "You know tears are a self-indulgent luxury. Coddling only encourages her self-indulgence."

Nina smoothed a hand over Hayley's back. Her daughter still clung to her but at least she'd stopped crying. "I'm comforting her—not coddling. She's hurt."

"She hurt her pride more than her backside." He reached for Hayley. Short of using her daughter in a game of tug-of-war, Nina had no choice but to let her go. Trey set her on the floor and laid a hand on her head. "You're fine, aren't you, princess?"

Hayley sniffed. "Yes, Daddy."

Trey winked at her. "That's my girl. Now, go into the kitchen with your brother. I need to speak to your mom. Alone."

Nina forced a smile. "If you wash your hands, you may each have one cookie. One. Understand?" They nodded. "Good. Now say goodbye to your father."

Hayley threw her arms around Trey's legs and tipped her head back, her lips puckered. "Bye, Daddy."

"Bye, princess." Trey kissed her and patted her back before disentangling himself from her hold to accept Marcus's quick, one-armed hug. "Goodbye, son. Next weekend remember to bring your math book."

"Okay," Marcus mumbled. "See ya."

"Nina," Trey said when the kitchen door swung shut behind Marcus, "cookies so close to dinnertime?"

Her back to him, she rolled her eyes. "One cookie

isn't going to spoil their appetites. Besides, we're eating at my parents' so dinner will be a little later."

He sighed, his you're-such-a-trial-to-me sigh. "I don't like them out late on school nights. You know that."

Yeah. She knew. She knew how he felt about all of her transgressions, each one of her faults and her many failings.

Trey was nothing if not vocal in his opinions.

She began to tuck a wayward curl behind her ear but stopped at Trey's disdainful expression. During their marriage, she'd straightened her hair and pulled it back into a low ponytail because that's how he'd liked it. But their marriage ended long ago and she'd be damned if she'd give him any more control over her life.

She twisted the loose strands around her finger. "They need to see their grandparents and aunts and uncles. And this is the only night that works for everyone. They'll be home and in bed at their regular bedtimes."

"I hope so. I wasn't happy with Marcus's last report card. A boy that bright getting a B in math...."

"I don't think it'll hurt his chances of getting into a good college. Besides, he's doing his best—"

"No, he isn't. Clearly. He can do much better."

And didn't that sum up every problem she and Trey had had during their marriage? She'd done her best to please him, to make him happy. And it had never been good enough. He'd found her lacking. Her looks. Her intelligence. Her mothering skills. Even her skills in the bedroom.

"We met with his teacher, she said Marcus is doing fine—"

"She's enabling him to slide by. Let's have him switched to a different classroom."

He stepped toward her and she grabbed the serving tray off the table and crossed the room. "I have a lot to do before I can close up. Did you want something else?" she asked as she cleared the dishes from Dillon's table.

She didn't want to argue with him. She'd done enough of that during her marriage. Besides, she'd learned long ago that standing up to Trey was a waste of time and effort. She couldn't win.

But she could divert and evade—the only tactic that had ever worked for her.

Trey's mouth thinned. Either he was angry she had the nerve to try to change the subject or he blamed her for getting sidetracked from his original goal.

"What was going on with you and Dillon Ward?" he asked, his hands on his narrow hips. "What if someone walked by and saw you two in here, alone, after closing? Do you realize how that looked? What people would say?"

At the next table she loaded dirty coffee cups onto her tray. "It's snowing like crazy. I doubt anyone in town is out walking or peeking into storefront windows."

"That's not the point," Trey said stiffly.

"We were just talking—"

"Men like Dillon Ward don't just talk to women. More than likely, he sees you as an easy mark. You're single, own your own business and are ripe pickings for someone like him."

She tossed dirty silverware onto her tray with a loud clang. "Ripe pickings? What am I, a piece of fruit?"

"You're being overly sensitive. All I'm saying is that

you can't let your guard down around someone like him. You're an attractive woman." His gaze skimmed over her. "Even with those few extra pounds."

She spun on her heel and walked back behind the counter, her stomach churning, her face heated. She shouldn't let his words affect her. But God, she hated how looking into his eyes made the memories rush to the surface. Made her feel like less than nothing.

She shut off the industrial coffeepots as if they demanded her full attention. Every self-help book she'd read during the past two years said the only way someone could hurt you is if you gave them power over you. She gripped the counter, the hard edge digging into her palm. But she didn't give Trey power. He took it. And she ended up feeling worthless, fat and inadequate.

Just like he always told her she was.

"Dillon isn't interested in me," she said, brushing past Trey. She placed a chair upside down on the table. Someone like Dillon wouldn't look twice at her. She was too vanilla—plain, boring and unnoticeable. "We were discussing his eviction."

Trey grinned, the same grin that had wrapped her around his finger all those years ago. She still remembered how her stomach had fluttered the first time he'd smiled at her like that. How shocked she'd been that he'd noticed her. How flattered.

How stupid.

After double-checking to make sure the table was clean, he leaned back and crossed his arms. "I'm glad you listened to my advice. This is best for everyone concerned. Ward is dangerous."

She moved to the next table. "Of course you're glad. You got what you wanted."

He shook his head, his expression magnanimous. Composed. As if he was talking to one of his patients. "It's not what I want that matters, Nina. Even though things didn't work out between us, I still care about you. I don't want to see you get hurt."

She bit her lip. Cared about her. Right. Which was why he made her feel worthless. And then left her for the tall, thin, sexy—and let's not forget successful— Dr. Rachel Weber.

"You made the right decision," he assured her as he patted her shoulder. She twisted out of his reach, but either he didn't notice or didn't care that she couldn't stand him touching her. "I've got to get going. I'll pick the kids up at six Thursday. Please have them ready on time."

As he walked out, she slammed the next chair on the table and imagined it was his head. Her pulse raced. Talking to Trey always made her feel like she'd just run a race.

And lost.

"Marcus had three cookies," Hayley said as she skipped into the room.

Marcus, hot on his sister's heels, said, "Nu-uh. I had two."

"Daddy says Marcus needs to stop eating so much 'cause he's getting fat."

Nina fisted her hands. While Marcus had put on some weight since the divorce, her son was far from fat. But Trey wouldn't tolerate anything less than per-fection. Especially in his children.

"They were small cookies," Marcus mumbled, his cheeks flushed pink. "I'm pretty sure they equaled one regular-size cookie."

"Well, *I'm* pretty sure I told you one cookie," she said, forcing a brightness she didn't feel into her voice. She ruffled his mussed hair. "But not because I'm worried about your weight. I just want to make sure you eat the dinner Grandma's making. You can work up an appetite by helping me put the rest of the chairs up on the tables."

Hayley tugged on Nina's jeans. "I want to help, too."

"Run and get the broom and dustpan. And no more tattling."

Hayley raced off while Marcus dragged his feet toward the first table. "How was your weekend?" she asked.

He shrugged. Turned a chair over before hefting it in place. "Dad signed me up for the indoor soccer league."

She helped him lift the next chair. "I didn't know you wanted to play soccer."

"I don't. I want to play basketball."

"Then why—"

"Dad wants me to."

"Well, it might be fun—"

"No, it won't. None of my friends are playing and I think soccer's boring, but Dad wants me to play it because he says I'm not good enough to start at basketball, which means I'll be on the bench for most of the games and won't get enough exercise."

She crouched in front of him and placed her hands on his shoulders. "Dad just wants what's best for you.

Come on, give it a try. If you don't like it after a few weeks, I'll talk to your dad about quitting."

Marcus frowned, but it wasn't the anger on her son's face that made her throat constrict. It was the disappointment. "No, you won't. You always say you'll talk to him but it never changes anything."

She sat back on her heels. "Honey, that's not true. Dad and I may make decisions that you don't like but we're only thinking about what's best for you."

"Basketball's what's best for me."

"Well, then," she said slowly, "I'll discuss it with your dad."

He searched her face. "Promise?"

The idea of confronting Trey, of subjecting herself to his put-downs and arrogance made her palms sweat. But for her son, for that hopeful look on his face...

"Of course I promise." Something crashed in the kitchen. Nina stood. "Could you please check on your sister?"

As she watched her son leave, his back stiff, she couldn't help but wonder if she was doing the right thing. She wanted to teach her kids how to get along with their father. To protect themselves from his stinging comments and wicked temper. So why did she feel like she was failing them?

And in the process, failing herself?

ONE GOOD THING about his latest foster parents. They had decent taste in music.

Kyle Fowler loaded AC/DC's "Back In Black" into the SUV's CD player and cranked the volume. He switched on his high beams but that made it harder to see in the heavy snow.

Their vast CD collection was the only good thing about Joe and Karen Roberts. Sure, during the past seven months with them they'd given him a cell phone—to use in case of emergencies—and bought him some new clothes. But they were no different from any of his other foster parents.

He slowed enough to make sure there was no other traffic and then coasted through a Stop sign. No other foster parents had given him anything except a hard time. But Joe and Karen had bought him things just so they could take them away again.

What kind of sick head game was that? They were getting off on their power, that's what they're doing.

Jeez, it was just a little pot. It wasn't like he was cooking up meth or something really bad. Pot never hurt anyone. Besides, they shouldn't have been snooping around his room. They were the ones who were wrong and yet they thought they could ground him?

Who the hell gets grounded anymore?

None of his other foster parents had ever cared if he got in trouble. Okay, so maybe they cared—but only how it affected them and their check. Oh, once in a while he'd have someone bitch him out, maybe slap him around a bit but nobody lectured him like the holier-than-thou Joe and Karen.

On a straight stretch by the high school, he accelerated and flipped the bird to the empty building. He wasn't going back there, that's for sure. The SUV fishtailed on the slippery, snow-covered road, but he easily kept it under control.

He remembered Karen's disappointment, Joe's anger, as they'd sat him down earlier this evening. He'd felt almost sick when Joe tossed the baggie of weed onto the coffee table in front of him. And when they'd both said how disappointed they were in him, he hadn't been able to breathe.

Karen claimed she found it when she was cleaning up his room. She was always doing stuff like that— cleaning his room, putting away his clothes. Acting all nice and sweet, as if she enjoyed having him around. But he knew the truth would come out eventually. She and Joe were just messing with him. Acting as if they liked him, cared about him.

His hands tightened on the wheel. What bullshit.

He reached into his coat pocket and took out a pack of smokes. He'd just forget how nice Karen pretended to be, how she smiled at him and laughed at his jokes. How she asked him what he wanted at the grocery store and never complained that he ate too much. How she'd made him a cake for his birthday.

No one had ever made him a cake. No one had even remembered his birthday before. But Joe and Karen took him to a restaurant and when they got back home, they had the cake with candles and everything. They'd even sung to him.

It was freaking embarrassing. He was fifteen, not five.

The worst part was, when Joe had hugged him and Karen kissed his cheek, he'd thought maybe, just maybe, this time would be different.

His eyes burned. And it was different. But it was also

worse. Because he'd thought they were cool. But the way they flipped out over a little bit of pot was whacked.

He had wheels, a full tank of gas and, thanks to his helping himself to the extra cash around the house and in Karen's purse, he had money. Almost two hundred dollars. That would last him until he was far enough away to ditch the car. He'd get a job and start fresh. Make his own way.

And to hell with everyone who'd ever held him back. To hell with anyone who tried to stop him.

With his cigarette in his mouth, he lifted his hips and dug in his front pocket for his disposable lighter. Steering with his left hand, he lit the cigarette with his right and blew out smoke. He glanced at the speedometer. He was going fifty down Main Street. He should probably slow down but nobody in this hick town was up anyway.

Not even the cops.

He pushed a button to roll the window down a crack. He took his eyes off the road for a second to flick the ash off his cigarette but when he looked through the windshield again, he was heading straight for the sidewalk. Swearing, he dropped his cigarette and jerked the wheel to the right at the same time he slammed on the brakes. His tires locked up. The SUV spun out of control, jumped the curb and crashed through the front of Sweet Suggestions.

Nina was sure it wasn't as bad as it seemed. It couldn't be.

Because it seemed really, really bad.

Two of the three large, glass display cases were

smashed. Tables and chairs were in pieces across the room. Donuts, pastries and loaves of bread covered the floor, along with rubble and glass. Both large windows were demolished. The outside wall was gone.

And a banged-up SUV sat in the middle of the room, halfway through the wall separating the kitchen from the front.

The frigid air cut through her sweatpants. She shivered and flipped the hood of her heavy down coat over her snarled hair. When Police Chief Jack Martin had called and woke her, she'd tried to take off in her sweats and the ratty Hello Kitty T-shirt she slept in. Luckily, her mother—whom she'd called to watch the kids—had shoved Nina's arms into the coat. She just wished she'd had the good sense to pull on wool socks instead of slipping her bare feet into these ancient canvas sneakers. She could no longer feel her toes.

Outside, the lights from two police cars were flashing while bright orange flares burned at the intersection. Her father was talking to one of the policemen while the tow truck driver hooked his winch to the SUV. Nina's teeth chattered and she blew on her hands in an effort to warm them.

Jack had asked Nina to wait inside. From the look on his face as he spoke to Dora Wilkins—the editor-in-chief of the *Serenity Springs Gazette*—out on the sidewalk, he wouldn't get to Nina for a while.

"You all right?"

"I'm fine," she answered automatically, then realized how foolish a lie it was. She exhaled heavily and glanced at Dillon. His hair was mussed, his green

T-shirt wrinkled, his work boots untied. "On second thought, I'm not fine. This is a disaster."

He turned over an unbroken chair and used the sweat-shirt crumpled in his hand to brush it off. "Could've been worse."

"Worse?" she asked as she sank into the chair. She gestured wildly. "There's an SUV in my bakery. There's a huge hole in one wall and the other wall's completely gone. *Gone.* How can it be much worse?"

"A few feet to the left—" he crossed his arms; she noticed his skin was covered in goose bumps "—and he would've taken out your gas meter. That would've been worse. As it is, you'll have to shore up the supporting wall, get new windows and a door, a couple of tables—"

"Tables and chairs and new display cases. Maybe even new flooring. Not to mention priming and paint-ing those new walls." Her throat tightened painfully with unshed tears. She dropped her head into her hands. "Everything's ruined. What am I supposed to do now?"

"You're supposed to handle this," he said simply. "Does it suck? Yes. But sitting around whining—"

"I am not whining." She stood and flipped her hood back. When he raised an eyebrow, she sighed. "Okay, maybe I am whining. Just a little bit. I'm entitled."

"Look," he said hesitantly, "I realize we don't...know each other very well, but since I've lived here I've seen you handle your kids, late deliveries and rude custom-ers. Believe me, you can handle this."

Her mouth popped open. "That's...that's the nicest compliment I've had in a long time." And what did that say about the sad situation of her life that it came from the man she'd recently evicted? She skimmed her fingers over his cold hand, just the briefest of touches, but it left her fingertips tingling. She rubbed her hand down the side of her leg. "Thank you."

He stepped back, looking so uncomfortable she almost smiled. "It's no big deal. Just calling it like I see it."

She cleared her throat. "You know, that sweatshirt might do you more good if you actually put it on."

"It might," he agreed as he unwound the cloth to show her the dark blood staining it, "but I'd rather not."

"What happened?" She swept her gaze over him. "Are you hurt?"

"It's not his blood," Jack said as he carefully stepped over glass to join them. "It's Kyle's."

Her knees went weak. "Kyle? Kyle who?"

"Kyle Fowler," Jack said. "He's the one who was driving."

She held her hand out. "Wait a minute. Isn't that the Roberts' foster son?"

"He is." Jack rubbed the back of his neck. "Seems he got mad at Joe and Karen and took off."

"Took off?"

"He stole their car," Dillon said, balling his shirt up again. "Some of their cash, too. The kid's in deep sh… uh…trouble."

"He's lucky he walked away with only a few bruises and a broken wrist," Jack added.

"If he wasn't hurt," Nina said, "where did all the blood come from?"

"He hit his head against the window, got cut up. But it's not as bad as it sounds." Dillon held up his shirt. "Or looks. Head wounds always bleed a lot."

She didn't even want to think about how or why Dillon would know such a thing. "I'm glad Kyle's okay."

"You're taking this pretty well," Dillon commented.

"What do you mean?"

"If some kid stole a car and crashed into my building, I don't know if I'd be quite so understanding."

"Understanding? Is that what I'm being? Maybe it would be better if I said I wanted to go to the hospital and tear into Kyle for his stupid, reckless actions?"

"I'm not sure about better, but it might be more honest."

"Yeah, well, honesty's overrated," she muttered. The few times she'd allowed her temper to get the better of her, she'd ended up with a lot of bruises. Besides, she couldn't get mad at some troubled teenager. The town would probably pass out collectively in shock.

And take away the halo they'd branded her with.

"There will be consequences," Jack told her as one of his officers called his name. "Kyle's facing some serious charges. And this isn't his first offense. It could mean time in juvenile hall for him. Excuse me for a minute," he said before walking away.

While she was glad Kyle wasn't seriously hurt, she just couldn't feel bad for him. He'd only been here a few months, and he already had a reputation as a troublemaker. Although truth be told, he'd arrived with the stigma in place. Everyone had been concerned when Joe, a local accountant, and Karen, an elementary school teacher, had become Kyle's foster parents. Married for close to twenty years and unable to have children of their own, they'd chosen to take in a juvenile delinquent instead of adopting an infant.

"You're allowed to be pissed," Dillon said.

She laughed and rubbed her temples. "That's a new one. Usually people are telling me not to bother getting mad. Especially over things I can't control."

"I'm just saying you have the right to be angry. Most people would be."

She dropped her hands. "I don't want to be angry. I just want this to not have happened. I want to close my eyes and open them to discover this is all a bad dream."

"That's not how life is."

"No kidding."

He thumped his fisted hand against his thigh several times. "Since you can't blink and make this disappear—"

"What if I wiggled my nose?"

He smiled and the effect was so sexy, she caught her breath and lowered her gaze. The last thing she needed was her hormones taking notice of Dillon Ward.

Of course, it'd been so long since she'd been aware of a man, she'd begun to doubt she even still *had* hormones.

The tow truck driver got into his truck and started hauling the SUV out. Dillon took a hold of her elbow and led her to the far corner.

"Unless your magic powers suddenly materialize," he said, bending close so she could hear him over the noise, "you're going to have to decide what your next step is."

He still hadn't dropped her elbow. His hand was large and very masculine against the bright pink of her puffy coat. His hold on her was light. Supportive. And steady. She could really use some steadiness now.

She swallowed. "I…I guess the next step is to call the insurance adjuster."

"Yeah, but right now the exterior wall needs to be boarded up and, since the interior wall is weight-bearing, it'll have to be jacked up temporarily." He leaned back, his jaw tight, his eyes steady on hers. "I could take care of the exterior wall. I wouldn't be able to do anything inside until tomorrow, though. That is, if you want my help."

Her pulse skittered. Before she could answer, her dad barreled toward them. His weathered cheeks were red from the cold, his knit ski cap pulled down low over his ears.

Dillon dropped her arm and stepped back. Nina forced a smile for her father. "Good news, Dad," she said, trying to ignore the sudden tension, "Dillon's offered to board up the wall tonight. Dillon Ward, you know my father, Hank Erickson, don't—"

"That won't be necessary." Her dad's mouth was turned down at the corners. "I already have a contractor on his way."

Dillon looked at her as if…what? "Thank you so much for offering, Dillon, but—"

"No problem," he said. "Good luck with the renovations." His expression hard, he nodded at Hank and walked away.

Hank squeezed her shoulders and dropped a quick kiss on her head. "We'll take care of this, honey. I called Jim Arturo to handle the repairs. Don't you worry about a thing."

She stiffened and slipped out of his hold. "Don't worry? This is my livelihood we're talking about."

He patted her arm. She wanted to bite his hand. "I know it's upsetting, but let me handle this. Now," he said, taking his cell phone out of his pocket, "you have your insurance with Todd Alexis, right? I'll call him and get things moving along."

She opened her mouth to tell him she could call her insurance agent herself but he was already dialing a number as he walked into the kitchen. She slumped into a chair. She had a bank loan to repay and Christmas gifts to buy, not to mention her ancient minivan needed new tires. And she'd kicked out her tenant, the only source of income she could count on.

She blinked back tears. But she wasn't supposed to worry. Or be strong enough to solve her own problems.

The sad part was, even though it grated on her last nerve, she knew she wouldn't stand up for herself. She was so damn tired. And scared. And since everyone expected her to stay in the background and let them take care of her, that's what she'd end up doing.

Even if she did want to take charge of her life.

CHAPTER THREE

"You didn't have to come in today," Allie said from behind the polished, horseshoe-shaped bar.

"Yeah, I did." Dillon sat on a stool and shrugged out of his jacket. Early morning sunlight filtered through the windows, casting The Summit's barroom in shadows. Despite a jukebox filled with classic rock songs, Allie hummed along to some bubblegum song playing on the radio underneath the bar. He grimaced as the singer hit a high note. "How can you listen to this crap?"

She flipped her heavy, dark hair over her shoulder. "It's pop music, not crap. And I like it." She did a little shimmy and shake to the chorus. "Besides, if I have to listen to 'Hotel California' one more time, I'll stick my head in the oven."

"It's electric."

She waved that away. "So it'll be a symbolic gesture." She turned the music down. "I drove by the bakery on my way here. The damage is pretty extensive. What's Nina going to do about it?"

"Her father was there last night, said he'd take care of getting a carpenter to do the repairs."

Yeah, Mr. Erickson had jumped in real quick. Nina's father hadn't wanted the town's most dangerous citizen anywhere near his precious daughter.

Dillon's shoulders tensed as he remembered how Nina had brushed off his offer to help. An offer he never should've made. She had enough people around to help her. He wasn't going to lose any sleep over her.

Allie polished a beer glass, her eyes narrowed in concentration. He didn't bother pointing out that water spots weren't going to keep her clientele from drinking their booze. "Joe Roberts called me before you got here. Wanted to get my opinion on what was going to happen to Kyle."

"Are you putting your lawyer shingle back out?"

Regret flickered across her face but was quickly gone. "Hardly. I'm a business owner now."

Allie had been a successful defense attorney with a high-class law firm in New York City before returning to Serenity Springs last year. The few times he'd asked what had happened to send her back to her hometown, she either changed the subject, evaded his question or went into some long, boring dissertation about the legal system. His least favorite subject.

If her ability to talk for thirty minutes straight and not say a damn thing was anything to go by, she must've been a hell of a lawyer.

"So why'd they call you?" he asked.

"My mom is friends with Karen's mom and she told them to call me."

"Sounds like legal work to me."

Having wiped each and every spot off the glass, she set it down and picked up another one. "Only work I'm doing is figuring out how to keep a bartender longer than two months."

"Smart choice."

He was glad she wasn't going to allow herself to be dragged back into trying to save people. Talk about a thankless—and futile—endeavor. He'd spent the first half of his life trying to save his mother from her addictions and Kelsey from abuse—and her own rebelliousness. And it hadn't helped any of them.

He'd almost stepped back into that bottomless pit again when he'd offered Nina help last night. Luckily her lack of backbone had come to his rescue.

"I don't know," Allie said, holding the glass up to the light before putting it away. "After talking to Jack—"

"If you're not working the case, why talk to your brother about it?"

"I wanted to get a feel for what's going on. Kyle's in big trouble. It's a shame. He was doing so well with Joe and Karen."

"He stole from them."

"I know, but he was upset and he's only fifteen. Poor kid's been in the system most of his life. He's had it tough."

Dillon shifted and hooked his foot on the rung of the stool. Fought to keep the bitterness from his voice. "Lots of people have it tough."

His own childhood—if you could call it that—had hardly been ideal. His father died from an overdose when Dillon was four and his mother spent most of her time drowning her sorrows in vodka.

But he'd survived. He'd sucked it up and taken care of his mom and Kelsey. And even though there had never been enough money, he'd never resorted to stealing. He'd made sure Kelsey hadn't, either.

Until she'd stopped listening to him.

He frowned as he realized there were more than a few similarities between his sister and Kyle. When Dillon helped Kyle out of the SUV last night, he'd seen defiance in the kid's expression, the to-hell-with-the-world-I-don't-need-anyone attitude. But he'd also seen the kid's fear.

All of which he'd seen plenty of times in Kelsey growing up.

Compassion warred with his hard-earned good sense. Even after all that happened to him, his protective instincts still drew him to those in need.

Like the kid. And Nina Carlson.

"Kyle will be punished, that's for sure," Allie said. "He'll probably be sentenced to juvenile hall."

"Is that what you told his foster parents?"

"I told them the truth. And advised that it wouldn't hurt to have Kyle try to make amends somehow. If he's lucky and gets Judge Williams, showing remorse will go a long way toward a lenient sentence."

Did that really work? When Kelsey got busted for shoplifting or underage drinking, she never made amends. Just got into more trouble. Trouble he'd then do his damnedest to get her out of.

He rolled his head side to side but his neck muscles remained tight. He hoped for Kyle's sake, Allie's idea worked. Being locked up changed a person. He'd hate to see that happen to a kid.

He drummed his fingers on the bar before slapping it lightly with his palm. Not his problem. Even if it was, he was in no position to help.

"Allie, we need to talk."

She didn't take her eyes off of the stubborn spot she was trying to rub out. "I thought men hated to talk."

"We do." She set the glass down and looked at him expectantly. He scratched his jaw. Between his late night and wanting to get this conversation over with, he hadn't taken the time to shave. "Listen, this…thing between us—"

She tossed the towel on the bar. "I knew this would happen."

"What?"

She pushed up the sleeves of her dark green sweater. "This." She gestured between them. "Us working together every day. It got to be too much for you. The tension. The attraction. And now, you've fallen for me. Why must I be so irresistible?" she asked the heavens. She squeezed his arm. "It'll never work out between us. You have to see that. I'm not what you need."

What a smart-ass. God, he was going to miss her. "What I need is for you to swallow your ego and be serious for a minute."

"Why?" She leaned on her elbows, her face in her hands. "You're being serious enough for both of us."

"Allie…" He slid to his feet. "I'm leaving."

She swatted him on the arm as she straightened. "Don't be such a drama queen. I'll stop. I promise I'll be good."

"No. I mean I'm leaving Serenity Springs."

"What?" Her smile disappeared. "But why?"

"It's time I moved on. And now that I've been evicted—"

"Nina evicted you? No way."

He nodded. "She said she wanted to expand. I figure

she'd just been biding her time after buying the building to kick me out. Can't say I blame her for not wanting a murderer living above her place of business."

Allie's eyes flashed. "She can't refuse to rent to you because you were in prison. We'll take her to court. I can't believe she would pull something like this. And to think, she used to be so...so *nice*."

"Put away your law degree. We're not taking anyone to court for anything. And Nina hasn't changed. She told me—very nicely—that I was evicted. It's no big deal."

He didn't want Allie and her high ideals to go after Nina. The ex-lawyer would smash the cupcake into crumbs.

He hadn't been lying when he'd said Nina was nice. Too nice. And she'd seemed so...lost last night. Fragile. She'd acted as if she wanted to take charge, but just didn't know how or what to do first.

Allie hurried out from behind the bar. "But what about the rest of the work here?"

"There *is* no more work here. And after the false accusation of Shannon's murder, Serenity Springs just isn't the place for me."

"It could be," she said softly. "You could have a second chance. And if you need a place to stay, why not move in upstairs—"

"No." He shoved his hands into his pockets. "I'm leaving after the wedding. I'll get my tools out of here today."

She crossed her arms. "But I don't want you to go." She pouted. "I'll miss you."

He smiled. "Last week you told me I was a bigger pain in your ass than your brother."

"So? Doesn't mean I don't like having you around."

He chuckled. "You'll be fine." Before he could change his mind, he squeezed her shoulders and kissed the top of her head. "Thanks for being a good friend."

She patted his waist, sniffed and walked away. Dillon tipped his head back and exhaled. Leaving was for the best. He just hoped the next two weeks flew by.

IF ONE MORE PERSON told her how sorry they were for her, she'd shove a stale Danish down their throat.

And it would be even more effective and surprising because it came from sweet, easygoing, good-girl Nina Carlson.

She kicked the table leg. Pain shot up her foot. Ouch. She hobbled over to lean against the counter. See why she never bothered to get angry? All it did was leave her feeling empty and guilty.

And in pain.

She picked up the contractor's estimate and crumpled it in her fist. No, anger wouldn't help. It was past time she took control.

Headlights illuminated the kitchen as a truck pulled into the parking lot. Finally.

Nina shoved the wadded paper into her pocket and hurried across the room, ignoring the ache in her toes. She yanked the door open and dashed out into the cold air. "Dillon!"

Getting out of his truck, he stopped and looked over his shoulder at her before closing the driver's side door.

She crossed her arms and lowered her head against the stinging wind as she jogged across the parking lot. It had stopped snowing but the wicked cold blew through her threadbare Harvard sweatshirt, and snow soaked her sneakers.

Two feet from him, she slipped, her arms windmilling as she started to fall.

"Easy," he murmured, stepping forward and taking a hold of her upper arms.

She clutched him until she found her balance. At least the embarrassment heating her face eased the tingle of cold in her cheeks.

He scowled at her. "Where's your coat?"

"Inside." Her breath came out in bursts of frost. She inhaled and forced herself to meet his eyes. "Dillon, I…I need you."

He let go of her and stepped back. "I'm flattered."

She blew on her frozen hands—spring couldn't come soon enough. "Look, I've had a really rotten day and I don't mean to be rude, but I don't have the time or inclination for innuendos right now, okay?"

"My mistake."

Ack. Did he have to be so…unflappable? Especially when she was always so flustered.

"What can I do for you?" he asked, but there was no curiosity on his face. Merely patience.

"I…are you almost done at The Summit?"

He raised an eyebrow. "I finished up today."

"That's great." Her teeth chattered. "Can…can we go inside? I have fresh coffee."

He was going to refuse. She could see it on his face. What could she do to change his mind? To persuade him to hear her out? Kelsey would make some wise remark and bait him. Nina's older sister Blaire used her stunning looks to manipulate men.

Since she didn't have Kelsey's nerve or Blaire's looks, Nina silently prayed.

"I have a few minutes to spare," he said.

She smiled, relieved, noticing the way his eyes narrowed slightly before she trudged back toward the bakery. But at least he was following her.

Inside, she poured two cups of coffee, took a moment to doctor hers with a heavy dollop of cream and preceded him into the dining area. A chill racked her and she wrapped her fingers around her warm mug.

He sat and nodded toward the plywood covering the hole in the exterior wall. "Looks like you have things under control here."

She choked on her coffee. Coughed so hard, her eyes watered. Once her vision cleared, she studied him. The man had the emotionless thing down pat.

"I wouldn't say things are under control." She rapped a staccato beat on her cup with her fingernails before setting it on an empty table. "As a matter of fact, I don't have anything under control."

"That so?"

"My father asked Jim Arturo, you know, from Arturo and Sons Builders?" He inclined his head. She took that as a yes. "Anyway, Dad asked Jim to meet us here earlier today." She took out the paper, smoothed it out and handed it to Dillon. "Jim gave me this."

He glanced at it as he sipped his coffee. "Pretty sizable estimate."

"That's not the problem. The problem is, he can't start working here for at least two months. *Two months.* Do you know how long that is?"

"Eight weeks? Give or take a day or two."

She gave him the look she used on her kids to warn them they were two seconds away from being banished to their rooms. Dillon didn't seem the least bit intimidated. Figures.

She began to pace. "There's no way I can afford to lose two months' worth of business, especially during the holidays. Besides losing local sales, I'll be missing out on a huge chunk of revenue generated by tourists—"

"Kitchen's still functional."

She stopped so quickly, her ponytail hit her cheek. "But I don't have a place to display what I've baked. Plus, without any place to sit and eat, I'll lose the breakfast and lunch crowds, not to mention foot traffic from people out shopping. Even if I put up a sign that says we're still open, how many people are going to notice in all this mess?"

He set the estimate on the table. "Yeah. That's tough."

"Tough?" Her voice rose. "I've worked my butt off trying to make this business a success. I have daily specials planned for the entire month. I've even booked a few holiday parties plus a girl's eighth birthday party where the kids can eat lunch, play games and bake and decorate their own cookies." Her breathing grew ragged, and spots formed before her eyes. "Where am I supposed to do all of that? In the kitchen?"

Nina tried to catch her breath, to get herself under control again. She'd blown it. She'd overreacted, just like Trey always said she did. Lost her temper when she knew better. She rubbed her cheek. If she raised her voice to Trey and his oh-so-reasonable tone didn't get her to calm down, his stinging slaps did.

"What does any of that have to do with me?" Dillon asked, seemingly unaffected by her outburst.

She frowned. That was it? The man really was an enigma.

"You said you were finished at The Summit and I was hoping…" She swallowed, then rushed on so fast her words slurred together. "I want to hire you to do the renovations."

She held her breath until the silence stretched out so long, she grew dizzy and had to exhale.

Finally Dillon stood and asked, "What makes you think I don't have other jobs lined up?"

She rubbed the base of her bare ring finger. "I heard no one will hire you after the murder investigation."

After a second of stunned silence, he asked, "You always believe everything you hear? Because if I did, I'd believe you were emotionally crushed when your ex-husband left you. And that if he ever returned, you'd take him back in a flash." He waited a beat. "At least that's what I've heard."

She remembered being the top subject of the rumor mill. But instead of letting her humiliation overcome her, she made a show of looking him up and down. "What are you, a secret member of the Red Hat Society? I thought only old women gossiped."

His lips twitched. "Maybe you can hold your own after all."

"I can," she lied. "But just because you shouldn't believe everything you hear, doesn't mean there isn't some truth in rumors, either."

She'd rather use margarine and artificial sweetener in her recipes than go back to Trey, but she *had* been crushed when he'd left her for another woman. Oh, not her heart—that had just been bruised—but her ego. Her pride.

She'd give just about anything to get even a tiny bit of that pride back.

"So. Do you have any other jobs lined up?" she asked.

"Nope."

"Great. So will—"

"No."

She shook her head. "What?"

"I won't work for you."

"But why not?"

"I'm not going to be here." The intensity of his gaze pinned her to her spot. "You wanted me gone, remember?"

She opened her mouth. Shut it again. Shoot.

"Thanks for the coffee," he said. "Good luck finding someone to take the job."

She leaped forward. "You can stay," she blurted, clutching his arms, "in the apartment. It's not like I can afford a tearoom now anyway."

His brown eyes were guarded. "You didn't evict me because of a tearoom."

"That was nothing personal—"

"Doesn't matter." His hands were large, warm and surprisingly gentle as he disentangled himself from her grip. "I've come to expect people to treat me a certain way, and so far, they haven't disappointed me."

Shocked, she stared at him. Is that what she'd done? All she'd wanted was to get her family and Trey off her back. And yes, maybe to give herself some peace of mind by asking Dillon to leave.

But she hadn't meant to hurt him.

"Dillon, I'm so sor—"

"Don't be. You did what you had to do and now I'm doing what I have to do. Find someone else for the job because I'm not interested in saving you."

HER CHEEKS TURNED PINK. He wondered if Nina's skin was a soft as it looked. Man, she smelled good.

"But, if you don't have any other jobs, you could work here," she insisted. One thing for her: she might be a cupcake, but she was a stubborn cupcake. "I'm sure you'd be done by the end of the month."

"You're right," he acknowledged. "Except I'm leaving after the wedding."

"You could wait. Aren't you celebrating Christmas with Kelsey and her family?"

"I hadn't planned on it."

"Please," she said hoarsely. "Please."

Damn it. He didn't want to feel bad for her.

"Nina?" A middle-aged man with salt-and-pepper hair and round, wire-rimmed glasses opened the door, holding it wide for Kyle to walk in. The kid's too-large feet shuffled against the linoleum, his thin frame lost in a pair of baggy jeans and sweatshirt, his left wrist wrapped in a light blue cast.

The man glanced at Dillon before focusing on Nina. "I hope this isn't a bad time. We're on our way back from our lawyer's and Kyle has something he'd like to say to you."

The kid's shoulders slumped, his eyes hidden by his

shaggy, brown hair. The man—Dillon assumed he was the kid's foster father—cleared his throat.

Kyle lifted his head and shook his hair back giving them all a glimpse of the nasty purple bruise on his forehead. But he still didn't meet Nina's eyes. "I'm sorry for the accident. For the trouble."

Nina's lips tightened. She opened her mouth, then shut it, her face flushed, her eyes flashing. Dillon's lips twitched and he ducked his head as he waited to see what she'd do next.

She inhaled and her expression cleared. Dillon suspected he was the only one who realized her smile was completely fake.

And the way she kept hiding her true feelings from everyone was really starting to bug him.

"Accidents happen," she said in a high, chipper voice. "I'm just glad you weren't hurt."

"Nina," the other man said, "can I talk to you? In private?"

"Of course. Come on in the kitchen."

"I'll be right back," the guy told Kyle who just shrugged.

Dillon needed to leave, too. But instead of heading out, he heard himself say, "That was a piss-poor excuse for an apology."

The kid snorted and rolled his eyes. "Her insurance will cover the damages."

"Heard you might get sent away for this."

"Listen, just because you helped me last night doesn't make you my savior."

"True." He wasn't anybody's savior. Not anymore.

Dillon started to leave before turning back. "You been to juvie before?"

"Not yet." Kyle smirked. "You can fill me in since you know all about being sent away."

Dillon fought to keep his expression neutral, to not grab the kid and try to scare some sense into him by telling him exactly what it was like to be put away. If he got sent away, he'd learn soon enough how things worked behind bars. He'd experience it all first hand.

The kid's smart-ass attitude wouldn't help him then.

"Besides, maybe Joe can talk the bakery lady into helping us out," Kyle said.

Hope. The one thing Dillon had numbed himself against while in prison. The first thing he'd lost when he'd been locked up. The one thing he'd never gotten back.

"I'm sorry. I didn't introduce myself before," the man said as he reentered the room and held a hand out to Dillon. "I'm Joe Roberts."

"Dillon Ward."

"I know. Nina told me. Thank you for your help last night."

"All I did was get the kid out of the car," he said uncomfortably. "The EMTs bandaged him up."

"Still, my wife and I appreciate it." He crossed to Kyle and laid a hand on the kid's shoulder. "We'd better get going. We're supposed to pick up dinner. Thanks again."

After they left, Dillon stared blindly at the door. Kyle reminded him of Kelsey as a kid. She'd always been reaching out for something. And while he'd believed he'd been protecting her, he hadn't really. He'd told her to smarten up but hadn't done enough, hadn't made those big gestures that show people what they mean to you. Show them the difference between right and wrong. He should've taken Kelsey away as soon as possible, gotten guardianship or something. Instead he'd just hoped she'd listen to him and not cause problems. And that their stepfather, Glenn, wouldn't hurt her.

Look how well that had turned out.

Why hadn't Nina returned from the kitchen? Obviously she didn't want to see him again. He crossed the room but couldn't force himself to walk out.

He lowered his head. Why did he have the feeling he was about to make a really big mistake?

But what the hell? It wouldn't be the first time.

CHAPTER FOUR

DILLON WALKED INTO the kitchen and stopped short when he noticed Nina at the small table.

Damn.

He stared down at the top of her bent head. Her shoulders shook and she was making these soft, hiccupping sounds—as if her entire world was crumbling.

He rubbed a hand over his face. Tears. God, he could handle just about anything. Imprisonment. Having the living hell beat out of him by three other prisoners. The days he'd spent in solitary confinement because he'd had to…protect himself.

But not a woman's tears.

Indecision made him edgy. Should he put his hand on her shoulder? Murmur useless platitudes about how everything would be fine?

At a loss and way out of his element—not to mention his comfort zone—he scowled. "You going to swallow those tears back?" Startled, Nina lifted her head, her cheeks wet, her lips parted. "I never would've taken you for one of those women," he added gruffly.

She sniffed and wiped her cheeks. "One of those women?" she asked, her tone surprisingly frigid for someone who'd just been bawling her eyes out. "What is that supposed to mean?"

"One of those women who cries when things don't go their way, instead of standing up for themselves. Who whine and complain but never do anything to change their circumstances."

Women like his mother.

"If I want to cry because my business, my finances and any chance I have at giving my children a decent life are all in danger, then I'll damn well cry," she told him as she stood. With her hands on the table, she leaned forward. "And if you can't suck it up and take a few tears, then leave."

Huh. Maybe Nina wasn't like his mother after all. Leigh never stood up to any of the many guys who used her and she sure as hell didn't stand up to Glenn or try to leave him. No matter how badly he hurt her or her kids.

"That Joe guy say something to you to set you off?" he asked.

"Of course not. He just wanted to let me know that Kyle's not really a bad kid." The disbelief in her tone made it all too clear how she felt about that. "The court-appointed psychologist thinks Kyle was testing his foster parents. Seeing if he could push them away before he got too close to them."

Smart kid.

"You think that's what happened?" he asked.

She straightened, her hands fisted at her sides. "You know what? I don't give a rip about what Kyle was doing when he crashed that SUV. My life is in the toilet, but I'm the one feeling guilty. Like I should be more understanding. More forgiving." Her voice broke and she turned her back to him.

Dillon ordered his feet to move. But knew he couldn't walk away. "When do you want me to start?"

She faced him again. Wiped the back of her hand under her pink-tipped nose. "Start what?"

"The job. Tomorrow soon enough?"

"I thought you weren't interested in saving me." Her venomous tone made him want to smile. "What changed your mind?"

"A couple of things." He shrugged. "I figured I might as well make some money before I move. And my working here will piss off all the people who wanted me out in the first place." He paused. "All the people you listen to."

Her pretty mouth popped open. "So this is revenge?"

He couldn't tell if the idea appalled her. Or thrilled her. "Does it matter?"

"I…" She shook her head and rubbed her temples. "You know, at this point, I'm not even sure."

He grinned. He couldn't help it. She was just too damn cute with her nose wrinkled in disgust.

Thank God he didn't find cute appealing.

"You might want to decide," he said. "The offer's not going to be on the table forever. But before you make up your mind, you should know I do have one condition."

"Virgin sacrifices every morning?" she mumbled.

He froze, unsure if he heard her right. Then he allowed his gaze to roam over her lush curves.

Color flooded her cheeks. "What's the condition?"

"I want Kyle to work with me."

She blinked. "What?"

"I want him to work with me so he can show he's

taking responsibility for what happened and wants to make amends."

"No," she said, stepping around the table in front of him. "No way."

"You told his foster father you would forgive and forget."

She tossed her hands in the air. "What was I supposed to say when they were both staring at me like that? Joe expects me to forgive, to be the nice girl—"

"Well, now you can be the nice girl and surprise a few people at the same time."

"How do you figure that?"

"Not only will you be showing some backbone by hiring me, but having Kyle work here will tell people there's more to you than meets the eye."

"I don't want to surprise anyone," she said, crossing her arms. "I just want to get on with my life."

"It's a deal breaker. Take it or leave it."

He held out his hand.

She stared at it and pressed her lips together. Then gave him a jerky nod. Dillon kept his hand out.

Nina rolled her eyes but she stepped forward, closing the last distance between them and put her small, soft hand in his. "Fine. I'll take it." Her handshake was firmer than he'd expected, but the bigger surprise was when she didn't let go immediately. Instead, she moved closer. Close enough that her sweet scent filled his nostrils and her warmth permeated his clothes. "I'll take it, but I won't like it."

Dillon forced himself not to step back, to ignore the prickly heat pooling in his lower stomach. He squeezed her hand, leaned toward her and said quietly, "Cupcake, nobody's going to like it. Least of all me."

DILLON HAD BEEN RIGHT. No one—and by *no one* she meant her overprotective family—liked him working for her.

And they had no qualms about letting their opinions be known.

Her mom had stayed at Nina's house to get the kids ready for school, but Nina's father and younger brother, Luke, met her at the bakery at 7 a.m. to help her clean the mess. They'd both been surprised when Dillon arrived and began sweeping up the broken glass by the smashed interior wall—without making eye contact or saying a word.

Man, how she wished her dad and brother would be that quiet.

"This isn't a good idea," Nina's father said—for the third time—when he returned from taking a load of garbage to the Dumpster out back. Hank snatched his hat off and crushed it in his big hand. "I'll call Jim Arturo. See if he can move some jobs around so he can get to you sooner."

Nina shoved a loaf of stale, dirt-encrusted bread into a large garbage bag. "Don't bother. Jim said there's no way he can get to me until after the first of the year. Besides, this isn't a big deal." She glanced at Dillon who studiously ignored them—though she knew darn well he could hear every word they said—as he tore out damaged drywall. She lowered her voice. "Dillon's doing me a favor—"

"A favor?" Luke, hauling a broken table, frowned

down at her, his eyes—gray like her own—narrowed. "And what will he want in return?"

She slapped him upside his too-good-looking head. "You are such a pervert."

Holding on to the table with one hand, he smoothed down his wavy, dark blond hair with the other. "I'm a guy. That's what guys do. And it's the reason you shouldn't allow some dangerous criminal—"

"Dillon's not a criminal," she hissed, grabbing Luke by the arm and walking a few steps farther away from the man in question.

"Not a criminal? The man was in prison."

"Because he protected his sister. What would you do if you caught somebody attacking me or Blaire?"

"I'd rip his heart out."

That was exactly why Nina never told him, or anyone in her family, about Trey's abuse.

"So how can you think Dillon's dangerous?" she asked.

"Look at him." Luke lifted his chin in Dillon's direction. "He rarely speaks, he never smiles and his eyes look dead. Like he'd just as soon slit your throat than talk to you."

"I'm sure Dillon's…reserve is just a way to protect himself."

"Nina, the man has no friends and from what I've heard, he doesn't even speak to his own sister—the woman he killed a man for. That's not self-protection, that's just cold."

She glanced at Dillon's rigid back. Okay, so Luke had a point. A lot of points, actually, but she'd come this far she couldn't back down now.

Could she?

"Luke," Hank said as he joined them, "why don't you go about your business? I'd like to speak with your sister alone."

While Luke picked up the table and headed out back through the kitchen, Nina trudged after her father to the far corner and sat at one of the few unbroken tables. See? This is what she got for asking her family to help her. But she was already behind a day and she couldn't in good conscience ask either of her two employees to help clean.

And while she appreciated all her family had done for her, she couldn't deny that they were starting to get on her last frazzled nerve.

Hank sat and clasped Nina's hands in his on top of the table. "Sweetheart, I'm worried about you. I realize your grandparents gave him the benefit of the doubt but I think hiring Dillon Ward is a mistake." He gently squeezed her fingers. "Having someone with his…reputation and past work here could negatively affect your business."

"What do you want me to do, Dad?" she asked, pulling her hands away from his and crossing her arms. "I've already hired him."

"I want you to tell him you've changed your mind. That he can't work for you."

Her heart thumped heavily in her chest. Ever since she'd agreed to Dillon's deal, she'd suspected this moment would come. The time when she'd have to explain and defend her decision to hire Dillon. But she'd figured she'd be explaining and defending herself to Trey. Not to her family.

Her pulse kicked up and an unknown—unnamed—fear seized and took hold of her. Made her dizzy. She had to stand up for herself, for her beliefs. And if ever there was a time when she needed to stand up, it was now.

Even if it meant facing her father's disappointment.

"I'm sorry," she forced out through her constricted throat, "but I won't do that. I hired Dillon and I stand by that."

His graying eyebrows drew together as he sat back. "The last time you ignored my advice, it proved a big mistake."

She stiffened. "True," she said, knowing full well he was referring to her decision to marry Trey when her dad wanted her to wait until she'd graduated from college.

She just hoped he wasn't right this time, as well.

"But it was my mistake, my choice, to make." She swallowed but the painful lump in her throat remained. She clenched her hands together in her lap and looked over at Dillon who continued to work as if he was alone in the room. "And if you can't support me—fully support me, no-holds-barred—then…maybe it'd be best for both of us if…" She couldn't believe she was about to say this but she knew it had to be done. "If we kept our distance from each other for a while. At least until the bakery's up and running again."

Shock and hurt crossed her father's handsome, weathered face, causing the laugh lines around his eyes to stand out in sharp relief. He opened his mouth only to close it again. Nina almost apologized, but she couldn't. Wouldn't. She needed to surround herself with people who believed in her. Or at least, supported her. The last thing she needed was someone who doubted her every move. Her every decision.

She doubted herself enough as it was.

Finally, her dad stood. "If that's the way you feel, I guess I'll head back up to the lodge. Tell your brother not to hurry back, I'll handle the food delivery." Nina's parents owned and operated a successful ski resort outside of town and had recently brought Luke in as full partner. Halfway to the door, Hank stopped and turned back. "If you need me, you know where to find me."

Nina nodded. The door shut softly behind him and she rubbed a hand over her aching heart. Luke came back into the room, raised an eyebrow at their father's disappearance and shook his head. Then, without a word, he grabbed two broken chairs and headed back outside again.

Well, she'd done it. She'd stood up for herself, made her position clear. She'd also disappointed her father and now had her younger brother looking at her like she was an imbecile.

And it wasn't even 9 a.m. God, she needed more coffee.

She stood as the front door opened. "Hey," Blaire said, stomping snow off her stacked-heel boots. "I just passed Dad. Where's he going?"

Nina crossed to where she'd left her trash bag. "We had a…disagreement. He's not comfortable with certain decisions I've made." She glanced at Dillon. "So he decided to leave."

Blaire's expression softened. "Don't worry about

Dad," she whispered, giving Nina a hug. "He'll come around."

Nina bent down, slipping out of her sister's hold to pick up a few smashed muffins. What did Blaire know about it? She'd never disappointed their parents. Blaire's life was as close to perfect as you could get. Happily married to pharmacist Will Elliott with two great kids, Blaire, a stay-at-home mother, was the golden girl and always had been.

Her designer jeans hugged her long legs and slim hips, and a puffy, white vest was left unzipped to show the hint of cleavage beneath her V-necked, emerald-green top. A wide headband held her silky, honey-colored hair back from her face, her makeup subtle yet perfect.

Nina tightened her scraggly ponytail and tried to remember the last time she'd worn mascara or even blush. Heck, she couldn't even remember the last time she'd used moisturizer.

It was as if she'd forgotten how to be a woman.

"Why don't I pick the kids up from school?" Blaire asked. "They can eat dinner with us, do their homework. I know you have a lot of work to make up for—"

"That's not necessary." While Marcus and Hayley loved hanging out with their cousins, seven-year-old Adam and four-year-old Tyler, the last thing Nina needed was more help from her family.

"You don't have to do everything on your own," her sister said, clearly hurt.

Nina sighed. It wasn't Blaire's fault she felt frumpy and as appealing as a two-day-old donut in her threadbare Levis and tattered sweater. Just as it wasn't Blaire's fault Nina's life was a mess—had been one since she'd first fallen for Trey.

She forced a smile. "You're right. And I'm sure the kids would be thrilled to go to your house for a while. Thanks."

"Great." Blaire started taking off her ski vest. "Can you call the school and let them know? In the meantime, what do you want me to do?"

Nina put her to work helping Luke take the bigger pieces out to the Dumpster. She finished filling her garbage bag and tied it closed when Dillon approached her.

"I'm heading out to pick up the new drywall," he said as he slipped on his coat. "About half of the framing lumber is still usable, but I'll need a few more pieces."

"Okay. We should have the rest of the garbage out of your way by the time you get back."

He nodded, but didn't leave. "It's not too late, you know."

"Too late for what?"

"We can still end this. I'll go my way, you go yours."

"Are you backing out on me?" Frustrated and tired, her voice rose. "Because I've already defended you to my brother and gave an ultimatum to my father—which he took, as I'm sure you're well aware, seeing as how you've witnessed every conversation I've had today. And now you just want to what? Walk away?"

"Simmer down. I'm not quitting. I just thought…" He shrugged, watching her steadily. "Maybe if I left, it'd be easier on you."

Okay, that was sort of…sweet.

"I wouldn't blame you for wanting to forget about

this whole thing," she said. "Not after what you must've heard."

He lifted one shoulder. "I hear lots of things. Most of it rolls off my back."

"Well, even though you have ducklike tendencies, I want you to know I'm sorry you had to hear any of it. And, for the record, I told them I wasn't changing my mind about hiring you." She attempted a smile. "It looks like we're in this together."

He looked at her blankly for a moment, then turned to go. She could've sworn she heard him mutter, "God help us both."

"WHATEVER HAPPENED TO child labor laws?" Kyle asked, his tone pissy.

His foster mother laughed. "I don't think working a few hours a week constitutes slave labor."

"It should," he muttered, slouching down in the passenger seat of her car. He could've walked the mile from the high school to downtown, but Karen had insisted on leaving her fourth-grade class so she could drive him. Like she knew he'd skip out if she didn't personally deliver him to the bakery.

Jeez, it wasn't community service or anything. It wasn't even mandatory—just some dumb thing Joe had agreed to.

Kyle stared out the window, squinting into the bright sunshine as Karen pulled over in front of Sweet Suggestions. He'd seen the boarded-up building yesterday when Joe had dragged him down here to apologize, but the sight still made his stomach feel funny.

Karen shut off the car. "Come on," she said, sliding her sunglasses on top of her head. "It won't be that bad."

He snorted and stared out the window again. "Right. I mean, I'll just be working for a convicted murderer. What could happen?"

"Are you...do you think he'll hurt you? Are you afraid to work with him?"

He straightened. "I'm not afraid of anything." He glanced at her. Noticed the way her hands were clenched together in her lap. The worry on her face.

She was such an easy mark. He could push her to talk to Joe, get him to change his mind about this. She'd already bitched Joe out last night when Dillon Ward had called about Kyle working there.

Karen studied him, probably trying to figure out what he was thinking. She was big on wanting to know what was going on inside his head, as if by sharing his thoughts and feelings over every little thing, it'd somehow magically make them a family.

It'd somehow morph him into the kid she'd always wanted.

"You don't have to do this," she said.

See? She was way too soft. Too...nice.

"It's okay. It's only for a couple of weeks, right? Besides, like Joe said, it'll look good to the court."

"Are you sure?" she asked, twisting a chunk of her chin-length, brown hair around her finger. "Your wrist isn't too sore, is it?"

"It's fine." Did she have to hover? Ever since the accident, she'd been constantly asking him if he was in any pain. If there was anything she could do for him.

As if he hadn't stolen her car and gone through her purse.

She'd even cried Sunday night when she'd seen him at the hospital. Instead of yelling and telling him what a complete screwup he was and how she couldn't wait to get rid of him, big tears had slid down her cheeks. She'd gently touched his face. Then she'd hugged him tight.

She'd held on to him for so long, her tears soaking his T-shirt, that Joe had to make one of his stupid jokes to get her to let go.

Kyle cleared his throat. "Listen, it's no big deal, okay?"

"Okay." She smiled again, but it didn't reach her eyes. "I'll pick you up at six."

He nodded and gripped the door handle. Karen leaned toward him and he froze. She wasn't going to hug him or anything, was she?

Either Karen sensed his feelings or she hadn't planned on hugging him, because all she did was pat his arm. "See you in a few hours."

"Yeah," he said, telling himself he was glad she hadn't gone all mushy on him. "See ya."

At Sweet Suggestions, he stopped and waved. Karen waved back. After a minute, he rolled his eyes and pulled open the heavy door. She wasn't going anywhere until she saw him walk into the building.

He let the door slam shut behind him. Nickelback blasted from a portable radio in the corner by Dillon Ward's feet. Dillon was tearing out pieces of what was left of the wall, and tossing the chunks onto a large pile in front of what used to be a window. Kyle shoved his hands in his pockets and waited. He didn't want to scare the guy. Old dude like him would probably have a heart attack and Kyle'd get the blame.

"You're late," Dillon called over the music without looking up. There was no way he heard Kyle enter. Must have some sort of freaky psychic ability.

Probably got it in prison.

Dillon reached over and flicked off the music. Instead of silence, Christmas music—the song with all the pa rum pum pum pums—filtered in from the other room. He thought he saw Dillon make a face, but it was gone so fast, he couldn't be sure. "I said, you're late."

"Yeah, I heard you. What are you going to do? Dock my paycheck?" He sneered. "Oh wait, I guess you can't since I'm not getting a paycheck."

Dillon took off his gloves and slapped them together. A small cloud of dust exploded in the air before dissipating. "Paychecks are reserved for people who earn them. What you're doing is making restitution. And you can start by taking these pieces of drywall out back to the Dumpster."

He held up his bandaged hand. "I have a broken wrist."

Dillon picked up his hammer. "I noticed. I also noticed that your other wrist and your legs are fine." Then he turned the radio back on and started tearing at the wall again.

Kyle frowned. What the hell? He stood there for at least five minutes, but Dillon didn't say anything else. Didn't bitch at him to get going, didn't add a slap to help him move.

Blowing out a breath, he trudged over to the drywall pile, searching until he found the smallest piece. Hey, he had a bad wrist and a head injury—maybe even a concussion. Even though that stupid doctor in the emergency room hadn't said so.

He wasn't taking any chances.

Kyle expected Dillon to act like a prick about it, to tell him to not be a wuss and to take a bigger piece, but he didn't even glance his way.

Slapping the piece of drywall against his thigh, he went through the door Dillon had indicated. The bakery lady was at the counter, rolling dough. She wore a plain apron that had streaks of purple and blue across it. The sleeves of her pink shirt were pushed up to her elbows, and her hands were covered in flour.

And while she didn't smile or seem overjoyed to find him standing in her kitchen, she didn't look like she'd just sucked on a lemon, either. "Hi," she said, over the Christmas tune blaring in the background. "I didn't know you were here."

"Uh…yeah." He ducked his head, studied the toes of his sneakers. "Dillon wanted me to take some stuff out to the Dumpster. Out back?"

"Oh." She sipped from a glass of water and glanced at his bandaged wrist. "Are you sure you should be doing that?"

Guilt, something he'd never had to deal with until he moved to this stupid town, pinched him. This chick had a screw loose. He'd wrecked her bakery and she was worried about his wrist? Jeez, she was as bad as Karen. "Yeah, it's okay."

He took his time crossing the small room. The kitchen smelled great, like when Karen made pies and stuff for Thanksgiving. His stomach rumbled and heat crept up his neck. He hoped the bakery lady hadn't heard. Maybe he shouldn't have spent the lunch money Joe had given him on cigarettes.

He trudged outside and hunched his shoulders against the cold. Tossed the drywall over the side of the Dumpster. For over two hours he repeated the process.

Juvie was sounding better and better. He had to take several cigarette breaks just to keep his brain from leaking out his ears in complete boredom.

Finally, the clock on the wall said six. About freaking time.

He headed to the door. Had his hand on the knob when Dillon shut off the music and said, "Don't bother coming back tomorrow unless you're ready to work."

Kyle shook his hair out of eyes. "What the hell is that supposed to mean? I did work."

Dillon's expression didn't change. The guy was like some sort of cyborg. "You dragged ass, carried a fourth of what you could handle and at least five times you were outside for fifteen minutes. What happened? You get lost?"

"I was taking a break."

"You work for three hours. If you need a break, you can have ten minutes at four-thirty."

"What are you, my warden?"

"I'm your boss. And no smoking while you're working for me. The last thing I need is for your parents—"

"Foster parents."

"The last thing I need is for anyone to ride my ass."

Kyle clenched his hands into fists. "This is stupid. What are you trying to prove? It's not like this is going to make a difference to anybody. Besides, I can handle juvie."

Dillon just stared at him. Made him fidget the way he studied him, no expression on his face. Didn't the guy ever get mad?

"You think having no privacy is no big deal? Sleeping with guys that have done things you can't imagine? You think you're such a badass that they can't touch you? Hurt you? That you'll waltz in there and be running the place?" His voice was mild, curious almost. "You want to spend a few months or even years in a place where you can't even take a leak in private? Where if you look in someone's room or make eye contact with the wrong person you'll get jumped?"

Kyle lifted his chin. "Hey, if someone messes with me, they're the ones who end up being sorry."

Dillon shrugged. "Maybe you're as tough as you claim. But that doesn't matter. You'll never be the same if you get locked up. There's no hope. No joy. There's not even fear anymore. You have to deaden all of that or you'll never survive. And sometimes, even knowing you're getting out eventually, there are times when you no longer care if you live or die."

"What were you expecting when you killed that old guy? A day camp?"

Something flashed across Dillon's face and for a moment, Kyle wondered if he'd gone too far. He stepped back. But Dillon shook his head and once again, his face was expressionless.

"You have a chance here to avoid all of that," Dillon said quietly. "But you have to decide whether or not you're going to take it, or if you're going to walk away and prove everyone right. Prove that you're nothing. A nobody. And that you'll never be anything else."

What a bunch of bullshit. He wasn't nobody. He'd make something of himself no matter what—and he'd do it all on his own.

He'd show Dillon. He'd show them all.

A car horn honked twice—Karen had arrived right on time. With one last glare at Dillon, Kyle stormed outside, slamming the door behind him. He walked out in the cold, suffocating under his fears, anger and the unfairness of it all.

CHAPTER FIVE

"THINK HE'LL BE BACK?"

Dillon whirled around to find Nina leaning against the remaining display case. Damn it. How long had she been standing there? How much had she overheard? His gaze slid over her and something in his chest tightened.

Her jeans were ancient, her sweatshirt stretched out beyond hope, but a flush brightened her cheeks and some tendrils of hair had escaped her braid to frame her face in honey-colored corkscrews. One long curl caressed the soft curve of her jaw. His fingers tingled to tuck it behind her ear. He clenched his hands.

"Yeah," he said, crossing the room, putting distance between him and temptation. He lifted the hinged lid of his standing toolbox. "Kyle will be back."

"What makes you so sure?"

"The kid's not dumb." He grabbed his nail gun's orange plastic case and set it on the floor. "He knows this could be his last chance."

He knew when Nina moved closer to him. Knew when she stood right behind him, if he shifted back, he'd bump into her knees.

He reached for an extension cord, used the movement to edge forward a few inches.

"If he does come back, I hope his attitude improves."

Dillon glanced up. "He give you a hard time?"

"No," she admitted grudgingly. "But he didn't seem too happy to be working here, either."

He hadn't exactly been thrilled himself to spend most of the day under the watchful eyes of Nina's family. Luckily, her brother had left right after lunch and her mother and sister took off a few hours after that.

Dillon straightened and took a step back. "You always happy about doing the right thing?"

"I don't sulk as if my world's just come to an end." When he raised an eyebrow, she pursed her lips and added, "Well, at least, not much."

He didn't smile until he'd turned to set his nail gun in the toolbox. "Kyle's just being a teenager," Dillon said. "Most people overreact to their mood shifts."

"I know you're not talking from experience since you only seem to have two moods—stoic and brooding."

He scowled at her. "I don't brood."

"Right. And I didn't get these hips from testing all my recipes."

Did she think there was something wrong with her shape? He jerked his gaze from her hips back up to her face. "Actually, I am speaking from experience. I spent my teenage years making sure Kelsey kept out of trouble. Or at least, trying to. As you might've heard, it didn't always work."

"She's doing okay now."

He snorted. Yeah, Kelsey seemed to be doing all right for herself. He just hoped her rebellious streak didn't ruin the life she'd worked so hard for. Not that he believed his sister had completely changed her ways and would be content to settle down with someone as straitlaced as Police Chief Jack Martin.

"What about you?" he asked, snapping the case shut. "Were you a moody and rebellious teen?"

"Please. So far my biggest rebellion has been hooking up with you." She blushed. "Hiring you," she added quickly. "My biggest rebellion has been *hiring* you."

See? She was just too damn sweet. "That's it? No smoking in the girls' room? Didn't you sneak out to see your boyfriend?"

She nudged his metal, portable toolbox with her toe. "I never even stayed out past curfew. That would've ruined my image." She sounded disgusted. As if she was upset that she'd been a good person. He couldn't figure her out. Did Serenity Springs' sweetheart have a hidden yen to be bad?

Her forehead wrinkled and she swung her foot again, this time connecting with the toolbox hard enough to send the tools inside clanging against each other. "I got good grades and never did anything wrong. Never stayed out late or came home with hickeys on my neck."

He picked up the toolbox before she kicked it through the wall he'd just spent the day repairing. "Don't sound so disappointed. Hickeys would only mess up your pretty skin anyway."

Her hand flew to the side of her neck. She dropped her hand and shrugged. "I guess."

He put the toolbox away and shook his head at her disappointment. He didn't understand women.

When she turned, she was next to him, holding his drill. "Thanks," he said, careful not to touch her as he took it. "You don't have to stick around and help me clean up."

He needed her to go, to give him some space. When she was around, he felt edgy, irritated.

But instead of taking his cue to leave, she looked up at him with those big gray eyes, her teeth nibbling on her full, lower lip. "So, what you were saying about trying to keep Kelsey out of trouble…was that what you were doing with Kyle? You know, when you told him about life in prison? About not having any hope or joy. About not caring if you lived or died. Was that really how it was for you?"

He kept his face expressionless. "We need to get this place running full-time again so you're not forced to eavesdrop to get your gossip fix."

"So it wasn't true?" she persisted. "You just made it up to scare him?"

"You'd like to believe that, wouldn't you?" he asked gruffly.

She frowned and wiped a hand over her hair, but the curls just bounced back around her face. "It was a simple question. I thought maybe you were exaggerating—"

"That's not how I work. If anything, I toned the truth down for the kid."

"So you…you did feel that way?" she asked hesitantly. "You didn't care if you lived or…"

"Died?" He unhooked his tool belt and set it on the floor next to his Thermos—instead of throwing it against the wall like he wanted. "I wasn't suicidal, if that's what you mean. But being in prison…it takes something from you."

She nodded. "Your freedom."

"That's sort of the whole point about prison, isn't it?"

Her frown deepened. "It seems so unfair. You were protecting your sister—"

"I killed a man," he said, slamming the heavy lid to his lockbox shut. Bitterness filled his mouth. "I don't need anyone to sugarcoat it or to forget it. I sure as hell won't."

"It just seems like you were given a…a harsher sentence than you deserved."

Couldn't she just shut up? "I paid for my crime. But don't think for a moment that I got more than what I deserved just so you can feel better about letting an ex-convict work for you."

She stepped backward, looked as if she might run out. Except she didn't, in the end she stood her ground. "That wasn't what I was doing. I just…wanted you to know I'm sorry. For what you went through."

And the last thing he wanted was her sympathy.

He edged closer to her. "You feeling sorry for me, *cupcake?*" he asked and she visibly stiffened. But she didn't step back. "I could use that, couldn't I?"

"Use what?" Her voice was husky, her expression wary.

"I could use that big heart of yours against you. I could play on your sympathy."

"Why would you do something like that?"

He skimmed a finger down her soft cheek. "So I could feel your skin. Get close to you," he continued, as he took hold of her waist and yanked her to him. Their thighs brushed, her breasts grazed his chest. "To see how you fit against me."

She gasped, a soft sound.

"I don't want your pity," he growled, tightening his grip on her. "It won't do me any good. Not now."

Her fingers curled into his shirt. "What do you want?"

He leaned forward a few inches. Allowed his gaze to drop to her mouth before meeting her eyes. "I want you to remember that everything you've ever heard about me is true." She winced as he tightened his fingers on her waist. "I really am the most dangerous guy you'll ever know."

NINA'S MOUTH WAS DRY. Her head was light, she couldn't catch her breath.

If he let go of his hold on her, she'd probably fall at his feet.

She tried to step back, to break the contact between them. But his large hands, placed so intimately, didn't budge.

"I...I don't pity you," she told him, forcing herself to breathe more slowly, in and then out. Beneath her hands, she felt the hard planes of his chest. Felt the strong beat of his heart against her palms.

"I know all about not wanting pity," she said as she met his gaze head-on. "I've had enough of it since my divorce to last a lifetime."

He shook his head. "Not quite the same thing. You didn't deserve what you got." He slowly, ever so slowly, pulled her even closer—impossibly close—until her whole body was pressed against him. "I did."

His gaze fell to her mouth. She couldn't move now... even if she wanted to. She closed her eyes. Waited.

"Stop me," he murmured.

Her eyes snapped open. His words had been a plea.

Her lips parted but no sound came out. How could she stop him when he looked at her with such…intensity. Such hunger? How could she stop him when he made her remember how it felt to be held by a man. Touched by a man.

Wanted by a man.

She stared up at him. His expression was harsh, his jaw set, his eyes narrowed. She kept her hands on his chest—as if keeping that slight distance between them would be enough to save her.

It wasn't.

He lowered his head and touched his lips to hers. She was taken by surprise at the softness and warmth of his mouth and, yes, the pleasure of his touch. When he settled his mouth on hers a second time, she slowly slid her hands up to his shoulders.

He cupped her neck with one hand, held her head still. It'd been so long since she'd been held and kissed—really kissed… A low moan escaped her. She pressed her hips against his.

An answering sound rose from his throat and he pulled her up against him so that her toes only grazed the floor. He stroked his tongue across the seam of her lips and she opened them. The slow rasp of his tongue against hers made her heart pound. The feel of his hand on her lower back and his large, solid body against hers—she felt…wanted. Desirable. Maybe even daring.

And, good Lord, it was wonderful.

Until she realized she was acting like a sex-starved divorcee. She was kissing Dillon Ward right there in front of God and anybody who just happened to walk by—or worse, into—the bakery.

What would people say?

Panicked, both at the idea of getting caught and at her own unwanted reaction to him, she leaned back and pushed against Dillon. This time he immediately dropped his hold of her and turned around in one smooth motion. His broad shoulders rose and fell with his rapid breathing. Her breathing was none too steady, either, and she locked her knees to make sure she remained upright.

He lowered his head and muttered something, but she couldn't make out the words.

His shoulders slumped before he faced her. And she wanted, more than her next breath—or even that new mixer she'd had her eye on for the past year—to be able to read his thoughts.

"I apologize," he rasped. "That never should've happened."

She wanted to rub her fingertips over the stiffness of his jaw, but when she opened her mouth, nothing came out except a humiliating squeak. She squeezed her eyes shut. God, she really was an idiot.

She cleared her throat. "No harm done."

He stared at her as if she was a few donuts short of a dozen and shook his head. "Right. So I guess I'll see you tomorrow."

Without waiting for her response, he swept up his tool belt, Thermos and lunch pail and walked out without so much as a backward glance.

Nina moved to the nearest table and slid into a chair. She bit her lower lip. *No harm done?* She said that to her kids when they spilled milk at the dinner table. She lowered her head until her forehead hit the cold tabletop with a thump.

And because she deserved it for being so reckless, she tapped her head against the wood twice more.

She figured as far as penances went, a headache was a small price to pay.

The door opened followed by the sound of footsteps. "Nina. Are you all right?"

She didn't have the energy to lift her head so she turned her face just enough to see Trey crouching next to her, concern etched on his handsome face.

Perfect.

"Are you hurt?" he asked as he gently smoothed her hair off her forehead. "Did you hit your head?"

His touch, combined with his concern, made her straighten. "I'm fine," she said pulling away from him. "I just…" *Experienced the best kiss of my life with Dillon Ward.* Not something her ex-husband would be happy to hear. "I have a headache is all."

Trey didn't seem convinced. But instead of harping at her, he sat down and unzipped his jacket. "You're under a lot of stress here. It's no wonder you're feeling beat up." His tone was sincere and soothing. So sincere and soothing she knew he was up to something.

"Was there something you wanted?" she asked wearily.

"I heard about the problems you've been having." Trey leaned back and crossed one designer shoe over the sharply creased knee of his pants.

And here it came. He was there to lay into her for hiring Dillon. "Listen, I'm handling things here. It might not be the way you'd like—"

"Hey, no, that's not it at all." He dropped his foot and sat up. "I'm not here to argue with you, Nina."

She narrowed her eyes. "You're not?"

"Of course not. Even though we're no longer together, we both still want what's best for our family. Our kids."

"Is that why you're here? To discuss the kids?"

"In a way." Trey rested his elbows on his thighs and linked his hands together to hang between his knees. "Hank called me a few hours ago. He told me you hired Ward—"

"What?" She jumped to her feet. Her chair wobbled and she steadied it by slamming it under the table. "My dad called you?"

"Now, don't get upset. He's worried about you." Trey stood, as well. "We all are."

Her hands curled into fists, but when she spoke, she kept her tone calm and cool. No way would she give Trey or her father the satisfaction of knowing she was about one patronizing pat on the head away from going ballistic. "What right do either of you have to discuss me or my business? And don't you dare tell me you're worried about me. You gave up that right two years ago."

Trey winced. "That's not fair," he said. "You know I never meant to hurt you."

She pressed her lips together and wished she'd kept her mouth shut. The last thing she wanted was for him to think she cared about him enough to give him the power to hurt her. His affair with Rachel had bruised her pride, but even when she'd been at her lowest point, Nina had known his leaving was the best thing to happen to her.

No, his deserting their marriage hadn't hurt—but he'd done plenty that had hurt her. Emotionally. Physically.

And each time he called her an ugly name, tromped on her self-worth, or pushed or slapped her, he always apologized and sometimes even blamed his outbursts on his stressful job.

Usually, though, he blamed her. Her nagging. Her unrealistic expectations of him. Her inadequacies.

He'd been wrong. She knew that now, she knew all of his failings were his own fault, his own weaknesses, but she hated that he could still put her on the defensive. To have her saying things better left unsaid, to make her question herself.

And if she'd turned to her family, if she'd told them of Trey's verbal and physical abuse, she doubted they'd be calling him for backup. But she hadn't. Just one more bad decision she had to live with.

"Dad doesn't need to worry," she said. "I have everything under control here."

She held her breath and waited for a lightning bolt to fry her where she stood at the blatant lie.

"You're a bright, capable woman," Trey said as he stepped closer to her. "But sometimes, you're too stubborn for your own good. This is just like after Marcus was born. His colic kept you up night after night but you refused to ask your mother to come and stay."

"What could she have done? I wouldn't have been

able to get much sleep knowing he was screaming in the other room."

Besides, as much as she'd longed for a few hours of uninterrupted sleep, Marcus had needed his mommy. And she hadn't been about to admit failure at something she'd wanted from the time she was a little girl.

"Seeing as how you won't ask for assistance, I'm offering it instead." He reached into his inside jacket pocket, pulled out a folded check and handed it to her.

She about choked on her own spit when she saw all the zeroes at the end of the amount. And that it was made out to her. "What's this?"

"Now you can hire whoever you want. For this amount, I guarantee they'll drop their other jobs and work here."

She didn't doubt it, seeing as how it was three times the amount quoted for the job.

She held it out with an unsteady hand. "I can't take this."

He frowned but made no motion to take the check. "Of course you can."

She waved it at him and stepped forward. "I don't want it."

"Nina, don't be ridiculous. I want to help. And, well, to be honest, I always felt bad you didn't ask for more of a financial settlement during the divorce. This is my way of making it right."

She blinked. Oh, sure he'd felt bad. So bad it'd taken him two years to offer her any sort of financial help. And only when, she was sure, there was something in it for him.

Against her divorce attorney's advice, she hadn't

asked for any money except child support. She'd never regretted it. Yes, she'd struggled financially—especially compared to the lifestyle she'd had with Trey—but her kids were well fed, clothed and had a decent roof over their heads.

More importantly, they were loved. And safe.

"No." She took a shaky breath, lowered her voice. "Thank you, but I don't need this."

Impatience flared in his eyes. "If it makes you feel better, we can call it a loan. I know you'll pay me back when you can."

That was even worse than it being a gift. And either way, it all boiled down to one thing: she'd owe him.

"I'm not in any position to be taking any loans." She shoved the check against his chest until he took a hold of it between two fingers.

"This isn't like you, Nina,"

"What? Saying no? Standing up for myself?"

"Putting your own wants before what's best for our children. Do you really think it's safe to have them around a convicted murderer?"

She gripped the back of the chair with both hands. "I would never let anyone hurt my kids." She remembered how patient Dillon had been with Kyle. How he'd tried to get through to the teenager about straightening his life out. "Besides, I don't believe Dillon would ever hurt them—or anyone."

"This is exactly what worries me." Trey slapped his hand on the table and she jumped. "You're too naive. It's obvious Ward's already playing on your good nature just so you'll keep him around."

Okay, she'd had enough. "You—and Dad and anyone

else in town who's worried—can relax. Dillon isn't taking advantage of me. He's doing a job and once that's over, he'll be on his way."

"I hope you're right," Trey said, crumpling the check in his hand. "Because you've already strained your relationship with your father because of Dillon Ward. Don't make the mistake of risking more than you care to lose."

CHAPTER SIX

SATURDAY MORNING, DILLON pushed his lockbox across the bakery's dining room. Nina's son, Marcus, had spent the past forty-five minutes at a corner table. His hair was mussed, his sneakers untied and his head was bent over some sort of handheld video game. Every time Dillon looked over, he caught the kid watching him—like a warden on the lookout for a jailbreak. When he'd catch Dillon looking, he'd quickly lower his gaze.

Dillon set the lockbox underneath the boarded-up window. He had enough problems just getting this job done; he sure didn't need an audience. He'd figured it'd take him a week, ten days at the most, to finish at the bakery. No such luck.

He picked up a stack of chairs. Instead of two days to tear out the drywall and replace the ruined two-by-fours in the damaged walls, it'd taken him four. And the electrician couldn't get there until Tuesday, which meant Dillon couldn't install the insulation or hang the new drywall today. So he'd decided to skip ahead a few steps and work on the floor in the hopes of still finishing before Kelsey's wedding.

Kyle walked by, dragging a single chair in his wake, his long, wavy hair held back by a wide, black bandana.

"Aren't you, like, way old to be listening to Metallica?" he asked with his usual sneer.

"You know," Dillon said as he switched off the CD player, "if you put as much thought into your work as you did into your wiseass comments, my life would be a lot simpler."

"Dude," Kyle said, his expression serious, "I live to make your life easy."

Dillon pinched the bridge of his nose. "If only that was true."

The kid rolled his eyes. "Whatever."

"Marcus," Hayley said as she pushed through the kitchen door, her pale hair in two braids tied with pink ribbons that matched her sweater, "Mommy says you have to give me a turn."

Dillon couldn't hear Marcus's response. Whatever he said didn't make his sister happy, though, as her little face scrunched up in a fierce frown. "But Mommy said you had to!"

"You can have it," Marcus said, not even looking up from his game, "as soon as I finish this level."

Hayley's eyes filled with tears and Dillon's chest tightened. Man, it was bad enough he had to deal with a pissy teenager and be watched by an overly serious nine-year-old, he didn't need Nina's daughter bawling while he worked, too.

"Can I take a break?" Kyle asked.

"Sure. I mean, you've already worked almost thirty minutes this morning. You must be exhausted."

"Cool." He grabbed his coat and went outside.

Dillon stared at the door. For someone who spewed

sarcasm with every breath, it was funny how Kyle missed it when it was aimed at him.

He shook his head. Guess he wouldn't mind a quick break himself. He picked up his Thermos, crossed to the table and sat down. Both kids looked at him, but he ignored the wariness on Marcus's face, the way Hayley edged closer to her big brother.

"Marcus won't let me play," Hayley said, as if, just because he was an adult, he was somehow an authority.

Man, was she whining up the wrong tree.

"Mommy said it was my turn," she continued, "and I want to play Sonic Rush."

He poured coffee into the Thermos's lid and took a sip. Sonic Rush? Sounded like a grunge rock band. Or maybe a fast food chain.

"Sorry, kid, can't help you," Dillon said, causing her lower lip to stick out. "Guess you'll just have to wait."

Dillon reached over and opened the pastry box in the middle of the table. Donuts. He groaned. Hayley tilted her head at him.

He cleared his throat as he studied the choices in the box, thankful that Nina always made sure they had plenty to eat. And she kept Kyle happy—and on a caffeine buzz—by making sure he had an endless supply of that yellow soda he drank like it was some sort of magical elixir.

Dillon chose a donut dusted in powdered sugar, bit into it and grinned as thick, sweet, raspberry jelly filled his mouth. He finished it in three bites, then wiped his mouth with his hand.

He sipped his coffee and debated whether to go for the plain cake donut or the glazed twist next.

"We're helping Mommy today." Hayley smiled shyly at him. From what he'd seen, she wasn't half as gregarious as Emma. Maybe he didn't have to worry about her bringing up any uncomfortable subjects. Like baby making.

"Oh, yeah? Well, you did a good job with the donuts."

She giggled. "We didn't make those. We help Mommy cook at home but we can't here 'cause of the health spector."

"Health *in*spector," Marcus corrected without missing a beat of his game.

Hayley's smile widened, showing the gap where her two front teeth should be. "We usually get to go to Gramma and Papa's house but Mommy's mad at Papa 'cause Papa told her not to let you be here and Papa's mad at Mommy 'cause she still let you work for her."

"Hayley," Marcus said.

"What?" she asked, all blue-eyed innocence.

Marcus shook his head in disgust. "You can have the game now. You can use the headphones, too."

Hayley grabbed it. "Yay! Thanks."

"Don't drop it," Marcus ordered as Hayley climbed onto a chair.

"I won't," she promised, then hooked up the headphones. Within thirty seconds, her little forehead puckered in concentration as she saved the world from whatever evil Sonic Rush battled.

Giving him a wide berth, Marcus walked over to where Dillon had his tools lined up out of the way. Dillon picked the glazed twist and sat back. Took a bite, chewed and swallowed before saying, "I'm impressed."

Marcus spun to face him. "Huh?"

"You know, with how you handled your sister."

"She's such a baby. She doesn't know…"

"When to keep quiet?"

Marcus stared at his shoes, shrugged one shoulder.

Dillon polished off his donut. "I know what you're going through. I had to watch out for my baby sister, too. She didn't know when to keep quiet, either. Still doesn't, if you want to know the truth. Careful," he said mildly when Marcus ran a finger over Dillon's nail gun.

Marcus jumped back and shoved his hands behind him. "Sorry," he blurted, his round cheeks red.

"Hey, it's no big deal." Dillon narrowed his eyes at the kid's reaction. Kelsey used to behave in the same way when she was young and had done something wrong. Of course, that was because she'd learned that disobeying their stepfather in any way meant a few bruises. Like the time Kelsey had been about Marcus's age and had taken Glenn's badge to school for Show and Tell without his permission. She'd ended up with a split lip.

Dillon pushed the memories—and the never ending anger that went with those memories—aside. "I just didn't want you to get hurt. You know, that whole 'you'll shoot your eye out' thing."

"Oh." Marcus backed up a step. Then another. "Okay."

"Since you're stuck here all day," Dillon heard himself say before he could think better of it, "you want to help me out?"

"How?" Marcus asked.

"I could use another set of hands tearing up this carpet and hauling it to the Dumpster. That is, if you're interested."

The kid's expression told Dillon he was more than interested. But then he glanced at the closed kitchen door. "My mom probably won't let me. She told me and Hayley not to bug you."

Dillon stood. "You're not bugging me if I ask for your help, are you?"

"I don't know. I mean, I guess not. But she'll probably still say no."

"Why don't you let me worry about your mom?" Dillon asked, as if he didn't already worry enough about Nina and the way he'd obviously scared her the other day.

He'd wanted to prove to her that he was dangerous, that she should be frightened of someone like him. And he'd succeeded. A little too well. To make amends, and for his own peace of mind, he'd kept his distance from her ever since.

The door opened and Kyle came back inside, reeking of cigarette smoke. "What's going on?" he asked as he nudged his way between Dillon and Marcus to grab a donut.

"I hired Marcus to work with us today," Dillon said. "Seeing as how you could only handle one chair at a time, I figured we could use someone with a bit of muscle."

Kyle smirked but surprisingly kept his wisecracks to himself. "That's cool," he said around a huge bite of donut. "This guy—" he jerked his head in Dillon's direction "—can use all the help he can get."

Cool? Dillon wouldn't have put it quite that way.

But Marcus had puffed up with pleasure to have some positive attention from Kyle, which was good, right? It meant Kyle could act like a human being. What wasn't so cool was that Dillon now had to convince Nina to let her kid work alongside a juvenile delinquent and a convicted murderer.

He would've been so much better off if he'd just stayed in bed today.

THERE WERE TIMES in a woman's life when she had to just suck it up and admit defeat.

Nina knew all about those times. Trying times like when a three-year-old Hayley threw the mother of all tantrums in the middle of the grocery store because Nina wouldn't buy her an ugly rubber frog she'd wanted.

Depressing times such as when she'd subsisted on nothing but cabbage soup, water and the occasional piece of fruit only to gain three pounds.

Hard times like after her divorce, when she'd had to ask her parents to loan her money so she could buy her kids school clothes.

So yes, Nina was smart enough—and secure enough and sometimes desperate enough—to know when to quit.

This wasn't one of those times.

But she really wished it was.

Because she had a better chance of making a flourless, low-fat chocolate cake that didn't taste like crap than she did of catching up with her increasing workload. And because she was already two hours behind schedule—and was going to be even further behind since Lacy, her assistant, called in sick with the flu.

Nina rolled out the dough for her cinnamon rolls, grunting with the effort. If she ended up getting sick, she was going to be mighty ticked off.

She used the underside of her wrist to rub at an itch on her cheek. Not even the Christmas CD could cheer her up. But that didn't stop her from singing along loudly—and, okay, badly—to "Deck the Halls."

"Do you have a minute?"

She jumped, lifting the heavy wooden rolling pin like a club even as her cheeks heated at being caught fa la la la la-ing. Dillon entered the room, scowl firmly in place, which did little to slow her racing heart.

She turned the music down and looked over her shoulder at the empty kitchen before meeting his eyes. "You talking to me?"

He stopped at the other side of the wide work counter. "Yeah, De Niro, I'm talking to you. You see anyone else here?"

She poured brown sugar into a large, ceramic bowl. "Considering you haven't done more than grunt a word or two at me since…"

She pressed her lips together and kept her gaze on the cinnamon she was adding to the bowl. The book she read last night said she needed to be assertive. And if she couldn't be assertive, it recommended taking the old fake-it-until-you-make-it approach.

So she'd fake being in control.

She inhaled and forced herself to look up at him. "You've been avoiding me since the other day. I'm just wondering what makes today so different?"

He studied her as if he was trying to see her thoughts. "Do you have a minute or not?"

"Sure. If you don't mind if I keep working." She went to the stove and added butter to a small saucepan. Flipped the burner on to low. "I'm behind."

She didn't think it was possible but his frown deepened. "Where's Little Mary Sunshine?"

"Who?"

"Your assistant. The redhead."

"Lacy?" She smiled at his description of her bubbly young assistant. "I guess she is a bit...sunny."

"She's like a damn supernova."

"Well, not everyone can be blessed with your unenthusiastic disposition."

He tugged on his earlobe. "If you're done zapping me with your clever one-liners, I'd like talk to you about your kids—"

"Are they bothering you? I'll get them," she promised, wiping her hands on her apron as she walked past him, "I'm sor—"

He stopped her with a hand to her wrist and then just as quickly let go. "They're not bothering me. They're good kids."

"Then what do you want to talk to me about?"

"Is it okay if I give Marcus—and Hayley, if she's bored—a few bucks to help me out? Just carrying scraps and stuff," he said when she began to protest. "Nothing dangerous."

"Yeah, he leaves the dangerous stuff to me," Kyle said as he walked in and headed straight for the soda machine. He filled a plastic cup, sneered at them, then walked out.

Nina raised her eyebrows at Dillon. "He's such a delight." She crossed to the stove, turned off the burner and carried the saucepan back to her work counter. "It must be exhausting being that angry all the time." She paused, looked pointedly at Dillon. "Well, you'd know all about that, right?"

"I'm not angry," he grumbled.

"No? Then what do you call it when you stomp around here all day, scowling, only grunting at me when absolutely necessary?"

He held her gaze. "My usual unenthusiastic disposition, remember?"

She blushed and averted her eyes. "I'm sorry. I'm just a bit...stressed."

Dillon ignored that. "So what do you say about the kids helping me out? Marcus seems to want to."

She paused in the act of rolling her dough. "You already mentioned it to him?"

He picked up a star cookie cutter, frowned at it. "It came up."

"It came up or you've already asked him if he wanted to work for you?"

He dropped the cookie cutter. "I asked him."

"I wish you hadn't done that," she said irritably as she wiped her hands on her apron. "If he wants to and I say no, then I have to deal with his disappointment."

"You afraid of being the bad guy with your kids?"

"It's not a matter of being the bad guy." She covered the dough with a clean towel and grabbed a bag of pecans. Ripping it open, she sprinkled a generous amount into a baking pan. "It's that you had no right to offer him a job—you had no right to offer him anything—without consulting me first. I have enough people in my life who either ignore what I want or run over me.

And to be honest, I don't have time to deal with adding you to that list."

"So you're saying you don't want Marcus to work for me."

His question was innocent enough, but for some reason, the nape of her neck tingled. "It was really...nice of you to offer, but it's not necessary." She grabbed a stick of butter, waved it as she spoke. "Marcus will find some way to occupy his time—he brought his video game and I have a portable DVD player and DVDs. Beside, I'm sure you have better things to—"

"You worried about having your kid around me?"

Her head snapped up at his sharpness. His face was expressionless, his hands relaxed by his sides but she knew he was angry—and hurt. "Of course not."

What worried her was Trey's reaction to their kids being around Dillon.

"You know what?" he said, sounding almost as snide as Kyle. "Just forget I mentioned it."

"Dillon, wait. I didn't—" But it was too late. He'd already strode out of the room. Nina clenched her hands, smooshing the stick of butter. With a curse, she tossed it on the table and hurried after him.

And walked into the room just as Dillon told Marcus, "Sorry, buddy. I'm not going to have much for you to do today after all. Maybe another time?"

"That's okay," Marcus said, and even from across the room, Nina could clearly see her son's disappointment. It seemed she was constantly letting people down.

Especially her kids.

And why hadn't Dillon told Marcus the truth? Why had he accepted the blame for disappointing her son?

Trey never had any problem placing any and all blame squarely on her shoulders. Hadn't he let everyone know that their failed marriage was all Nina's fault? And when Marcus or Hayley misbehaved or, God forbid, got below a B average in school, he made it clear she'd failed as a mother. Because she wasn't disciplining them properly. Or gave in to them too often.

Yeah, he'd been a real prince. And yet she refused to let her son do something he wanted because she was afraid of Trey's reaction.

He wasn't even there and he was still controlling her.

No more.

CHAPTER SEVEN

MARCUS'S SHOULDERS DROOPED as he shuffled back to the table and took a seat next to his sister. Hayley, spellbound by the tiny video game in her hands, hadn't looked up since Dillon had come back into the room. Out of the corner of his eye, Dillon noticed Nina approach the table, her expression determined.

He crossed to the far corner. He wasn't running away from Nina. Why would he? Her views of him didn't matter. And though Marcus had been disappointed, it wasn't his problem or his responsibility. Hell, he wasn't responsible for anyone other than himself. Which was just how he wanted things. No ties. No commitments.

No chance of being disappointed by people. Marcus needed to take a lesson from him.

"Break's over, Kyle," he called. "Let's get this done."

Kyle stopped beside him. "Yeah?"

"The baseboards of these two walls need to be torn out."

"No problem. I'll just yank them out with my teeth."

Dillon pinched the bridge of his nose. Times like this, he wished he was the praying type.

"Or," Dillon said, proud of his even tone, "I could show you how to use this pry bar. Your choice."

Kyle shrugged, which Dillon took as an affirmation. He shimmied the pry bar behind the baseboard, tapped it in with his hammer and then placed a scrap piece of plywood behind the bar to protect the wall and give the bar stability. One swift, hard tug and the baseboard popped loose.

"Think you can handle it?" he asked.

"Duh." Kyle knelt down and took the pry bar from Dillon.

"Great." Dillon stood as Kyle struggled to tap the pry bar in place without smashing himself. Not an easy task, considering the cast on his left hand. "When you're done, just take all the boards out to the Dumpster."

Luckily, Dillon couldn't make out Kyle's muttered response.

He picked up his razor knife, crouched and sliced through the carpet so they could tear out manageable sections. He shifted to his left to repeat the process.

But Nina stood next to him, blocking his progress. "Dillon, I—"

"Apology accepted," he grunted, using more pressure than necessary to cut through the layer of carpet and glue.

"What makes you think I want to apologize?" she asked.

He glanced up at her. "Don't you?"

She blushed and shifted her weight. "Yes." She sighed. "I'm—"

"Save it." He stood and moved again, forcing her to step out of his way. Back on his knees, he cut more carpet. Her apology was part of her I'm-just-a-nice-girl-trying-to-do-the-right-thing act. "I've already absolved you. So why don't we forget the whole thing?"

But instead of taking the out he'd given her, she crouched next to him. "I know you're angry—"

"I'm not."

"Okay," she said slowly, "hurt, then."

He stabbed the knifepoint through the carpet and into the wooden floor beneath. Swearing under his breath, he wrenched it loose. "To be hurt, I'd have to care what you think about me. Now, in case you haven't noticed, I'm trying to work. And," he continued, unable to hide his bitterness, "you wouldn't want to get me angry would you? Who knows what someone like me is capable of."

She stiffened. "You know, you're being a real ass." He detected a very real hint of anger threading her words.

Good. Why should he be the only one who was pissed? "Just doing what's expected of me."

"I know all about meeting expectations," she said after a significant pause. "And so far, I've done everything but what's expected, starting with hiring you. So do you think you could cut me some slack when I mess up?"

He pressed his lips together. She hadn't messed up. He had. By expecting her to be different.

"You're making too much of this." He rested his weight on his left hand and dragged the knife through the carpet with his right. "After all, you have to do what you think is right. Especially when it comes to your kids."

Before she could respond, Hayley screamed, a piercing sound that made the hair on his arms stand on end. He jerked to his feet but Nina was already racing toward her kids. A wet feeling spread across his left hand. He went to wipe it down the side of his jeans when he noticed the blood. At the sight of the deep gash between his thumb and forefinger, he bit back a curse. He hadn't even felt the sharp blade slice his hand. But when the pain caught up with him, it was going to hurt like a son of a bitch.

"Mommy, Marcus took the game from me and I wasn't done!"

Nina straightened and put her hands on her hips. "Hayley Ann Carlson! What have I told you about screaming like that?"

Hayley sniffled. "I'm not s'posed to yell unless there's a 'mergency."

"That's right. And because you yelled like that, you're restricted from the video game for the rest of the day. And," she turned to Marcus, who stood off the side in an attempt, Dillon figured, to either become invisible or at least go unnoticed for a few more moments, "that goes for you, as well."

"What? But why?" Marcus asked as Nina snatched the game from him.

"For taking it away from your sister. And the next time I hear a scream like that," she snapped, "there'd better be broken bones or blood involved."

"No need to wait," Dillon said as he held his injured hand in the air. "There's plenty of blood involved now."

NINA FROWNED. "What?"

She inhaled sharply. Dillon stood between the tables and the kitchen door, trying—and failing—to capture with his right hand the blood that dripped from a nasty cut on his left hand.

She rushed over to him, Marcus and Hayley on her heels. "What happened?"

"Knife slipped," Dillon said. He wiped his hand on the front of his jeans and pressed the hem of his dusty T-shirt against the cut.

"Sweet." Kyle's eyes were bright as he stood on tiptoe to peer over Dillon's shoulder. "You sliced it good. Look at how deep that sucker is. Do you think we can see bone? Or at least some muscle?" he asked excitedly as he pressed against Dillon's back trying to get a better view.

"Get out of here," Dillon said, pushing his head gently away from him. "What are you, a vampire or something?"

Blood seeped through Dillon's shirt. Nina glanced around for something to stop the bleeding.

"Hey," Kyle said when she pulled the bandana off his head.

"I'll buy you a new one," she promised. She swatted Dillon's uninjured hand away when he tried to stop her and wrapped the bandana around the cut. "Come into the bathroom off the kitchen so I can clean and bandage this properly," she said, pulling on his elbow.

He didn't budge. "It's fine—"

"It's not fine," she said in her sternest mother voice. "Now quit being so stubborn and get your ass in the bathroom." When he hesitated, she narrowed her eyes. "*Now.* Marcus, you and Hayley help Kyle until I get back. For God's sake," she said as she led Dillon through the kitchen, "don't bleed on anything. I still have to finish those cinnamon rolls and I have five dozen cup-cakes, a carrot cake and a Yule log to make. All before lunch."

"I'm touched by your concern."

She flicked the light on in the small bathroom and tugged him inside.

He held his hand up by his head. "Are you sure you know what you're doing?"

"I've given birth—twice—and doctored more bruises, scrapes and cuts than you can imagine. All I want to do here is clean and bandage your hand, not perform surgery."

He lowered his hand and she took a hold of his wrist. His skin was warm and his pulse jumped under her fingers. She placed his wrist on the edge of the sink and unwound the bandana. And wished she could've used the bathroom off the dining room—the one currently filled from floor to ceiling with supplies.

This bathroom was too small. Too crowded. With the backs of her knees pressed against the toilet, her thighs brushing his and her head inches from his chest, it was way too intimate.

No wonder she was having a hard time just breathing.

She tossed the blood-soaked bandana in the sink and tried to hide her grimace at the sight of the deep gash.

"It's still bleeding, but it's not as deep as I first thought." She turned on the water and grabbed a handful of paper towels from the wall dispenser. Soaking them, she wiped the blood off his hand so she could see the wound. She bit her lower lip. "I'm no expert, but I don't think you'll need stitches."

"Great," he muttered. "But it still hurts like hell."

"I'm sure it does," she said briskly, even as she locked her knees so she wouldn't slide to the floor in a heap.

Comforting him the way she would one of her kids, she patted his chest. "You'll be fine once we get it cleaned up and bandaged."

He made a noncommittal sound and she looked up. Which was yet another mistake. Because they were too close, their bodies touching, her hand holding his. And he was way too sexy with that dark hair across his forehead and the sulky expression on his face.

"What's going on here?"

Dillon stiffened. Nina glanced past Dillon's shoulder to see Luke glowering at her from the doorway. "Dillon cut his hand." She shoved Dillon's injured hand in her brother's face. "What do you think? Is this deep enough for stitches?"

Luke turned an interesting shade of gray and then stumbled back out of the bathroom and slammed the door shut.

"Okay," she said, "now that he's gone, let's get you bandaged up."

"Well done," Dillon said.

She smiled. "Worked like a charm, didn't it?" She bent down and opened the cabinet below the sink, took out the first-aid kit. "My entire family is squeamish when it comes to blood."

"I can still hear you," Luke called through the closed door.

"So no one in your family can stand the sight of blood?" Dillon asked. "Including you?"

She opened the kit and set the hydrogen peroxide and

a tube of antibiotic cream on the sink. "I can stomach it long enough to get the job done."

"And after that?"

Her face heated. "I usually throw up."

He chuckled, a low sound that she could've sworn she felt rumbling through his chest.

She leaned back, and the sink dug into her lower back. "You might want to hang on to your amusement," she said, holding his hand over the sink, "because I have to clean this and it's going to hurt."

Before he could respond, she poured the peroxide. He flinched, hissed out a breath and tried to pull away, but she held on firm. "Holy shit! Are you trying to kill me?"

"Don't be a baby." But since she could only imagine how much it stung, she raised his hand and blew on the cut. She lifted her head and caught him staring at her in surprise—and she realized she must look like a complete dufus. She quickly lowered their hands. "Better?"

He cleared his throat. "Yeah. Thanks."

Thankful for the diversion, she dug a packet of gauze out of the kit and ripped it open. "I'm sorry."

"It's no big deal. It doesn't hurt much anymore."

"No. Not about the cut." She raised her head. "I mean about before. About Marcus and what happened in the kitchen."

"Forget it."

"I don't want to forget it." She carefully smoothed antibiotic cream over the cut. "I was wrong. And if you still want the kids to help, to give them something to do, it's fine with me."

"I shouldn't have said anything to him without talking to you first."

"No, you shouldn't have. But I realize it seemed like I didn't trust you around my kids, which isn't it at all. It's just that I have some…people around me who aren't too thrilled with my choices of late."

"You knew they wouldn't be."

She placed gauze on the cut. "And that was part of it, wasn't it? You told me I'd be proving I could stand on my own two feet, thumb my nose at people by hiring you, by allowing Kyle to work here. Guess I wasn't quite prepared for what that would really mean."

"You knew what you were getting into."

Did she? Although she and her father were still on speaking terms, he hadn't come back to the bakery since the day they'd argued. The rest of her family acted as if she'd lost her mind, and once Trey found out the kids were around Dillon all day—and she had no doubt he would find out—she'd have even more problems.

Luke knocked on the door. "Are you done?"

"Almost," Nina said, wrapping tape around the gauze. "Want to come in and hold the edges of skin together for me to cut back on the scarring?"

Luke made a gagging sound and Dillon and Nina shared a smile.

She finished wrapping his hand, cut the tape and smoothed it over the bandage. "That should do it. If you were one of my kids, I'd offer to kiss it to make it better," she joked.

She raised her head and her grin slid off her face. She froze as he reached out and tucked a loose strand of hair behind her ear, his fingertips grazing her cheek. "Not a good idea," he warned huskily, "because if I took you up on that offer, we'd both end up getting more than we bargained for." His gaze dropped to her lips and his hand fell back to his side. "More than either of us need."

She shivered. Tried to work some moisture back into her dry mouth. He was right. She knew he was right but that didn't stop her from wanting to kiss him. To experience that rush of desire again, to forget about her financial and business problems and just feel. To stop being Nina Carlson, Trey's ex-wife, Serenity Springs' most upstanding resident and just be Nina. Even if only for a few moments.

But she was afraid those few moments could cost her everything she held dear.

CHAPTER EIGHT

DESPITE THE PROMINENT Closed sign, someone knocked—
or rather, pounded—on the temporary door to Sweet
Suggestions. Damn it. Can't a man work ten freaking
minutes without any interruptions?

The pounding continued.

Obviously not in this town.

Dillon tossed down the razor knife, got to his feet
and yanked open the door. Whatever he'd been about
to say—something pretty close to a snarled "Get
lost!"—died when he came face-to-face with Kelsey.
He frowned. Seeing her always brought back too many
memories. Reminded him of his many failures.

And hit him with too many emotions. Emotions he
didn't want to name or acknowledge.

"Hey," he said, stepping back to let her in. He went
back to where he'd left his tools.

Kelsey closed the door and stomped her feet on the
heavy cardboard he'd set down. She shook her head and
snow flew across the rough-hewn subflooring.

"What happened to you?" she asked.

He glanced at the bandage covering most of his left
hand. Dr. Cupcake had been mistaken. When his cut
hadn't stopped bleeding, he'd had to go the E.R. Now

he had five stitches in his hand to remind him how dangerous distractions can be to a man's health.

Something he wouldn't forget ever again.

"Work-related injury," he said.

"Ahh…is that why you're not further along here?" She unwound her scarf and took off her green knit hat. Static left her short, red hair sticking up in sharp spikes. Of course, with Kelsey, that was probably a fashion statement instead of hat hair. "You worked a lot faster at The Summit."

"I had fewer distractions there."

She scanned the empty room. "Yeah, I can see where all this quiet would really take its toll on you."

He stood and used his good hand to pull the strip of carpet he'd cut loose. "This is just a lull in the action." He stepped forward, shifted his grip and pulled again. "Between customers traipsing through constantly, wanting to buy a box of homemade fudge or a loaf of seven-grain bread, and Nina's kids here before and after school wanting to help, I'm not getting as much done as I'd planned."

"I'd have thought you'd be ahead of the game, what with that kid helping you and all."

"Kyle spends most of his time sneaking off to smoke." He rolled the strip of carpet and set it aside.

"Well, you should be used to dealing with a rebellious teenager with a shitty attitude, right?"

Dillon studied his sister. Something was…off with Kelsey. Nothing he could put his finger on, but her smart-ass comment lacked her usual bite and humor. Her smile was strained, not cocky. And he wasn't even going to guess why she'd lost the sparkle in her eyes.

A sparkle that'd been all but permanent ever since Jack slid that rock on her left ring finger.

"I'd forgotten what a thankless job it is to be responsible for someone else."

She winced and dropped her gaze. What the hell was that about? One thing about Kelsey, she looked you in the eye no matter what.

"I've got to talk to Nina," she said, her voice cracking.

She brushed past him and fled into the kitchen. Just got the hell out of there without any kind of overture for them to get together, to bond over their past and shared DNA. She hadn't invited him to join her new little family for dinner or made him extremely uncomfortable by bringing up how grateful she was to him for saving her life all those years ago.

How she owed him.

Which was good. He didn't want to be reminded of what happened that night. Kelsey's gratitude—though sincere—always left him cold.

Being around her just reminded him of his mistakes. Of what he'd lost.

When all he wanted was to forget both.

With one last look at the closed kitchen door, he went back to his work. He'd been stacking the carpet strips to the side to give Kyle something to do when he came in after school. The kid still had to finish taking the remaining baseboard off since he'd spent most of Saturday afternoon begging Dillon to let him see his cut. And when blood had soaked through Dillon's bandage, Kyle had even offered to stitch him up. He'd claimed he needed a needle and some fishing line and Dillon would be as good as new.

Honest to God, what did these kids watch on TV nowadays?

Kyle had been so clearly disappointed when Dillon had told him there was no way he'd let him within ten feet with a needle, Dillon had taken Kyle to the E.R. to watch him get stitched up by a professional.

No doubt about it, Kyle was some sort of freak.

So now he was even further behind than he'd been Saturday. He didn't need to waste more time worrying about his sister.

But when five minutes became ten and Kelsey still hadn't come back out, he glanced at the kitchen door. Maybe he should take a few rolls out to the Dumpster… just to get them out of his way.

He grabbed the carpet, set it on his shoulder and pushed through the kitchen door.

"And I m not sure about the appetizers," Kelsey was saying as she paced the length of the room. "Maybe we should have more choices? What about those tarts with the grilled vegetables in them?"

"Sure, we can add those," Nina said. She sat at the table, a pen in her hand, a thick binder opened in front of her. "Do you want them in place of the fresh vegetable platter?"

Kelsey nibbled on her lower lip. "Uh…we could do both, right? Oh, and maybe we should add a few more choices to the dessert tray?"

Nina tapped her pen against the table. "I think you need to be careful about offering too many choices. Or people might not eat dinner. Or have room for cake."

"I just want everything to be perfect."

Dillon raised an eyebrow at Kelsey's bitchy tone as he walked out the back door. He never would've pictured Kelsey as a Bridezilla. Weddings must turn even the most level-headed women into lunatics.

He tossed the carpet into the Dumpster and went back inside in time to hear Nina demand, "What do you mean, you want to change your wedding cake?"

Kelsey waved a hand in the air, not concerned in the least that Nina now stood with her hands on her hips, a crazed, do-not-even-think-of-messing-with-me look on her face. "I still want a white cake with raspberry filling. I just want to…tweak the design."

Nina made a sound—sort of like a teakettle whistling— and shut her eyes. Her lips moved as she silently counted to ten. Or twenty. He poured himself a cup of coffee and snatched a sugar cookie off a tray. And waited for the fireworks to start.

He bit into the cookie. Damned if he could figure women out. Nina was about to blow a gasket but was fighting it for all she was worth. He already knew she hated confrontations—which was why she got pushed around so much. And Kelsey…well…suffice it say his sister didn't mind confrontations. Some would even say she relished them.

But he had a feeling more was going on in Kelsey's head than a sudden urge to yank Nina's chain.

Nina exhaled heavily. "The wedding is in five days. It's a little late notice to be changing—"

"If you can't handle a few minor changes," Kelsey snapped, "then we'll just go somewhere else."

As Nina stood there with her mouth working, Kelsey

spun on her heel. Dillon stopped her impressive display of pissiness by taking a hold of her arm when she attempted to storm past him.

"I'll bite," he said. "What's going on?"

Kelsey attempted to pull away, but he refused to let go. Her sharp features took on a mulish expression. "Nothing's going on. I just want my wedding to be perfect. Is that okay with everyone?"

"It's more than okay with me and I'm sure Nina's all for helping you get what you want, but we both know there's more going on here, don't we?"

She shrugged.

"Hey," he said and squeezed her arm gently. He read the sadness in her eyes, the fear. "I know you, remember? You don't have any problems making decisions— especially over appetizers and cake designs."

"I made a mistake!" she cried.

"It's all right." Nina rubbed her temples. "I'll figure out a way to make it work—"

"No!" This time when Kelsey pulled away, Dillon let her go. She tugged both hands through her hair. "That's not what I mean."

"Then what—"

"I can't do it!" Her eyes filled with tears and Dillon felt sick. "I can't marry Jack."

NINA BLINKED. ONCE. TWICE. She even shook her head in case she hadn't heard correctly, but Kelsey's words seemed to echo in her brain.

"You have to marry Jack," she said, her voice rising. "As we've already mentioned, your wedding's in five days."

"Better quit now than down the road, right?" Kelsey, back to pacing, paused long enough to nod at Dillon as if seeking confirmation. "I mean, what was I thinking? That I'd be a good wife? A mother? What a joke. I'll probably be just like Leigh."

Nina frowned. "Who's Leigh?"

Dillon, seemingly not upset in the least by this turn of events, sipped his coffee. "Have you climbed inside a bottle of vodka lately?"

"Of course not," Kelsey said wearily. "But that doesn't mean I won't screw this up."

He studied his sister. "You know, at first I thought you were reverting back to the Kelsey I knew growing up. The one who ran at the first sign of trouble—"

Kelsey snorted. "Yeah, trouble I usually caused."

"Trouble you *always* caused," Dillon corrected her. "But now, I can see this isn't about you rebelling or even being reckless."

Kelsey froze, staring at her feet.

When she couldn't stand the silence any longer, Nina said, "Well, I give up. What is it about?"

"She's scared," he said quietly.

"Of course I'm scared!" Kelsey blurted, tossing her hands in the air. "Emma called me Mommy last night!"

Nina crossed to stand next to Dillon. "And?" she asked.

Kelsey looked appalled. "And? Isn't that enough?"

"Yeah, it is," Dillon said. Nina shot him a look that he, of course, ignored. "So why don't you run? Why are you even here telling us this?"

"I should run. I mean…what if marrying Jack is a huge mistake? What if you were right when you told me people couldn't change, that I'm not what Jack and Emma need?"

Nina glared at him. "You told her that?"

He shrugged. "Just speaking the truth."

Kelsey took hold of his arm. "Dillon, what if I hurt them?"

To Nina's shock, he patted Kelsey's hand and said, "You should leave. Get out now while you can."

"What?" Nina dropped her head into her hands. "I'm surrounded by lunatics."

But Kelsey didn't seem surprised by Dillon's agreement. She just seemed…scared. "I…I should. Maybe you could lend me your truck? I could get my stuff out of the house while Jack's at work and Emma's at school. I could head back to New York before Jack and Emma and I get even more involved."

"How much more involved than engaged can you get?" Nina asked.

They both ignored her. Story of her life.

Dillon straightened. "You know, Kelsey, you were always reckless and rebellious. And wild. But you were never stupid." He smiled. "Until now."

Kelsey jerked her chin up. "Excuse me?"

"You love Jack and Emma."

"Yes, but—"

"You want to be that little girl's mother and Jack's wife more than you can say but you're scared you'll blow it. Maybe it won't happen today, maybe not even this year, but sometime down the road you figure you'll mess up. Instead of facing those fears, you want to run. I can't believe I'm going to say this but…" He shook his head. "You're a coward. And cowards run." He crossed his arms and nodded toward the door. "So go."

Nina caught her breath. Waited.

Kelsey turned to Nina, her shoulders straight, her green eyes flashing. She jerked her head toward Dillon. "He used to try that reverse psychology on me when I was a kid, but it only ticked me off."

With her red hair surrounding her head like flames and an angry flush on her face, Kelsey reminded Nina of a lit fuse. Fiery. Explosive. And dangerous. "What about now?"

"Now?" Kelsey shook her head. "It worked like a charm."

Nina slumped against the counter. "You two are so weird."

Kelsey shrugged. "You're much better at talking me down than you used to be," she told Dillon.

"Maybe you're just better at listening."

"Maybe." She threw her arms around Dillon's neck and gave him a loud kiss on his cheek. "Thank you."

Then she held her brother tight. Nina's heart warmed to see Dillon's arms go around his sister. To see the love for her on his face. Love he obviously didn't want anyone else to know about.

Especially Kelsey.

But then he disentangled himself and held her away from him. "Don't thank me. You still have five days to change your mind."

"I won't." She rubbed a hand over her stomach. "I'm still scared, yeah...I mean, the thought of hurting Jack or Emma kills me, but you're right. I do want this. More than anything."

"Good luck, then," he said. "You'll need it."

"And I'm sorry about freaking out," she told Nina. "Everything's great. The food, the cake. We don't have to change a thing."

"No problem," Nina said, because really, what else could she do? "Pre-wedding nerves happen to most brides."

Kelsey laughed. "It's nice to be normal about some things, I guess. I'd better get out of your hair. I know you both have a lot to do. See you Saturday."

Nina stared at Kelsey's retreating back. "You were great with her. Who knows what she would've ended up doing if you hadn't stepped in."

"I was just trying to avoid bloodshed," he said, looking uncomfortable with her compliment. "When she said she couldn't marry Jack, I thought your head was going to explode."

Nina's face heated. "I hated the thought of her hurting Jack and Emma. She's such a sweet little girl and he was devastated after his wife died. I didn't think he'd ever get over it."

"I thought maybe you were pissed about the idea of losing more business."

"That never crossed my mind," she said indignantly. When he raised an eyebrow, she hesitated. "Okay, so maybe I did think of that. But then I remembered I'd still get to keep the down payment they made last month."

He grinned. She was close enough to feel his body warmth, to see the flecks of gold in his eyes.

He cleared his throat. "Now that that crisis is averted, I guess I can get back to work."

Nina laid her hand on his arm. He stared at her fingers resting against his sleeve, then into her eyes.

Before she could change her mind, she rose onto her toes and pressed her lips against Dillon's cheek. He stiffened, even though the kiss was soft. After two heartbeats, she leaned back slightly. Their mouths were barely an inch apart. She waited, holding her breath. She wanted his kiss, wanted to press her mouth against his, but didn't have the nerve.

He shifted forward and her lips parted. But then his lips thinned and he leaned back.

"What was that for?" he asked gruffly.

"For what you did for your sister," she said, though she knew that was only part of it. The only part she was willing to admit. "You're not as inhuman as you'd like everyone to think."

"Are you sure about that?"

"I definitely saw hints of humanity. You care about Kelsey, even if you don't want anyone to realize it. What you did for her was very sweet."

"You don't know anything about me," he said harshly. "You wouldn't think I was sweet if you knew the things I've seen or worse, the things I've done." He took another step back, his expression a hard mask. The coldness in his eyes made her shiver. "You want to try and pretty me up, make me less of a threat to you and your safe little life but—I'm not the one who'll be hurt if you insist on believing I'm something I'm not."

CHAPTER NINE

THURSDAY AFTERNOON, DILLON walked into the bakery's kitchen and said, "You look like hell, Nina."

That probably hadn't been the smartest thing to say to the woman who'd hired him, but it was the truth. Nina's apron was stained, she had dark circles under her eyes and her ponytail was frizzier than usual.

She stopped pouring some sort of thick, creamy batter into large muffin tins long enough to glare at him. "Thank you for not only noticing that," she said, scraping the last of the batter out with a spatula, "but for saying something about it."

"I aim to please." He pulled his insulated lunch pail out from under his arm and set it on the counter. "Aren't you eating lunch?"

"I'll grab something as soon as I'm done." She measured brown sugar into a bowl, added flour, cinnamon and a stick of butter. "I just want to get these muffins in the oven first."

He shrugged. It didn't matter to him if she didn't eat. Or that she'd been working so hard she resembled a fluffy-haired zombie and snapped at everyone who came in contact with her.

The phone rang. Nina wiped her hands on her apron as she crossed the room.

"Sweet Suggestions," she said into the receiver. "Hello, Mrs. Bradley." As she listened, she tipped her head back, closed her eyes and mouthed something that looked suspiciously like, "Why me?"

"Of course that's no problem," Nina said with forced cheer.

Her baking skills may be top-notch but her acting skills sucked.

He bit into his peanut butter and jelly sandwich as Nina hung up. She wrote something in a spiral notebook and then hurried back to her work area. She mixed the butter into the dry ingredients, then tossed in chopped nuts and sprinkled the remainder over the batter in the muffin tins.

"Do you think that's a good idea?" he asked.

She looked at him as if he'd hit himself on the head with his hammer. "These wouldn't really be cinnamon streusel muffins without the streusel, would they?"

He opened a bag of chips. "I'm talking about you taking more orders when you're already behind."

"I had to take that order." She brushed her hands together and carried the trays to the oven. "Theresa Bradley is one of my most loyal customers. And as you just pointed out, I'm already behind, so making a cake for her daughter's birthday party shouldn't make much of a difference either way."

"It shouldn't," he agreed and bit into a chip, "as long as she doesn't want this birthday cake before Saturday."

Nina wiped her work area clean. "She needs the cake tomorrow."

Dillon paused, a chip halfway to his mouth. "And you still said yes? Are you stupid?"

Her head snapped back as if he'd slapped her. With a low growl, she wound her arm like a baseball pitcher—with terrible form—and threw the dishcloth at him.

"Hey," he said when it hit him in the chest with a damp splat. Still holding his sandwich in one hand, he set his chips down and brushed at the wet spot on his shirt. "What bug flew into your cookie dough?"

"Don't you ever, *ever* call me stupid," she said, her voice shaking. She strode over to him, not stopping until her toes bumped his. "In case you haven't noticed, I'm running a business here, a business I want to make a success. What's so wrong with that?"

He held his hands up. "Whoa, there's nothing wrong with wanting to get ahead. Unless you kill yourself for it." She crossed her arms, her cheeks flushed pink with fury. "And for the record, I don't think you're stupid."

"Oh, really? Then why did you say that?"

"Rhetorical question?" he asked hopefully. She rolled her eyes. "But you're not going to do anyone any good, including your kids or your business, if you don't take care of yourself and get some rest. Oh, and you might want to eat something every now and then."

"Fine." She grabbed his hand and bit into his sandwich. "Happy now?" she asked, around her mouthful.

Damn. Why did he have to find her so adorable? "Thrilled."

He used the pad of his thumb to wipe jelly away from the corner of her mouth. Staring at her, he slowly raised his hand to his mouth and licked the jelly off his thumb.

She ran the tip of her tongue over her lips where his thumb had been and his body tightened. He imagined his own tongue tasting her there. His mouth pressing against the dimple in her cheek before sliding over to take hers.

He shoved the sandwich they were both still holding under her nose. "You finish it," he said gruffly. "I have two more."

She took a hasty step back. "Give them all to me."

"If you're going to throw them at me, I'd rather not. I'm hungry."

She raised her eyebrows and held out her hand. He handed her the sandwich she'd bitten into and then reached into his lunch pail for the other two.

She went to the stove, put a frying pan on the burner and turned the flame on. "I'm sorry I hit you with that dishcloth." She buttered the sandwiches then sprinkled them with cinnamon and sugar. "I guess I'm more stressed out than I thought."

Stress he could handle. Hell, he could even handle her throwing things at him. What he couldn't handle was how fascinating he found her. How attractive.

He popped another chip in his mouth. "Seems to me I hit one of your hot buttons."

"Trey used to call me names. Said I was stupid," she said dully, laying the sandwiches on the frying pan. The smell of melting butter filled the air.

Dillon tensed, crushing his remaining chips. Had she put up with her husband's verbal abuse? Stood up to him like she'd just stood up to Dillon?

Or had she been like his mother and sat there, tears streaming down her face as she apologized for whatever transgression—real or imagined—had set her husband off? And if Carlson was such an asshole to his wife, did that mean he treated his kids just as badly?

He couldn't imagine Nina standing idly by while Carlson abused—verbally or otherwise—her kids. But did he really know Nina? When Carlson lost his temper with Marcus or Hayley, had Nina protected them?

Or let them fend for themselves the way he and Kelsey had had to?

"You should hire another assistant," he said while she placed the sandwiches on a plate. "Especially since Lacy can't be bothered to show up for work until two hours into the day." He carried the plate to the table knowing if he didn't force her to sit down, she'd eat standing up, baking as she did. "Where is she, anyway? That girl works less than anyone I know. Except Kyle."

"She works two jobs and goes to school part-time." Nina cut the sandwiches in half and warm peanut butter and jelly oozed out. She picked up a section and blew on it before taking a bite. "Right now she's out making deliveries for me."

He bit into his sandwich, surprised at how good it tasted. Who knew you could improve on PB&J? "Her being so busy is another reason for you to get someone else to help you out."

"I don't like too many people in my kitchen."

"What are you, Colonel Sanders protecting your secret recipe?"

She got a diet soda out of the refrigerator. "It's important to me to make this a success on my own. I'm so tired of everyone in town feeling sorry for me."

"Because of the wreck?"

She sat down. "Because of Trey. Because he left me for another woman after I dropped out of college to be with him." She opened her can and took a sip. "I'm just...tired of being Poor Little Nina."

"Being a boss and employing people doesn't make you dependent, just a smart businesswoman."

She grinned. "Point taken."

He drummed his fingers on the table. "Not that it matters but, despite your stubbornness, I think you're doing a damn good job."

"It does matter. Thank you."

"No problem." He jumped to his feet. "I'd better get back to work."

Her smile disappeared. "Oh. Sure. Thanks for lunch."

He got the hell out of there, back to the front room with the kitchen door shut behind him. He'd spent close to five years in a maximum security prison. And yet there he was, all tied in knots because a pretty woman had smiled at him.

Because what he thought meant something to her.

He was an idiot. He thought he knew Nina? He didn't know anything about her.

Was she really the devoted mother and take-charge woman she was obviously trying to be? Or just the town's pampered, protected princess who only worried about pleasing other people?

And did it even matter? Because in the end there was one thing Dillon knew about her for certain. She and her kids needed someone to watch over them. To stand up for them when they couldn't stand up for themselves. And he'd already done his time playing superhero.

"I WANT TO GO to Daddy's," Hayley cried, tears running down her red cheeks.

Nina heaved out a breath and added a teaspoon of salt to the mixing bowl. "I know, Hayley, but you can't." She turned the mixer on and, out of the corner of her eye, noticed Dillon enter the kitchen. "Mommy has a lot of work to do so you need to just—"

"Then I want to go to Gramma's," Hayley wailed. "I don't want to be here! You're mean. You're the meanest mom in the world!"

Nina shut the mixer off. "Great. Do I get to wear a crown?"

"No. No crowns and I'm not going to give you a Christmas present, either." Hayley crossed her arms and stuck out her lower lip. "I'm going to call Gramma and have her come get me." She stomped off, her feet making an incredible amount of noise for someone who weighed less than fifty pounds.

"If you so much as pick up that phone," Nina warned, "you're going to lose television privileges for a week."

Dillon came up next to her. "You do realize you're fighting with a six-year-old, right?"

She glanced at him, too tired, frustrated and, to be honest, clinging to the end of her very short rope to even be embarrassed. "She started it," she mumbled.

"Mommy's mean," Hayley said, running over to Dillon. "She won't let us go to Daddy's."

"We can't go to Dad's," Marcus called from the table, a book opened in front of him. "He's not going to be there, remember?"

"But he promised to take us to the movie."

The disappointment in her little girl's voice broke Nina's heart. She crouched in front of her. "Honey, I'm sorry, but your dad and Rachel had to go out of town. You'll see them Thursday."

"Then can Gramma take me to the movie tonight?"

Nina caressed her daughter's silky hair. "The wedding reception is at Grandma and Papa's lodge, so they have a lot of work to do tonight to get ready. Besides, you get to have a sleepover at Grandma's tomorrow. But only if you behave tonight. Do you understand?" Hayley sniffed and nodded. "Good. Now, go and play with your brother while I finish up a few things, okay?"

"Okay," she said, sounding so long-suffering Nina struggled not to smile. "Do you want to play with us?" she asked Dillon.

Before he could answer, Nina said, "Mr. Ward's done working for the day, honey. He has to get home."

"Why don't you let Mr. Ward figure out when he has to leave," Dillon suggested.

"Is there a problem?" she asked. "Didn't you and Kyle get the windows hung?"

"No problem. And yes, the windows are hung."

"Great." At the sink, she washed her hands. "So we're still on track for the grand reopening."

"As on track as we're going to get."

She patted her hands dry with a paper towel. She had big plans scheduled for a week before Christmas. She had an ad reserved in the *Serenity Springs Gazette* and had come up with a list of specials and sales to draw customers back.

She laid the ball of dough on the flour-covered counter. "Do you really believe we'll be ready to reopen by Wednesday?"

"Should be."

"That doesn't exactly ease my mind." She kneaded the dough. "You're not very good at assurances."

"Some things are out of my hands, like the electrician pushing us back on his job list. If you need coddling, I suggest you look elsewhere."

She slammed the dough down onto the board. She'd just wanted a bit of reassurance. Someone to tell her things were going to work out, that she'd made the right decisions. Was that too much to ask for?

She glanced at Dillon. His T-shirt was dusty, the short sleeves hugging his biceps. His mussed hair and dark stubble gave him a sexy, dangerous edge. She averted her gaze.

Maybe she didn't want assurances. Maybe what she really wanted stood across from her, all strong and steady and more than capable of offering her the one thing she couldn't ask for.

Comfort.

"Knock it off!" Marcus yelled.

She sighed. Marcus and Hayley were playing tug-of-war with the video game. "If you have to fight, could you at least keep it down to a low roar?" she asked them wearily.

They lowered their voices. She heard a hissed, "stupid face," followed by a whispered, "doo-doo head."

"You're not going to break that up?" Dillon asked.

"Kids need to learn to deal with some problems on their own. That includes arguments." She wiped her hands on her apron. "Besides, Hayley's already informed me I'm Queen of the Mean Moms, so it's not as if I'm worried about losing Mother of the Year."

"Yeah, she was pretty ticked at you when I came in."

"She's just disappointed. Something else she's going to have to learn to deal with. Although I have to admit, it kills me to see her that upset."

"Your ex bailed on them, huh?" His tone was mild, barely curious.

She tossed the dirty utensils into the mixing bowl, nodding.

Trey had been more upset about Nina's angry re-action than the thought of letting his kids down. He'd had no qualms about letting her know how unfair she was being.

Right, she had no reason to be angry just because she'd have to not only deal with the fallout of his bailing on the kids, but also because she'd had to rearrange her work schedule yesterday. And to make matters worse, she'd had to listen to Trey's self-absorbed condescension while he explained how she was overreacting.

"It is what it is," Nina said. And how Zen was that? Maybe all those self-help books really were working. "The kids will get over it. But in the meantime, they need to keep themselves occupied and out of my hair for a few more hours—"

"Hours? It's already past five. How much more do you have to do?"

"I just have to finish up a few things."

He studied her and though she told herself not to, she couldn't help but fidget under his intense scrutiny. "How many is a few?"

"I need to prep for the appetizers tomorrow—slice the vegetables, make the dough and dips. Plus I still need to make the cookies and fruit tarts…and Kelsey wanted a couple of cheesecakes along with her wedding cake—"

"And you thought you could get all of that done tonight? By yourself?"

"Actually, I thought Lacy would be able to help me, but she had to cover the check-in desk at the motel. And…well…that's not all." She exhaled, ruffling the curl that had fallen across her forehead. "I still have to finish the wedding cake."

He straightened and glanced at the corner where the cake was assembled, frosted and surrounded by dozens of icing flowers. She still had to decorate it.

"Let me get this straight. My sister's wedding is in less than twelve hours and you still don't have the cake done?"

"Well, I meant to finish it. It's just that somehow my week got away from me."

"It got away from you because you refuse to tell anyone no—and because you're too stubborn to ask for help. Now your back's up against the wall."

"I know that, all right?" she burst out as the enormity of everything she had to do sunk in. "It's not like I planned it this way. I knew I shouldn't have taken on so much extra work, but I couldn't say no and miss an opportunity to show everyone what I'm capable of." Her chest constricted and she found it hard to breathe. She broke out in a cold sweat. "And each time I took on more work I figured one more thing wouldn't hurt, that I'd somehow find the time. And now I'm at least eight hours behind schedule and I won't be able to work tonight because my kids need me but I still have all the piping and decorating to finish. And that doesn't even count the other prep work I'll have to do in the morning so that there's enough product here so Lacy can work while I attend the wedding and—"

"Stop." Dillon grabbed her by the upper arms. "Take a breath."

She placed a hand over her racing heart. "I…I can't."

"You can. Lower your head," he told her as he gently nudged her head forward, kept it there with a warm hand to the back of her neck. "Now inhale."

She squirmed, panicked when the air she sucked in didn't fill her lungs.

"Shh…" He massaged her neck. "You're doing great. Inhale again and count to five. Good. Exhale."

She followed his instructions—inhale, count to five, long exhale—several times until her dizziness passed.

"Better?" he asked.

"I think so." She lifted her head and his hands fell back to his sides. Was she a wimp if she admitted she missed the contact? "Thank you."

"Mommy?" Hayley asked, standing next to Marcus. "Are you okay?"

"I'm fine." She smiled, knew it was shaky but it was the best she could manage. "I just…" What? Lost her mind? That seemed to be the most reasonable explanation.

And unfortunately, she didn't have the time—or the energy—to search for it.

"I just need to buckle down and get back to work," she told them, ruffling Marcus's hair. "Everything will be okay."

Her kids didn't look convinced. Neither did Dillon. She pulled her shoulders back, clapped her hands together and forced a laugh. "Stop worrying. I'm fine. Why don't you go out front and make sure the Closed sign's flipped over?"

Once her kids were out of the room, she shut her eyes. Could feel Dillon still watching her, feel his body heat. "The only expectations I will worry about are those I put on myself," she murmured. "I will open myself to the possibility of success and success will be mine."

"What are you doing?" Dillon asked.

"The book I'm reading suggests using affirmations as a way to get through stressful situations. I can do this," she chanted, "I can do this. I can—"

"Damn right you can."

She opened her eyes. "What?"

"You don't need affirmations and you sure as hell don't need me to tell you that you're smart and capable and tough. You hired me and Kyle—the two baddest badasses in this town. I have complete faith you can accomplish whatever you set your mind to."

She blinked. "I can?"

"Yeah. And I'm going to stick around to make sure you do."

CHAPTER TEN

FIFTEEN MINUTES LATER, Dillon descended the steps from his apartment, his arms piled high with blankets and pillows. As he reached the bottom, he thought about Nina's hesitation to accept his offer to hang out with her kids.

It wasn't brain surgery. Just keeping two little kids occupied, happy and out of their mother's hair for a few hours.

How hard could it be?

He pushed open the kitchen door. Nina stood between Marcus and Hayley, one hand on each of their heads keeping them apart as they tried to tear into each other.

"Marcus, apologize to your sister," a frazzled Nina said.

"Why should I?" Marcus pulled away from his mother's hand. "It was her fault."

"Is it time for Friday night wrestling?" Dillon asked as he came in. "Should I make popcorn?"

"Marcus took the game away from me." Hayley rushed over to Dillon and grabbed his leg. "And he didn't give it back, even though Mommy said he had to."

"I'm not done with it." Marcus's face was red, his mouth set in a stubborn line. "How come she gets everything she wants?"

"It's because I'm a girl," Hayley said matter-of-factly, "and Daddy's princess."

"There are no princesses here," Nina said, "no matter what your daddy says."

"Yeah," Marcus added with a sneer. "Princesses are stupid."

Hayley's lower lip began to tremble. The kid could flip on the waterworks on a whim.

"You don't want to be a princess anyway," Dillon said.

She sniffed. "I don't?"

"Nah. Being a princess would be boring."

"But they wear fancy dresses and pretty jewelry and go to balls and dance with princes."

Dillon shook his head. "You need to cut back on the fairy tales there, short-stuff. Besides, princesses don't have great adventures—"

"Ariel had a adventure when she got human legs," Hayley said, blinking innocently. "And Jasmine rode on a magic carpet. And—"

"They don't get to have adventures like we're going to have," he said.

"We're having an adventure?" Marcus asked. "What kind?"

Dillon shifted the load in his arms. "Let's go into the front room and I'll fill you both in."

Their argument forgotten, the kids raced out of the room.

"Are you sure you want to do this?" Nina asked, her forehead furrowed.

"Don't worry about it. If I have any problems, I'll let you know."

She smiled. "Well, if you're sure…"

Hell, when she looked at him like that, as if he'd just set the freaking moon—instead of watching her kids for a few hours—he wasn't sure of anything.

"What kind of adventure are we having?" Marcus asked when Dillon went into the other room.

Hayley skipped up to him. "Is all that stuff part of our adventure?"

"The kind that keeps you both out of your mother's hair," he said to Marcus, setting the blankets and pillows on a table before turning to Hayley. "This stuff is going to be our construction materials." When they both looked at him blankly he added, "We're going to build a tent."

Hayley poked at a blue blanket. "But it's too cold to sleep outside."

"You don't have to be outside for a tent, dummy," Marcus said, his big-brother disgust clear on his face and in his voice.

Hayley's face fell.

"Marcus," Dillon said, "why don't you help me move this table so we have more room? Hayley, can you put all the pillows on that chair over there?"

Once he and Marcus were out of Hayley's hearing, Dillon said, "Do you know what a bully is?"

"Sure, they talk about it at school all the time. A bully is someone who picks on you or maybe even hits you."

Dillon nodded and crouched down to be eye level with the kid. "That's right. And a bully can pick on people by making fun of them or even calling them names." He paused. "Like calling your sister a dummy."

Marcus blushed and ducked his head. Maybe Dillon should've kept his mouth shut but he'd known too many bullies in his lifetime. People like Glenn who used fear and intimidation to get what they wanted.

But still, Marcus wasn't his responsibility. It wasn't his job to correct him or to want better from him. "Listen," Dillon said as he straightened, "forget I—"

"Hayley," Marcus called, his chin raised, "I'm sorry I called you a dummy."

"That's okay," Hayley replied.

Dillon patted Marcus on the shoulder. "Okay, you two," he said, "let's build a tent."

It took them a good half hour, but they managed to build a fort that didn't fall on their heads. Even with the fourth side pinned back, Dillon had to keep reminding himself there was plenty of air.

He sat closest to the opening.

"Did you camp a lot when you were a kid?" Marcus asked as he helped himself to a second slice of cheese pizza.

"I slept out a few times," Dillon said, finishing off his third. "Why?"

Marcus shrugged. "You're pretty good at building tents."

He should be. When he and Kelsey had been young and she'd had a nightmare, she'd come into his room and he'd build her a safe place to spend the night. And now she was getting married tomorrow. The realization hit him hard.

"I had you two to help me," Dillon said, shoving aside the unwelcome feelings. "Anyone like another root beer?"

"Daddy says sodas aren't good for us." Hayley sipped from her can. "He says it rots teeth and is one of the reasons why Marcus is getting fat."

Marcus blushed and he set his pizza down.

The more Dillon heard about Dr. Trey Carlson, the less he liked the asshole. He kept his face expressionless, his voice neutral when he asked, "What does your mom say about soda?"

"She says we can have some on weekends, but no more than one and only if there's no...no..." She scrunched up her face and looked at Marcus.

"No caffeine," her brother said.

"Right. 'Cause that keeps us up and we need our sleep."

"Soda can rot your teeth," Dillon said smoothly, "but only if you drink too much of it. And Marcus is just the right size."

Hayley nodded. "Marcus told me not to tell Daddy we helped you the other day and that we shouldn't tell him you watched us tonight."

"Hayley," Marcus growled, "you have a big mouth."

"What?" she asked. "You did say that."

"It's not a lie," Marcus told Dillon quickly, as if he were some sort of judge as to what was and what wasn't a lie. "I just didn't want him to get mad at Mom."

"Daddy use to yell at Mommy and make her cry," Hayley confided, snuggling closer to him, her head on his arm.

"He said you were bad," Marcus said, "and that Mom needed to learn she couldn't trust just anyone. So I thought it would be better if he didn't know we'd helped you."

Dillon nodded, not knowing what to say to these kids. "That's probably a good idea. But if your dad finds out, I don't want you to lie. And I'm sure your mom wouldn't want you to, either."

"I don't think you're bad or scary." Hayley grinned up at him. She put her warm—and slightly sticky—hand on his arm. "I think you're nice."

He wanted to shake her hand off, wanted to growl that he wasn't nice.

But he couldn't. So he forced a smile and, as gently as possible, extracted her from his side and put a movie into their portable DVD player.

Hayley soon became engrossed in the film—some holiday, feel-good fantasy about a train heading to the North Pole. Dillon picked up the mess from their dinner. He tossed the paper plates and napkins into the trash and set the soda cans aside for recycling, turned—and about jumped out of his boots to find Marcus behind him.

"Jeez, kid," Dillon said, "you practicing to be a ninja or something?"

"No. I…what you said before, about bullies? So… does that mean if someone says something mean and makes someone else cry all the time…is he a bully?"

The kid seemed worried, like whatever answer Dillon gave was really important.

Talk about pressure.

"I'd say anyone who picks on someone or tries to make them feel bad on purpose is a bully." He studied the kid. "Why? Is someone at school bothering you?"

"No. Not at school." Marcus fidgeted. "But…what if

you're too afraid to stand up to a bully? Even if they're hurting someone else?"

How the hell did he know? When it came time for him to protect Kelsey, he had.

"I guess," Dillon said slowly, "if there's no adult around to help you, then you have to do what you feel is right."

What the kid didn't need to know was that sometimes doing the right thing ended up costing you everything.

"ARE THE KIDS ASLEEP?" Nina asked when Dillon came into the kitchen. She'd resorted to ingesting copious amounts of caffeine.

So now she was jittery and running to the bathroom every thirty minutes.

"Hayley's been out for about ten minutes," he said as he crossed to the refrigerator. "Marcus is nodding off."

"Did everything go okay?"

He raised an eyebrow. "You should know. You checked on us at least six times."

"I didn't want them to give you a hard time. They're both tired and at each other's throats tonight…"

"And you thought I'd beat them bloody and toss them out into the nearest snowbank."

Hadn't they been through this before? "If I didn't trust you," she said carefully, "I wouldn't have agreed to your offer to watch my children in the first place."

She'd left her kids in his care, hadn't she? What more did the man want? A written declaration?

"Thanks for watching them," she said when he remained silent. When she'd peeked in on them—and it had been three times, not six—they'd been smiling and happy. What more could a mother ask for?

He pulled out the pizza box, set it on the table and lifted the lid. "You haven't eaten yet."

"I've been—"

"What have you eaten since lunch?"

She pursed her lips. There was something about him tonight…he seemed edgy and restless.

"Nothing," she admitted hesitantly.

He took the piping bag out of her hand. "You need to eat. Look at you, you're shaking."

"Too much caffeine," she muttered, trying to get her bag back. He raised his arm and she gave up. She was too old for games like this. And too tired to fight.

"After you eat," he told her, "you can have this…" He glanced at the frosting bag. "This thing back."

"Fine," she grumbled. She picked up a piece of pizza and took a huge bite. "You know," she said around her second bite, "you're the only person who encourages me to eat. Most people tell me to stop eating."

"People like your husband?"

The pizza stuck in her throat. She took a long drink of water to help wash it down. "He…wasn't happy when I didn't lose the baby weight right after I had Hayley so he'd…encourage me to watch my calories."

Dillon's gaze slid over her with an intensity that upset her equilibrium. "Why'd you get involved with such a jerk in the first place?" he asked quietly.

Having lost what little appetite she'd had, she set the remainder of her pizza down. How could she explain to Dillon something she wasn't sure of herself?

Or, to be more accurate, something she didn't want to admit, even to herself.

"When we first met, Trey already had his practice up and running. He was smart and so handsome and charming, he swept me off my feet." How many times since then had she wished she'd kept both feet planted firmly on the ground? "When Trey first asked me out, I couldn't believe he wanted me. I'd never had anyone, any guy, give me that much attention."

"I find it hard to believe you didn't have guys chasing after you."

"That's sweet, but no, I never had guys chasing me. Not like my sister. I was so used to being Blaire and Luke's sister, the middle child. The quiet one. The smart one." She shrugged as if didn't matter, but it had. It had mattered way too much to her. "Not as pretty as Blaire, not as popular as Luke."

"You're not competing with your brother and sister," he pointed out.

"I know that now. But as a teen? Not so much." She took the piping bag from him and went back to adding scroll designs to the top layer of the cake. "I fell into the role of good girl and just…never got out of it. The one time I did go against my parents' wishes was when I married Trey."

"They didn't want you to marry him?"

"They wanted me to finish college first. But I was in love." She rolled her eyes. "And they eventually supported the idea when Trey convinced me we should get married right away."

And she'd been so enamored, so enthralled with his

looks, his charisma and with the idea of him loving her, wanting her, that she'd chosen to ignore his faults.

What a mistake.

"I dropped out of college," she continued, adding another scroll to the cake, "and Trey and I were married that September. Our wedding was so perfect, I thought it must be an omen, you know, that we were destined to have this fairy-tale life." She cursed softly when too much frosting squirted out. She set the bag down and tried to pull herself together. "The fairy tale never came true. I dealt with it—am dealing with it."

"Why did you stay with him so long? And...why are you afraid of him?" When she didn't answer, he gently turned her to face him. "Nina?" He lifted her chin with one finger, held her gaze. "Did he hit you?"

Humiliation washed over her, made her nauseous. "Not all the time." Dillon cursed, his fingers tightened on her momentarily. "The first time I had a hint of his true nature was at our engagement party. I'd been talking to one of Luke's friends. I had no idea of the extent of Trey's anger until he got me alone in my parents' backyard. He pushed me against the wall, accused me of flirting with another man. When I started crying, he apologized. Blamed his outburst on the stress of starting his own practice, the wedding—and his fear of losing me. He promised it'd never happen again."

"And you believed him?"

Instead of the derisiveness she deserved, Dillon sounded both understanding and exasperated. "I chose to believe him, yes. I *wanted* to believe him. And I kept right on believing him until the first time he hit me."

She tugged herself away from him and faced the

sink, curled her fingers around the edge of the counter. "We'd gone out to dinner with some of Trey's colleagues. Marcus was an infant and I was so anxious about leaving him for the first time, I kept excusing myself to call and check on him. Everyone seemed to take it in stride—even Trey. But when we got home and sent the babysitter on her way, he…he slapped me." She shut her eyes. She could still remember the sting, the surprise—both that he'd raised a hand to her and at how much it had hurt. "He said I embarrassed him in front of his influential friends. I was so shocked, so angry, I packed up Marcus and left Trey."

"But you went back."

She turned and leaned back against the counter, hugging herself. "I went to my parents' house but they wanted me to think things through. Told me how all new marriages went through rough spots and that having a baby changed things. That Trey and I needed to work together to make our marriage succeed."

Dillon stepped in front of her. "How could they encourage you to go back to an abusive man?"

"They thought I'd left because I was under stress, not enough sleep due to the baby. Trey had charmed them—continued to charm them until he left me for Rachel. And I never let on that he was anything other than what they wanted to see."

"You didn't tell them he hit you."

"I couldn't. I was too ashamed. I believed it was…"

"It was your fault?" he asked softly.

She nodded and swallowed past the lump in her throat. "Plus, I…God, this is humiliating to admit but… I didn't want to be seen as a failure." She hadn't wanted anyone to know the mistake she'd begun to think she'd made. "So when Trey came over in the middle of the night carrying a dozen roses and begging my forgiveness, I took him back. I told myself that if I didn't make him angry, if I'd just be the wife he wanted—the wife he deserved—he'd change."

"My mother used to say the same things." Dillon's eyes were hooded, his body—so close to hers she could feel his warmth—tense. "Every time Glenn hit her she'd blame herself. If I tried to intervene, she accused me of making it worse. Of getting in the way of her marriage. And if Glenn took his temper out on me or Kelsey, it was because we deserved it."

She winced at his bitterness. The accusation. "I would never let Trey hurt my kids."

"He already has. Or do you think they didn't see what he did to you? How he treated you? Do you really think he'll treat them any differently?"

And there, right there, was her greatest fear. That she hadn't done enough to protect her children. That she still wasn't doing enough.

She pulled her shoulders back. "I know I've made mistakes—"

"Mistakes your kids are paying for."

She felt chilled. "No. That's not true. Even if I wasn't proactive in my marriage, even if I hadn't left Trey when I should have, I'm free of him now. And I'll do whatever it takes to stay free of him. To keep my kids safe."

"I hope so," he said slowly. "Because from what I can see, your kids are pretty great. They don't deserve to spend their life in fear."

"I don't need you to remind me how great my kids are," she grumbled, crossing her arms again. "Just as I don't need you to question my devotion to them."

He frowned. "I wasn't—"

"Weren't you?"

He scratched the back of his neck. "Look, I'm not trying to put down your mothering skills. I just…hate the thought of them being treated badly." His eyes flashed. "Almost as much as I hate the idea of that bastard hurting you. Or you being so paralyzed by fear that you didn't get away from him earlier."

She sighed. "Okay, fine. Let's just…drop it for now. I have a lot of work to do still. Thanks for watching—"

"Need any help?"

What was it with him? Two weeks ago, if someone would've asked her what Dillon Ward was like, she wouldn't have hesitated. Cold. Hard. Frightening.

Now she had no idea. All she knew was that he still scared her.

But for very different reasons.

"What do you know about making pastry dough?" she asked.

"Nothing."

"Well," she said, taking his hand and pulling him away from the counter, "I'd say it's past time you learned."

CHAPTER ELEVEN

IF ANYONE ASKED, he'd deny it, but as Dillon stepped inside the cool, dim foyer of St. Francis Church Saturday afternoon, he held his breath. When lightning didn't strike him dead, he figured he'd make it through the wedding ceremony.

He slipped into the last pew—which was thankfully empty—and sat. He'd arrived in time to hear the organ music start and to see the backs of Jack Martin's parents as they walked down the aisle.

Dillon adjusted his tie. It was just his imagination that it was choking the life out of him, right? He tugged at his collar. Damn thing felt like a noose.

He winced and glanced up. Nothing. He relaxed his shoulders, forcing himself to stop messing with his neckwear before he got into even more trouble with the guy upstairs.

Seemed like he'd already used up his quota of trouble for one lifetime.

As Jack's parents took their seats, Dillon scanned the rows of people but didn't see Nina's familiar honey-colored curls anywhere.

He drummed his fingers on his knee. He didn't care if he saw her or not. He just wanted to make sure she'd made it to the ceremony after working so late last night.

Not that he cared if she made it or not.

He couldn't help but compare Nina to his own mother, but unlike Leigh, Nina wasn't an alcoholic. And she loved her children and put them first.

But, even though she'd deny it, Nina was someone who needed to be taken care of.

He shifted in his seat. A stoic Jack, dressed in a dark suit, stood at the head of the church between the priest and the best man, blond New York detective Seth Valentine, in a matching dark suit.

The music switched and as one, the congregation turned to the back of the church. Allie stepped into view, the small bouquet of white flowers she held stark against her black strapless dress. He'd never understand what held a dress like that up. It gathered at her waist and swept the floor as she walked. Her dark hair had been pulled into a pile of curls on top of her head, showing off her toned shoulders and all that golden skin. She gave Dillon a wink and began her measured walk to the front.

Emma skipped into view looking adorable in her froufrou white dress, her smile wide, her face flushed with happiness. The kid was so excited, he'd be surprised if she didn't bust one of those fancy pearl buttons off the back of her dress. She carefully sprinkled red rose petals from her basket over the white runner as she made her way toward her dad.

The familiar opening chords of "The Wedding March" filled the building. Everyone got to their feet and looked back expectantly.

Dillon didn't stand. Couldn't breathe. This, his coming here, was a mistake. For the past twelve years he'd tried to distance himself from Kelsey—for both their sakes. And since she'd moved to Serenity Springs, he'd tried even harder. He should leave *now*. As soon as he could catch his breath—in, out—he'd slip through the heavy wooden doors to freedom.

Just then, his sister came into view. She was so… beautiful. Dillon slowly got to his feet, all thought of leaving gone. Kelsey's dress was low-cut and hugged her hips before falling to the floor. She'd somehow managed to get some curl into her supershort hair and had added a few sparkling clips.

She looked…beautiful.

And so scared, Dillon wouldn't have been surprised if she'd picked up the hem of her dress, turned around and bolted out of the church. Just as he'd wanted to a moment ago. What a pair they were.

Their eyes met and something shifted inside him. Made him remember all the times he'd protected Kelsey growing up. All the responsibility he'd felt for her.

How much he'd loved her.

And for the first time in a long time, that love didn't feel suffocating.

It felt right.

Dillon walked over to her as Kelsey took her first, hesitant step forward. She stopped, her eyes filled with tears even as she smiled.

Then she took his offered arm so he could escort her down the aisle to her future.

"You need to go for it."

Nina glanced at her sister in the large mirror over the sinks in the ski lodge's ladies' room. The reception was well under way in the main dining room but inside the bathroom, the music and voices were reduced to a low hum. "Go for what?"

Blaire smoothed a hand over her hair. "Dillon Ward, of course."

Heat climbed Nina's neck and filled her cheeks. She was surprised she didn't pass out.

"I don't know what you're talking about," she muttered, taking her lipstick out of her evening bag. She leaned forward and slicked the color over her lips.

She should've known Blaire had wanted more than a joint trip to the bathroom when she'd accosted her on the dance floor.

"Mom's worried you have a crush on him."

Nina tossed her lipstick back into her bag. "A crush? What am I, ten years old?"

"No need to get defensive." Blaire twisted in an effort to see the back of her understated—sexy—little black dress in the mirror. "I'm just repeating what I heard."

Nina pulled the bodice of her dark blue dress up in an effort to hide some more cleavage—no such luck. "Well, I don't have a…crush…on Dillon."

"Really?" Blaire crossed her arms and raised her eyebrows. "Then what would you call it?"

"It's…complicated."

Yes, that was it. Her feelings for Dillon—and she wasn't saying she actually had feelings for him—were complicated. And confusing.

And so very, very scary.

"Hey, complicated isn't such a bad thing," Blaire said. "I noticed all those glances you keep sending him. And Mom's usually right on track with these things—

she knew I was in love with Will before I could admit it to myself. Trust me on this, she has some sort of sixth sense about her kids' love lives."

"Then I have nothing to worry about. I don't have a love life." Some days she wondered if she had a life period. "And I'm certainly not in love with Dillon."

The door opened, letting in noise from the reception along with Seth Valentine's mother.

Great. Just what she needed. One of the biggest gossips in town hearing her protest her feelings for the local ex-convict. But if Mrs. Valentine had overheard, she gave no indication. Just gave them a sloppy grin before disappearing into one of the stalls.

No sooner had the stall door shut when Blaire said, "Of course you're not in love with him. You're much too sensible for that. But that doesn't mean you don't want him."

"Shh…" Nina grabbed Blaire and pulled her into the corner by the entrance. "Keep your voice down."

"Why?" She followed Nina's pointed look toward the occupied stall. "Oh, please," Blaire said, but at least she lowered her voice, "the way she's been hitting the open bar, I doubt she'll remember her own name tomorrow, let alone what she overheard in the bathroom."

"Still," Nina persisted, "I don't want everyone to think I'm…lusting after Dillon."

"Why not?"

Because he was dangerous and exciting and sexy. Because people counted on her to do the right thing, to make the right decisions.

"I…I'm afraid," she admitted softly.

Blaire wrapped an arm around Nina's shoulders and squeezed. "What are you afraid of?"

Nina almost laughed. What wasn't she afraid of? Seemed she lived her life in fear. Fear of making another mistake. Fear of disappointing others.

Fear of her growing feelings for Dillon.

"I am attracted to Dillon," Nina said as she laid her head against her sister's shoulder, "but I shouldn't be. I don't want to be."

"Because of his past? Or because of your past? Or because of what people will say?"

Nina sighed. "All of the above, I guess."

The toilet flushed and the stall door swung open. Mrs. Valentine stumbled in her low pumps, giggling as she caught her balance and continued toward the sink. "Lovely wedding, wasn't it?" she asked, drying her hands.

"Beautiful," Blaire agreed.

The older woman gave a little finger wave before she pulled open the bathroom's door. Once they were alone again, Blaire said, "I know this is none of my business and you didn't ask for my advice—actually, you never ask for my advice." She shrugged. "But that's a whole other conversation. Anyway, what I want to say is, trust yourself."

"Thank you, Obi-Wan. When do I get my light saber?"

"Ha ha. Your wit amazes me." Blaire shook her hair back. "Now, as I was saying, you're smart, beautiful and talented but you don't give yourself enough credit. You need to trust that you know what's best for you."

Nina crossed her arms, tucking her bag against

her side. "You mean like I trusted that Trey was best for me?"

Blaire wrinkled her nose. "Honey, Trey fooled all of us. Our entire family thought he was a good guy until he cheated on you. But somehow, after all you went through, you kept going."

She shrugged and one of the cap sleeves of her wide-necked dress fell down. "As if I had a choice. I have two kids, remember?"

"We all have choices. You could've chosen to hide in bed. You chose to trust yourself enough to get up every day—for your kids, yes, but for yourself, too." She squeezed Nina's hand. "You trusted your instincts about buying the bakery from Grandma and Pop, about the changes you wanted to make and you were right. So why can't you trust yourself when it comes to your personal life as well?"

Nina's throat constricted. What if Dillon didn't want her?

"What have you got to lose if you do make a mistake?" Blaire asked. "And even more important, is what you want worth the risk?"

DILLON SIPPED HIS beer and tried to pretend he wasn't watching at least fifty people—including the chief of police, a prominent attorney and several small business owners—shake their groove thangs to the Village People's "YMCA."

If the DJ played the macarena, Dillon might just have to hurt him.

He'd never had reason to visit the lodge before and had to admit he was impressed both with the reception and the building itself. A makeshift dance floor had been set up in front of the massive stone fireplace with round, white-covered tables taking up the rest of the large room. A full bar sat in an alcove next to the hallway that led to the restrooms and, most likely, the kitchen.

The cathedral ceilings were broken up with criss-crossing, glossy cherry boards. Before the sun had set, the floor-to-ceiling windows that took up the entire front wall afforded a breathtaking view of the snow-covered mountains.

He'd gone above and beyond in his brotherly duty—not just in walking Kelsey down the aisle, but by spending the day with 200 people who were all too afraid to make eye contact with him. He'd kept to himself, eating alone at the bar and not speaking to anyone unless specifically spoken to. An easy enough task, considering the only people brave enough to approach him so far had been Kelsey, Jack and Emma.

He'd even stayed long enough to witness all the hokey traditions—from the bride-and-groom dance, to the cake-cutting, to the tossing of the bouquet and garter.

And to be honest, watching some guy—even a guy who'd just married her—reach up his sister's dress for her garter was its own kind of torture.

Hell, he didn't know what he was doing here.

He took another drink. Okay, so he knew why he'd stayed so long. He may have come to the wedding for Kelsey but there was only one reason he'd endured three hours of this.

Nina.

She looked amazing. Her blue dress hugged her breasts and waist, flaring to just above her knees. And her sexy, silver heels… He couldn't stop staring at her. Even her hair. He'd never seen her wear it in anything other than ponytails and braids, but today it fell past her shoulders in golden, corkscrew curls.

His fingers itched to touch it. To find out if those curls were as soft as he imagined.

"You know," Allie said as she sidled up next to him. "I can honestly say that, in all of my life, I have never been stood up." She paused. "Until last night."

The music changed to "Livin' On A Prayer." Dillon glanced back at the dance floor to see Nina smiling as she danced with some guy in an Army uniform. "I got tied up."

"If you mean that literally, and in the best sense possible, I'll forgive you."

"I had to…help a friend."

She squealed in delight. "What? You've made your first friend? I'm so proud."

He smiled. "You are such a wiseass." He turned the beer bottle in his hand. "Nina needed some help—"

"Aaah…"

He scowled. "There is no 'aaah.' She was in a bind and I gave her a hand."

"What did she need help with?"

"I just…hung out with her kids," he said quietly. Nina's entire family had attended the wedding and while he'd noticed the kids left about thirty minutes ago with their grandparents, Nina's sister and obnoxious brother were still around. And the last thing Nina needed was for them to know he'd spent most of the night with her and the kids.

"You babysat Marcus and Hayley?"

"It's no big deal," he said, embarrassed and edgy. "Sorry I didn't show up last night, though. Let me make it up to you by buying you a drink."

"It's an open bar."

He grinned. "I'd still be happy to order it for you."

"In that case, I'd love a glass of red wine." He turned and placed the order and within two minutes handed her the wine. She thanked him and took a sip. "Well?"

He kept his gaze on the dance floor. "Well what?"

"Aren't you going to comment on how I look? Tell me I did a good job walking down the aisle? Anything?"

"You're gorgeous," he said, "as you well know since every man in here can't take his eyes off you."

"Not every guy." She nodded. "Anything you want to share with your old buddy?"

"Nope." He finished his beer and set the bottle on the bar behind him.

"You're not going to tell me what's going on between you two, are you?"

He leaned back against the bar. "Nope."

She sighed. "Fine. I guess we'll just make small talk, then. Wasn't the wedding beautiful?"

What was it with women and weddings? "It was good."

"Careful, your romantic side is showing." She wrapped her arm around his. "And it was more than good. It was perfect. Just look at how happy they are," she said, pointing at Jack and Kelsey on the dance floor.

Allie was right. They looked happy. Complete. He

was glad Kelsey had found that sort of connection, that sense of belonging. He'd never thought it possible for either of them.

It gave him hope.

He just wasn't sure he wanted hope. Because the only thing worse than not having any hope, was having it dashed.

"Now that the small talk is out of the way," Allie said, "we can get to the meaty stuff. You have a thing for Nina, huh?"

He tore his eyes off the woman in question to glare at Allie. "Don't go there."

She just grinned. "Fine. And I don't have to go there since she seems to be coming to you."

He stiffened. Allie didn't move, kept her arm wrapped around his, her body pressed to his side. When Nina reached them, she looked nervous and unsure. And so damn beautiful, he couldn't breathe.

She smiled tremulously. "Hi."

He nodded.

Her smile faltered. "Hi, Allie. You look beautiful."

"Thank you," Allie said. "You, too. That blue is amazing on you."

Nina tugged her sleeve back onto her shoulder. "Thank you." She rubbed her forefinger and thumb over the base of her left ring finger. "Uh…the wedding was lovely."

When he kept silent, Allie said, "Yes, it was." Then she gave the back of his arm a vicious pinch. He pressed his lips together and glared at her. Of course, she just ignored him. "The appetizers were delicious. And the cake was beautiful."

"I had a lot of help," Nina said, glancing at him.

In the background, the DJ announced the next song, Norah Jones's "Come Away with Me," and Allie once again broke the tense silence. "Oh, I love this one and I haven't had a chance to dance with the groom yet. Would you two excuse me?"

She didn't wait for an answer, just squeezed between them and hurried off.

Nina swallowed before straightening her shoulders. "Would you…would you like to dance?"

He opened his mouth to tell her no. He didn't think he could touch her, hold her and have her pressed against him without wanting more. Much more.

But Nina looked up at him with those big gray eyes, her question hanging in the air between them. Then she held out her hand.

And he realized how brave she'd been to approach him in front of her family and friends.

He couldn't say no.

He took her hand.

CHAPTER TWELVE

TRUST YOURSELF. Trust yourself.

And whatever you do, don't throw up.

Nina's stomach roiled as she led Dillon onto the small dance floor. His hand was warm and steady in hers, his skin rough. She felt the curious gazes of people but kept her eyes straight ahead.

She'd wanted to approach him all evening but hadn't the nerve until Blaire's bathroom pep talk. To be honest, it wasn't Blaire's advice so much that helped Nina to ask Dillon to dance as much as it was Nina's own realization that, even though she was free of Trey, she was still afraid of making waves. Disappointing people. Getting hurt again.

And she was oh so tired of living in fear.

She wove her way between couples on the dance floor, not stopping until she reached the far corner. Only then did she face him. After a moment's hesitation, he placed his hands on her waist and began swaying to the music.

Disappointed he didn't crush her against him—seemed her fantasies were getting the better of her—she laid her hands on his shoulders. His muscles tensed under her fingers. Norah Jones's breathy voice surrounded them, wove a sensual spell.

"I hadn't realized you were going to walk Kelsey down the aisle," she said, thankful her heels added a few inches so she could speak into his ear.

"It wasn't planned."

She tilted her head back. "She didn't ask you to give her away?"

"She asked. I said no."

"What changed your mind then?"

For a moment, she didn't think he'd answer her. But then he shrugged. "She needed me."

Nina almost stumbled. How could she fight her growing feelings for someone who not only watched her kids, helped her bake until three in the morning, but also stepped up to do the right thing for his sister simply because she needed him?

Nina took a small step closer to Dillon, to his strength and his heat, but he shifted.

She frowned. Was it her imagination, or had Dillon just backed away from her?

She looked up into his face and froze. In his eyes she saw heat, desire and…nerves.

What on earth could Dillon be nervous about?

Wait a minute. What if…what if he was nervous about…her?

The idea of dangerous, in-control Dillon Ward being nervous about holding her was ludicrous. And, well, rather intoxicating.

She smiled and his gaze fell to her mouth. A muscle jumped in his jaw before he jerked his eyes up to stare somewhere over her left shoulder.

Okay, so maybe she was right. But to be positive, she had to test her theory.

Before she could change her mind, she clasped her hands together behind his neck. Her breasts brushed his chest and she felt, more than heard, his sharp intake of breath. She lifted her face, her forehead bumping his chin lightly. His expression was heated. Intense.

He pressed his hands to her lower back, his fingers splayed just over the curve of her butt. Heat licked its way into her stomach.

"You're killing me," he growled into her ear.

A shiver raced up her spine at his admission. At the desire roughening his voice.

The music ended, but before Dillon could walk away, she forced herself to meet his eyes.

"Will you take me home?"

JUST BECAUSE A woman asked a man to take her home, didn't mean she wanted him in her bed.

A fact that Dillon repeatedly reminded himself as he stood shivering in the snow outside the lodge's front door. He flipped the collar of his suit coat up and blew on his frozen hands. By unspoken agreement, they seemed to have decided they shouldn't be seen leaving together. So she'd gone off, presumably to gather her things, while Dillon went outside, brushed snow off his truck and started the engine to warm it.

But now, a good ten minutes later, he couldn't help but wonder if he'd imagined her request.

And then the door opened and Nina, wrapped in a long, black coat, gingerly stepped out onto the snow-covered parking lot. They walked to his truck side by side. He should've taken her elbow, helped her manage in her impractical—but beyond sexy—silver heels, but he didn't want to take the chance of anyone seeing that and thinking the worst.

He opened the door for her and she climbed into his truck with surprising ease. In the process, flashing him a generous amount of leg.

As he drove to her house, the cab of his truck seemed to shrink. Grow warmer. Hot air blew out of the vents, swirling her scent around him. He stole a glance at her and wondered what she was thinking.

Had she changed her mind? Or perhaps she hadn't meant her question to sound so…propositional? Either way, he felt like a damn teenager on his first date.

Nina lived on the other side of town in a small development of similar-looking ranch-style houses, most of which were dark when he pulled into her driveway. He shut off the engine but kept the keys in the ignition. And his hands safely on the steering wheel.

They both stared at the house.

"The kids are spending the night with your parents, right?" he asked.

"How did you know?"

"They told me last night."

"Oh, right. Yes, they're…they'll be gone all night. Do you…" She stopped. Took an audible breath. "Do you want to come in? For coffee?"

His fingers tightened on the steering wheel. "No."

He sensed her studying him in the dim cab. "Oh," she said. That soft sound, filled with disappointment almost undid him.

She fumbled with the door handle but before she could open the door he said, "I don't want any coffee."

She turned toward him, her hands clenched in her lap. "You...you don't?"

The porch cast her face in shadows but he clearly saw how nervous she was. How uncertain.

He knew he should let her go.

"No," he admitted. "What I want is to touch you."

"I want that, too," she whispered.

"Do you? Because before you invite me in, I need you to be sure."

"I've only been with one man," she blurted, color washing her cheeks.

Her words hit him like a solid one-two jab. "That doesn't make me want you any less."

Truth be told, it made him want her more.

He had to let her know what she was getting herself into. What they were both getting into. "I want to touch you. Taste you. Every inch of you. I'm not some smooth college-educated guy who can sweep you off your feet. I'm not the kind of guy you can bring home to your parents, and I can't be paraded around town as a good catch. I've seen things...done things that you can't even imagine." He lowered his voice. "No matter who I am, what I lived through will always be a part of me."

"I don't want...I don't need you to be anything other than who you are," she said. She touched the side of his face, her hand warm and soft against his skin. "Honest. Strong. Honorable."

If he was so honorable, why didn't he get the hell out of there? If he was strong, why was his heart racing?

Why did she make him feel so weak?

He took her hand from his face and tugged her toward him. "You tempt me, Nina, more than any woman ever has."

She laced her fingers through his and squeezed. "Come inside with me. Please."

He dropped her hand, took the keys from the ignition and walked around the front of the truck to open her door. He wasn't noble enough to say no a second time.

At the front door, she fumbled with her keys. Her unsteadiness settled his own nerves.

He followed her inside and shut the door behind them. Nina flipped on the lamp on a narrow table. The house had an open floor plan with the kitchen—to his left—separated from the large living room by a breakfast bar. The rooms were done up in blue and gray with white accents.

While the house was no match for the house Dillon had imagined she'd shared with her wealthy ex, it was warm and inviting. In a settled, comforting sort of way.

Nina set her purse down and twisted her fingers together. She looked so nervous, he wasn't sure whether to be flattered or insulted.

"Are you sure I can't get you something? Soda? Or I might have a beer…" She headed toward the kitchen but he caught her by the wrist and pulled her back.

"I don't want anything to drink." He wrapped one of her soft curls around his finger. "The only thing I want," he continued, realizing what he was about to say was a truth so real, it scared the hell out of him, "is you."

NINA ATTEMPTED TO work moisture back into her suddenly dry mouth. "Oh."

Dillon studied her, his shoulders slouched in a negligent pose. Despite his shaggy hairstyle, he should've seemed bland and non-threatening in his dark suit coat and tie. Sort of like an accountant, or one of those catalog models.

But no civilized demeanor could hide his rough edges. His raw sex appeal.

"This is going to sound idiotic, but I...I don't know what to do," she admitted.

He flashed her a heart-stopping grin. "They say it's like riding a bike."

She burst out laughing. "That's not quite what I meant." Although, dear Lord, what if she had forgotten how? Was that even possible?

"I see your brain working," he said, his hands in his front pockets. "It's not too late to change your mind."

"Do you...have you changed your mind?"

He gave one, quick shake of his head. "It would kill me to walk away from you now, but you have to want this. And be here, with me, totally."

"I'm here. There's no place else I'd rather be."

He smiled. "All I can say to that is, thank God."

She returned his smile but then gestured between them. "Is this awkward? I mean, is it supposed to be this...weird? What do we do first?"

"Why don't we take it step by step?" he asked.

Mesmerized by the fire in his eyes, she could only nod in agreement.

"Step one," he murmured, moving forward, forcing her to back up until she bumped into the side table.

Her pulse pounded in her ears. Closing her eyes, she nearly jumped out of her skin when he tucked her hair behind her ear.

He traced her ear with the tip of his finger. She shivered. He then dragged that finger down the side of her neck and over her shoulder to the sleeve of her dress.

"Step two is to tell you how amazing you look tonight," he said roughly. But his touch was still whisper-soft as he skimmed his finger down the edge of her dress to the top of her breast. "I couldn't take my eyes off you."

He drew his finger over her breast. She reached behind her and gripped the table with both hands. Caught her breath. Her nipples beaded, pressed against her dress. Heat pooled low in her stomach. Between her legs.

"Your skin's so soft." He rubbed his finger back and forth across the skin just above the bodice of her dress. He paused to dip his knuckle in the space between her breasts. "Lovely."

He cupped the back of her head, his fingers in her hair. "Step three," he murmured before pressing his mouth against the side of her neck.

A shiver ran up her spine and she laid her hands against his solid chest for balance. For a touchstone to reality. His shirt was cool and silky. A decided contrast to the heat of his mouth.

He brushed his lips over her sensitized skin. She gasped and curled her fingers into his shirt. He used both hands to sweep her hair to the side, wrapped one fist around it and tugged lightly until she tipped her head to give him better access. He scraped her pulse with his teeth and she jerked and tipped her hips toward him.

Her nerve endings thrummed. Unable to stop herself, she pressed against his chest, trapping her hands between the hard planes of his chest and her breasts.

Dillon groaned, yanked her against him and kissed her with a hunger that made her knees weak. She threw her arms around his neck, thankful for the heels that aligned their bodies. They kissed, a heated mesh of tongues and teeth, greed and desire. His erection pressed against her stomach and she arched against him.

Still kissing her, he tugged her bodice down. Lifting his head, he stared at her bared breasts. She held her breath only to release it on a long whoosh when he bent and sucked one nipple into his mouth. She slid her hands into his silky hair and allowed her head to fall back against the mirror nailed to the wall, her hips pressed forward by the narrow table. The wet suction of his mouth made her squirm against him, trying to find relief from the ache building between her legs.

Turning to her other breast, he gathered the skirt of her dress in his hand and lifted it above her waist, pinning it there with his lower body. Pulling her panties down her legs, he laid his hand flat against her.

She should've been embarrassed, standing in her foyer with a gorgeous man's mouth on her breast. His hand between her legs. The fact that she was breathing hard and already so wet for him should give her pause. But it didn't. She wanted this, wanted Dillon.

So when he placed his large, callused palm on her inner thigh, nudging her legs apart, she couldn't refuse him. And when he finally touched her, when he slid one finger, and then two, inside her, she moaned and undulated against his hand.

He groaned and shifted his hand, his thumb rubbing

her where she needed it most. She panted as she climbed toward release, moving her head back and forth against the mirror. And when he gently rolled her nipple between his teeth, she bucked hard against his hand and cried out as she came, her body quivering.

Thank God Dillon was there to support her as she recovered. He held her in his arms, his face against her shoulder, his breathing ragged, his rigid body still vibrating with need.

Her eyes filled with tears at the sweetness of what had happened between them, at how he held himself back. She blinked the tears away. She didn't want anything—not her stupid sentimentality or her very scary growing feeling for Dillon—to ruin this night.

"If those were just the first three steps," she said, bending down and wiggling back into her panties, "I can't wait to see what you have in mind for steps four through ten."

He lifted his head, his upper lip dotted with sweat, his jaw tight with tension. "What makes you think there are only ten steps?"

She raised her eyebrows even as she tugged her dress back up over her breasts. "You have more?"

"Cupcake, I have so many things I want to do to you, I'm not sure I could get to them all in just one night."

She smoothed a lock of hair off his forehead. "Well, in that case, we'd better get started on number four."

CHAPTER THIRTEEN

DILLON'S HEART hammered. He yanked Nina into his arms and kissed her. She felt so incredible. The heat from her skin scorched through his clothes, and her face and chest were flushed. Her hair was a wild tangle of curls.

Better yet, she still trembled from the strength of her orgasm. The orgasm he'd given her. Pure male satisfaction filled him.

"Bedroom?" he asked in between kisses as he backed her down the dark hallway.

"Last door...on the right."

At her bedroom door, Dillon pressed his body against hers, trapping her against the wall. He shoved both hands into her hair and held her head immobile while he deepened the kiss. Her body was so soft, so responsive he couldn't help but roll his hips against hers. Her soft moan and the way she arched against him left him insane for her. With a low growl, he spun them into the room.

Still kissing her—he didn't think he'd ever get tired of kissing her—he tugged the zipper down the back of her dress. The sleeves fell off her shoulders. He pressed his mouth against her clavicle, flicked his tongue over the pulse that beat erratically at her neck.

But it wasn't nearly enough to satisfy him. He had to see her.

With one arm wrapped around her waist, he reached around the wall until he came in contact with the light switch. He flipped it on.

"Wait," she said. "Dillon, stop."

Her words, and the fact that she was pushing at his chest filtered through the desire muddying his thoughts. He shook his head and blinked until his vision cleared and he saw the very real apprehension in her eyes.

Though it took an act of superhuman will, he forced himself to let her go.

She clutched the fabric of her dress against her breasts and stepped back.

"Do you want me to go?" he asked.

She frowned. "What?" He could see realization dawn in the widening of her eyes. "No. I was just wondering if we could…keep the lights off?"

"We can do whatever you want," he said carefully, "but I'd love to see you." His voice dropped to a husky whisper. "I've been dying to see you."

She swallowed. "It's just that I'm…I have stretch marks. And…well, it's no secret I'm carrying around a few extra pounds…and I've…never done this except in the dark."

Dillon raised his eyebrows. So that's what this is about?

No way would he let Nina continue to believe whatever bullshit her ex had told her. But since he sucked at expressing how he felt, he'd just have to show her.

"I'm not him." His tone wasn't harsh but she winced anyway.

"No, I know you're not."

"Do you?" He skimmed his fingers over the hand that still clutched her dress to cover herself. "Then let me see you."

He dropped his arm back to his side. His breath hitched as he watched the emotions cross her face. Anxiety and uncertainty mixed with desire. And finally, thankfully, trust.

Nina unclenched her hand. His head buzzed with anticipation as she inhaled and slowly—ever so slowly— slid one sleeve, then the other, down her arms then tugged at the dress until it slithered past her hips to pool at her feet.

The air left his lungs. Her silk panties were black, a decided contrast against the paleness of her skin. And seeing as how panties—and her shoes—were all she wore, he held on to his control by a very thin thread.

"You're beautiful."

Her blush deepened and she dropped her gaze. He didn't have the words to convince her he was speaking the truth. What he felt when he looked at her.

"Come here," he ordered as he shrugged out of his jacket and loosened his tie.

When she hesitated, he tossed his coat onto the armchair but made no move to close the distance between them.

After another long moment, she stepped over her dress toward him.

He laid his hands on her hips, hooked his thumbs under the elastic waist of her panties. "Did I tell you how much I like those shoes?"

She laughed shakily. "No, you didn't." Pulling his

tie off over his head, she undid the top three buttons of his shirt. Her trembling knuckles brushed against him. "I never would've figured you as the type of guy to have a shoe fetish."

He rubbed his thumbs back and forth across the incredible smoothness of her skin. "Maybe it's more of a curiosity of how women even walk in those things." He dragged her closer. "I'm just glad someone invented them."

She lifted her head at the same time he leaned down to capture her mouth with his. He slipped his hands into her panties and caressed the top curve of her rear while she fumbled with the buttons on his shirt. After a moment, she growled in frustration. The next thing he knew, she'd torn his shirt and the last few buttons popped off.

He wrapped both arms around her waist and carried her to the bed, letting go of her only long enough to strip off his ruined shirt before settling on top of her.

He braced himself on his elbows. He had to slow down. He wanted to touch her, bring her back to the edge of pleasure again. But it was hard when she tasted so damn sweet and the soft sounds she made were such a turn-on. Still, he fought his need and slid his hands over her breasts.

Her own hands moved over him, over his shoulders and down his chest and stomach. She lightly brushed his erection and he sucked in a harsh breath. Exhaled heavily when she worked his belt loose and undid his pants. She slipped inside his briefs and wrapped her warm, soft fingers around him. He cursed brokenly at her touch.

He bent his head and took one nipple into his mouth, sucked as he smoothed his hands down her rib cage to her silky stomach. He placed soft, biting kisses across her collarbone and up her neck until their mouths met again. Kissing her, he skimmed his hand over her panties, tracing tiny, featherlight circles over them. She arched against him.

"Dillon, please," she gasped. "Now."

Beyond control, beyond reason, he toed off his shoes and kicked away his pants while Nina lifted her hips and wiggled out of her panties. He grabbed a condom from his wallet, sheathed himself and settled between her legs. Bracing his hands on either side of her head, he kissed her deeply and entered her.

He reached under her hips and lifted her so he could imbed himself in her more fully. She moaned and raked her nails down his back and he plunged into her again and again. Sweat covered their bodies. The sound of their breathing, the scent of their lovemaking filled the room.

He grasped her behind her thighs, wrapped her legs around his waist. Her high heels dug into his back. Her hands clutched his biceps. He quickened his pace and her breathy moans turned into pants. Her body contracted beneath his. Her eyes clouded.

"Dillon," she gasped.

And the sound of her saying his name sent him over the edge with her. His heart racing, he collapsed on top of her. Her fingers tightened in his hair. When his breathing returned to normal and his body stopped trembling, he rolled to the side and pulled the end of the comforter over them.

Then he tucked her against him. Her head on his shoulder, she placed her hand on his chest. A few minutes later, her breathing deepened. He smoothed her hair back, kissed her forehead and sighed as he let his head fall back.

Ah, hell.

THE PHONE RANG. Nina sat up, the receiver to her ear before she opened her eyes.

"Hello?"

"Hey, it's me," Luke said. "Hope I didn't scare you but we've got a little situation here."

Nina squinted at the blurry numbers on her alarm clock. 3:53. "Luke?" She cleared her throat, brushed the hair out of her eyes. "What's the matter?"

"Hayley got sick."

"Hayley?" She swung her feet over the side of the bed. "She's in bed sleeping."

"Wake up, Neen. The kids spent the night with Mom and Dad after the wedding, remember?"

Nina frowned and rubbed her forehead. The wedding. Of course. She turned around so fast, she fell off the bed, landing on the carpet with a thump.

"Hey, you still there?" Luke asked.

"What?" She peered over the edge of the bed but Dillon must've shut the light off and she couldn't make out anything. Not even a lump. "Uh, you said Hayley's not feeling well?"

"She threw up. She doesn't have a fever, so Mom thinks she probably ate too much at the reception. But she was crying and wanted to come home—"

"I'll be right there." Oh, her poor baby. Nina got

to her feet and wobbled, balancing herself against the nightstand. Dear Lord, she still had her shoes on.

And nothing else.

"Don't bother," Luke said. "I'm already on my way."

"What?" She reached around, found the lamp and switched it on. Blinked against the sudden light.

"Mom asked me to bring Hayley into town. It's snowing pretty hard and she didn't want you driving out here."

A chill racked Nina's body. She faced the bed, not surprised to find Dillon leaning on his elbows watching her out of heavily lidded eyes.

She gripped the phone tightly. "Uh…what do you mean, you're on your way?"

"I just passed the Glicks' house. Hey, do me a favor and unlock your door. Hayley fell asleep a couple of miles back so maybe we can get her into her bed without waking her. See you in a few minutes."

The dial tone buzzed in Nina's ear. Her entire body tingled—and not from the effects of two fabulous orgasms. No, this was good old-fashioned panic.

"Everything all right?" Dillon asked, his voice husky from sleep.

"You have to leave," she told him as she spied her underwear on the floor. Pulling them over her hips, she gathered his clothes and threw them at him.

"What the…" Dillon caught his pants before they hit him in the face. "What's going on?"

"I don't have time to explain." She flew across the room, opened her middle dresser drawer, grabbed the first shirt she saw and pulled it over her head. "What are you waiting for?" she cried when he hadn't moved.

"Get dressed." She picked out a pair of flannel pajama pants and, using the dresser for balance, put them on. "You have to go. Now. Right now."

Dillon stood and pulled his pants on.

She tugged her hair back into a high ponytail, tying it with a hair band she'd snatched off the dresser and glanced at the clock. 3:55.

"Listen, I'm sorry, but I don't have time to explain." She practically shoved his arms into the sleeves of his shirt—both to hurry him along and because, well to be honest, the sight of him standing there barefoot and bare-chested was more than her jacked up system could take at the moment. "Luke said he was by the Glicks' house, which is only two miles away, which means he'll be here any minute."

"Is Hayley okay?" Dillon asked.

"Fine." Nina tossed his tie and coat at him, whirling around as she searched for his shoes. Aha. There they were, by the bed. She rushed over, picked them up and shoved them at him. "I mean, I guess she's fine. A stomachache from too many sweets."

Another look at the clock. 3:56. Dillon still hadn't moved, just stared down at her, an unreadable expression on his face.

She grabbed his hand and pulled him toward the door. "I'll tell you everything later. I promise. But right now you need to—"

Headlights illuminated the hallway.

She cursed and pushed him back into the room. "It's too late, Luke's already here. Promise me you'll stay in the bedroom. And be quiet."

He opened his mouth but before he could say anything, Nina stepped out into the hallway and shut the door. She hurried to open the front door for Luke.

"She's out," Luke whispered, carrying Hayley inside. His gaze flicked from the kitchen to the living room. "She didn't even stir when I unbuckled her."

Nina swept her baby's hair back and felt for any signs of fever but found none. "Let's put her in bed."

Luke laid Hayley down. She didn't even wake when Nina took her coat off and tucked her under the covers. Nina didn't waste any time hauling her rear back out into the hallway. A good thing, too, since Luke was staring pensively at Nina's closed bedroom door.

She steered him down the hallway, not stopping until they were in the kitchen. "Thank you so much for bringing her home."

"Is she still sleeping?"

Nina nodded. "I'll stay on her floor tonight, in case she gets sick again." She forced a smile, crossed her arms. Uncrossed her arms. "Anyway, it's late and I'm sure you want to—"

"Nina?" He stood with his hands on his hips. "What the hell is Dillon Ward's truck doing in your driveway?"

"Dillon's truck?" Damn.

"Yeah. His truck. The one covered in snow—which tells me it's been here for quite some time."

"Uh…well…I…uh…had a few glasses of wine, you know, at the reception? And…uh…I didn't want to drive home, so Dillon was nice enough to…" Heat climbed her neck. "Drive me home."

"That doesn't explain why his truck is still here."

She swallowed. "He…uh…" She wiped her hands down the front of her pants. "His truck. It wouldn't start. I mean, after we got here, something…it made this sound like 'ping ping.' We were lucky to even make it this far."

"Ping ping, huh?"

"Yeah." She licked her lips. "So Dillon walked back to the bakery. He said he'd call a tow in the morning…"

"I see. Well, that makes perfect sense."

Her shoulders sagged. "Right. Well, now you know. So, thanks again for bringing Hayley home. Good night." She turned to get a bucket from under the sink.

"So tell me," Luke said, "when did you get that hickey on the back of your neck? Before or after the ping ping?"

She slapped a hand to her neck and straightened. "It's…it's not what you think—"

"What I think is you've lost your mind," he hissed. "You barely even know this guy. And what we do know should send you running from him, not sleeping with him."

She really didn't need this. She hadn't had time to even figure out her own feelings about what had happened between her and Dillon. She didn't need to listen to her brother's opinion.

She dragged him down the hall. "I'm done discussing this with you." She opened the door and was blasted with cold air. "It's late, I'm tired and I need to check on Hayley. And if you even think about telling anyone— and I mean anyone—about this, I'm going to make sure the entire town knows how you used to dress up in Blaire's dance costumes."

"I was four!"

"Were you? Seems to me you were much older. More like…fourteen?"

He scowled. "Don't even—"

"Good night."

She shoved him onto the porch and slammed the door in his face. Leaning back against it, she listened to him pull out of the driveway.

She shut her eyes and sighed. Who knew? Maybe she had a future with this bad-girl stuff after all.

"You're in my way."

Her eyes flew open. Not because Dillon's voice was harsh or even all that loud.

But because it was so cold, it chilled her to the bone.

Worse, though, was the anger in his eyes. And the disappointment and hurt.

She rubbed her hands over her arms. "Dillon, I'm sorry—"

"Sorry about what, exactly?" He was dressed in his wrinkled coat, his tie balled up in his hand. He edged toward her, his walk so predatory, the look on his face so fierce, her stomach pitched. "Sorry your daughter got sick? Sorry your brother came over? Or just sorry we had sex?"

He towered over her, his hair on end, stubble covering his cheeks and chin. Had she thought he was dangerous before?

She kept pressed against the door but slid two steps to the side. Her throat constricted. But this was Dillon, she reminded herself. Not Trey. Dillon would never hurt her.

Would he?

She pushed away from the door. But when he raised his hand, she couldn't help but flinch and shrink back.

His expression twisted into a sneer. "And you thinking I'm going to wail on you is the perfect ending to a completely shitty situation."

He opened the door. "Dillon, wait. I didn't mean—"

"Save it." He jerked away from her and stepped onto the snow-covered stoop.

Her mouth fell open. What had she done? What had she said?

"Oh, and you might want to do yourself a favor," Dillon said over his shoulder. "The next time you invite an ex-con to spend the night with you? Make sure you cover your tracks better."

CHAPTER FOURTEEN

AT THE BAKERY Monday after school, Kyle dipped his paint roller into the tray of white primer and then slapped it on the new drywall. "This sucks."

Dillon, priming the wall next to him, grunted.

Kyle plopped his roller back into the primer. "My arm's tired." He glanced down and swore at the white specks covering his favorite Rush T-shirt. "And my shirt's ruined."

"I told you to wear old clothes."

"Yeah, well, you can just buy me a new shirt. Hey, I know, why don't we get one of those spray painter things? You know, you fill it with paint and then—" He held up his roller and swept it from side to side like a spray painter—or machine gun. "The whole room's done in, like, twenty minutes. That would be sweet."

"Watch it," Dillon snapped. "You're getting paint all over the floor."

Kyle lowered the roller to his side. "Isn't that what the drop cloth's for?" he muttered.

Dillon's lips thinned. "I'd like less paint on the ground and more on the walls."

"Fine." Jeez, no need to get hostile. He glared at Dillon. Mr. Tightass didn't care about anything like, oh, having fun.

He ground his back teeth together. Hell, he'd even started thinking maybe this gig—working with Dillon and all—wasn't so bad.

Guess not.

He'd sort of liked Dillon up until now, but he understood that things changed. And that he needed to trust his first instincts when it came to people. Look what happened when he'd started thinking Joe and Karen could be different—even if they still treated him decent. But he couldn't forget how they freaked over a little pot.

Adults. Who needed them?

"You're putting too much paint on your roller," Dillon said coming up behind him. "You've got drips everywhere."

"So? We're just going to sand it tomorrow, right? And that better be with an electric sander, 'cause there's no way I'm doing it by hand."

"I'm the boss. You're the worker. You'll do what I tell you to do, how I tell you to do it. Got it?"

"Dude, did somebody stick something up your ass over the weekend, or what? You are seriously tripping."

Dillon stepped forward, his expression dark. Ignoring his sweaty palms, Kyle pulled his shoulders back and straightened to his full height. So what if Dillon had at least five inches and a good fifty pounds on him? The guy got in his face, Kyle had to show he couldn't be pushed around.

Dillon just shook his head. "Forget it. Just…get back to work."

He stalked back to his own corner of the room. Kyle laid the roller against the wall. His hand trembled. He hadn't been afraid. It was just adrenaline. He could've held his own against anything Dillon dished out.

He wiped his free hand down the front of his jeans. Not that he had anything to worry about. Nothing made Dillon lose his cool.

The door opened and Hayley and Marcus ran inside, followed by Nina. Hayley took her book bag over to the corner and started digging through it.

"Hi, Kyle," Nina said, giving him one of her dimply smiles. "How's it going?"

He shrugged. "It's okay."

Her smile became strained and her dimples disappeared when she faced Dillon. "Can I get you two anything? A drink or—"

"No," Dillon said, not even looking at her.

Kyle raised his eyebrows at Dillon's abrupt, do-not-talk-to-me tone. He caught Marcus's eye, shrugged a shoulder. He had no idea what the sudden tension in the room was all about. But he couldn't wait to find out.

Nina took a cautious step forward, as if Dillon was a chained dog and she wasn't sure if she should get too close. "Are you sure? I made some—"

Dillon's pissed-off look shut her up real quick. "I'm sure."

Nina shrank back. Sort of like his last foster mother used to when her old man raised his voice. Which was smart, since once that bastard raised his voice, he usually raised his fist as well.

"Here, Kyle." Hayley held out a folded piece of green construction paper.

"What's this?"

He opened it. Inside was a crayon-drawn Christmas

tree, a bright yellow spot he guessed was some sort of star and colorful squares under the tree that must've been presents. On the left were the words: Thursday. 7:00. And My School.

"It's a invitation to my Christmas pageant," she said, skipping over to Dillon. "I made one for you, too. It's Thursday night and we get to dress up and sing three songs and then we'll have cookies and drinks." She clasped her hands together and smiled up at Dillon as he opened his invite. "Will you come? Please?"

Nina laid her hand on Hayley's shoulder. "Honey, Dillon and Kyle might be busy…"

Hayley's eyes filled with tears.

Dillon sighed. "I'll be there."

"Yay!" Hayley threw her arms around Dillon's leg before turning to look at Kyle.

He slapped the paper against his palm. Hang out at a grade school watching a bunch of kids sing dorky Christmas songs? Yeah. That sounded like a great time. Then again, he was still grounded. But if Joe and Karen thought he was going to the Christmas show thing, they might give him the night off.

He grinned. "Sure. I'll go, too."

Hayley clapped her hands and did a little hop. Then, since she got her way, she ran over to bug Marcus who now had his video game out and his headphones on.

Out of the corner of his eye he noticed Nina approach Dillon again.

She was either really stubborn. Or really dumb.

"Dillon. Can we please—"

"I need to get something out of my truck," Dillon said, and he left.

Nina nibbled on her lower lip, her shoulders hunched as she stared after him.

Kyle went back to his work. Huh. Looked like someone could make Dillon Ward lose control after all.

SHE BLEW IT. Again.

"I have to…uh…do something in the kitchen," Nina said to her kids. "You two get started on your homework, okay?"

She hurried out to the back door, but couldn't seem to make herself walk outside. She tugged at the edge of the turtleneck sweater she'd worn to cover Dillon's hickey. She couldn't go one more minute with this awful tension between them.

She stepped outside. Dillon stood behind the open tailgate of his truck. She hugged her arms against the chill and crossed the parking lot.

He shoved a toolbox across his truck. It hit the back of the truck bed with a clang and tipped over. He slammed the tailgate shut. "Feeling brave today, huh?"

She took the blow without wincing. "I guess I deserved that for what I…for my reaction the other night—"

"You mean for shrinking from me at the door as if I kick puppies for entertainment?"

She shivered. "It was a…knee-jerk reaction."

"Right. Because I'm just like your ex-husband. Or maybe, given my violent history, you figured I always beat on women who piss me off. After all," he said, crowding her until the backs of her thighs pressed against the cold bumper, "I am a killer."

"I know you would never hurt me."

She reached out but he stepped back. "You really don't want to touch me right now."

She fisted her hand. "Listen, I didn't mean to push you out of the house. I just didn't want Hayley to wake up and find you there."

"You think I'm pissed because you put your kids first?"

She frowned and stomped her feet in an effort to return feeling to her toes. "Well…what else could it be? The way you left, the things you said—"

"I respect how you put your kids first. I can't remember how many times I woke up as a kid to find some guy sitting at our kitchen table eating the cereal and milk that was supposed to be for me and Kelsey. You think I want your kids exposed to that? Or that I want to put you in the same category as my mother?" He shoved his hands in his pocket. "Your opinion of me keeps getting worse and worse."

"Then, tell me what I did. I want to under—"

"You didn't stand up."

She blinked, her teeth chattering. "Excuse me?"

"To your brother." The wind mussed his hair, made him hunch his shoulders. "You wanted me to stay hidden in your room, but not because of Hayley. Or at least, not just because of her."

"That's not—"

"When Luke said you'd lost your mind, that you should be running from me, you should've told him to stay out of your business. Should've made it clear that you're strong enough to pick who you want in your life and in your bed. But you're afraid." Before she could defend herself, he added, "And I don't have the time, patience or desire to slay your dragons for you."

"I…I…" She tried to find the words, the things she wanted to say. She didn't need him to slay her dragons. She was a strong, capable woman who could handle herself, thank you very much. She didn't need his help conquering her fears.

She wanted to say all those things. But she couldn't. Because they weren't true.

She couldn't admit her failings—such as her miserable marriage. Or the humiliation of knowing she stayed with a man so abusive and manipulative that she couldn't free herself or her children from him.

She couldn't change who she'd always been, who people expected her to be. She wasn't even sure she wanted to try. Because the idea of standing up to her family, of going against their expectations, or worse, of confronting Trey and her mistakes, left her stomach churning and her palms sweating.

But she'd hurt Dillon. She could see that now. And that was worse, so much worse than just making him angry.

"You've got this all wrong," she insisted. "I wasn't ashamed of being with you. I would've hidden any man Luke caught me with. Except I don't want just any man. Dillon…I want you."

"Don't. We just need to move on. What happened Saturday night was a—"

"Don't you dare say it was a mistake," she said, her voice shaking. "Or I might just be the one who resorts to violence."

He studied her. "If not a mistake then a reminder.

And a really good reason for us to keep our distance until I finish the job and leave town."

He walked back into the building. Despite the cold, she followed slowly. Why did she feel so empty…as if she'd just lost something important? Something vital.

But that couldn't be, she rationalized as she entered the kitchen. She'd never had Dillon—well, not his heart. And as he'd pointed out, she wasn't strong enough to face other people's opinions, their disappointment or derision if she and Dillon were a couple in an open relationship.

She shut her eyes. She really was a wuss.

But that didn't mean she had to continue to be afraid her entire life, did it? If she didn't want to live this way, she had to be the one to change things. To take chances.

Be rebellious.

And not just any rebellion. She didn't want to be a bad girl; she just wanted to be herself.

And she wanted Dillon. No matter what people said.

Now all she had to do was convince him of that.

She partially opened the door to the dining room, saw Hayley at the table with the headphones on playing a video game. Dillon rolled paint on the wall while Marcus stood next to him. Kyle was nowhere to be found—which meant he'd gone out back to sneak a smoke.

"I heard you say you were going to Hayley's pageant thing," Marcus said to Dillon, who grunted a response. "The little kids are singing and us bigger kids are doing a play but I just did set design since I like to draw so much."

Dillon dipped his roller into the tray of paint at his feet. "Cool."

"Yeah." He shifted his weight from one foot to the other. "I...I don't want you to get mad or anything but I probably won't talk to you." His hair hung in his eyes. "My dad will be there and he doesn't want me or Hayley to talk to you."

Her son's voice trailed off and Nina's heart lodged in her throat. She ducked out of sight but kept the door open enough to see and hear them.

"Don't sweat it," Dillon said as he continued his even strokes. His expression gave none of his thoughts away. "We'll pretend we don't know each other."

"I wish I didn't have to. I wish I could sit with you instead of Dad and Rachel, but that's our night to go to Dad's house." He lowered his voice so that Nina had to strain to hear him. "I don't even like going there but the judge says I have to. Plus, I need to make sure Hayley doesn't do anything that will make Dad mad."

She covered her mouth to keep from sobbing. Oh, her poor baby.

Dillon stopped painting and crouched so he was eye level with Marcus. "You know, I admire the way you take care of your little sister."

"You do?"

Dillon nodded. "When I was your age I had to take care of my younger sister so I know how hard it can be. But you're doing a great job."

Marcus blushed with pleasure. "Can I help you work today? I got my homework all done."

"Wouldn't you rather play your video game or watch a DVD?"

"Nah. I like helping you. You don't call me a baby or stupid if I make a mistake."

For a moment, Dillon looked as stunned as Nina felt. She knew Marcus was talking about Trey. How many times had her son been put down or belittled by his own father?

How many times had she thought she was protecting him by finding excuses for Trey's behavior? All because she was afraid of rocking the boat?

"I could use some help," Dillon finally said. "You ever paint a wall?"

"No."

"Then I guess it's time you learned how."

She closed the door. Pressed a hand to her unsteady stomach. She'd made so many mistakes and now those mistakes, her failings and weaknesses were being pushed on her kids.

And she'd be damned if she'd let that happen.

AS SOON AS the Annual Serenity Springs Elementary School's Christmas Pageant ended, Dillon jumped to his feet and headed to the nearest exit. The noise level rose as kids, parents and grandparents—all of whom had just sat through two hours of torture disguised as entertainment—started talking.

He couldn't wait to get out of here. Nina had insisted he sit with her. And spending two hours with Nina on one side of him, her uptight, stiff parents on the other, had been another form of torture separate from listening to kids butcher holiday songs.

Even though the school gym was packed with people, Dillon didn't have any trouble working his way through the crowd. He simply scowled fiercely, lowered his head and moved forward.

Everyone gave him a wide berth. Sometimes being the town outcast had its perks.

The lit EXIT sign beckoned, promising him solitude and escape. Just when he thought he was home free, someone ran into him, knocking him back two steps.

Dillon glanced down and frowned. Damn. Waylaid by a three-foot Santa. What were the chances?

"Sorry," Santa—or in this case, the kid dressed up as Santa—mumbled before racing off to get in line for cookies and punch.

He took a step forward.

"Dillon, wait," a small voice called.

He looked at the door longingly. So close.

No sooner had he turned around than Hayley, dressed in the same shiny, pink dress and white sweater she'd worn to Kelsey's wedding, skidded to a stop beside him.

She grabbed his hand and grinned up at him. "You came!"

Well aware people were watching them—including Trey and his skinny wife—Dillon gently squeezed Hayley's hand and then let go. "Hey, I said I would, didn't I?"

"Is Kyle with you?" she asked as Nina joined them. "I didn't see him anywhere.

"Sweetie, I don't think Kyle made it," Nina said.

Hayley frowned. "But he said he'd be here."

"Maybe he wasn't feeling well." Nina brushed a hand over Hayley's braids. "Now you'd better get yourself a cookie before they're all gone."

That perked the kid up. "I hope they still have those frosted ones." Hayley took two steps, stopped and turned around. "I'll get you both cookies too, okay?

Mommy made the chocolate chip ones and they're really yummy," she told Dillon before running off.

And so he was stuck.

"Thanks for coming," Nina said.

He nodded and looked over the people milling around the room. Anywhere but at Nina. Not when she stood so close and looked so good in her black slacks, high-heeled boots and clingy, red turtleneck sweater.

She shifted her coat from her left arm to her right. "Uh…so did you enjoy the show?"

Was she kidding? But she seemed serious enough. And very nervous. He wasn't about to feel bad about the things he'd said to her. A man had the right to protect himself.

"Emma and Hayley's song was the best," he said, since Nina still looked at him expectantly.

She smiled. "True. Although I thought the Christmas rap song the fourth grade did was…unique."

He raised an eyebrow. "Not as unique as that kid in the elf costume who break-danced."

She laughed and several people close by sent them quizzical looks. Probably wondering what the hell she was doing talking to him, never mind what he was doing there in the first place.

Something he couldn't help but wonder about, as well.

"Nina."

She stiffened as Trey reached them. "Hello, Trey."

"You look lovely." He leaned forward as if to kiss her cheek, but she edged closer to Dillon's side. Trey narrowed his eyes but kept his fake smile firmly in place as he nodded toward Dillon. "Ward. What are you doing here?"

Dillon looked over Trey's shoulder to where Marcus was standing with his grandparents and stepmother. Remembered what the kid had said the other day about Trey telling Marcus not to talk to him. "My sister's stepdaughter was in the pageant."

"Yes, I saw Jack and his new wife. You didn't sit with them."

"Hayley invited Dillon to come tonight," Nina said, shocking the hell out of him. And, by the lemon-sucking expression on Trey's pretty-boy face, him, too. "Dillon's been so great with both the kids—"

"Are you telling me," Trey asked as he stepped closer to them, "that you allow a murderer around our children?"

"Dillon's past is just that," Nina said. "It has nothing to do with the man he is now."

"He killed a man. A fact you seemed to have conveniently forgotten. While your naiveté is…refreshing…" Trey's voice practically dripped with condescension. What a prick. "I need to know I can trust you to keep our children safe."

Nina drew herself up to her full height. "I'd never do anything to endanger my children. They're safe with me. And with Dillon."

Trey shook his head as if he couldn't believe what he was hearing. "I hate to do this, Nina, but if you insist on associating with criminals, you leave me no choice." He nodded a greeting to a middle-aged woman who passed by and then turned back to Nina. "I'm going to ask the court to grant me full custody."

Nina's face lost its color but before she could respond, Dillon said, "No need for the courts to get involved. I'm leaving town in a few days."

"No." Nina pushed past him to face Trey. "You can't bully me, Trey. If you want to take me to court, go right ahead." She shook her hair back, her back ramrod straight. She looked like a fluffy haired, pissed-off Christmas angel. "But I'll fight you every step of the way. I'll fight back."

Dillon couldn't help but lay his hand on her lower back. He just hoped she could feel what he couldn't say. That he was behind her—literally and figuratively. That he believed in her.

Trey pinched the bridge of his nose. "Nina, what have you gotten yourself tangled up in this time? I warned you about getting involved with him. How could you be so stupid?"

"Watch it," Dillon warned.

Trey kept his eyes on Nina. "You've always suffered from low self-esteem." To anyone who happened to overhear, Trey's voice had just the right mixture of earnestness and caring.

But Dillon saw the anger in his eyes.

"That," he continued, "plus the loneliness and inadequacy... That must be why you're behaving irrationally."

"You really are a piece of work," Dillon said in awe. He glanced at Nina. "You aren't buying any of this, are you?"

"Not a word." But her voice shook. "Shall we go, Dillon?"

She took his arm, but before they got away from

Trey, her ex said, "For God's sake, Nina, have some self-respect. Do you want everyone here to know you're his whore?"

"No," Nina pleaded softly when Dillon took a step forward. His hands were already fisted and he could taste the need for violence, for vengeance for everything Trey had ever said and done to Nina, on his tongue. "Please don't," she said, pulling on his arm. "He's not worth it. Let's just walk away."

He somehow allowed Nina to tow him along. One step. Then another. But at the third step, Trey's low laugh reached him.

"She must've really improved in bed since I was with her."

Then, the only things Dillon heard were Nina's soft gasp and his own blood roaring in this ears.

And the sound of bones cracking when his fist connected with Trey's pointy nose.

CHAPTER FIFTEEN

BLAIRE HANDED NINA a wet paper towel. "Here. You have some blood on your cheek."

"You're kidding." Nina grabbed the paper towel and raced into the small bathroom off Blaire's kitchen. After leaving the school, she'd driven straight to her sister's house with the kids—she wasn't about to let go with Trey after what he'd pulled—then sent Marcus and Hayley upstairs to play with their cousins. Quickly, she filled Blaire in on what had happened.

Nina switched on the bathroom light and grimaced at what she saw in the mirror. She scrubbed at the tiny dots of blood covering her right cheek and jawline.

Dots of Trey's blood.

Who knew a broken nose splattered blood like that?

"This is a nightmare," she said as she returned to the kitchen. "I can't believe Dillon punched Trey. At the Christmas pageant, in front of everyone!"

Blaire poured red wine into two tall glasses. "Well, I can't believe I missed it. Of all the years to skip the cookies and punch. You think anyone got it on tape? Just about everyone there had a video camera."

"God, how would I know?" Nina perched on one of the high-backed stools at the wide, granite-topped island. With its stainless steel appliances and dark cherry cabinets, the room was a gourmet cook's dream. She shook her head when Blaire set a glass in front of her. "I can't drink this."

"Honey, if anyone needs a drink, it's you."

True. Nina lifted her glass with a trembling hand and sipped.

Blaire sat across the island from her. "So tell me what happened after Dillon punched that bastard."

"Not much to tell. Trey stood there, blood gushing—"

"Did he do a Marcia Brady?"

Nina frowned. "What?"

"You know." Blaire covered her nose with both hands. "'Oh, my nose!'"

A smile tugged at Nina's lips. She fought it. "No, he sort of grunted and swayed and then…well…he passed out."

"What a wimp," Blaire scoffed. She crossed her legs and sipped her own wine. "Okay, so Trey's passed out on the floor, I assume pandemonium broke out amongst the kiddies and their parents—"

"Not quite," Nina mumbled, remembering how the gym had gone almost completely silent. How everyone had stared at them. Pandemonium would've been preferable.

"What happened then?"

"Well, of course, Rachel rushed over to Trey and Dillon just…looked at me…" She shivered. She doubted she'd ever forget the expression on his face—the anger. The barely leashed violence. His white dress shirt splattered with blood. "And then he said he was sorry."

He'd said he was sorry but she'd turned away. Her

fears, her doubts, had all converged, and she'd realized that she didn't know Dillon Ward at all. She'd wanted to believe he was different. That he was more than his past. But what if he wasn't? What if everyone around her had been right?

And she'd been wrong. Wrong to believe in Dillon.

So she'd done the only thing she could. She'd gathered her children—who'd luckily been ushered into the hall by their grandparents—and walked away. Left Dillon standing in the middle of the room surrounded by people who mistrusted and feared him.

Left him to deal with it on his own.

"If you ask me," Blaire said, "Trey deserved a punch in the nose for what he said about you. Did he talk to you that way when you were married?"

Nina avoided her sister's shrewd gaze. But even now, she still couldn't admit how bad her marriage had been.

"That's not the point," she insisted, supporting her aching head in her hands, her elbows on the cool countertop. "Dillon kept telling me I needed to stand up for myself, be who I want to be, take control. But when I did that, when I asked him to walk away from Trey, he wouldn't."

Blaire reached over and squeezed Nina's knee. "Honey, he was defending your honor. That's nothing to be upset about, that's something to appreciate."

"But I didn't want him to defend me. I wanted to handle it on my own." She fisted her hands in her hair. "I was the one Trey insulted, Dillon should've respected me."

"He's a guy. What did you expect him to do? Even my mild-mannered husband would take exception to someone insulting me. What's this really about? You're not letting what Trey said get to you, are you?"

Nina wiped at the tears coursing down her cheeks. "I was scared," she admitted just above a whisper.

"Of Dillon?"

"Not of him—he wouldn't hurt me. But of the situation. Of his reaction." She groaned and squeezed Blaire's hand. "I'm such a coward."

"Oh, honey, you're not a coward." Blaire smoothed Nina's hair back. "But if you're not scared of Dillon, I can't help but wonder what you're so afraid of."

"Dillon kept telling me not to forget his past. What he'd done." What she hadn't wanted to face. "What if he was right? We both know I'm no good at reading people. Look at how Trey had me fooled."

"Dillon's not like Dad," Marcus said from behind them.

Nina wiped her eyes and got to her feet. "Marcus, what—"

"Dillon's not like Dad," her son insisted. "He'd never hurt anyone."

Nina crouched down and laid her hands on Marcus' stiff shoulders. "You know what happened tonight. Dillon hit your dad."

Marcus pulled away, his chin set stubbornly. "That's because sometimes you have to stand up for what's right and face down a bully, even if it's hard or gets you in trouble."

"Out of the mouths of babes," Blaire murmured.

Nina suddenly felt dizzy. She staggered and reached out for the stool for support. "Oh, my God. What did I do?"

She knew what she'd done. She'd blown it. Again.

But this time, she would make it right. No matter what it took.

"Can the kids spend the night?" she asked Blaire.

"Of course. What are you going to do?"

"I'm going after Dillon. But first, I have a phone call to make."

KYLE JOLTED AWAKE, his arms flailing as he fell out of the chair he'd been sprawled in to land on his hands and knees on the floor. "Huh? What?"

He squinted his eyes against the bright light and realized he'd woken up because someone had slammed a door hard enough to scare the crap out of him. As soon as the room stopped spinning—the result of pounding six beers in less than two hours—he was going to kick some serious ass.

"What the hell are you doing here?"

Kyle followed the sound of the voice to where Dillon stood in the middle of the kitchen, a major pissed-off expression on his face.

Kyle struggled back onto the chair. "I was waiting for you."

"How'd you get in?"

"It was easy." He reached under his knit hat to scratch the side of his head. "You should get a better lock."

Dillon's face turned so red that for a moment, Kyle thought the guy's head was going to explode. Boom! Like a cartoon or something. Which would be messy, but sort of cool, too.

"Well, Einstein," Dillon muttered under his breath,

"the next time you break into someone's apartment, you might want to close the door."

Kyle sat up. He hadn't shut the door? Weird. But that would explain why he was so cold. Despite the coat and hat.

He got to his feet and saved himself from a header by placing both hands flat on the wooden table. "Can I crash here tonight?"

"No."

"What?" he asked as Dillon left the room. He staggered after the man. "Why not?"

"Because you're stoned." Dillon went into his bedroom and switched on the light.

Kyle leaned against the doorway for support. "I'm not stoned. I just had a few beers—"

"You're wasted," he said, his voice cold and flat.

"So I got a little buzzed. What's the big deal?"

Dillon jerked open a drawer and took out a T-shirt, slapping the cloth against the top of the dresser. "The big deal is that you're underage, on probation and you skipped out on Hayley's pageant."

"I was going to go to the pageant thing," he mumbled, "but then I ran into a couple of buddies—"

"Bullshit." Dillon was as angry as Kyle had ever seen him. "You never planned to go."

"I told you," he declared between his teeth, "I was going to go." He snatched his hat off and hit it against his thigh. "Just let me crash on your couch and tomorrow I'll make it up to her. I've already missed my curfew—" Yeah. Three hours ago. "And if I go back to Joe and Karen's tonight, they're going to freak."

"Not my problem." Dillon sat on the bed and pulled

his shoes off. Threw them—literally threw them—into the closet. Kyle raised his eyebrows. The guy was seriously torqued about something. Then Dillon met Kyle's eyes and he couldn't move. "You promised Hayley you'd be there and you weren't. If you're not man enough to keep your promises, then you shouldn't make them."

"So I got a better offer. The kid'll get over it. Besides, she needs to learn how to handle disappointment."

Dillon stood, disgust clear on his face. "You're a hell of a teacher."

He shrugged out of his coat and let it drop to the floor. Kyle's mouth popped open.

"Dude, is that blood on your shirt?" he asked breathlessly. He moved into the room as Dillon, his movements jerky, unbuttoned his blood-splattered shirt, yanked it off and tossed it on top of the garbage can. "What happened? You get in a fight?"

"You need to leave. Call Joe to come and get you. Now."

A thought struck Kyle. "Holy shit. You didn't kill someone else, did you?" Dillon turned so quickly, so angrily, that Kyle backed up two steps. He held up his hands. "Hey, it was just a question."

"No, I didn't kill anyone," Dillon snapped as he bent and picked up his coat. "I broke Trey Carlson's nose."

"Nina's ex?" Kyle asked as he hurried after Dillon down the hallway and back into the kitchen. "Why'd you break his nose?"

"He deserved it." Dillon sat and pulled on his work boots.

"I thought you were at the pageant thing."

The guy yanked his laces so tight, Kyle thought they'd snap in two. "I was."

"You got into a fight at the Christmas Pageant? Bet that livened things up."

Dillon got up and put his coat back on. "Go. Home."

Kyle stood in the kitchen, staring at Dillon's back as he walked away. Just like that. What was it about him, Kyle, that made it so easy for people to just walk away?

To give up on him?

His chest tightened. He flew down the stairs, the cold air blasting his face. He caught up with Dillon at the back door to the bakery and swung him around.

"Who the hell do you think you are, riding my ass about disappointing Hayley? How do you think she felt about you beating on her old man?" Dillon flinched. "Yeah. That's what I thought."

"I screwed up." Dillon shrugged as if it didn't make a difference. "And don't worry about working tomorrow. You're off the hook."

Kyle began to shake. Just the cold, he told himself. "What are you talking about?"

"I shouldn't have given you the impression that if you worked hard enough to show remorse you'd be forgiven. That if you played by the rules you could have everything you wanted." The wind blew Dillon's hair. But it was as if nothing, not even the cold, could penetrate his tough exterior. "Life doesn't work out that way for guys like us. Yeah, you've got it good with the Roberts, but so what? You'll just screw it up. Hell, you already have. Think they'll give you another second chance? How much longer until they get tired and kick you to the curb?"

"Go to hell," Kyle spat, his fists clenched.

"Already on my way there, kid." Then he stepped inside and shut the door in Kyle's face.

He rubbed at his burning eyes. He hadn't cried since he was four; he sure wasn't going to bawl over some loser like Dillon Ward turning his back on him.

He shivered. And realized he'd left his favorite hat in Dillon's apartment. Halfway up the stairs, the queasiness in his stomach returned with a vengeance. He bent over the banister and threw up. When his stomach was empty, he wiped the back of his hand across his mouth and continued up the stairs on shaky legs.

In Dillon's kitchen, he searched through the cupboards until he found a clean glass. Got some water from the sink and rinsed the nasty taste out of his mouth. His head pounded. He couldn't stop shaking.

He wanted to go home.

Except, he didn't have a home, did he? He'd never had a home. Just a series of bedrooms in a series of houses. Each one sucked more than the last. They were never really his. Just as the foster parents weren't his parents. Weren't his family.

Except Joe and Karen.

What if he'd screwed up the best thing that'd ever happened to him?

Before he could change his mind, he picked up the phone on the table. Karen answered on the first ring, her voice laced with worry.

"It's me," he said. He used the heel of his hand to rub away the single tear that slid down his cheek. "Can you…could you come get me? I want to come home."

DILLON STORMED THROUGH the bakery's kitchen and into the dining room. He headed for his tools but tripped over an empty paint can—a can he'd told Kyle to toss in the Dumpster yesterday. He cursed and viciously kicked the can across the room. It hit a chair with a loud crack and spun on its side.

He tipped his head back. Attempted to get his anger and his breathing under control. But it was no use. He wanted to kick the can again. Or the wall.

Or somebody's ass.

Kyle needed something—or someone—to shake him up. The kid was un-freaking-believable. And so like Kelsey as a teen—rebellious, unrepentant and way too cocky—that Dillon couldn't believe he'd come to hope Kyle would be okay. That he'd straighten his life out before it was too late.

One more hope shot all to hell.

He'd taken it upon himself to try to give the kid a hand, to help him out of a bad situation, but he'd learned his lesson. Again.

The only person he was looking out for from now on was himself.

He yanked the corner of a drop cloth up and whipped it over to the opposite edge. He folded it in half, crouched down and folded it again when someone entered through the back door. He froze, alert. His pulse racing.

Because only one person would show up there in the middle of the night. The last person he wanted to face.

"You don't want to be here," he told Nina.

"Yes. I do." She stepped farther into the room. "I've

been so worried. I stopped by the police station but they said you'd been released."

He laid the drop cloth on top of his lockbox and began folding the next one. As per his shitty luck, Jack Martin witnessed Dillon breaking Trey's nose and, in his capacity as chief of police, had arrested Dillon for aggravated assault.

He flexed and clenched his sore right hand. At least Jack hadn't handcuffed him. Not that his night could've gotten much worse—not after Nina turned her back on him.

When he didn't speak, she said, "I didn't know what to do so I called Allie—"

"You told Allie?" he asked, making the mistake of facing her. She was so damn beautiful it hurt just to look at her.

"I thought maybe she could help," Nina said uncertainly.

Allie had helped. She'd saved him from his worst nightmare—being locked up again. Even if it would've only been a night in the local jail.

Too bad he couldn't find it in himself to be grateful.

"When I was at the station," Nina continued, "I told Jack what happened, what Trey said—"

"I don't want anything from you."

She flinched. "What are you doing?"

"I'm packing my stuff." He tossed his paint trays and rollers into the lockbox and shut the lid. "Hire someone else to finish the painting or do it yourself. Either way, I'm done."

"What? No. Dillon, please, listen, I—"

"Save it." He tucked the drop cloths under his arm and picked up his toolbox. "I'm not interested."

"I realize you're angry," she said, walking backward and blocking his way as he tried to cross the room. "And I don't blame you but when I left, it wasn't because of you. I had to get the kids out of there. I didn't want them to see—"

"You don't owe me anything." He moved to the right but she blocked him. "Least of all an explanation."

He should've left weeks ago when she kicked him out of the apartment. Instead, he got sucked into caring about her and her kids and Kyle. Which just proved he shouldn't care about anyone. They just let you down.

He faked a move left, which she fell for, and then slipped past her on the right.

"I know you're angry, and I don't blame you," Nina repeated, following him through the kitchen. She pushed in front of him and plastered herself against the door. "But if you'd stop running away from me, from any problem we might have, maybe you'd see my side."

The flash of temper in her eyes made him pause. "Your side?"

"I asked you to walk away!" she cried.

"Because you were afraid of what I'd do to him."

For a moment, she looked like she wouldn't mind punching Dillon in the nose.

"Because I didn't want you fighting my battles for me. Because I want to be with a man who listens to me and respects my wishes."

"Of course I respect you," he said, truly appalled.

"But not my decisions. Any time I don't act just as you think I should, you get pissed and walk away. I'm willing to accept you for who you are—why can't you do the same for me?"

He couldn't. Even though he knew she was right.

He scowled at her. "You're in my way."

The scowl had no effect. "I'm going to stay in your way until you listen to me. Dillon, I...I care about you."

He stepped forward. He didn't really want to scare her and he'd die before he'd physically hurt her, but if it took intimidation to get her to move, then he'd use his size and his anger to do it.

She stood her ground. "We both know Trey baited you into that fight. Why on earth did you fall for it?"

"I lost control." His fingers flexed on the handle of his toolbox. "Just like the night I killed Glenn."

"You were protecting Kelsey—"

"I killed a man. And no one, least of all me, is ever going to forget that."

He couldn't let himself forget. Or forgive.

"What happened tonight is different."

"Then why didn't you want me to protect you?" he asked, feeling as if the words were ripped from his throat. He dropped the cloths and toolbox, which clanged against the floor. Nina jumped, her eyes wide. She opened her mouth, but he didn't give her a chance to speak. "I'll tell you why. You were afraid of me. Afraid I'd lose control."

"No. God, no. That had nothing to do with it." Her eyes welled with tears and she blinked furiously. "I wasn't afraid of you. But maybe I was...I hate to even admit this but...I *was* worried about causing a scene. Worried about what people would think."

He snorted. "I used to believe in doing what's right,

too. I spent half my life toeing the line, trying to protect my mother, staying after Kelsey to keep out of trouble but none of it did me one damn bit of good when it mattered."

She nodded. "The police in your hometown let you down."

He narrowed his eyes. "What do you know about it?"

"I…I called Kelsey tonight. I had to know," she rushed on when he swore. "I wanted to understand what happened that night."

"What's to understand? I lost control."

Tears streaked down her face. "No. You protected your sister from being raped. You saved yourself and her." She stretched her hand out to him but he stepped back, out of reach. Hurt, she slowly lowered her arm. "But the judge who sentenced you didn't know that, did he? He was never shown pictures of Kelsey taken after the attack. Never heard Kelsey's statement."

"You think I got an unfair sentence, cupcake?" he asked fiercely as he once more closed the distance between them. "You think I should've been let go after what I did with that bat?"

He grabbed her by the upper arms and yanked her up onto her toes. She gasped but didn't try to pull away from him. "You feeling sorry for me because my own mother wouldn't testify on my behalf? Because she not only blamed me for taking her husband but she turned her back on me like she always did, even when I was protecting her from Glenn?"

Nina, sobbing openly now, pressed her hands against his chest. "Like I turned away from you tonight. Oh,

Dillon," she said, barely above a whisper. "I'm so very sorry."

No, damn it. He didn't want her pity and he sure as hell didn't want her apology. He wanted to be free of her.

"You don't get it." His throat hurt. "I don't deserve pity or apologies. I spent five years in prison. Five years that turned me into a man I didn't want to be. And tonight just proves I'm still that same guy, minus the prison uniform. I have no hope. No control." His voice broke. "I have nothing."

"That's not true." She lifted his face until their eyes met. "You have me."

CHAPTER SIXTEEN

DILLON SHOOK HIS head and let go of her. He tried to step back but Nina clung to him. No way would she let him go. Not now. Not ever.

"Listen to me," she demanded, "you do have me. I admire your strength and patience and sense of honor. Even if you don't believe in yourself, in your worth, I do."

She rose on her toes, pulled his head down and kissed him, pouring everything she had, everything she felt for him, into the kiss. His mouth was unyielding under hers. She wrapped her arms around his neck and pressed against him. Nibbled gently on his lower lip before stroking the seam of his lips with her tongue.

He groaned, shoved his hands in her hair and held her head while he took over the kiss. Her immediate relief was replaced by mindless passion when Dillon yanked her sweater down and kissed her neck. She let her head fall back against the door. His other hand went under her shirt to cup her breast. He rubbed his work-roughened palms across her nipples until her thigh muscles weakened.

Frantic with need, with love for him, she slipped her hands under his shirt and returned the favor. Scraped her nails lightly over his nipples. He moaned into her mouth, pressed his hips against her.

They tore at each other's clothes. She knew nothing other than the sensations roaring through her body and her desperate need for him. While she fumbled with the button on his jeans, he shoved her clothes down her legs. Took off her shoe and pulled her left leg free. She managed to get his jeans unbuttoned and he made quick work of his zipper. Kicked his clothing aside while she stroked him.

He hissed out a breath and kissed her again while he gripped one of her thighs in each of his hands. She guided him to her opening, swirled the tip of his erection around her moisture. His fingers dug into her skin as he entered her in one smooth move.

The feel of Dillon inside her, stretching her, felt so delicious, so incredible, she arched her hips in an attempt to take him deeper. He lifted her legs, wrapping them around his waist. She crossed her ankles as he pumped into her, banging her against the door with each powerful thrust.

She squeezed her thighs together as the tension built and coiled through her system. Her shirt stuck to her skin, her hair damp with sweat. He shifted his hands to her butt, bent his knees and increased their already frantic tempo. Her orgasm built, fast and intense, overtaking her body and her senses.

Dillon pressed his face into her neck, dug his fingers into her rear and emptied himself inside her with a low moan.

She unlocked her ankles and lowered her legs. Luckily, he still supported her as her muscles had disintegrated. She laid her head against his shoulder, inhaled his scent.

And couldn't help but smile.

Everything would be okay. She knew it now, was as certain of it as she'd ever been of anything in her life. She and Dillon were meant to be together.

"I was thinking," she said, running her fingers through his hair, "since you said you didn't have plans for the holidays, you could come to my parents' on Christmas Eve. My mom does this whole big dinner with everyone at the house. Turkey, the works and—"

Dillon cursed. A chill racked her body as he let go of her and pulled his pants up.

She pushed aside her worry as she got dressed. "Is something wrong?"

"I'm not going to be here for Christmas Eve," he said flatly. He yanked his zipper up and buttoned his jeans. Picked his keys up off the floor. "Nothing's changed."

Her mouth popped open. "Of course things have changed. Starting with me." She grabbed his keys out of his hand and strode to the middle of the kitchen. "And by God, you're going to stay right here until I prove it."

She dug her cell phone out of her purse and dialed the familiar number. Listened to it ring. It was past time Dillon had someone stand up for him.

And when she was done standing up for him, if he still wouldn't listen to reason, then she'd just have to stand up *to* him. Even if it meant knocking some sense into his thick head.

DILLON KNEW HE should leave but short of wrestling his keys away from her, he was stuck.

Plus, his damn curiosity got the better of him.

"Mom," Nina said into the phone. "It's me."

His head snapped back in surprise.

"No, no. Everyone's fine," she said. "I'm sorry to call so late but I wanted you to know I'm with Dillon." She took a deep breath. "And I plan on being with him. No matter what."

Tears filled her eyes and he turned away. It killed him to see her upset, to know he was the cause of it. Why did she have to be so stubborn?

"I'm sorry you feel that way," Nina said and he glanced at her. She held the phone so tightly, her knuckles were white. Her eyes were on him as she said, "Yes, I know you're worried about me but, Mom, I'm…I'm not a child anymore, okay? You have to trust me. Trust my decisions." She used the back of her hand to wipe away a couple of tears. "Even if you don't agree with me, I need you to trust me."

There was a pause and then Nina shook her head and, in a show of emotional strength that shook Dillon, she said, "Then I guess there's nothing left to say."

She cut the connection and carefully set the phone on the table.

"Why'd you do that?" he demanded.

"I wanted to show you I meant what I said." Her voice was unsteady and she kept blinking.

"Alienating your family isn't going to change my decision. All you've done is made things worse."

"No, I haven't. Not for me—things are going to be much better. I stood up for myself." She cleared her throat. "I'm strong enough to live with regrets. And I'm ready to start living for myself."

His frustration—at her family, at her for not letting well enough alone and at himself for letting his guard down in the first place, for wanting her as much as he did—threatened to boil over. "Damn it," he exploded, his fists clenched, his arms shaking with the effort it took to not punch a hole in the wall. "Now do you see that this...thing between us is only going to hurt you?"

"No. All I see is that it's past time my family trusted me to make the right decisions for myself and for my kids." She closed the distance between them and he had to force himself not to back up, especially when she took his hand in hers. "And no matter whether my parents like it or not, I know what I want. You."

The emotion in her voice and the warmth in her eyes made it impossible for him to speak.

"I want to be with you. I care about you. And I trust you—with my kids and—" she laid his hand over her breast "—with my heart. Dillon, I love you."

"Don't say that," he snapped, yanking his hand away.

"Why not?" She smiled at him. "It's the truth. I love you."

Did she have to repeat it? The way Nina turned her back on him earlier, the way Kyle let him down tonight, only proved that hope was for fools.

"You're delusional if you want someone with my history by your side," he said, "and part of your kids' lives. You think you can trust me? Depend on me? Lady, you barely know me."

"I see you clearly. Do you?"

"I'm not dependable." He hardened his heart against the hurt in her eyes and went for the final blow. "And from what I've seen, neither are you."

She stepped back. "No. Don't say that. I made a mistake—"

"We've both made mistakes. Let's not make them worse." He held out his hand. "Now, be a good girl and give me my keys."

AS IF IN A TRANCE, Nina dropped Dillon's keys into his palm and walked away. It wasn't until she reached the table that anger began to trickle through the pain.

She didn't even realize she'd picked up her cell phone until it hit the door—barely missing Dillon's head.

He jumped and turned around. "What the hell—"

"How dare you throw my feelings back at me and then just pat me on the head?" Her voice was raw. She stormed over to the counter, grabbed the half-empty bag of flour and heaved it with all of her might.

He ducked. The bag exploded in a white haze against the wall, covering Dillon's head and shoulders. "Damn it, Nina—"

She marched over to the baking racks and started unloading day-old donuts at him. He didn't even move as they hit him on his chest, just stared at her as if she'd lost her mind. Who knew? Maybe she had. It was about time. "I've already given up so much, lost so much all these years by worrying about meeting other people's expectations." She squeezed a donut so hard butter cream filling oozed out. "And if I don't fight for what I want, I'll continue to lose more of myself and my kids' respect."

And worse, much worse, she'd lose Dillon.

With both arms she swept the counter clear. Dishes,

mixing bowls, utensils, sugar and flour crashed to the ground.

"Nina," Dillon said firmly, "that's enough."

But it wasn't. The way she felt, it would never be enough.

She shoved the rolling baking rack toward him. It teetered and fell over with a loud crash, rolls and muffins scattering across the floor. "Do you know how long I let Trey tell me 'enough'?" She picked up a rolling pin.

"Don't even think about it," he warned.

She couldn't say the thought didn't cross her mind but she still had enough self-control that she didn't whip it at his head. But she did fling it to the side. It hit an upper cabinet, denting the wood before falling into the sink. "I didn't walk away from my marriage even though I knew Trey was cheating on me." She threw a loaf of raisin bread at Dillon's stubborn, beautiful head.

"Hey." He batted it away. "Damn it."

"I stayed married to someone who made me feel so bad about myself that I started to believe I was as worthless as he claimed." She flipped a chair over. "When Trey left, you know what I felt? Relieved. I didn't mind being thought of as Poor Nina because I was free. But I should've minded, I should've set people straight."

She should've been the one to walk away.

All this time she thought no one had faith in her because they felt sorry for her—for Trey leaving. For all the mistakes she'd made. But how could they believe in her when she didn't believe in herself?

Bone weary and as spent as if she'd just run a marathon, she let her hand drop to her side. "I'm through doing what's expected," she said quietly, her words seeming even softer after the noise of her trashing her kitchen. "I love you."

He stepped forward, the expression on his face conflicted. "Nina—"

She held up her hand to stop him. "But even though I love you and want to have a future with you, even though I want you to love me back," she said, her voice breaking, "I'm strong enough to let you go if that's what you want."

For a second, she thought he'd take her into his arms. But then he bent, picked up his toolbox and walked out the door.

Leaving her to slide down the wall, lay her head on her knees and cry alone in the mess she'd made.

THE WEEKEND PASSED in a blur for Nina. After Dillon walked out, she'd sat in the kitchen until her tears and anger were spent. Leaving only the pain. Leaving her to wonder what she could've done differently. What she should've said to convince him to stay. What she should do next.

That's when she knew she'd do what she always did next. She'd get up, brush herself off and take care of her kids and her business.

And worry about getting through each day one at a time.

Facing the destruction she'd caused in her kitchen hadn't been easy but cleaning it had been therapeutic. Even if it had taken her the rest of the night and a good chunk of the morning.

She hadn't seen Dillon again but she'd heard him go up and down the stairs as he hauled his possessions out of the apartment. When Lacy showed up for work Friday morning, she seemed to know better than to ask Nina why she looked like hell. Instead, she ushered Nina out the door, promising she'd take care of everything as long as Nina went home and got some rest.

When Nina returned a few hours later—she hadn't slept but she had showered and felt marginally human—Dillon's tools and truck were gone. Lacy had silently handed Nina the keys to both the apartment and the bakery that Dillon had left. That was it. No note. No goodbye.

She'd willed back tears. Stuck the keys into her pocket and knew she'd get through.

And the first step in getting through was to contact her attorney about revisiting her custody agreement with Trey. After Trey had threatened to fight for full custody—and the ugly way he'd acted at the pageant—Nina hadn't wanted to let her kids near him, even for his weekend visit. Except her attorney was worried that keeping the kids from Trey would backfire and hurt her chances of winning any future custody battles.

Not to mention Trey would probably have the police legally enforce his visitation rights.

So she'd had Trey pick the kids up from Blaire's house Friday afternoon. And she hadn't stopped worrying about them since.

The only bright spot of the weekend was when Kyle showed up and offered to finish the work Dillon started. He'd seemed so sincere—and almost as hurt as Nina was by Dillon leaving them—that she couldn't say no. Thank God she hadn't. The changes in him were subtle but noticeable.

Truth be told, he was capable of being a nice kid. Who knew?

Sunday afternoon, she flipped the Closed sign on the front door. "Wow, it looks wonderful," she said. "You did a great job."

Kyle, tapping a lid onto a can of half-used paint, shrugged and ducked his head, but she didn't miss his small smile.

She leaned back against the table next to him. "So, I guess that's it, huh? You're all finished?"

"Yeah. I guess."

She checked her watch and tried not to worry that Trey was ten minutes late bringing the kids home. She couldn't get in to meet with her attorney until after Christmas but once she did, Nina was going to do whatever it took to keep her kids safe.

"I was wondering," she said, as an idea popped into her head. She started to question herself, but she needed to trust her instincts. If she made a mistake, she'd deal with it later. "What do you think about working here part-time?"

He looked up at her from underneath his shaggy bangs. "You mean, work for you?"

"That's the plan. How about…three days a week to start, including one weekend day. We'll see how it goes and if you want more hours than that."

"I don't have to bake anything, do I?"

"Do you know how to bake?"

"Hell…uh…I mean, heck no."

She laughed. "You'll be working up front and maybe waiting tables if need be. The tips are pretty good."

"Sure. That'd be cool."

"Great." See? Things would be okay. Life goes on, and all that. The door opened and, to her immense relief, Marcus ran inside. "Hey. How was your weekend—"

"Fine," he mumbled as he rushed past her.

She stopped him before he made it to the kitchen. "What's the matter?" He shook his head and she knelt down, placed a finger under his chin and turned his face toward her.

Everything inside of her froze to see the tear tracks on his face. And the bright red spot on his left cheek.

"What happened?" She forced the words out.

"Nothing," he said trying to pull out of her hold.

Hayley came in and threw herself at Nina, almost knocking her off balance.

"Mommy," her little girl cried, "I don't want to go to Daddy's house anymore. He hit Marcus!"

CHAPTER SEVENTEEN

NINA SAW RED. She was surprised steam didn't billow from her ears. She patted Hayley on the back. "Okay, okay. Calm down so we can all talk about this." She turned to Marcus. "Is that true? Did your father hit you?"

He lowered his eyes and nodded. She pulled him to her and held him tight.

"Daddy told Rachel he didn't think you deserved to keep us," Hayley said, laying her head against Nina's shoulder. "He called you a bad word and Marcus told him to stop it and Daddy hit him."

After what Trey had said at the Christmas Pageant, she can only imagine what he'd called her. And her poor baby had tried to stand up for her, tried to do the right thing and gotten hurt.

Oh, God. She'd followed the rules, done the right thing legally and her son had gotten hurt. She was done playing by anyone's rules but her own. Starting right now.

"Where's your dad?" she asked Hayley.

Hayley sniffled. "He's talking to some old lady out on the sidewalk."

"Okay." She nodded and turned to Marcus. "I'm so sorry this happened."

"It's not your fault," he said.

"It is," she said firmly. "But I'm going to take care of it. I'm not going to let your father hurt you ever again. I'm proud of you." She gently cupped his cheek and attempted a smile. "Kyle," she said knowing he'd clearly heard their conversation, "could you please take Marcus and Hayley into the kitchen for a snack?"

"Sure." He picked Hayley up and touched Marcus on the shoulder. "Come on, guys."

They pushed through the kitchen door just as Trey came inside. At least he looked like hell. She'd avoided him since the night of the pageant but now she wished she'd faced him earlier. He had a bandage on his swollen nose and both eyes were black.

She couldn't find it in herself to feel even the tiniest bit sorry for him. As a matter of fact, she wished Dillon had hit him even harder.

"Where are the kids?" Trey asked.

"What did you do to Marcus?"

"Obviously they get their overly dramatic tendencies from your side of the family." He made a show of looking around. "I see Ward's truck is gone. Dare I hope you've come to your senses and he's left for good?"

"Dillon is none of your concern," she said fiercely, "and neither am I. Now what did you do to my son? Did you hit him?"

He narrowed his eyes. "Don't overreact," he said as if he was talking to a deranged person. "Marcus mouthed off to me so I gave him a little love tap."

"You left a handprint! That's abuse."

"I said it was nothing. Just a disagreement between a father and his son. And none of your concern."

"What happens to my children is always my concern."

He waved his hand in the air as if swatting away a pesky gnat. "Don't blow this out of proportion like you did at the pageant. You and I both know Ward's vicious attack on me was unprovoked." He lightly pressed two fingers to the bridge of his nose and winced. "You should've known better than to bring him to the school. Honestly, Nina." He sighed. "I blame myself for how low you sunk in order to get attention from not only the opposite sex, but from your family—and, I suspect, me, as well."

She shook her head, not sure she heard him correctly. "What are you talking about?"

He looked at her with such pity, she almost bared her teeth and growled at him. "It's obvious you were, in some sense, trying to punish me for leaving you. And trying to make me jealous of your relationship with him."

She rubbed at her temple. "You are unbelievable."

"And you are in serious denial." He patted her arm and she twisted out of his reach. "You're obviously in no mood to see reason. We'll discuss this when I pick the kids up Thursday night."

He walked away and opened the door.

"No," she said, proud of how strong her voice sounded. How steady.

He turned back. "Excuse me?"

"No, you can't manipulate me and the situation to your own benefit. No, I'm not going to listen to your reason—not ever again." She laid her hand over her queasy stomach. "And no, you won't be picking the kids up Thursday."

There was nothing overtly threatening in the way Trey walked back toward her but that didn't stop her heart from racing. Her palms from sweating.

"Of course I'll pick them up on Thursday," he said as if speaking to a recalcitrant child. "Our custody agreement clearly states that I get them every Thursday night."

"I'm going to petition the court first thing Monday morning to have your custodial rights terminated until you get the help you need to control your temper." Though it was one of the hardest things she'd ever done, she stood her ground. Even when he moved closer. "I won't let you have the kids until I know for certain they'll be safe with you."

His mouth flattened. "And you really think they'll grant it?" He shook his head. "Nina, everyone in town knows you've changed. If you go to court, the entire town will know the only reason you're doing this is to get back at me. They'll see it for what it is, a cry for help. Just as they'll see you for who you are. A woman out for revenge."

"Some people might believe you," she admitted. "You are, after all, a respected member of town. And those same people will wonder about my true motives. I'm sure there'll be talk. Whispers and rumors."

He smiled. "I'm glad you see things my way."

"You didn't let me finish," she said coldly. "There will be whispers and rumors. And I couldn't care less."

Two bright spots of anger appeared in his cheeks. Something flashed in his eyes, something that warned her he'd lost his battle with his temper but before she could move, he slapped her, hard, across the face.

"You'll do no such thing," he told her as he grabbed her upper arms in a grip so tight, she knew from experience she'd have bruises tomorrow morning. "You think you can embarrass me publicly?"

"Get the hell away from her!"

Kyle came flying out of the kitchen and tried to pull Trey away from her. Trey went right for Kyle's weak spot—his bandaged wrist—seized the teen's hand and twisted. Kyle cried out and Nina, her cheek stinging, her eyes watering, picked up the first thing she saw—a sheet of cookies off the top of the display case.

Cookies flew in every direction, scattered on the floor as she hit Trey on the shoulder as hard as she could. He roared, probably more from anger than pain but she didn't care. He let go of Kyle, who immediately placed himself between Nina and her ex.

She stepped forward so she and Kyle were side by side and held the tray like a baseball player ready to hit a home run. "Get out of here," she told him, so furious her voice shook, "or I swear to God, I'll knock you upside the head. You're nothing but a bully and I refuse to be bullied anymore."

Trey rubbed the shoulder she'd hit. "You'll regret this," he said, his eyes bright. "I'll take you to court and sue for full custody of the kids."

"Oh, please do. I'd love nothing better than to tell everyone in town exactly what type of man you really are."

"You'll be hearing from my lawyer," he promised before slamming the door shut behind him.

Her arms trembled as she lowered the pan. She felt light-headed with relief—and triumph. She did it. She'd stood up to Trey and had actually gotten him to back off.

It'd been the scariest thing she'd ever done. But she did it anyway.

"Mommy? Are you okay?" Hayley asked from the doorway. She and Marcus wore identical wide-eyed expressions.

"I'm fine. How about you?" she asked Kyle.

"I'm good." But he held his wrist in his free hand and his face was strained. He lowered his voice. "Would you have really hit him over the head with that?"

Nina followed his gaze to the pan now leaning against her leg. She glanced at her kids huddled together and then back at Kyle. "Oh, yeah," she said with a smile. "I would've kicked his ass."

DILLON STARED THROUGH his truck's windshield at Kelsey and Jack's house. White icicle lights hung from the porch, while colored lights decorated the small bushes and a leafless tree in front of the picture window. Snow fell gently, giving the yard a pristine cover of white.

Like a Norman Rockwell Christmas Eve.

His hands tightened on the steering wheel. He could only imagine how excited Emma and Hayley and Marcus were tonight about Santa's impending visit.

He wished he could see them, see the excitement in their eyes. Hear their giggles. Hell, he wouldn't even mind seeing Kyle's perpetual smirk or hearing the kid's never-ending sarcasm.

Mostly, he wanted to see Nina.

The door to the house opened and Kelsey came outside and ran across the yard. She wore a denim miniskirt, a snug, long-sleeved top and a pair of snow boots.

Must be her version of holidaywear.

She opened the passenger door and climbed in. "You coming inside?" she asked as she shut the door and shivered. "You've been sitting out here for fifteen minutes."

"No." He couldn't make himself get out of the truck. "I just wanted to drop off a few things."

She flicked the heat up higher and held her hands out over the vents. "Like what?"

His cheeks warmed. He was too old and way too cynical to get embarrassed. He jerked a thumb to the bags on the seat in the extended cab behind him.

She grinned. "Dillon, are you playing Santa Claus?"

"Look, I saw something I thought Emma would like and I got it, okay?"

She widened her eyes and held up her hands. "Hey, it's okay with me. You can buy her presents whenever you want."

"Good," he muttered.

"So, where'd you run off to after punching Trey Carlson?"

"I didn't run anywhere."

"Please," she said with an exaggerated eye roll, "you were like one of those cartoon characters, you know when they take off so fast they leave puffs of smoke behind."

"Where do you get this stuff?"

"Vivid imagination." When he just shook his head, she grinned. "Hey, believe me, Jack appreciates how imaginative I can be."

He dropped his head so that his forehead smacked against the steering wheel. "I'm in hell."

And there wasn't a damn thing he could do about it.

"If you're in hell, it's certainly not because of me or my husband's appreciation of my many talents. But, wherever you've been hiding yourself the past five days," Kelsey said, "you missed all the excitement."

He lifted his head. "I've had about all the excitement I can stand, thanks."

"Well, yeah, punching a guy in front of a bunch of kids and their parents was pretty exciting, but that's not what I'm talking about." When he didn't say anything she turned in her seat and bent one leg under the other. "Oh, don't beg, I'll tell you what happened. Seems Nina has filed for full custody of her kids. From the sounds of it, it's going to be a nasty court battle."

"What? Why would she do that now?"

"Probably because she's accusing Trey of child abuse."

Dillon went rigid. "Tell me everything you know."

"Okay, but you have to remember I'm getting my information mostly from Hayley. Nina won't talk about it even when I asked her outright." She scratched her knee. "All I know is that Trey slapped Marcus for something minor, Nina found out and went ballistic. When she confronted Trey, he hit her—"

"I'll kill him," Dillon said.

"Not so fast. Nina handled it. With a little help from Kyle. See, after Trey hit Nina, Kyle came to her rescue, except then he needed rescuing so Nina ended up whacking her slimy ex with some sort of cookie tray."

He almost smiled at the image. He wished he

could've been there to see Nina and Kyle take that ass-hole down a couple of notches. "But they're all okay, right? Nina and Kyle and Marcus?"

"No permanent damage done." She studied him, her green eyes steady. "Although I'm not sure why you'd care if they were hurt. I mean, you were the one who took off."

He slid her a narrow look. "Why don't you leave the reverse psychology to me? You suck at it."

"Fine. Then I'll just straight out ask. What are you doing? Why are you throwing away this chance? It's obvious Nina's in love with you."

Damn it, didn't she think he knew that? Hadn't he re-played Nina telling him she loved him a thousand times? Did she think he didn't wish things could be different?

"It doesn't matter. I'm no good for her. Even if you or she can't see that, everyone else in town does."

"What else do you expect from them when you glower at anyone who looks at you? The only reason people haven't given you a chance is because you won't let them."

He wanted to deny it, but he couldn't. Not when he knew she was right.

"You'd better get back inside," he said, his throat tight, "get back to your family."

"Argh!" She slapped his arm. "What is wrong with you? You'd rather hold on to your past than take a chance on loving someone as awesome as Nina? Aren't Nina and her kids worth the risk? Aren't you?" She fell back against her seat and crossed her arms. "You're pretty dense, you know that? And that's not reverse psychology, either. Just the God's honest truth."

He grit his teeth. "This really has nothing to do with you."

"Bull. I'm your sister and I love you. And you love me, too, which is why you helped me face my fears about marrying Jack. About being Emma's mother. Can't you see you're facing those same fears? But you're letting them win. And that's not the brother I knew growing up."

"What if he's gone?" Dillon asked quietly. "What if I'm never able to get back to the man I was? The man I want to be?"

Kelsey squeezed his arm. "Maybe it's time to let that man go. Yes, what happened to you, what you lived through changed you. It would change anyone. But deep inside you're still the same guy who ate dry cereal so I'd have the last of the milk. The brother who took care of me and protected me. And I'll always be grateful to the brother you were…but it's the man you are today that I want a relationship with, that Nina wants in her life."

"What if that man's not enough?"

"What if he is," she asked, "but you're too scared to find out?"

He'd spent the past four nights in a dive motel about sixty miles down the interstate. Sure, he'd been eating and sleeping and breathing—but not really living. Just like when he'd been in prison and his main concern had been to just get through each day—and worse, the endless nights.

Now, he'd created his own prison by shutting out the people he cared about. Who cared about him.

He really was acting like a coward.

"Get the gifts and get out," he said.

Kelsey's face fell. Before she had a chance to move, he covered her hand with his and squeezed her fingers.

"I'll stop by tomorrow to see Emma, but right now I need you to get out so I can go get my family." He grinned at her. "I'm late for Christmas Eve dinner."

NINA STOOD IN her mother's kitchen and spooned mashed potatoes into a serving bowl while her mom hurried out the door carrying a platter of sliced ham. The doorbell rang, and Nina glanced at Blaire. "Are we expecting anyone else?"

"Not that I know of." Blaire took the pan of sweet potato casserole out of the oven. "Luke probably invited one of his friends and forgot to tell Mom." Blaire grinned at her as she used her hip to shut the oven door. "Guess it runs in the family."

"Hey, I told Mom I'd invited Kyle and Joe and Karen." When she'd found out Joe and Karen had no other family, she'd gladly extended the invitation that they join her family for dinner. The more the merrier.

Especially since the more people around meant she kept busy pretending she didn't care that Dillon was gone. Or that she hadn't cried herself to sleep every night since he left.

"Do we have everything?" Blaire asked.

Nina picked up the bowl of potatoes and looked around the cluttered kitchen. "Yep. Let's eat. I'm starved," she said, forcing a smile.

"That smile is just pitiful and not fooling anyone. You sure you're okay?"

"I will be." She pursed her lips at Blaire's disbelieving look. "Really. I mean, I don't have any other choice, do I?"

"Hmm...I guess not. But you know, if you ever want to talk about it—"

"I know," Nina said. The idea of discussing Dillon held about as much appeal as eating unsweetened baking chocolate. "Thanks. But I'm okay."

Blaire nodded and went out the door. Nina's shoulders sagged. Not that she didn't appreciate her family's concern because she did, but she wouldn't mind if they'd give it a rest. At least for Christmas.

After she'd stood up to Trey, she'd finally found the courage to tell her family what her marriage had been like. How Trey had treated her. They'd been hurt that she hadn't come to them sooner, and while they weren't quite ready to embrace her feelings for Dillon, they were willing to give her the benefit of the doubt. That she knew what she wanted and what was best for her and the kids.

And they'd promised to support her no matter what happened. Which was all she'd ever wanted. And what she'd need if she went after Dillon like she planned.

But she wasn't going after him tonight. Right now, she just needed to get through the holiday. She took a deep breath, plastered a smile on her face and walked out of the kitchen. And slammed to a stop when her mother led Dillon into the dining room.

His eyes immediately locked on hers and so many emotions crashed through her at once—joy, hope and lingering anger that he'd left in the first place—she swayed from the force of them.

"Breathe," Blaire whispered as she came up beside her and took the bowl out of Nina's hands.

She let out a shaky breath, her eyes still on Dillon's. His coat was open and his T-shirt was wrinkled. He had a few days worth of dark stubble, his hair was mussed and dark smudges circled his eyes.

How she loved him.

For those few seconds, everyone seemed to freeze, but then Hayley gave a little cry of delight and launched herself at Dillon. Marcus followed suit, running over and hugging him around the waist while Blaire took her seat. Nina's father got to his feet but her mother touched his arm. Their eyes met and something passed between them, something that needed no words. Hank's shoulders relaxed and he slowly sat back down.

Nina's heart warmed as she looked at her parents. But Dillon didn't seem to notice her family's mini-drama. Instead, he closed his eyes and hugged Hayley close before shifting her to his hip so he could tousle Marcus's hair. "Hey, you two," he said gruffly. "I missed you." His mouth turned up in a lopsided grin as he looked at Kyle and then met her eyes again. "All of you."

"I thought you took off," Kyle said, his old sneer back in his voice.

"I did, but now I'm back."

"Nina," her father said, "why don't you take your… friend into the living room so you can talk?"

She wiped her hands down the side of her black suede skirt.

"That's not necessary, sir," Dillon said before she could move. "What I have to say, I can say in front of all of you." He searched her face. "That is, if Nina doesn't mind."

She nodded, just the barest of movements but he seemed to understand. He seemed so nervous, so unsure that she wanted to tell him to never mind. That he didn't have to tell her anything. That his being there, her daughter in his arms, his hand on her son's head was enough.

"First," he said to Marcus, "I want to apologize to you and your sister for not being around the past few days."

"Why'd you go away?" Hayley asked. "Was it something we did?"

"No, absolutely not." His mouth thinned. "The truth is, I was scared."

"You're not scared of anything," Marcus declared. "I know it."

"I *was* scared," Dillon said softly. "You see, I wanted to be with you and your sister and mother so much but I was scared you wouldn't want me. Scared I wasn't good enough for you. And I was really afraid I'd do something to hurt you." He inhaled deeply. "But if you all—" his gaze landed on Kyle and then on Nina "—give me another chance, I promise I'll never leave you again."

Everyone looked at her expectantly, but she still couldn't speak. God, it took all she had just to keep breathing.

What if he hurt her again?

"You should give him another shot," Kyle told her. He shrugged when all eyes went to him. "He promised. And Dillon always keeps his promises."

"Right," Hayley piped in. "Plus it's Christmas and you should forgive, especially at Christmas."

Dillon kissed Hayley's cheek then set her down. Everyone followed his movements as he crossed the room to stand in front of Nina.

"I've been scared many times in my life," he said quietly, "but nothing compares to the fear of losing you and the kids." He reached out and touched her hair. Rubbed a curl between his fingers. "You were right the other night when you said I was hiding. But no more. You gave me hope." His voice was low, sincere and full of emotion. "You're brave and so much stronger than I am. And even though you don't need me, I need you. Nina, I love you."

Her heart swelled and soared. He loved her. He needed her. And he'd just declared his feelings for her in front of all the people she cared most about in the world.

She couldn't have asked for a more perfect Christmas present.

Her mother cleared her throat. "Should we set another place at the table?"

"Could we hold off on that please," Dillon asked, his eyes still on Nina's, "until I'm sure I'm wanted there?" He looked at her, love, hope and uncertainty clear in his eyes. "What do you say, Nina? Am I wanted?"

Tears slid down Nina's face even as she smiled. "Yes. Yes, I want you."

He shut his eyes and pulled her into his arms. "Thank God," he murmured before lifting her off her toes and kissing her.

A few people clapped, someone—Kyle, probably— let out a wolf whistle but still Dillon didn't let go.

"Don't make me bring out the hose," Nina's father warned, his voice half exasperated, half serious.

Dillon broke the kiss and set her back on her feet. "Sorry, sir."

Hank nodded and then, after a moment reached over the table. Dillon looked at her father's outstretched hand, then at her. She smiled encouragingly and he shook her father's hand.

"What are we waiting for?" Hank asked as he set his napkin on his lap. "Dinner's getting cold. Luke, go on and get another place setting. Blaire, make room for Dillon next to your sister."

Dillon took his seat beside Nina but wouldn't let go of her hand, not even when Hayley climbed onto his lap. "Santa's coming tonight," she told him.

He smiled. Nina knew she'd never get tired of seeing him smile. "I've heard that rumor," he said.

"Did you ask him to bring you a present?"

Dillon squeezed Nina's hand, their eyes met and held over Hayley's head. "Looks like I didn't have to. Old St. Nick knew just what I wanted."

* * * * *

We hope you enjoyed reading

TRYING PATIENCE

by *New York Times* bestselling author

CARLA NEGGERS and

A NOT-SO-PERFECT PAST

by reader-favorite author

BETH ANDREWS

Both were originally **Harlequin** series stories!

Discover more heartfelt takes of family, friendship and love from the **Harlequin Special Edition** series. Romance is for life, and these stories show that every chapter in a relationship has its challenges and delights, and that love can be renewed with each turn of the page!

SPECIAL EDITION

Life, Love and Family

When you're with family, you're home!

Look for six new romances every month from
Harlequin Special Edition!
Available wherever books are sold.

***

She exhaled noisily and collapsed on the other end of the couch. "Casey—"

"I just wanted to see you."

She slowly closed her mouth, absorbing that. Her fingers tightened around the glass. She could have offered him one. He'd been the one to introduce her to that particular winery in the first place. The first time she'd invited him to her place after they'd moved their relationship into the "benefits" category, he'd brought a bottle of wine.

She'd been wholly unnerved by it and told him they weren't dating—just mutually filling a need—and to save the empty romantic gestures.

He hadn't brought a bottle of wine ever again.

She shook off the memory.

He was here now, in her home, uninvited, and she'd be smart to remember that. "Why?"

Love the Harlequin book you just read?

Your opinion matters.

Review this book on your favorite book site, review site, blog or your own social media properties and share your opinion with other readers!

HARLEQUIN®

A *Romance* FOR EVERY MOOD™

Stay up-to-date on all your
romance-reading news with the
Harlequin Shopping Guide,
featuring bestselling authors, exciting new
miniseries, books to watch and more!

The newest issue will be delivered right to you
with our compliments! There are 4 each year.

Signing up is easy.

EMAIL

ShoppingGuide@Harlequin.ca

WRITE TO US

HARLEQUIN BOOKS
Attention: Customer Service Department
P.O. Box 9057, Buffalo, NY 14269-9057

OR PHONE

1-800-873-8635 in the United States
1-888-343-9777 in Canada

Please allow 4-6 weeks for delivery of the first issue by mail.